OTHER PLACES, OTHER TIMES

ROBERT WEXELBLATT

Other Places, Other Times by Robert Wexelblatt

978-1-949790-76-4 (paperback)

978-1-949790-77-1 (ebook)

Copyright © 2023 Robert Wexelblatt

Cover images:

Portrait of Emperor Wen of Sui by Yan Liben, Tang Dynasty

La Bella Principessa, attributed to Leonardo da Vinci

Layout and Book Design by Mark Givens

First Pelekinesis Printing 2023

For information:

Pelekinesis, 112 Harvard Ave #65, Claremont, CA 91711 USA

Library of Congress Cataloging-in-Publication Data

Names: Wexelblatt, Robert, author.
Title: Other places, other times / Robert Wexelblatt.
Description: Claremont : Pelekinesis, 2023. | Summary: "Other Places, Other
   Times is a collection of twenty-six historical fictions. Thirteen of the
   stories are about Chen Hsi-wei, an imaginary peasant/poet of the Sui
   period, circa 600 C.E. As a boy, Hsi-wei served the emperor on a
   perilous mission. He turned down the offer of material rewards in favor
   of an education which made him a poet. Hsi-wei travels the empire making
   straw sandals and verses. The narratives account for Hsi-wei's poems,
   which are also included. The other thirteen stories are set in various
   times and locations, from post-war England to Renaissance Italy, Paris
   in the Fifties to post-war Germany, South America in the sixteenth
   century to Hesse in the mid-nineteenth, Ruthenia in the seventeenth, and
   the American West after the Civil War"-- Provided by publisher.
Identifiers: LCCN 2022040347 (print) | LCCN 2022040348 (ebook) | ISBN
   9781949790764 (paperback) | ISBN 9781949790771 (ebook)
Subjects: LCGFT: Short stories.
Classification: LCC PS3573.E968 O84 2023 (print) | LCC PS3573.E968
   (ebook) | DDC 813/.54--dc23/eng/20220912
LC record available at https://lccn.loc.gov/2022040347
LC ebook record available at https://lccn.loc.gov/2022040348

www.pelekinesis.com

OTHER PLACES, OTHER TIMES

Robert Wexelblatt

ACKNOWLEDGMENTS

"Property" first appeared in *Indian Review*

"The Rio Rosa Crisis" first appeared in *Amarillo Bay*

"Three Noons" and "Irretito Animae" first appeared in *SN Review*

"Petite Suite Littéraire" first appeared in *BlazeVOX*

"City of Caesars" first appeared in *Vulcan*

"Hsi-wei at the Moon Festival" and "Hsi-wei and the Worn-Out Brush," first appeared in *Sortes Magazine*

"Hsi-wei and the Three Proverbs" and "Hsi-wei and the Little Straw Sandals" first appeared in *Lowestoft Chronicle*

"Hsi-wei, Song Sidao and Shi Xing" and "Hsi-wei and the Fall of the Sui" first appeared in *Modern Literature*

"Kristyrmishl," "Marche Militaire," "Egon Gleicher," "Count Mactenburg," "Philharmonia," "Luciana di Parma," "The Dreams of Count Wenzel von Geiz and the Jew Eisik," "Hsi-wei in Huaiyang," "Hsi-wei and the Murders in Licheng," "Hsi-wei in the Gardens of Shun," "Hsi-wei and the Great Wall," "Hsi-wei and the Wood-Block Printer," and "Hsi-wei in Wuyan" first appeared in *Offcourse Literary Journal*

Contents

KRISTYRMISHL

On a fine April Sunday in 1669, a crowd of citizens poured from the gates and spread out along the western wall of the Ruthenian city of Kristyrmishl. Lit by the afternoon sun, the stones, pockmarked with mementos of three recent wars, turned a warm orange. Market women had set up stalls selling chicken, potatoes, and stew with dumplings. There were also pears and marzipan on offer. Three tradesmen made a bar of a bench and served up home-made plum brandy and beer straight from the barrel. These provisions were for the common people; the gentry brought their own provender, trunks of it lugged by servants, many in livery. For their comfort, Turkish rugs and silk pillows were laid over the new grass. Some even brought chairs. The wealthiest of the grandees, the sort of men who always contrive to hide jewels and gold during wars, ordered that they be placed as far as possible from the rabble. Something about the affair made them uneasy yet they did not want to miss it, despite the unruly mood of the crowd and the dubiousness of the whole business.

A monsignor and a prior stood by a copse monitoring the scene. "It's almost a pity that nothing's going to happen," remarked the monsignor.

"Let's hope the mob doesn't tear the charlatan to pieces," said the prior. "Like Dionysus."

The monsignor made a face. The prior was, as usual, attempting to impress him. "The dismemberment of Dionysus marked the winter," he explained coldly. "It had to do with pruning back the vines. But this is Eastertide, not December."

"Quite right."

The monsignor gestured upwards to the budding branches above them. "Resurrection."

"Just as you say, Monsignor. I only meant. . . . But what if something *does* happen?"

"Then we shall be obliged to request the secular arm to arrest the man. And so on."

"Doesn't the fool realize his danger. I mean what he's in for whether he succeeds or fails?"

"Vanity, Father. His recent success with parlor tricks has gone to his head. Vanity."

"And hubris," added the prior.

A rough platform had been erected about thirty feet from the wall. Dymytrii Lemko, a lean young man with a well-trimmed beard and wearing a royal blue cloak, ascended it by means of a ladder. He was followed by a boy of fifteen, the little Jewish servant he pompously referred to as his famulus.

While it was under Polish administration, Ruthenia experienced an influx of Jews and Armenians. The prosperity no less than the population of Kristyrmishl was expanded by these enterprising and grateful immigrants. They got on with one another perhaps because neither was welcomed with much warmth by the local population; but, of the two communities, the Jews were by far the more mistrusted and despised, the Armenians being at least Christians of some kind. Still, social relations in the city were stable until the Khmelnytsky uprising, the Russo-Polish War, and the Swedish invasion known simply as The Deluge. These blows came so quickly upon one another as to be virtually continuous. Kristyrmishl was besieged four times, occupied twice, partially destroyed and left to rebuild without help from a central government. In fact, the city had changed hands so often that nobody was entirely certain under whose rule it fell. One consequence was that the Church exercised unusual political influence. After the death of Archbishop Ryazanov, an anxious and not exceedingly bright cleric, the Pope appointed as the new bishop of Kristyrmishl a stern Silesian named Alardus who, less for reasons of state than out of personal conviction, stirred the people up against the Jews. The inevitable pogrom broke out on Good Friday, 1666. Two of the city's three synagogues were razed and Torah scrolls desecrated. Nearly a hundred people were murdered and many more injured.

Among the dead were Reuben's parents Yehuda and Malka, also his sister Brina. Their tailor shop was attacked late in the afternoon and set alight. As the three fled, they were grabbed by the mob and dispatched like cattle, with clubs and axes. Reuben ben Yehuda, twelve at the time, survived only because he had been at the study-house preparing for his bar mitzvah. Though it too was attacked, he managed to crawl out a small rear window. When order was restored the following Monday, Reuben was discovered hiding in the cellar of a bakery. As the baker did not know what to do with the orphan, he thought it best to turn the boy over to the Church.

Dmytryii Lemko's father had the knack of buying cheap and selling dear. Before the wars, he supported his wife and four children in comfort. He himself was uninterested in luxury and amusements; he was obsessed with profit and loss and seldom left his place of business. He was an all-powerful absence in the lives of his children, a God who provided bounteously but was essentially indifferent to them. The exception was the older of his two sons, Rodyon, but only because he had to be prepared to take over the firm. If the other children saw too little of their father, then Rodyon saw too much. As for Dmytryii, he was impulsive, egoistic, fond of books and card games; he liked pulling practical jokes, teasing his sisters, mocking his brother, and saying indecorous things at table. He was occasionally indulged by his mother and frequently punished by his father. Despite his cleverness, both regarded him as a disappointment. His father delivered his verdict on his younger son in memorable words, "You're not even ornamental." The boy yearned to escape Kristyrmishl. Like many adolescents, he felt a powerful but unfocused ambition to win fame.

When he turned seventeen Dymytrii managed to persuade his father to send him to the University of Krakow, an institution which had been in decline for nearly a century. Here he would, he insincerely promised, master the Law and so make himself an asset to the family.

In the middle of his second year in Krakow the wars closed the university and Dymytrii had to return to Kristyrmishl. During his time in Krakow, he seldom attended lectures, preferring to spend his nights in taverns and whorehouses, his days in the Jagiellonian Library, the university's one unquestionable glory. The collection was deemed so precious that the books were attached to their cases with chains just long enough to reach the massive oak reading tables.

One day, while exploring the depths of the old Gothic pile, Dymytrii happened on a door whose lock had all but rusted through. It took little more than a nudge to open it and this Dymytrii did not hesitate to deliver. The door opened on a small closet with shelves holding about a dozen tomes, all unchained. Dymytrii picked one at random. The title, *Cabala del Cavalla Pagaseo,* meant nothing to him, but the name of the author did. It was by Giordano Bruno. These were, he realized, forbidden books. With a mixture of audacity and prudence, Dymytrii appropriated three books, Bruno's and two others he only chose because they were slim and would be easy to smuggle past the proctors. One turned out to be a heretical Albigensian tract on dualism, the other a volume written in two languages neither of which he could understand, though he recognized that one was Hebrew.

After a perilous journey from Krakow, Dymytrii arrived home to find his father expiring and the business also on the point of death. His sisters had been hastily married off, and his mother sat beside by his father's bed in a state of catatonic stupor. And what of Rodyon, the hope of the family. During what was supposed to be a truce, he had gone personally to deliver a consignment of Macedonian figs to a wealthy customer in Szepes and had been caught in the crossfire of a skirmish. Dymytrii, inheritor of the moribund family firm, liquidated what remained of the stock, consigned his widowed mother to the care of one of his sisters, and took two rooms in the city's poorest quarter. With its low taverns and eight whore houses, the district suited him. It was much like Krakow without the lectures and the library. But he had his forbidden books.

The pogrom broke out a week after Dymytrii's return and, when he heard of the Jewish orphan nobody wanted, he went to the bishop's palace, begged for an audience, and offered to take the boy on as his servant. To this Alardus assented with a tight smile and an indifferent wave of the episcopal hand. To him, this was the fortuitous solution of a minor problem.

"What's it about?"

"Tricks, sir."

"What do you mean, tricks?"

"Tricks with coins and cards, with water, iron bars, with rabbits, pigeons, keys, apples and peppers. All sorts of things."

"Then it's a book of magic?"

"Magic?"

"It was forbidden for a reason."

"Perhaps only because the people who banned it weren't able to read it."

"Are you mocking me?"

"Oh no, sir. These tricks aren't magic. Just sleight-of-hand. At least the ones in Hebrew."

Dmytryii, always mercurial, was formulating a plan. These notions always came to him in images. Already he saw himself among finely dressed people, all of them smiling, applauding, and slipping him fat velvet purses.

"What's the other language?"

"What my people spoke in Spain. It's sometimes called Ladino."

"You understand this Ladino?"

"A little only, sir, very little. My grandmother sometimes spoke it."

"What's it say?"

"I'm not sure. Maybe just more tricks."

"Jewish tricks, eh. From Spain. Good. Work it out, boy.

That's why I'm feeding you."

"It'll take some time, I think."

"Don't shirk. In the meantime we'll work up the Hebrew tricks."

"Sir, you'll need an assistant."

"Then I'm lucky I've already got one."

That winter, with peace restored, life in Kristyrmishl gradually began to settle into something like normality. Rebuilding commenced, at least for the well off. The city fathers allocated money for reconstructing the City Hall tower but, at the insistence of the bishop, forbade the rebuilding of the destroyed synagogues. In addition, they issued new restrictions. Jews were now to be crowded into a ghetto sharply reduced in size and certain trades were forbidden to them, including goldsmithing. Business and social life both picked up; villas were refitted and places of business restored. The bishop was pleased and the wealthy were in a celebratory mood.

Dymytrii practiced until he had mastered three card tricks, then two with coins, plus an impressively complicated illusion with four iron bars. Reuben translated the instructions and flattered his master's performances even as he corrected them.

Through the influence of an acquaintance of his late father's, Dymytrii secured an invitation to a dinner party in the home of a furrier. He promised to provide entertainment for the guests. In the days leading up to his debut his beatings of Reuben decreased in proportion to his need for reassurance. He bought some used clothes for Reuben who would serve as his assistant. The evening of the furrier's dinner, Dymytrii was frightfully nervous, by turns whining and short-tempered. Reuben had all he could do to calm his master down. "I'll be right at your side," he said sooth-ingly, as if to a child.

"Oh!"

"Ah!"

"How clever!"

"Bravo!"

"Simply splendid!"

It was all just as Dymytrii had imagined it. He basked in the delight of his audience, the ladies and gentlemen, also the squeals of the children, who had been allowed into the parlor to watch.

Soon he was being invited to more parties, and Reuben always stood right next to him as he pulled off his illusions. Dmytrii pushed Reuben to teach him more Hebrew tricks. The boy translated patiently, gently correcting his master's errors until perfect execution was achieved. It was Reuben who suggested the royal blue cloak and also the theatrical value of appearing to fail once in a while.

Dymytrii Lemko was happy yet unsatisfied. There must always be something novel, after all, something more impressive. Every day he pestered Reuben about the Ladino translation. The truth was that Reuben had completed it long before, but, for his own reasons, pretended to be making only slow progress. His intention was to wait until Lemko's reputation, income, and self-confidence had swollen up like drowned rats.

They moved to Schalkov, a better neighborhood with neither taverns nor whores but plenty of trees and carriages. Lemko began an affair with the young wife of an elderly dealer in crystal. Before leaving for an assignation, he would deliver a few blows to Reuben to encourage him to work harder on the Ladino tricks. "Stock needs renewing," he shouted at the boy. "A Jew ought to understand that!"

One morning Reuben woke Dymytrii, pretending great excitement.

"I've finished a whole chapter, sir. It's a spell."

"Spell?"

"Yes and, if it works, it will astound everybody."

Lemko was dubious. "A spell you say. Well, what is it, exactly. Some Jewish doggerel?"

"The book says it makes things disappear, sir."

"What. Anything?"

"Yes, sir."

Dymytrii threw back his new eiderdown and leapt from the bed. Gaudy pictures were forming in his mind of a triumph so astonishing that it would make his name not only throughout Ruthenia but across all of Europe. He pictured himself at the court in Vienna, in Paris.

They practiced for two weeks, with time out only for sleep. Reuben wrote the spell out phonetically and solemnly informed Lemko that to work it required both celibacy and fasting. If he wished to achieve success, he must consume no alcohol and eat only unleavened bread for at least two full days before pronouncing the spell; three would be even better. Reuben had invented these details himself and took spiteful pleasure in reminding Lemko of them. There was no way around it; the master must abstain. Lemko submitted to this, turned down all dinner invitations, and avoided his mistress.

They began with a rock. Reuben corrected Dymytrii's pronunciation and stood close beside him as he declaimed the incantation. "*Let the seen become unseen. Let this rock become a vanished dream.*" On the fifth attempt they succeeded. The rock simply vanished.

Next, they tried a worn-out boot, then a broken chair. Reuben, to whom Dymytrii now deferred, was careful to choose only worthless objects, things the master would not want back. Because he was intoxicated by his ability to make things disappear, by dreams of the fame and the wealth that such a skill would bring him, Dymytrii neglected to ask Reuben two vital questions, which was just what the boy intended. Could the spell be reversed. And, if so, how?

That spring was especially lovely, temperate, and fruitful. It was as if the whole of nature rejoiced in peace. Seeds were sown over former battlefields; orchards bloomed and wagon traffic crowded the roads. The rebuilding of the tower was completed. As Holy Week approached, Dymytrii had bulletins printed and nailed up all over the city. These promised a grand demonstration of his abilities on the Octave of Easter, in the afternoon. The population of Kristyrmishl was encouraged to gather outside the city walls to witness an unforgettable spectacle. In accord with a suggestion from Reuben, there was no mention of what the spectacle was to be. "To keep it secret will raise interest and discourage scoffing," said the boy drily.

On Easter Sunday, Bishop Alardus delivered a sermon excoriating the Jews, after which, in Frunzi Square, the guilds mounted the old passion play.

During Holy Week, Dymytrii resumed his adulterous affair and gorged himself on beef and fish, fortifying himself for the fast Reuben reminded him he would have to begin on Friday at the latest. Lemko also drank heavily and, one night, when he had fallen into a drunken sleep, Reuben paid a visit to the Jewish quarter. He climbed over the gate which, in the Venetian fashion, was locked each night. He made straight for the sole remaining synagogue where he roused Rabbi Yitzak and told him that the Jews had to depart the city that very week; moreover, he cautioned, in so far as they could, they must do so in secret. The sleepy rabbi listened but asked no questions. He merely mumbled a prayer for the boy's family and yawned until Reuben approached him and whispered a Hebrew phrase in his ear. The rabbi's eyebrows shot upward. Reuben left with a final plea, unsure whether he had convinced the rabbi.

The following night, the boy woke the priest at Saint Vartanatz's Church so as to deliver the same message to the Armenians. Father Arshag was angry at being awakened and, while he did not strike Reuben or even threaten to turn him over to the authorities, he did curse him. With a heavy heart, Reuben begged the priest to spread the word quietly among his people then, not without compunction, he stole away into the night.

Dymytrii Lemko stood on the platform in his royal blue cloak. Reuben, close by his side, held his transliteration of the spell which he had somewhat expanded for the occasion. Dymytrii was so nervous that, unwilling to trust his memory, he had to ask the boy for the parchment.

The picnicking crowd was noisy and some jeered, but everyone fell silent when Dymytrii turned away from them and faced the high wall. Then he began to read with a quavering voice and in a strange language.

> *Let the seen become unseen.*
> *Let Kristyrmishl become a vanished dream.*
> *Let it disappear like Purim treats,*
> *its wicked lanes and vile streets.*
> *Let the seen become unseen.*

Nothing happened. There were jibes and the mob began to roar with laughter and disappointment. But then Reuben shouted out the phrase Dymytrii had never heard because, when they were practicing, Reuben had whispered it under his breath, just as he had to the rabbi. According to the Ladino text, the words *"Bashem El Chai V'Kayyam"* activated the spell. *Do this in the name of the living, the enduring God.*

In the blink of an eye, the city of Kristyrmishl vanished, everything and everyone in it. Where it had stood was only empty land.

The crowd stood hushed and stunned. Reuben took the opportunity to scramble down the ladder and run as fast as he could for the high road. On the way, he stopped by the beech tree under which he had concealed an old pilgrim's knapsack. As for the forbidden book, he had burned it the day before in the courtyard at Schalkov as Dymytrii napped.

The monsignor and the prior were as dumb-struck as everybody else. Kristyrmishl was gone, truly gone. It was no illusion. Surely this was the blackest of black magic.

"Lemko will go to the stake," hissed the prior.

The monsignor did not reply at once. "Then how do we get our city back?" he said at length. "Who else can restore it?"

"Ah," said the prior. "Ah, hmm. I didn't think of that."

Dymytrii Lemko was sent to Szepes where he was thrown in a dungeon, repeatedly questioned and tortured, though not so as to threaten his life.

"The Jews," he groaned desperately as the screws were tightened.

"Not this time, Lemko," growled his inquisitor. This was the monsignor himself, heir apparent to the vanished bishopric of Kristyrmishl.

HSI-WEI AND THE MURDERS
IN LICHENG

The Tang Minister Fang Xuan-ling took a particular interest in the verses of Chen Hsi-wei, the peasant who became a poet. Like all those who had come through the examination system, Fang knew the ancient masters thoroughly; however, unlike most of his peers, for whom poetry was chiefly a means to an end, Fang loved poetry and enjoyed conversing about it. When he praised Chen Hsi-wei's verses, most of his colleagues said they had never heard of him while others expressed contempt. It was hard to tell if the contempt was owing to Hsi-wei's lowly background or because he hadn't the distinction of being dead for three hundred years.

Hsi-wei flourished during the brief Sui Dynasty, with its impressive accomplishments and spectacular failures. It was under Emperors Wendi and Yangdi that Hsi-wei wandered through the Empire leaving behind him straw sandals and poems. The sandals stayed with the peasants who bought them, but his verses spread over the country, giving him a measure of fame among the common people but also some of the elite, like Lord Fang Xuan-ling.

Toward the end of his life, Hsi-wei retired to a small cottage granted him by the Governor of Chiangling. Fang was informed that the place was a stingy gift; it had only two rooms, a tiny patio, and a vegetable garden, and that it lay in the middle of farmland three *li* from the city. Nevertheless, Hsi-wei was deeply grateful for it, his first and last home.

When Minister Fang learned that Hsi-wei was alive and where he could be found, he wrote to the Governor in Chiangling to announce that he would be visiting the city. The Governor wrote back at once inviting this important man to be his most honored guest for as long he chose. When Fang arrived in Chiangling with his entourage, the Governor and his entire family greeted him with deep bows. The Minister was, of course, to stay in the Governor's own villa. Having moved his two daughters to smaller quarters, he gave Fang their splendid suite of rooms and offered to provide for his escort's food and accommodation, but the Minister insisted on paying. This was an insult and intended as such, meant to show the Governor that the Minister disapproved of the shabby place he had allotted to Chen Hsi-wei. To make the point clearer, he then disappointed the Governor by declaring that the sole purpose of his visit was to see the retired poet, whom he referred to as Master Hsi-wei. The Governor took the point. What could he say.

Fang spent a week in Chiangling, riding to Hsi-wei's cottage each morning and staying until the moon rose. The Minister was a methodical man. He had prepared many questions about Hsi-wei's poems, especially their origins, took notes on their conversations and recorded them each night in his extensive and invaluable diary.

One morning as they sat in the patio Hsi-wei was pleased to call his courtyard, Fang asked about the poem the literati of the capital called "Clear Air on the Kunlon Mountains" but which the peasants had given another title, "The Madness of Nüwa." Fang said he found the poem obscure.

Hsi-wei looked pained.

"I didn't mean to upset you by calling it obscure, Master. I only meant that there are things I don't understand."

"It's not that, my Lord."

"The memory of why you wrote it upsets you?"

"Yes. That poem is the bitter fruit of a terrible event."

Fang was intrigued. "Then it's about something you witnessed?"

Hsi-wei nodded. "It was an event in which I became personally involved," he said sadly.

"In what way, Master?"

Hsi-wei took a moment to collect himself and his memories.

"It must have been at least fifteen years ago. I was traveling through Yuzhou at the time and stopped at the town of Husian where I discovered the younger brother of one of my old schoolmates had recently been appointed magistrate. Yang Bogin had only just passed his examination; he was still quite young and without a wife or children. Though a fine student and a decent man, determined to do his new job well, he was, of course, inexperienced and, having spent all his life in the capital, knew little of the peasants.

"Yang received me courteously. He said that his brother had often spoken about the peasant who was so relentlessly abused by Master Shen Kuo. He told me his brother spoke of me as a kind of curiosity—a peasant out of place. He also told me he had heard the story of how, during the wars, I carried a message to the south then turned down the usual rewards for the service in favor of an education— that is, being tormented by Master Shen Kuo. It appeared that my old schoolmate occasionally got hold of a poem of mine and shared it with his brother. 'Like me,' said the young man, 'he's no literary expert, but I believe he's rather proud of you.' For his own sake, he said, as much as for my old schoolmate's, he invited me to stay with him.

"Yang's villa was pleasant but not large. He apologized for being able to offer me only a small room behind the kitchen but, accustomed to putting up in sheds and stables, I assured him that for me it would be luxurious. After that, he went to his office, and I headed for the marketplace to look for customers. I found a place beside two elderly sisters, with whom I made friends. One sold vegetables, the other fruit. They took amused themselves by teasing one another, each accusing the other of having romantic designs on me.

"Yang Bogin had been assigned the customary three assistants. Ruan and Pan were as inexperienced as himself, but the stout Xun was older and had seen some service with a magistrate in Jingzhou.

"Husian was a peaceful town and its citizens mostly content thanks to Emperor Wen's land reforms and reorganization of the government. Yang's unpopular predecessor had been officially retired, to the people's delight, and reassigned to the provincial capital in Dongdu. He had been appointed under the old system when magistrates were all local men who secured their sinecures from prefects through either nepotism or bribes. Yang came to Husian under Wendi's new system, one which I understand our new Emperor wisely intends to continue. central appointment from a list of those passing examinations with no magistrate allowed to serve in his native province. Because of these developments, Yang was well received in Husian, despite his youth. He and his assistants had little to do beyond resolving petty disputes about boundaries or wandering livestock, and sorting out the occasional drunken brawl.

"Yang's jurisdiction included the outlying villages. While we were finishing our meal that first evening, a peasant, a man on the far side of middle age, pounded at the door, begging to see the magistrate. He was breathless and in distress. 'There's been murder, Your Honor. *Two* murders!'

"Yang remained calm. He ushered the man into his parlor, made him sit, and ordered green tea for him. He then summoned his assistants and, turning to me, asked if I would be pleased to attend the interview. Of course, I agreed. And this is how a visit to Husian I thought would last no more than two days turned into a week's stay.

"Once he had regained his composure, the peasant gave his name and said he had come from Licheng. Licheng is quite near the town, only a few *li* outside the South gate. The peasant said a couple, Mr. and Mrs. Li, had been killed, their throats slit. Their daughter, Baozhai, reported that robbers had broken in during the night and that she hid behind her bed. Her brother, Deming, apparently slept through whatever happened. The village was in terror with no one in charge. Though the man knew the magistrate had to be fetched, he was afraid to leave his family. In the end, he had left them in the care of his neighbor Peng and rushed to Husian. He was keen to get home but frightened of being on the road alone after dark.

"Yang ordered his assistants to arm themselves, conduct the peasant back to Licheng, and begin a search for the murdering bandits. Ruan and Pan were keen, but Xun pointed out that a night search was unlikely to be of any use. 'And besides, Your Honor, we have too little information. No description. The daughter and son and their neighbors will need to be questioned first.'

"Yang considered this. He looked uncertain and asked my opinion. I said that Xun's reservations were reasonable;

and, if robbers were indeed responsible for the crime, they would have had half the night and all of the day to get away.

"It was decided the assistants would escot the peasant back to Licheng and the magistrate would join them early the next morning. Yang asked if I would care to accompany him. 'It will be an honor,' I said and added that I might find some customers in the village for my straw sandals. Yang looked at me quizzically. 'Some murders and all sandals come in pairs,' I observed. 'Customers sometimes like to gossip.'

"We mounted our horses at sunrise. Lacking his escort, Yang had me put on a helmet and carry a lance. 'For appearances,' he explained. I felt ridiculous. The burly Xun was waiting for us at the village gate. I noted that he could barely suppress a laugh on seeing me. I dismounted quickly and handed him the reins, then my helmet and the lance.

"Xun delivered a brusque report. 'Ruan and Pan are at the Li cottage with the son and daughter. I hope you'll pardon my presumption, but I thought you'd want to see the place and talk to them first. The victims are being seen to by the neighbors.'

"'Yes. Very good,' said Yang.

"I excused myself and headed for the village well.

"'Good luck to you, Sandal-Maker,' said Yang. 'And to you, Magistrate,' said I.

"Except for the infants and the senile, fear was on every face in Licheng. Because I was a stranger, I knew people would gather around, not to buy sandals, but to tell me about the terrible thing that had happened. They would be terrified by the murders but exhilarated too eager to talk. Tragedies and jokes—have you noticed that people love to share both, My Lord?"

Fang said that it was true, that the child in us loves the chaos of a storm while the adult fears the flood.

Hsi-wei nodded and went on with his story.

"I pretended to know nothing but let the peasants see my interest and learned all I could about the Li family from them. I discovered that Mr. Li was upright, hard-working, humorless, respected, and hard on his children, that Mrs. Li disliked gossip, didn't make good dumplings, and that both were strict Confucians of the old kind. People spoke with more warmth of the orphans. They told me Baozhai was sixteen, two years younger than her brother. The men spoke of how the brother, Deming, would now have to 'straighten his back' and work the land allocated to the family on his own. 'He's a good boy, always did just what Li told him to. Strong for his age. Poor fellow, we'll give him a hand." What interested the women was that Deming was in immediate need of a wife and would also have to find a husband for his sister. Already matchmaking, they exchanged suggestions—'Not *him*, surely!' 'Yes, *him*. And what about *her*; she'd be *perfect*'. To the women, marriage was the solution to everything. A capable wife would help Deming and a sound husband would settle Baozhai down. One woman explained: 'The girl can be a little flighty, emotional. When she was little, the Li shed burned down. They said it was an overturned lantern, but some of us were sure the girl set the fire. I always thought it was because her parents were so strict. Well, it's all in the past now.'"

"Yang met with the children and looked over the scene of the crime. Around mid-afternoon, we departed for Husian, leaving the three assistants behind. Yang gave them money for meals and lodging and ordered them to make inquiries in all the nearby villages about any robberies and whether strangers had been seen in the vicinity. On the ride back to town, he gave me a brief report. He described the Li cottage as a typical peasant dwelling and related what the brother and sister had said. Their testimony matched what we had been told by the peasant the night before. the sister saying their parents had been murdered by robbers, the brother claiming to know nothing.

"I asked Yang whether anything had been taken and how the siblings had behaved. He said it appeared nothing had been stolen from the cottage. As for the siblings, the brother was solemn, slumped with grief, and had little to say. The daughter, however, was beside herself, crying continually for her mother and striking her chest with her fist. Yang said that questioning her felt almost brutal. I asked if she was able to describe the robbers. No, she said it was dark and she was hiding. I asked why, if no one disturbed them, the robbers had fled. Yang said the girl believed they must have heard something that scared them off.

"I asked if he had noticed anything of value in the cottage.

"Yang thought this over. He said there was a small statue on a crude altar. The thing was not at all well carved, but it was jade. He didn't see anything else apart from pots, buckets, two brooms, and farming tools. He added that the family kept a pair of pigs, but neither had been taken or killed. It's possible the robbers alarmed the pigs, that they squealed and frightened off the murderers, but the nearest neighbors said they heard and saw nothing, just as the brother claimed. Yang shook his head, sighed, and said it was puzzling.

"We arrived back late at Yang's villa and ate a quick supper. The magistrate was tired out, yawning. He excused himself and retired. I went to my room and thought about what I had learned.

"In the morning, Yang had to preside over a hearing to

resolve a dispute over irrigation rights. I hastened to the marketplace, eager to speak with the vegetable and fruit sisters. Yang and I agreed to meet at his villa at midday by which time he hoped his assistants would be back with their report. 'I have a theory,' he confided, 'but everything depends on what they have to say.'

"The sisters made a fuss over me and began at once to accuse one another of flirting. The vegetable sister ordered a pair of sandals and, not to be outdone, so did the one who sold fruit. I turned the conversation to the murders in Licheng. I asked if the Li children often came to town on market days.

"'They came to a few when they were little, but it was usually just Mr. Li. But recently, Deming—such a fine-looking boy—would come along, you know, to learn how things are done,' said one sister. The other spoke of the daughter, Baozhai. 'A few months ago, the girl started coming too; but that hadn't much to do with radishes and cabbages." The sisters grinned at each other as old women do over the romances of the young. I asked why they were smiling.

"'It was to see that handsome boy from Shaohu,' said Fruit.

"'Shaohu's the village next to Licheng,' Vegetables explained. 'I saw them together right over there." She pointed to a shaded lane across the way and giggled in a way that was almost unseemly. 'They were standing *very* close to each other,' she added with a knowing nod.

"I asked if they happened to know the name of the handsome boy from Shaohu.

"'Of course. It was Li Honghui, wasn't it?' said Fruit. 'That's right,' said Vegetables. 'But it couldn't have been really serious. Just flirting. Honghui's to marry He Nuying.'

"'Her father's the richest man in Shaohu,' said Fruit. 'I've never seen the bride myself.' 'Nor have I,' said her sister, 'but people from Shaohu say she's very beautiful and spoiled.'

"On my way back to Yang's villa, I purchased straw for the sisters' sandals. When I arrived with my bundle, Yang was just taking off his official robe. His hat, the black futou with its wings, lay on a pillow at his feet. The assistants, he said with some irritation, had not yet returned. He ordered his cook to prepare tea and bing cakes for us but, before these refreshmens arrived, the assistants marched through the door.

"'Well?' asked Yang impatiently.

Xun gave a formal bow. 'Your Honor, there is nothing to report. We split up and went to the three villages nearest Licheng. No robberies and no strangers.'

"Yang nodded and smiled. 'But that's a most useful report, Xun.'

"The tea and cakes were brought in.

"'Here,' said Yang. 'You three take the cakes and drink the tea then go back to Licheng, arrest Li Deming, bring him back, and put him into the jail.'

"The assistants bowed. I overheard Xun whisper to his colleagues. 'See. What did I tell you?'

"I asked if I might accompany the assistants to Licheng. Yang asked why. I pointed to my bundle of straw and said it was to find more customers. He was not pleased.

"'Very well,' he said curtly. 'You can take one of the horses.'

"I was not yet sufficiently sure of my own ideas to share them with the magistrate. Yang could justly dismiss them; moreover, the theory I was forming was so monstrous that even to broach it might damage two reputations—one of them being my own. My purpose in returning to Licheng was to find a girl of sixteen or seventeen whose name I didn't know and who might not even exist."

At this point, Hsi-wei paused. He asked if Lord Fang were bored and, perhaps, hungry. "I confess," Yang said, "I'm caught up in your story. But yes, I suppose I am a little hungry."

Hsi-wei had been indeed speaking for a long time. Back at the Governor's villa in Chiangling, Minister Fang would be up far into the night trying to recall the details of the story and write them all down. But just then he was eager to know what happened when Hsi-wei returned to Licheng, the identity of the unknown girl he hoped to find there and, of course, who was guilty. It was frustrating that Hsi-wei chose this suspenseful juncture to suggest that they eat. But Fang didn't refuse, especially since he had brought delicacies for him from the Governor's kitchen— wood-ear soup, a baked fish and two pork dishes plus scallion dumplings and a quantity of the tea called black dragon pearls. He also considered that Master Hsi-wei might be even hungrier than he was.

Hsi-wei went into his cottage to start the fire while his guest remained on the little patio, watching the sun going down and wondering what Hsi-wei's story could have to do with a poem about the Kunlon Mountains.

The late afternoon air was still and pleasant and they dined by the light of an old bronze lantern. The meal was good, and the men agreed that the Governor of Chiangling was fortunate to have such a cook. Fang begged Hsi-wei to resume the story while they ate.

"Very well," said Hsi-wei, pleased that his listener was so eager to hear the rest of the gloomy story. "When I left off, I was on the way to Licheng with the magistrate's three assistants. During the ride, Xun delivered a lecture. 'I'll tell you what I learned when I was working with Magistrate Wu, a very shrewd man. He explained it all to me, solving cases like this one. "Xun," he said, "whenever there's doubt as to who committed a crime, you've only got to ask who gets the most out of it and that's how you'll find your culprit." Well, this wicked brother's going to take over the farm, isn't he. The cottage will be his and he'll be free of his strict parents into the bargain. As for his sister's story about the robbers, it's obvious her brother persuaded her to tell it. Magistrate Yang, I'm sure, has followed the same principle as my old boss. And that, Sandal-Maker, is why we'll be arresting Li Deming.'

"When we arrived in Licheng, I went with the magistrate's men to the Li cottage. I wanted to make sure that people saw me in their company. I stood by as they arrested Deming and bound him hand and foot. Xun tossed him brutally across the saddle of my horse. Baozhai protested the whole time then ran after them crying loudly and cursing Xun. I watched closely as a young girl of about Baozhai's age rushed from a nearby field and hugged Baozhai, trying to calm and console her, and then leading her back to the Li cottage. Then I went back to the village well. As I expected, people again gathered around to ask me for information. Why was Deming being arrested. Where was the magistrate. What about those murdering robbers. I said that no robbers had been found, that I didn't know why the magistrate suspected Deming but that he was a just man. Then I inquired about the girl who had run to help Baozhai.

"'Oh, that's Daiyue,' a woman said, 'the Changs' second daughter. The first was married two years ago to some skinny fellow with money from Husian. I felt bad for her.'

"I took two orders for sandals and, before the crowd dispersed, returned to the Li cottage. Daiyue was just leaving. I introduced myself and asked how her friend was. 'Poor Baozhai!' the girl exclaimed. 'She was beside herself. It was all I could do to keep her from following those brutes all the way to Husian. She's exhausted with grief and fear for her brother and now she's fallen asleep.'

"'It was good of you to look after her like that,' I said. 'You're good friends?'

"'Best friends,' said Daiyue shyly.

"It wasn't difficult to get the girl to answer my questions. She was eager to talk about her friend for whom, as she put, 'disasters have fallen on top of one another like loose tiles from the landlord's roof.'

"'Of course, the murder of her parents and the arrest of her brother,' I said.

"'Yes, but even before all that there was the business with Honghui.'

"'Honghui?'

"Yes. Li Honghui."

"And then she told me that Baozhai and Honghui, the handsome boy from Shaohu, were in love but she couldn't marry him. 'That Honghui didn't even wait. He went and did just what his parents ordered, the coward. He's going to marry that stuck-up Nuying." Daiyue's indignation turned to tears. 'Oh, my poor Baozhai!' she cried.

"I expressed my sympathy, thanked her, and promised to make her a pair of good straw sandals. When she asked why I would do that, I replied it was for being such a good friend to her unfortunate friend. Then I made my way back to Husian on foot, arriving late at Yang's villa. He greeted me, ordered food, and brought out a jug of yellow wine, 'to celebrate the resolution of this case." Then he retired to prepare for his interrogation of Li Deming in the morning. I wished him a good night.

"In the morning, the courtroom quickly filled up with people from both Husian and Licheng, including Baozhai and Daiyue. When everyone was seated, Xun struck the floor three times with the butt of his spear and Magistrate Yang entered from behind a screen at the back of the dais. In his formal robe and winged hat, he appeared older than his age, an impressive sight. He looked over the crowd gravely, took a scroll from his sleeve, and sat on a three-legged stool behind a tall baize-covered desk on which he laid out the scroll. After delivering a stern warning to keep silent and not interrupt the proceedings, he nodded to Xun, who pulled back a curtain at the side of the room. Pan and Ruan led in Deming who looked pale, distraught, and frightened. The two assistants forced him to kneel at the foot of the dais and stood on either side of him with their arms crossed. Xun took up a position to the right of the dais and frowned at the crowd, as if daring them to do anything of which he personally disapproved.

"The questioning started with the prisoner's name (he gave it), then the facts of his parents' death (their throats had been cut in the night).

"Yang then turned to the tale of the robbers. Had anything been taken from the cottage. (Not so far as he knew.) Did the prisoner see or hear these robbers or bandits. (No, he had worked hard in the field that day and had been fast asleep.) Was he aware of any recent robberies in Licheng or the adjacent villages. (He had heard of none.) Would he now inherit the cottage and household goods formerly belonging to his parents. (He supposed so.)

"Then Yang ordered Xun to report on the investigations made by Pan, Ruan, and himself. This the man did succinctly. 'Your Honor. We found nothing was taken from the cottage, no other break-ins in Licheng or any of the nearby villages, no reports of any robbers, bandits, or strangers in the vicinity.'

"'Then,' declared Yang harshly, 'the case against the prisoner is clear. Mr. and Mrs. Li were murdered in the night by the only person present with a motive for the terrible act. To make matters worse, the prisoner compelled his young sister to lie in order to cover up his crime.'

"At this Baozhai jumped up and began to scream. Daiyue tried but could not restrain her. The girl screamed and spoke at once so that it was impossible to make out anything she said except the words 'No. No!'

"Xun pounded the dais with his spear; Yang pounded the desk with his fist and in a loud voice ordered Xun to remove the girl from the courtroom. This Xun accomplished with some difficulty.

"When things quieted down, Yang told everybody what they already knew, that the prescribed procedure called for torture until the accused confessed. There were murmurs in the crowd, but no objections.

"It was at this point that I stood up and stepped to the dais. Yang looked at me almost angrily, but I begged for a word in private. 'It's important,' I whispered. Yang, still cross, considered, searching my face. He must have seen some of what I was feeling as he called a brief recess. We went behind the screen and into his office, a small room with bare walls, three shelves for scrolls, a low writing desk, and a short bench without pillows.

"'Well?' he said curtly. 'What's the important matter, Master Chen?'

"'There's a question I want to ask Your Honor and another I would like you to ask somebody else.'

"'And that's why you interrupted the proceedings. Well, what is it you want to ask me?'

"'Why didn't Li Demin support his sister's story about the robbers?'

"Yang's expression shifted from displeasure to perplexity. 'Hmm. I don't yet have an answer. What's the other question?'

"'I beg you to bring the sister, Baozhai, back into the court. I want you to ask her one question and carefully observe her reaction.'

"'You want me to ask her again about those imaginary robbers?'

"'No. The question is this. Who is Li Honghui?'

"'And you know this Honghui?'

"'He's a boy from another village.'

"Yang looked nonplussed but agreed to do as I asked.

"Baozhai, barely in control of herself, was conducted back into the court and led to the front of the room. She wrenched herself free from Xun's grasp, and stood up straight beside to her kneeling brother, and glared at the Magistrate.

"'Baozhai, who is Li Honghui?'

"At this, the girl exclaimed 'Oh!' and collapsed. Yang looked at me with raised brows. Daiyue and an older woman rushed to Baozhai and lifted the girl on her feet. 'Your Honor,' the older woman said, 'Can't you see these terrible blows have been too much for the girl. You shouldn't put her through more. We'll take care of her. We'll see that she gets home.'

"'Do so,' said Yang. 'Xun, take the prisoner back to the jail. If he doesn't confess tonight, the next phase of the proceedings will begin in the morning.'

"'No!' bawled Baozhai as she was led from the courtroom.

"Yang didn't wait long to ask me about Li Honghui. As soon as the hearing was adjourned he directed me back to his office. Baozhai's reaction to his question gave me the confidence to lay before him my theory of the appalling crime and the motive behind it. I told him that the violence of Baozhai's grief initially roused my suspicions. I related all that I had picked up from the peasants in Licheng, the market women in Husian, and from Baozhai's best friend. I said I believed that Li Deming was innocent, that there were no robbers in the night, and that—hard though it was to conceive—the terrible act was carried out by Baozhai, a teenager frustrated in love. Yang looked at me in amazement, as shocked that I could conceive of such a thing as that it might be true.

"'You believe that young girl cut her own parents' throats. But why?'

"I told him that Baozhai and Honghui had been seen concealing themselves in a lane off Husian's market square and that her friend had confirmed Baozhai's infatuation with the young man. 'But the crucial thing I learned was from their neighbors. They called Mr. and Mrs. Li strict Confucians, suggesting that most of the peasants of Licheng are not. In fact, I learned that most of them are Buddhists.

"Yang looked puzzled. 'Strict Confucians. What would that have to do with it?'

"I replied that it had to do with the traditional Confucian understanding of incest. 'The belief,' I explained to this sophisticated aristocrat raised in Daxing, 'has died out in the cities and large towns but still persists in many peasant villages, including the one in which I was raised. For orthodox Confucians, incest is determined not by blood but surnames. It is forbidden to marry anyone sharing your family name, even if there is no other relation. Honghui and Baozhai are not blood relations, but they share the surname Li, one of the most common in the Empire. I believe that for this reason Baozhai's strict parents vetoed her passionate wish to marry Honghui and that his impending marriage drove her to a tragic, mad, and bloody act.'

"Yang stared at me, dumbfounded. But he did not dismiss what I had told him.

"'And that's why you asked me to put the question to her, about Honghui?'

"'Yes.'

"He grunted. 'And that's why the brother didn't confirm her story of the non-existent robbers. Because it was invented to cover up *her* act, not *his*?'

"I nodded.

"I could see that Yang wanted to attack my theory, to pick out its flaws. What I had suggested was monstrous. At last he said, 'I need to think more about what you've told me, Hsi-wei. Meanwhile, things can stand as they are until morning.'

"Though I felt vaguely that this might be a mistake, I said nothing. I had sandals to make; Deming was safe for the night, and Baozhai was being looked after in Licheng. I will never forgive myself.

Fang said, "Never forgive yourself. What for, Master?"

Hsi-wei sighed and his shoulders slumped.

"'The women of Licheng did take Baozhai home and watched over her,' he said. 'They put her in her own bed and sat by her. But, when she was asleep, they left for their own beds. In the morning they found that the girl had hanged herself.'

After Hsi-wei said that, the two men were quiet for a long while. The moon was up by then, a waxing moon. With some compunction, Fang returned to his original question and asked what the terrible tragedy had to do with Hsi-wei's poem.

"My Lord, I wonder if you know the ancient myth about the origin of marriage—the origin of all of us, actually. I mean the story of Nüwa and Fuxi."

Fang said he might have heard the story as a child, that he had a nurse who told him the old myths which he took for fairy tales, but that he couldn't recall this one well. All he could recall was that it had something to do with the Great Flood.

"Yes, that's right. Nüwa and Fuxi were brother and sister, sole survivors of the Great Flood. According to the simpler version of the myth, the one told to children, the gods charged the siblings with repopulating the earth. They did this by molding thousands of clay figures and, with divine assistance, brought them to life. But there's another version. According to this, after the Flood, the siblings Nüwa and Fuxi found themselves alone. They fell in love and wanted to marry but felt ashamed of their wish. So, they went up into the Kunlon Mountains to be close to the gods and beg for their permission. 'If you allow us to wed, Great Ones, please surround us with a mist,' they prayed. At once, the peak was covered in a dense fog and the gods dictated the rituals of the wedding ceremony. Fuxi rejoiced but, in order to hide her shyness, Nüwa covered her blushes with a fan. That's why, to this day, peasant brides follow the custom of hiding their faces behind ornate fans. When I left Husian two days later, I gave the poem you asked about to Magistrate Yang. He must have sent it to his brother."

THE MADNESS OF NÜWA

Not the best time of the year for the toilsome
climb, but the thin cold air smelled sweet to her.
Down below, the waters were receding.
Bloated corpses were spread about like so
many verdigris boulders. The stink. The flies.
But he took her hand, helped her up the narrow
path, around the crashing falls, higher and higher.
He was so strong, so handsome. He was like her
only so much better. How she wanted him.
At the summit, in air so clear you could
look out on a score of peaks and down on
hundreds of drowned villages, they prayed
fervently for the sign, the mist of permission.
But there was nothing, just air. She didn't weep.
She shrieked and tore her robe and loosed her hair.
She beat her breast and cursed the unfeeling gods
and their pitiless rules. He sank down beside her.
silent, resigned. Or maybe he had already spotted,
far below, that graceful figure in a rose-colored robe.

PROPERTY

I

The hour was nearly up and Dr. Clough, feeling more like a referee than a tutor, was deciding how best to put an end to it.

The wood-paneled room was handsome and cold—all the rooms were. Cambridge was cold. England was cold, without enough butter, heat, or fun. Clough's eight M.A. candidates' serious faces looked pasty. They wore woolen sweaters and tweed—two were wrapped in mufflers, and one sported the fingerless gloves of a Dickensian clerk. This lot was, as his Francophile colleague would say, *bien engagé—un peu trop engagé*, he thought. Gerald Babcock, he of the fingerless gloves, was an ectomorphic Etonian Trotskyite, so there was no disputing with him. He himself argued a great deal, of course—Trotskyites can hardly help it—but the boy had a high-pitched voice, an unfortunate stutter, and expressed himself in such prefabricated clumps of words that nobody paid him much heed. In this class of bright young left-wingers, the really significant red-flag-bearer was Jane Redvers, one of two women in the herd. The Master had made a point of informing Clough that the daughter of the Earl of Telford—very gifted, he understood, and rather good-looking—would be among his charges that term. Clough thought the hint to be nice was clear; but he hadn't anticipated an enemy of the class system, practically an anarchist, and an exceedingly well-read one at that. He had gotten off on the wrong foot with Miss Redvers when on the first day of term he addressed her as *Lady Jane*. How was he to know she would take such umbrage. The few titled people he had met insisted on, seemed to revel in, their honorifics—Sir, My Lord, Your Grace, and so on.

The right wing was represented equally well, if uniquely, by Jack Moorcroft. Clough had gone out of his way to learn a little of Moorcroft. He knew the boy was not from money; on the contrary, his people only narrowly qualified as middle class. It was a maternal uncle, a bachelor, who was paying Jack's way. Clough discovered the uncle had prospered during the war when he converted his zipper factory to the manufacture of ammunition belts. Moorcroft was an exceptional scholar and dogged polemicist who regularly squashed Babcock. Jane Redvers, however, after some initial diffidence, proved herself his match. By comparison, the others were sticks of furniture. Clough had to work harder than he liked to prevent his classes from turning into debates. Redvers's and Moorcroft's frequent fencing and posing of questions he found it irritatingly difficult to answer made Clough recall some advice he'd been given by a jocular senior professor his first week at high table. "Do whatever you're able to keep your pupils away from the library, Clough. Libraries are places to find lectures."

Clough got to his feet as a sign that the proceedings were coming to a close.

"Before you run off to search for some place warm, I've a problem for you to think about for our next meeting. It's what our physicist friends call a thought-experiment." He focused for a full second on each of the eight faces while he propounded the problem.

"Suppose the eldest son of a rich man inherits his estate. This includes a large tract of good land. The heir is spoilt, foolish, and indolent. He allows the manor house to fall into disrepair and his fertile acres to sit idle. It's hard times. The local textile mill has closed, throwing hundreds out of work. The local families are desperate for land and housing. But, even pooling their meager resources, they can't come close to affording the land, let alone the cost of building on it. Now suppose there's a bright young fellow, a developer who has marvelous ideas on how to improve the land, innovative plans for inexpensive housing, and practical plans for new businesses.

"The question I want you to consider is to whom the estate ought to belong. the heir with legal title, the people with urgent needs, or the visionary with the brilliant plan."

Jane Redvers began speaking. "The people—' and, at the same moment, Jack Moorcroft did too. "Legally—" "Shh!" said Clough and put a finger to his lips. "Next week," he said, affecting an avuncular tone. "I hope you'll all enjoy our Monday holiday as much as I'm sure the bankers will."

On the way out Babcock stuttered at Clough. "It's no-not the own-*owner* but the bl-bloody *ownership*."

II.

Even considering how she insisted on provoking him, Jane's father had been more than usually short with her during the long weekend, the climax coming over the Sunday dinner of carrot and potato stew.

Before stalking away from the table, sheepishly followed by twelve-year-old Charles whom everybody called Chipper, the Earl leveled a finger at his daughter and offered first a comment then a prophecy.

The comment. "I'm damned sick of hearing you bang on about this Jack Moorcroft. You've been complaining about him since you got home—and all because, so far as I can make out, he holds sensible views—and yes, I *do* mean views like mine. If you can't bear the fellow, then it would be in good taste to stop talking about him so much."

The forecast. "You were a bluestocking at ten, Jane. Now at twenty-one you're a socialist. It's easy to see that by twenty-five you'll turn into the worst sort of feminist, and at thirty—a spinster!"

As he trailed after his father, Chipper glanced back at his sister ruefully, shook his head, and emphatically mouthed, "You won't."

When they were alone together in the sitting room, Jane's mother explained her husband's ill temper. "I'm afraid it's money troubles again, dear."

"So that's why he was on about the new taxes."

"He has a point, darling. The Labor government does seem intent on—"

"Annihilating a thousand years of unearned privilege. Quite right, too."

"This place means nothing to you, I know, but you might try to understand how deeply your father loves it and the things in it. He doesn't believe they belong to him personally, you see. He feels a profound responsibility, a duty."

"Oh," said Jane airily, "I understand all right. The property must be clung to and handed on intact to Chipper—preferably with a smoother lawn and a new folly at the bottom of the garden."

Lady Telford frowned, more disappointed than angry. "Sometimes, darling, I forget how very young you still are.

It must be those big, rather brutal words you like to use."

"Big words. The unanswerable argument of impolite diction. The naughty child must be sent to the nursery. *Brutal* words. That's just the sort of thing Jack Moorcroft would say if he hadn't a ready riposte."

"You know, your father has a point, Jane. You *do* go on about this Jack quite a bit. What's he like?"

"Infuriating—no, worse. He's the incarnation of *all* that's infuriating."

Lady Telford looked away and smiled. "I meant, what does he look like."

Jane shrugged and toyed with the hem of her skirt.

"It's no wonder your father's upset. We're going to be selling the five best paintings. No help for it, he says."

Jane was momentarily shocked. "Even the Reynolds?"

"And the two Turners, plus the Constable and the Van Dyke."

"The Reynolds?" By an effort of will, Jane recovered herself and said vehemently, "Good!"

"I know you're upset, darling, but apparently it's necessary."

"Upset. Of course I'm not *upset*. Those pictures all belong in a museum where everybody can see them."

"Only if the museum's the highest bidder, my dear."

"I'll tell you what. If they *do* wind up in a museum, I'll make Jack Moorcroft go and take a good long look at them. Art. . . liberated!"

Lady Telford was left still wondering what Jack Moorcroft looked like.

III.

Jack took the train down to London where he spent Friday night and Saturday at his parents' small apartment in Tufnell Park. On Sunday morning his uncle arrived from the Midlands in his Bentley for a brief visit with his sister and her husband. The big sedan carried the cook, Mrs. Hartley, and a cargo of groceries. Uncle Albert did the driving himself as the chauffeur had the weekend off. They all enjoyed Mrs. H.'s baked ham and pastries before, as planned, his uncle Albert plucked Jack away.

Albert Underhill had bought a Georgian manor in Norfolk near the Little Ouse, not far from Brandon. He was having the place refurbished and was eager to show it off to his nephew.

Albert kissed his sister, pumped his brother-in-law's hand, grabbed his nephew's arm, summoned Mrs. Hartley, and headed for the door.

Out by the curb, Albert threw the Bentley's keys to Jack. "Like to take the wheel?"

"Yes. Very much, thanks."

"Once we get shut of the city, the drive'll be picturesque. So's the new squat. I think you'll like it, and we won't be living rough," he said to Jack. "The work's nearly done and we've got the best cook this side of the Channel."

"Oh, what rot," said Mrs. Hartley clambering into the rear seat. "I feel like a duchess back here." She waved her hand regally. "Drive on, Jack."

Jack had known Mrs. H. since he was a child, and they had their private ways of expressing affection. They teased each other along the way by reminiscing. "Remember the time you ate the chocolate truffle cake, my whole blamed dessert?" "Oh, that divine cake. . . it was born of no earthly oven." "I don't know about that, but you were sick as poodle for two days." Uncle Albert was in high spirits too and spoke with boyish glee about the country house. Jack pleased him by asking after his new export markets and explaining why the Labor government's plan to turn London into Moscow was bound to come a cropper in months. As usual, Uncle Albert extolled Churchill; however, to Jack's surprise, he approved the new National Health scheme.

"Reasonable taxes, Jack, make reasonable civilization possible. And a reasonably civilized country *ought* to be reasonably civilized."

"Very reasonable," said Jack dryly. "By the way, who sold you the manor?"

"I suppose you're picturing some decadent aristocratic family, *pater* sitting out the war in the Admiralty while *mater* bravely kept the place above water by growing roses and brats—all of them pushed under by the Chancellor of the Exchequer."

Jack chuckled. "Something like that."

"Nothing of the sort. I bought it off Charlie Grimes. Known him for eons. Charlie was like me, you see. Did pretty well supplying leather goods during the war then went and invested too heavily setting up shop in the Punjab. Not wiped out, mind you, but he's had to cut back. I gather he got it from some debauched lord back in the Thirties. Anyway, thought I might be interested. Quoted me a hefty price but I didn't like to squeeze him."

"So," said Jack brightly. "A man of property now."

Albert scoffed. "Guess so but enough of that. Tell me what you've been up to in Cambridge."

"A good deal of arguing, actually."

"Oh?"

"There's this girl—woman, I should say—in my seminar."

"That would be political economy with, wait a sec, with Clough?"

"You *are* well informed."

"I keep an eye on my investments, Jack. Never forget."

"Oh, I don't. And I'm more grateful than I can say."

"So then, you like this girl. *Woman?*"

"What?"

"Simple question. Do you *like* her?"

This unexpected question acted like a catalyst and precipitated a realization that left Jack momentarily dumbstruck. He found he did like Jane Redvers; in fact, he liked her quite a lot. Jack's astonishment concerned only the top of his neo-cortex; his limbic system and reptilian complex had been aware of the attraction for weeks.

"Tell me about her. Pretty. Good stock?"

"Pretty. Very. Stock. I'm not so sure about that. She's an earl's daughter."

"*Lady* Jane, then?"

"God help the man who calls her that."

"Oh?"

"She's a Bolshie, maybe an anarchist."

"That happens," said Albert smoothly.

"What does?"

"*Noblesse oblige*—though they don't think of it that way, of course. Social conscience among the children of the aristocracy always begins with rebellion against their own class and romantic delusions about those below. It seldom lasts. Anyway, what are you going to do about it?"

"About what?"

"About liking Lady Jane, you dolt."

Jack stared at the road. "Exasperate her," he said with resolution.

Albert laughed and, from deep in the back seat, Mrs. Hartley gave a cackle.

Albert's new country house was large but tasteful and well proportioned. The limestone walls had a rosy tint and were partially covered with creeper and scaffolding on the north side. The drive cut through a park the featured ancient oaks.

"Well, what do you think?" asked Albert as Jack drove the Bentley slowly up the gravel drive.

"The England of an American's imagination. It makes me think of Mozart for some reason."

"Oh," exclaimed Mrs. H., sticking her head between theirs, "it's grand, grand."

They unloaded the food, then the luggage. After Mrs. H. expressed satisfaction with the kitchen, Albert showed her to her room, which, she said again, made her feel like a duchess.

Albert and Jack went upstairs. "There are six bedrooms in all. I had the builders finish three of them," said Albert. "I think we'll be comfortable enough."

Jacked stepped into his enormous room. "Comfortable?" he said. "I think the varsity eight could make themselves comfortable in here."

"There's going to be central heating, too," Albert bragged.

While Mrs. H. saw to dinner, the men took a stroll around the grounds. There were a couple of outbuildings, both in good repair, a thick hardwood copse, and a stream feeding a pool beneath a paved terrace with a stone balustrade.

"I'm thinking of getting some statues to put up here. Roman ones. What do you think?"

"Perfection," said Jack.

After a substantial dinner built around roasted lamb and new potatoes, Jack fetched his Conrad novel and the men adjourned to the library to enjoy their pipes. It was their custom to have a post-prandial read and smoke. Jack noticed his uncle was looking hard at a catalogue.

"What that?"

"Auction. There's something I'm interested in."

Jack put down *Chance* and got up to peer over his uncle's shoulder.

"Paintings, Jack. The walls need some good ones. I'm only an autodidact, of course, but these are first rate. Names even I've heard of. I might get one. Maybe more, if the bidding doesn't go too high."

Jack whistled. Constable. Reynolds. Van Dyck. Turner.

"Who's selling?"

"Anonymous, of course. Always is. But, when he alerted me, my agent said it's the Earl of Telford."

"But that's her *father*."

"*Her* father. You mean Lady Jane's?"

"Aye, aye, sir."

Albert turned in his chair and looked up at Jack with twinkling eyes. "Well, well. Tight little island, isn't it?"

Later in the evening, thinking of Jane Redvers and when he'd next see her, Jack told his uncle Dr. Clough's thought-experiment. "What do you think?"

"Me. Oh, I think Clough's a clever chap. It's a problem with which any economy has to cope, isn't it. There are always people who own resources but can't or won't use them and others who know how to use them but don't own them; and, of course, the majority of people need them but don't own or know how to use them."

"What about ownership itself. This house, the earl's pictures, investment capital. What about private property.

"What about it?"

"Jane Redvers' is of the property-is-theft school."

"And you?"

"Oh, I think it's a jolly good thing."

"Righto, and so do I. But then I have a good deal of it. So, tell me why you approve?"

Taken aback, Jack mumbled, "Lots of reasons."

"I'll listen to one or two," said Albert slyly. "It'll get you ready for Clough's class. You can rehearse your courtship by exasperation."

"*Court*ship?"

"Well, just the exasperation then, the vexing of Red Lady Jane."

"All right. Where there's no right to property there aren't any other rights, either. Hobbes the royalist and Locke the radical agree that the rights to life, liberty, and property derive from nature. The fundamental right is to life, but to live one needs both the liberty to choose one's way of living and property to sustain life. Governments don't confer these rights. The job of government is to make sure they're not snatched away, certainly not to do the snatching themselves."

"Not bad," Albert allowed. "But if our rights depend on property, then mightn't rights become proportional to the worth of that property. Not so long ago that's how it was with the vote, you know."

"True. Only a rule of law that divorces wealth from justice can prevent that. But no good society is perfect."

Albert smiled. "And no perfect society is good. You might use that on your radical classmate. But the imperfections can get in the way of a good society. I know this solicitor keeps a brass plaque in his office that's inscribed with a question. How much justice can you afford?"

"You're just provoking me. You don't agree with Jane Redvers one bit."

"Oh, I don't know, Jack. Probably not. But I haven't read as much as you—or, no doubt, as much as Lady Jane either. But I do hope you'll stick up for private property. I'm quite fond of mine."

Jacked pointed at the catalogue. "So, I imagine, is the Earl of Telford."

Albert squinched up his face and crammed his impression of an Oxbridge accent into one word. "Quite."

IV.

Early November and the room was chillier than ever.

"Well?" said Clough. "Any of you scholars find the time to contemplate my little thought-experiment?"

Up shot the fair hand of Jane Redvers.

Her position was unambiguous. "Control of the estate obviously ought to go to the visionary developer on the ground that this is most likely to ensure the greatest happiness of the greatest number of people." She turned toward Clough. "Two months ago, you warned us to avoid the vulgar error of thinking the greatest happiness principle belonged exclusively to the Utilitarians. You advised us, sir, to regard this principle as the goal of every economic theory, not just Bentham's but Smith's and Marx's as well. You were right to warn us against thinking it the *property* of any one of them. In the same way, it would be a mistake to think the *estate* belonged exclusively to a feckless twit simply because he happened to inherit it. Private property is the stumbling-block to happiness. According to Rousseau, it has been since the first man put a fence around a piece of ground, declared it his, and found fools to believe him. I'm only paraphrasing."

"H-hear, hear," cried Gerald Babcock.

Jane went on. "Bernard Shaw put it neatly half a century ago." Here she plucked an index card from the top of a stack of the things and did a rather good imitation of the Irish playwright's accent. "'Property, said Proudhon, is theft. This is the only perfect truism that has been uttered on the subject.'.

"Bravissima!" exclaimed Gerald.

Before Clough could speak, Jack asked Jane if she'd actually read Proudhon.

She glared at him. "Of course."

"Yes." Jack pointed to the index cards. "I can see you've prepared."

There was nervous laughter and even Clough smiled.

Babcock jumped to the defense. "I'd say P-Proudhon and Shaw got it right. And m-maybe someday *you* sh-shall too, Moorcroft."

Ignoring him, Jack fastened his smile on Jane and said, "*Semper paratus*?"

"It's a good motto and not the property of General Baden-Powell's acolytes."

The students laughed, thoroughly aware that they were an audience.

Clough, who did not want a prize fight, asserted himself. "Since Miss Redvers has brought him up, can anybody give an account of Proudhon's position—something more detailed than the famous slogan?"

Jack, always with his eyes on Jane, crossed his arms and smiled away. Everyone else was silent, waiting—even Gerald Babcock.

Jane shuffled through her cards.

"I've got the relevant passage here, Dr. Clough. It's from *What Is Property*, 1840."

Clough sighed. "Anyone *else*?" He looked around, settled on Jack, who shook his head and returned to grinning at Jane like a well-fed pirate.

"Very well, Miss Redvers. It appears you still hold the floor."

Jane read with much feeling, as if the words were her own. "'If I were asked to answer the following question: What is slavery? And I should answer in one word, It is murder!, my meaning would be understood at once. Why then, to this other question: What is property? May I not likewise answer, It is robbery!, without the certainty of being misunderstood; the second proposition being no other than a transformation of the first?'"

"Thank you, Miss Redvers."

But Jane wasn't finished. She plucked out another index card but didn't bother reading from it this time. "The same view of property was taken by the most progressive early Christians, in particular Saint Ambrose and Basil of Caesarea. Property equals theft. Brissot said the same thing."

Jack interrupted. "Brissot. That would have been shortly before his revolution cut off his head, I presume," he observed coolly. "A question, if you please, Miss Redvers. Do you think Karl Marx agreed with Proudhon and the blessed saints?"

"Of course," Jane scoffed.

"Well, yes, he did—at first. After all, a three-word, easy-to-remember slogan is punchier than workers of the world unite. But the fact is, after he'd thought through Proudhon's formula, Marx didn't. Agree, I mean. Actually, he had lots of objections." As he spoke Jack put his hand in his breast pocket and extracted some folded papers.

"Such *as*?" It was an indignant Gerald Babcock, the only one in the room who had yet to catch on that what they were witnessing was a duel.

"Mr. Moorcroft?" prompted Clough superfluously.

Jack opened up a sheet of paper and read. "'Theft as a forcible violation of property presupposes the existence of property.' That's Marx in 1865. He goes on to say Proudhon was guilty of—wait a second, here it is—'all sort of fantasies, obscure even to himself.'"

Jane almost chortled with scorn. "So, what then? You're saying Marx *approved* of private property?"

"Certainly. And capitalism, too."

The class was enjoying itself. Nobody thought of interfering, not even Clough.

"Really?"

"Never got over being a Young Hegelian, did he. Inevitable dialectic. Marx said an economy had to go through early and late capitalism before the great proletarian revolution could create utopia. Funny, by the way. Marx used to dismiss any leftists who didn't agree with him by calling them *utopians*."

"So then you *agree* with Marx?"

"You know I don't. I'm merely telling you it's Marx who agrees with *me*. But you say you agree with *him*, Miss Redvers. That estate Dr. Clough asked us to think about—call it Britain, call it the world—you'd hand it over to a 'visionary developer.' That would be Karl Marx, the man with the plan. Correct?"

Jane narrowed her eyes. "You're overstating things, as usual."

Jack sailed calmly on. "After some lamentably unavoidable bloodshed and a few hundred five-year plans, property, classes, the state, and history will reach a glorious quietus. It's like the Book of Revelations, only less specific."

Jane, with reddened cheeks, replied contemptuously. "And all this is in defense of letting a useless twit keep an estate?"

"You bet. It's *his*. By *right*."

This was too much for Jane. "Ever see a dog trying to imitate a wolf, Mr. Moorcroft. That's your petty bourgeois Tory."

This was personal and the class gasped. Clough spluttered but had lost control long before.

"Oh, I don't know," said Jack, unperturbed. "The dog may be ambitious and full of good sense. All dogs, after all, are wolves at heart. Wolf is a wolf to wolf," he joked.

"Precisely!"

"Better than a wolf attempting to imitate a mongrel."

This too was personal and evoked more gasps.

"Mr. Moorcroft, Miss Redvers," Clough finally cautioned sharply. "*Please*."

Jack, still smiling, unfolded his last sheet of paper and blithely read. "'In respect of property, harm and abuse cannot be dissevered from the good any more than debit can from asset. To seek to do away with the abuses of property is to destroy the thing itself; just as the striking of a debit from an account is tantamount to striking it from the credit record.'"

Jane, crossly: "And which apologist for the wretched status-quo is that?"

Jack suavely. "That would be Monsieur Pierre-Joseph Proudhon, having second thoughts and muddying the waters just as Marx said. *Confessions of a Revolutionary*, 1849."

Jane, angrily. "If there were no property, there would be no property owners."

Jack, from memory. "'What is owned by everyone is cared for by no one.' That was Aristotle, thinking of the bad idea Plato had long before Proudhon or Marx."

Babcock, fuming. "You're ab-absurd and a-arrogant."

Jack, always smiling. "As for your slur against the industrious bourgeoisie, what can I say. Yes, I'm middle-class—well, just barely."

Babcock, furious at being ignored, spit a little as he said, "H-Hold on, Moorcroft. L-Let's suppose *you* own a—"

"See?" said Jack. "The word *own* begs the question, don't you see. Besides I own hardly anything."

Jane looked down at her cards. "I didn't mean—"

"That people like me always identify with the interests of those above them and despise those below. No, of course you didn't mean that, Miss Redvers. Still, those who *are* in the middle—or near it—enjoy no repose. There's always the imperative to rise and the anxiety about falling. That tension is the motor of energy and imagination. It's why the middle class has taken the lead in every forward step we've made since the dissolution of the monasteries. Who advanced the doctrine of rights because they needed them so badly. Only aristocrats pretend it was a bunch of barons at Runnymede. And these precious rights must include the one to property. In the end your Proudhon himself conceded that liberty *is* property and so I hope, Miss Redvers, will you."

"I certainly won't."

"Well," said Jack with a shrug, "it was only a hope."

Things had arrived at an impasse and the energy level fell accordingly.

Clough offered a few awkward remarks about the unexpected treat of this lively debate and assigned the class an essay on the post-war Austrian currency crisis; then everybody, even the livid Gerald Babcock, jumped up and walked out, leaving a serene Jack and incensed Jane still confronting one another—not unlike the Russians and the Americans in Berlin, Clough mused as he gathered up his papers and made his escape.

V.

Sir Joshua Reynolds' *Portrait of Lady Caroline Redvers* depicts a handsome woman in her early thirties, fashionably dressed in satin of a blue that matches her eyes, seated on a gilded chair before a large window opening on a cerulean sky above a green world. The background is roughed so as not to distract from Lady Caroline's graceful hands and striking countenance. Reynolds managed something wonderful, a face expressing both sympathy and something like mockery—raillery, perhaps. This was a confident and lively woman. Lady Caroline liked politics and politicians liked her; even Tories were regular guests at Telford Hall.

Jane Redvers had no idea, taken all together, how many hours she had spent seated on the stairs looking up to and admiring Reynolds' painting of her ancestor. Its sale precipitated in her a contest of head versus heart, principle at odds with sentiment, pitting intellectual enthusiasm against childhood attachment. All property was theft and yet this picture—she didn't mind a bit about the others—belonged to her. No, it didn't; but also, yes, it did.

When Jack saw the Reynolds portrait in his uncle's catalogue he noted that it was the only picture of a Redvers family member. To part with it, he reckoned, meant the earl must really be in straits. This thought weighed on him and stimulated his imagination. He supposed that Jane must love this picture, and he began to dream of an impossible *coup*, *un beau geste*. The notion so took hold of him that the next time he went to Norfolk he found the nerve to speak to his uncle about it.

The childless Albert Underhill was tickled by his nephew's fantastic notion. Perhaps he liked the latter because he loved the former. In recent years, he found one of the things he most enjoyed about his prosperity was being Jack's rich uncle.

"I'd pay you back, of course," said Jack with impetuous earnestness. "Eventually."

"Not a bit of it. Take it as a gift, Jack. Anyhow, it's still a *sort* of investment, you know. But first we'll have to get hold of it."

The auction was on a Friday afternoon late in November. After a good deal of vacillation Jane decided to attend. She didn't tell her parents, who would, she guessed, have tried to forbid it. To watch that portrait go on the block, she told herself, would be an act of self-discipline, just penance for her unearned privileges. She thought of her running skirmishes with the maddening Jack Moorcroft and said to herself, "I'll be putting my money where my mouth is—*some*body's money, anyway."

Jack accompanied his uncle to the auction. The hall filled up quickly and they found seats on the far right of a middle row. It hadn't occurred to Jack that Jane Redvers would, like him, come down from Cambridge for the event. He was taken aback when he spied her standing behind a pillar at the rear of the hall and quickly ducked his head. "*She's* here," he whispered hurriedly to his uncle. "Don't want her to see me. Sorry. *Bon courage.*" Then Jack jostled his way through the late arrivals to the back of the hall and hid behind another pillar so that he could peer around it, keeping an eye on both Jane and the bidding.

The Turners both went high, as did the van Dyke. After that, quite a few people rose and left, demonstrably disappointed. With the diminished competition, Albert got the Constable for little more than the earl's reserve. As the pictures were knocked down, Jack detected nothing but indifference in Jane's face or posture. She lounged against her pillar with almost ostentatious nonchalance.

The Reynolds was the last in the lot. Jack was excited, his attention divided between the auctioneer and Jane. When the picture was brought in, he saw her step away from the pillar and cross her arms over her chest, as if suddenly cold. He got one good look at her face and the sight made Jack feel something sharp in the center of his body, pain at seeing Jane Redvers looking not nonchalant, exasperated, angry, frustrated, or self-righteous, but distressed.

There were only four serious bidders. It all went rapidly and, to Jack's delight, successfully. He was shocked that he could think paying two thousand pounds for anything a bargain.

As the gavel descended, Jack stepped back from his pillar. Jane was standing completely still, her head bowed like a mourning angel in a cemetery. Following an irresistible impulse, he went to her. She had a handkerchief in her hand and when she found him suddenly beside her, dropped it.

"You?"

"Me," he said softly and, true to his impulse, took her hand. "Come with me."

She was docile. He led her from the hall and around the corner to a pub.

They had a great deal less to say to each other than they did in Clough's tutorials yet communicated better.

Jack accounted for his presence at the auction by telling her about his uncle having bought a new house and wanting some antique furnishings for it.

Jane explained about the Reynolds, tried to make light of losing it and mocked herself for caring. "You'll call me a hypocrite."

"No," he said gently. "What was it Proudhon said— something about striking assets along with debits?"

"Won't your uncle be missing you?"

"Maybe. Probably. But I'm not leaving you," said Jack stoutly.

They took the five o'clock train back to Cambridge together.

VI.

During the weeks before Christmas Clough's tutorial turned suddenly placid, focused, and dull. On the whole, he was relieved; still, he was puzzled by the absence of the heat-generating abrasion between Mr. Moorcroft and Miss Redvers. The views of neither had altered. Both submitted first-rate, contradictory papers. Moorcroft had written an incisive essay on Adam Smith's critique of mercantilism while Miss Redvers' turned in a sympathetic exegesis of the views of the anarchist Johann Kaspar Schmidt, alias Max Stirner. The class made their way through the end of the syllabus, but all the energy had vanished.

Jack still sparred but half-heartedly, starting his discourses with phrases like "I take Miss Redvers' point, but. . ."

Jane still offered ripostes but began them with unwonted courtesy. "Though Mr. Moorcroft's no doubt better informed than I am, nevertheless. . ."

When he mentioned this to Mrs. Clough, a sensible woman and anthropology lecturer, she filled him in on the effects of sexual tension among the young and fertile.

"Ah," he said. "I see." Clough's excellent wife often made him feel stupid; it was the chief way he became aware of her excellence. Of her erudite husband, she once observed, "He knows everything—but that's all he knows."

On the last night of term, Jack invited Jane to his favorite restaurant, one of Cambridge's cheapest. Oil cloth on the tables, plenty of pasta on the plates.

Jack leaned across the small table and took Jane's hand, a gesture which she had learned not just to tolerate but enjoy. "Look," he said, "we'll both be with our families for Christmas."

"Tradition," she said. "In my family it comes with the air."

"Sure. I understand. And I'll be in London for the week. I'm not sure my father agrees, but my mother seems to think they don't see enough of me. However, my uncle's invited me down to Norfolk for the first week of January. His new place is about finished; the dear fellow's house-proud and needs to show it off. He begged me to bring somebody. May I tell him you'll come?"

"For the whole week?"

"Two, if you like."

She laughed, then frowned and squirmed a little. "This doesn't matter and of course it shouldn't, but, you see, my parents haven't actually met you and—"

"Fine. Then I'll meet them. You sort out the invitation and I'll bathe. If necessary, I'll shave and rent a dinner jacket, lie about my origins and talk posh—I might even manage a public school stutter like Babcock's if you think it would help."

"Enough, Jack!"

Jack received a written invitation to dinner at Telford Hall for the third day after Christmas. Jane and her father picked him up at the station in a pre-war Morris 8. "Lord Telford," said Jack, "thank you so much for the invitation and for this unexpected honor. Lovely car, by the way. A classic."

"Like my daughter," the earl observed dryly, "and nearly the same age."

Telford Hall was a Tudor pile with additions from later centuries, but signs of neglect were everywhere—uncleared brush and dead gardens, flaking stucco, crumbly cornices. The inside was much the same; that is, magnificent in general, decaying in detail. Jack thought the introduction to Jane's mother and brother went well. They were friendly, natural, not at all pompous. He felt himself welcome and, though an object of close scrutiny, not judged. Chipper was excited to have a male guest but restrained himself. "Jane says you're very smart but completely wrong-headed. Can you do Latin translations. I can't. I prefer cricket; in fact, I've got a collection of old bats. Maybe you'd like to take a look at them?"

Jack saw at once where the missing pictures had hung.

Dinner, vegetarian but ample, was served by an ancient fellow who kept mumbling at Chipper to sit up straight. Chipper ignored him. Jane had told Jack no dinner jacket was required. He looked presentable in his old Harris tweed and twills, improved with a new shirt and pair of oxfords. He was seated next to Jane and the focus of attention. Neither nervous nor completely at ease, he was determined not to disappoint. Many questions were lobbed his way, so he spoke a good deal and in his usual style—a mixture of the ironically formal, rigorously logical, and purely antic—which seemed to please Jane's mother and not to bore her brother. The earl was unreadable. Chipper roared at his story about how a class of undergraduates divided themselves into teams and played a term-long game of cricket by assigning runs and outs to the clichés which marred a certain professor's lectures. "He was so pleased when there were cheers at the end of his last lecture. So far as I know, he didn't even notice that they only came from the left side of the hall. It was a tight match, you see, and that the final *in point of fact* decided the contest."

After dinner, Jane's father ushered Jack into the library. Here he was treated to Jack's views on the Labor government and a persuasive prediction of its imminent collapse. The Earl could hardly believe such a level-headed young man had engaged the affections of his Bolshevik daughter, but he was delighted by it.

The consequence of the vetting was that Jane was granted leave to spend two days and one night in Norfolk.

Uncle Albert, not one to do anything by half, told Jack he had to take the Bentley to Telford Hall to pick up Lady Jane. "What do you think. Will her people will be impressed or offended?"

"Please don't call her that," Jack reminded him.

"Oh, but I *want* to, Jack. Especially now that I know she can be won over by exasperation."

Jack rolled his eyes. "You've been warned."

Separated for a week, the young people were so glad to see each other that they neglected to argue about anything at all on the drive. They talked only about their families, their childhoods, themselves.

Uncle Albert greeted them at the door.

"Welcome to my house, Lady Jane. Jack's told me I'm taking my life in my hands in calling you Lady Jane, Lady Jane, but I live dangerously, Lady Jane."

To Jack's surprise, Jane laughed and held out a regal hand to his beaming uncle who kissed it.

Mrs. Hartley popped out of the kitchen to have a look. She actually curtsied and offered Jack a furtive nod of approval followed by a thumbs-up. Jack hoped she wouldn't trot out the famous story of the chocolate truffle.

Jane was taken on a tour of the house and duly admired everything.

"I thought you were poor," she whispered to Jack.

"I am. It's my uncle who isn't."

"Evidently. What did it?"

"Zippers."

Dinner was jolly. The Christmas decorations were still up, Mrs. H. prepared a sumptuous meal, and the conversation was amiable, light, and entirely apolitical.

After dinner, Albert excused himself, saying he had to make a phone call.

Jack took Jane's hand. "I never gave you your Christmas present," he said.

"Present. I didn't give you one, either."

"True. And I'd have been desolated if I didn't know your views so well. Rousseau and Proudhon probably didn't give Christmas presents, though I suppose Saint Ambrose might have."

"I like your uncle."

"They don't come any better."

"Millionaires or uncles?"

"Don't tease."

"I can see how fond the two of you are of each other."

"Yes, we are. And since I'm every bit as fond of you and think Proudhon had the wrong end of the stick, I *did* get you a present. Wait here a minute. It's upstairs."

Jane was a little put out with herself for being excited to see what little trinket Jack had chosen for her.

He came back with something not small at all. It was big, oblong, heavy, and wrapped in silver paper that prettily reflected the light from the red Christmas candles on the table and the mantel.

Jane drew back her head and looked up at Jack warily. He leaned his gift against his uncle's empty chair and presented Jane with a pair of scissors. As she cut the wrapping paper a little cry escaped her. It might have expressed either joy or dismay, possibly both.

"My God. You're terrible," she growled.

Jack smiled at her serenely, as he had in Clough's tutorial and, as he had done then, quoted Proudhon. "'In respect of property, harm and abuse cannot be dissevered from the good any more than debit can from asset." We all have to accept the good with the bad, the losses with the gains, Jane. I hope you're pleased, a little, at least, even if it's against your will."

Jane cut away the wrapping paper and stared at the painting. She had never been so close to it. She touched her forefinger to its surface.

"What am I supposed to do with it?"

"Hang it back on the wall at Telford, stick it in the attic, cut it to ribbons, or give it to the National Portrait Gallery. Whatever you like. It's your property now."

Jane got to her feet and stood confronting Jack, who was holding his breath.

"You really *are* terrible, Jack Moorcroft," she said bitterly. "*Terrible*," she said sweetly.

Then Jane moved her face nearer to his until it was impossible to get any closer.

HSI-WEI AT THE MOON FESTIVAL

That summer, Chen Hsi-wei traveled through Liangzhou, the Empire's westernmost province. It had been seven years since the peasant/poet left Daxing to become a vagabond, selling his straw sandals and leaving behind those verses that would eventually win him a measure of fame. He was still in his twenties; it would be years before he would receive invitations to stay in the villas by high officials and to banquets by cultured wives wishing to show him off to their friends. Back then, Hsi-wei found shelter in the towns as he did on the road, whatever he could afford. He looked out especially for rundown inns. If the place had a stable, he could usually stay in it for hardly any money, sometimes for just a pair or two of sandals. If the weather was good, he could sleep out of doors; but when it was not, he would talk his way into barns, storerooms, pantries, and, on one occasion, a closet.

On the fifteenth of Osmanthus, shortly before noon, Hsi-wei passed through Yicheng's North Gate. Though it was the day of the Moon Festival, few people were on the streets. All morning, rain had been pouring down from a gloomy, sunless sky, and it was unseasonably cold. Hsi-wei arrived in the town drenched and shivering.

Not far from the gate he spotted an inn that still showed traces of red paint on its gray boards. Behind it was a small stable, which looked on the point of tumbling down. Hsi-wei went inside the inn hoping to warm himself but the main room was chilly and damp. However, at the far end, under a hole in the ceiling, the landlord had set up a brazier. The locals had pulled stools up in a tight circle around the fire where they drank and gossiped. Nobody looked at the dripping stranger shivering with cold.

Hsi-wei noticed a doorway and peered inside. A heavy-set man with an ugly mustache and a cleaver in his hand stood at a high table cutting up pork, cabbages, and spring onions. At one end of the table, a basket of eggs rested beside a big pot of water. Hsi-wei had heard that the local specialty was boiled pork prepared with a coating of egg white.

The innkeeper gave Hsi-wei a contemptuous glance and said, "You look like a half-drowned puppy."

"I would like to stay here tonight."

The man pointed up with his cleaver. "I have two good rooms up there. Clean ones. You don't look like you've got enough money for either of them."

"Most likely not, but I would be grateful if you would permit me a corner in your stable. I can pay with some good straw sandals."

"So, you're a sandal-maker. Well, it's late in the year for straw sandals and I don't need any, but I'll let you stay if you make a pair for my wife and one more for her mother. Both small."

Hsi-wei gave a short bow. "Thank you. That is agreeable."

The landlord grunted. "Then it's settled. Now, go in with the others before you start sneezing all over me and this pork."

In the main room, there was still no place by the fire. Just then Hsi-wei heard horse's hoofs outside. A minute later, the door swung open and a tall man in a dripping official's gown entered, shaking out a soaked fur cap. He was distinguished looking man, spare, about forty with a narrow, intelligent face and keen eyes. The men around the brazier looked over at him apprehensively. The man ignored them and called for the innkeeper who stuck his head out of the kitchen.

Seeing the official's gown, the landlord came into the room, gave a short bow, and adopted a deferential manner.

"What can I get for you, Sir. Wine. Perhaps you want a room. I have two, very clean."

"First, you can see that my horse is stabled and brushed dry," ordered the official.

"Yes, Sir. I'll send the boy at once."

Hsi-wei was still shivering by the door, right next to the newcomer who turned toward him and smiled.

Pointing at the rainwater that had gathered around their feet, he said, "We're both in the same sorry state." Then he nodded toward the circle of locals around the brazier. "It's cold over here but it looks warm over there."

"They won't make room by the fire," observed Hsi-wei.

The official grinned. "I believe I can fix that. Look, whatever happens, just stay where you are." Then he summoned the landlord again.

"What have you got to eat?" he demanded.

"I've been preparing our Liang pork, Your Honor. There's some ready now if you'd like."

"Excellent. Please put the meal in a bowl and take it out to my horse."

"What. To your *horse*?"

The official took out a purse and shook it so the innkeeper could hear the sound.

"Yes, take it to my horse and do it as quickly as possible. We've been on the road this whole wet morning and the poor beast's famished."

The men around the fire paid close attention to this astonishing exchange. Their mouths fell open.

The landlord scratched his head, looked at the purse, shrugged, and vanished into the kitchen. A few minutes later, he came out with a steaming clay bowl and headed for the stable.

All the men around the fire got up and followed. They'd never seen a horse that ate Liang pork.

As soon as they were gone, the official sat down on one of the stools closest to the brazier and motioned for Hsi-wei to join him.

The man stretched his hands toward the heat. "Now, that's better."

A minute later, the innkeeper came back with the bowl, followed by the locals.

"Your horse wouldn't touch the pork," the innkeeper complained.

"Well, that's a pity. But never mind. Just put the pork by the fire here. It will make a good meal for me and my friend. . ." The official glanced at the bedraggled poet and raised his eyebrows.

"Chen Hsi-wei. Sandal-maker. At your service."

The official gave Hsi-wei a nod that was friendly rather than imperious. "Wang Jiang-guo, Assistant Magistrate of Meishan. You'll join me in the meal?"

"Gladly," said Hsi-wei. "It's a clever way to get these warm stools and you're generous to share your horse's feast with a stranger."

Wang gave Hsi-wei an avuncular smile. "The brotherhood of distress."

The locals filed out, grumbling.

As it happened, Hsi-wei and Assistant Magistrate Wang had a good deal to say to one another. Though the conversation began with tedious comments on the deplorable condition of the roads and the nastiness of the weather, they soon moved on to more serious subjects such as the progress of Emperor Wen's land reform and his plan for distributing new coins. Wang spoke of the number of temples he had seen on the way from Meishan, which led to a discussion of the emperor's support for Buddhism. Though neither was a Buddhist, both men judged the policy a good thing, on the whole.

"So long as he doesn't neglect the sound teachings of Kong Qiu, of course," Wang cautioned.

"Will you be staying long in Yicheng?" Hsi-wei asked.

"No, not long. I'm just here to collect a report on some relatives of one of our big landowners in Meishan. The fellow is at the center of a complicated case having to do with the improper acquisition of land and evasion of the new laws. The man's in-laws are from Yicheng and it appears his wife's uncles are involved in the scheme."

Hsi-wei was surprised that someone like Wang would be given such a task. "All the way from Meishan just to collect a report?"

"Yes."

"But, with respect, wouldn't that be a job for somebody of lesser rank?"

Wang nodded. "Normally, yes. But the matter is urgent and no one at the magistracy wanted to be away from home during the Moon Festival. As it doesn't matter to me, I volunteered for the journey."

Hsi-wei noted the melancholy in Wang's voice. Either his new friend had no family, or he had one from which he wished to escape. Hsi-wei thought the former more likely.

"Tell me about yourself, young man," Wang asked. "How did you come to be an itinerant sandal-maker?"

"When I was a boy, my uncle taught me how to make sandals. I left Daxing two years ago and have been on the road ever since."

"Look, we're both here on our own on the day of the Moon Festival. The day's dreary but it's still a festival. It's unlikely we'll see each other again after today. Let's talk like new friends who pretend to be old ones. So, come now, I'm sure there's more to your story."

"It's a story that's hard to believe."

"Well, that's intriguing. Let's hear it."

Hsi-wei told about being sent to the capital as a boy because the government put out a request for illiterate peasant boys with fast-growing hair; how he was chosen to take a message to General Fu in the South; how his head was shaved and the words written on his scalp; how, after his hair had grown back, he was sent on his dangerous journey. Later, he learned that the message was from Yang Jiang himself and proved critical to the victory over the South that enabled him to unite the Empire for the first time in three hundred years and to declare himself Emperor Wen of Sui. Hsi-wei told Wang how on his return he had been offered the customary rewards but asked instead to be educated because of having words he couldn't read on his head. He described the strict Master Shen Kuo, compelled against his will to teach a peasant boy; how he had been beaten by Shen and mocked by most of his aristocratic classmates, though he also found among them some good friends. Then he tried to explain the strange thing that had happened, how from copying out he verses of the ancient masters he had begun to write his own. He concluded by saying that when he was old enough, he had left Daxing and took to the road. He did not say more about what led him to leave the capital. He kept to himself the story of his love for the young widow Tian Miao and how, with nothing to offer, he had gone away to clear the path for a well-off suitor who could make her happier.

"Why go on the road instead of returning to your village?"

"There was nothing to draw me back. My grandfather died when I was a child. I loved him very much. I loved my parents too, but both of them died of a fever while I was learning the classics and exasperating Master Shen with my terrible calligraphy."

"I see," said Wang.

"And you. There's no one you'd prefer to be with in Meishan tonight?"

Wang took a deep breath. "My wife died two years ago," he said stoically. "We had one child—or we would have. Mother and child died together."

There was nothing Hsi-wei could say to this, and so the two men ate in silence.

Suddenly Wang struck his thigh. "So," he said in a brighter tone, "do you still write poems?"

"I try."

"Recite one for me."

"I'm not used to reciting my verses."

"Indulge me. Pay for the pork."

"Very well. I'll try, if you please. In honor of the day, here's a poem about the moon." Hsi-wei recited *Yellow Moon at Lake Weishan*, the poem that became his most popular.

Wang squinted at Hsi-wei, clearly impressed. "You wrote *that*?"

"Yes, Sir."

"Well then, now I believe every word of your story."

Wang called to the innkeeper to bring them a jug of wine and two cups.

As they drank, Hsi-wei asked to learn more about the complicated case in Meishan. Wang obliged, taking professional pleasure in laying out the sordid story. Hsi-wei was attentive, asked questions about the men and women involved and even about some finer points of law. In this way, the two spent the afternoon, chewing over a criminal scheme and drinking yellow wine.

At dusk, Wang said, "Listen."

"What is it?"

"Nothing. No rain striking the roof."

"Yes, it's stopped."

"Perfect. Now that we've gotten warm and dry and a little drunk, what do you say we take a stroll through the town and see the full moon. It's a duty to look at the moon tonight."

Before leaving the inn, Wang bought another jug of yellow wine and paid the innkeeper for the cups too.

The streets and lanes of Yicheng had filled with happy children running about with lanterns, young couples strolling hand in hand, and old ones stopping to greet one another. Freed from the last ragged clouds, the full moon showered the town with a silvery light. Here and there, firecrackers were set off and, every few yards, women were selling mooncakes. People had set out small altars with clay or stone statues of the Moon Goddess. Passersby stopped to whisper a prayer for a child or an abundant harvest, for beauty, good fortune, long life, maybe for revenge or the death of a mother-in-law.

The sights and smells of the Moon Festival made the two men reflective, nostalgic and a little melancholy.

"This is my second Moon Festival on the road," said Hsi-wei as they watched two young couples laughing together and children squealing as they chased after each other. "In my village, we had special games during the Moon Festival. Have you heard of the one called 'Circle the Toad'?"

"Never heard of it. How's it played?"

"Boys draw straws and the one with the short straw has to stand still while the others make a circle around him and chant *Long life to the King of Toads! May he rule for a thousand years.* The chant's supposed to turn the boy into a toad—magic. Then he has to squat down and jump around like a toad until someone takes pity and sprinkles water on his head to turn him back into a boy again."

"I didn't play such games. We always spent the holiday at my grandparents' villa. My aunts and uncles all came. But my cousins were much older than I was, too old to play with me. My grandmother kept me near her, and every year would tell me the same story, the one about how the Sun God and the Moon Goddess are a married couple and the stars their children. She'd point up at the full moon and say that when she looks like that it means that she's pregnant and when she turns back into a crescent it means that a new star has been born."

"A pretty story."

"I used to believe it," said Wang with a wistful smile. "It's possible that she did."

They stopped so Wang could buy some mooncakes. He

asked the woman if she had any stuffed with red bean paste and when she said she did, he asked her for a whole basket.

"My favorite when I was a boy," he said offering one to Hsi-wei. "I liked sweets back then," he said staring up at the moon.

Hsi-wei did the same and fancied that though Wang was standing beside him in the moonlight of Yicheng he was also back at his grandparents' villa listening to his grandmother's story of the sun and moon and stars. Then Hsi-wei thought that it wasn't so different for him. Though he was chewing a sweet mooncake he was also a little boy in the middle of a circle of chanting children.

Their recollections made both men sad but happy, too. Nostalgia is like that.

They resumed walking toward the main square where they found an empty bench, sat down with their wine and cakes, and watched the lively crowd, listening to the greetings, laughter, and jokes. They felt like a couple of ghosts.

"My grandfather," said Hsi-wei, "also told me a story on the night of the Moon Festival. He must have told it to me every year until he died. You must know it, too—the story of Hou Yi and his wife Chang'e."

"Ah, of course. The elixir of immortality. There's more than one version of that tale—more than two. Can you remember how your grandfather told it?"

"I'm not sure I can, not all of it, anyway. It was long ago and it was complicated, like your case of fraud. I remember that the archer Hou Yi killed a monster or a devil of some kind and the gods rewarded him with a vial of the immortality elixir. But then for some reason he had to make a journey and, while he was away, his apprentice tried to steal the elixir for himself. But Hou Yi's virtuous wife Chang'e seized the vial first and swallowed it down. Hou Yi arrived home just as she was rising into the heavens and cried up at her helplessly. Chang'e longed to rejoin her husband but couldn't because she had become immortal. So, she settled on the moon to stay as close as she could to Ho Yi. According to my grandfather, whenever the moon was full, Hou Yi would honor his lost beloved by laying out her favorite foods in his courtyard. That was how my grandfather explained who the Moon Goddess was and that it is to remember Hou Yi's offerings to Chang'e that we make mooncakes on the day of the Festival and gobble them up at night. When he got to the mooncakes, grandfather would always pop one in my mouth." Hsi-wei laughed at the memory.

"Shall I pop a mooncake in your mouth?" said Wang.

Hsi-wei laughed.

"Well, your grandfather had one version of the story," said Wang. "The one I was told is nearly the opposite."

"The opposite. How's that?"

"My uncle, who had been a minister of Zhou during the wars, told it to me this way. He said that Hou Yi, the great archer, was asked by the gods to go to Shun and slay a monster that had been wreaking havoc there. Things had gotten so bad that the King of Shun himself had run away with his family. After Hou Yi dispatched the monster, the people of Shun made him their new king and the gods rewarded him with a jade bottle containing the elixir of immortality. As Hou Yi was still young and strong, he decided to lock the elixir in a special iron box, telling himself he would take it when he began to weaken and grow old. But power isn't good for some people. The hero the virtuous Chang'e had married, the brave and humane man she had followed to Shun, the skilled archer who had slain the monster, the monarch with the people's mandate, turned into a tyrant guilty of countless cruelties. Horrified by her husband's viciousness and the prospect of his going on harming people forever, Chang'e resolved to prevent that. She broke into the iron box and drank down the elixir. Then, just as in your grandfather's version, she rose into the heavens and became the Moon Goddess, watching over the people who worshipped her and prayed to her every autumn—the men for a good harvest and the women for healthy children."

Hsi-wei gave a nod. "I like your version better," he said. "Even though both stories are fables, yours seems closer to the truth."

Wang smiled. "I suppose a poet would know. Do you make fables that aim at the truth?"

Hsi-wei acknowledged this perceptive remark with a slight bow and then the two men again fell silent, each lost in his own chamber of memory.

At length, Wang gave a deep sigh.

"What is it?" asked Hsi-wei.

"The story of Hou and Chang'e has made me think about how I won my wife all those years ago. It was on this very night, that of the Moon Festival."

"If it won't cause you too much pain, I'd like to hear the story."

"Pain. A few years ago, I interviewed a woman whose husband had filed a petition to put her aside because of her constant complaining. She confided to me that the only thing that relieved the pain of her miserable marriage was whining about everything her husband did to hurt her."

"Did you think the woman spiteful?"

Wang gave a grunt. "Perhaps, but no more than her

husband. Well, I'll tell you what's hurting me now and maybe I'll feel better too. In my village, the Moon Festival was a time for matchmaking. There was a local tradition, a kind of formal game for the older children—more serious than your King Toad in the Circle. On the Festival night, young men would invite the marriageable girls who'd caught their eye to meet them at a certain clearing in the forest outside of the West Gate of the village. The girls would all come early and hide themselves in the thicket. When the boys arrived with their lanterns, they'd compete with one another in praising their chosen girls. This one's eyes, that one's smile, another's virtue, modesty, sweetness—and the beauty of them all. Then, at a signal, the girls would burst from the woods and go to their sweethearts. If they approved of what they'd heard, they would take their hands."

"And your wife took your hand?"

"Mmm. She did. On the night of the Moon Festival. This night."

Hsi-wei was suddenly overcome with homesickness and recalled something that had happened with his grandfather. They were walking through the village when the old man greeted a poor widow and discreetly slipped a few coins into her hand. The old veteran did this sort of thing all the time. "Grandfather, why are you so kind to everybody?" little Hsi-wei had asked.

"Because of the many men I killed and the more I saw being killed," was his grandfather's reply. At the time, Hsi-wei was too young to understand.

It grew late. The crowds dispersed. The lanterns burnt out. The children were all sent to bed by their parents. The jug of yellow wine was empty. The two men got up from the bench and, slightly tottering, circled back to the inn where they bid each other a quick, rather embarrassed good night.

There were no farewells in the morning. Wang left early for the magistrate's office while Hsi-wei slept late and then went to the square to buy straw for the sandals he owed the innkeeper and scare up some customers. Wang didn't return to the inn. He stayed in the villa of the local magistrate that night and left Yicheng the following morning. Hsi-wei stayed two more days, until he had filled all his orders for straw sandals.

Though the poet's visit to Yicheng was brief, it did have one lasting result, the short poem people called "Two Moon Festivals".

For two autumns I'd walked the Empire's rutted roads alone.
But that night in Yicheng, Wang Jiang-guo and I drank together.
We polished off two jugs of yellow wine, glad not to be alone.
We wallowed in memories sweet as mooncakes yet painful to tell.
All night, Chang'e watched over us as if sharing our homesickness.

MARCHE MILITAIRE

Olivier shivered in the chill of the November dusk, but his nose barely registered the smells of rot and mud, unwashed bodies, feces, and wood smoke.

His unit had been taken off the line and ordered to Souville and the safety of its buried fort for a few days' rest. They had been on the line for weeks, hunkered down under barrages then pushing the Germans back by inches. The officers read them dispatches lauding their progress but omitting to mention the butcher's bill. The Battle of Verdun was in its ninth month and gave every indication of being interminable, something bound to outlive them, like the war itself.

Carefully balancing his tin bowl and cup, Olivier made his way through the gravel and mud to a corner without any sprawled and sleeping bodies, without hysterical laughter or weeping, without men engaged in competitive complaining. He hunched down with his back against the wall and took a sip from his cup. The liquid might have been trying to be either coffee or tea but, in either case, without success. It wasn't even hot. He sniffed suspiciously at the slop that had been dropped in his bowl.

"What's this?" the man ahead of him had asked.

"A present from our great allies," cracked the cook and pointed over his shoulder to a heap of empty yellow tins.

Olivier squinted at the label on the nearest tin. Maconochie's Stew.

After the deafening barrages and terrifying advances against entrenched positions, after the machine guns, the grenades and barbed wire, after the unrelieved stench of corpses and latrines, after the rats, the lice, the trench foot and ulcers, after the deaths of Yves, Charles, Henri, and little Pierrot, who'd have thought the last straw would turn out to be a can of bully beef and colorless vegetables suspended in Aberdeen water. But that a Frenchman, even a lowly *soldat 1.eme*, should be given Scottish muck—it was simply too much for Olivier who, it must be said, might not have been altogether in his right mind, a consideration that later became a matter for some speculation.

His plan was rudimentary. He would wait until full darkness then slip away, make his way to the Meuse, and follow the river south to Langres from where it was only six kilometers to his parents' farm. Then he would hide out until either the war or the world came to an end. His father might need some persuading, might even want to turn him in; but Olivier would rather face the patriotic wrath of Carriveau père than another a bowl of British sludge, let alone another MG08.

During the evening, Olivier moved from one group to another, making sure he was noticed, supposing that this would mean it would take longer for him to be missed in the morning. When the snoring was going like a whole orchestra of pipe organs, Olivier gathered his gear—bedroll, gas mask, mess kit, and ammunition belt—and crept toward the entrance to the cave-like fort thinking of the hills and woods beyond. As a boy, he had hunted rabbits and fowl with his father and Uncle Bertrand. Olivier was a better shot than either and he had qualified as a sharpshooter. The rifle slung over his shoulder was fitted with a telescopic sight.

As he neared the entrance, Olivier prayed that it would be unguarded. As it happened, only a single sentry had been set, and he had fallen asleep on a stool with his back against the metal grating. Olivier took a deep breath and judged this to be an acceptable reply to his prayer.

Making his way through the woods in the dark was difficult, but once Olivier found the Meuse he began to make good progress. When he encountered troops or vehicles on the move, he hid either in the foliage beside the road or in the reeds on the riverbank. If hiding wasn't feasible, he stood to attention, saluted smartly, looked straight ahead and marched on as purposefully as though he were under strict orders to do precisely that.

It was shortly before dawn when the background noise of artillery grew louder, though it wasn't close enough for Olivier to tell from which side of the river it came. Had there been a German breakthrough, a probing action. Were the French advancing. Retreating. He kept moving forward but pulled up short outside St. Mihiel where he saw a French checkpoint being set up. There were sandbags and six armed men plus an officer. Something was up. They meant business. Bayonets were fixed. They'd certainly want to know why he wasn't with his unit; they'd insist on seeing his papers. He veered away from the road before they spotted him and headed into a thick stand of pines.

Olivier considered it would be prudent to make a large loop, working around the checkpoint and, if possible, all of St. Mihiel. The terrain had both forest and fields and he was heartened and refreshed to see trees that hadn't been blasted to stumps and skeletons, fields not pocked with craters or strewn with wire. He stuck as best he could to the wooded areas, avoiding open ground; but, for this reason, he found it hard to keep his bearings. In the early morning it had been easy to orient himself by the sun, but the day had grown overcast and he was unsure of his both direction and his distance from the river. He made a guess and pressed on, using his rifle to push back the undergrowth, clambering up boulders, always keeping well away from open country. It was as he came through a tangled patch of alders near the top of a ridge that he heard below him the burst of a "coffee mill"— a German heavy machine gun. He froze.

The 08 rattled again and Olivier, now focused intently on the sound, could tell it came from the other side of the ridge. He crawled carefully to the top and lay down on his belly.

The 08 had been mounted behind a stone wall and pointed at an open field. It was an ambush. There were the usual five men to service the weapon, all in field gray, plus an extra rifleman whose Mauser had a sight on it, just like Olivier's Lebel. Would that sniper also prefer to desert, Olivier briefly wondered.

Three poilus lay still in the high grass, wounded or dead. Olivier could make out others trying to hide behind the field's meager cover of rocks and fallen limbs. The machine gun raked the field. The wounded and terrified cried out. The German sniper, perfectly positioned to pick off any man attempting to stand and run, rested his gun on the wall, using it to steady his aim. It was just what Olivier would have done.

For an instant, he thought of slipping back down the ridge. He couldn't. He sighed. Careful to make as little noise as possible, he extracted two clips from his ammunition belt and placed them on the ground, took off his pack and his helmet, checked the scope on his rifle and laid it down beside the clips, assumed a prone position, then went to work. He took out the man firing the machine gun first, then the man next to him, the one who fed belts into the machine. One of the remaining Germans turned, having figured out where the shots were coming from. "*Da drüben!*" he shouted. Olivier dropped him before he raised his arm to point. One of the two men left dove for cover but moved too slowly and Olivier hit him square in the back with the last bullet in the clip. He fumbled to insert a new one as the sniper threw down his rifle and began frantically trying to turn the machine gun around. The big gun gave the man some cover. Though he was exposing himself, Olivier stood up, sighted over the machine gun, drew a bead just below the man's helmet and fired two shots.

Everything grew terribly silent. Then a shout went up from the Frenchmen in the field. They leapt up and ran from their cover, some to their fallen comrades, others to the German position, rifles at the ready.

Olivier knew he should just abandon his gear and run, run toward the Meuse if he could find it. But the men had seen him when he stood to shoot the last German. They were cheering. Half a dozen were already halfway up the ridge. It was no use.

Four days later, Général de Brigade Jean-Philippe Tourdonnet, a decent and therefore troubled man, convened a court martial. He personally made sure the three officers he appointed understood both the facts and the law. "Your job is to advise me," he said in a tone meant to relieve them. Then, standing at rigid attention, he added unnecessarily, "The responsibility rests with me."

Private Carriveau would be represented by a young officer, Lieutenant Étienne Plamondan, a law graduate who had served six months at the front in 1915 before losing an arm. After a short period of recuperation, he had requested reassignment to the Department of Military Justice. To prosecute, the General selected Colonel Lionel Marcou who had a reputation for being punctilious. A wit among his men said of Colonel Marcou that he was "strict but fair—in that order."

Olivier had been the guest of honor at a banquet the night after his escapade on the ridge. He was stuffed with leek soup, roasted chicken with buttered potatoes, and the better part of an authentic Gâteau St. Honoré. He was hailed with five toasts and enjoyed a whole bottle of excellent Malbec followed by two glasses of cognac. The troops insisted he must sleep on a decent bed and, to that end, commandeered a bedroom with a soft four-poster from a local landowner. By ten o'clock the following morning, however, Olivier was behind the bars of a basement cell. The official indictment wasn't precise in stating the charges and so, in the manner of a shotgun, broadcast them comprehensively: "desertion, disobedience, abandoning his post in the presence of the enemy, cowardice." At the same hour, Captain Armand Gautier, commander of the troops Olivier had rescued, was signing his recommendation that *soldat 1.eme* Olivier Carriveau receive the special decoration authorized by the government less than a year before, the Croix de Guerre.

Headquarters was in a commandeered château, and the court martial convened in what had been its dining room. Olivier was seated on a wooden chair with a guard standing behind him. The chair was uncomfortable; it was too small, as if it had been requisitioned from a primary school. Three bottles of mineral water and three tumblers had been set out on a deal table for the tribunal, two of whose members wore dress uniforms. The judges sat on upholstered chairs of normal size, no doubt three of those used by guests at pre-war dinner parties. The two advocates had matching chairs.

A sergeant-major stood by the side of the table, holding a folder. At a sign from the presiding officer, he opened the folder and read a concise account of Olivier's desertion from the fort at Souville as attested to both by his sergeant and the officer of the day. After a brief pause, he took a second paper from the folder and read Captain Gautier's commendation of his action against the German machine gun position in the St. Mihiel sector.

The presiding officer, a major who looked very grave indeed, asked if Olivier had anything to add to the statements or if he wished to challenge anything in them. Olivier might have put things somewhat differently, but just shook his head.

"Very well, then. Colonel Marcou, please proceed."

There was no podium, no lectern, not even a desk, so Marcou simply stood before the tribunal and delivered his argument forthrightly. He did so without notes, as if he had committed it to memory, like a schoolboy reciting Racine. It was very much to the point.

"The matter could not be plainer. Private Carriveau deserted. The penalty for desertion is death. This penalty is fixed, and the reason is self-evident. It is to be at once a deterrent to those tempted to make a similarly dishonorable choice and an encouragement to those patriotic soldiers with stouter hearts. Private Carriveau deserted the moment he departed the fort at Souville, which was his assigned post. Any actions he took subsequently are irrelevant. The principle of Carriveau's act in leaving the fort is clear and it is that principle we are to judge according to the law. In time of war a soldier leaves his post without permission. In doing so, he deprives the state of his service and endangers his comrades. We neither can nor should excuse such behavior since, by doing so, we would undermine discipline at a moment when the very existence of the Republic is in peril." Here, presumably for dramatic effect, Marcou fell silent for a couple of seconds before concluding in the style of Cato condemning Carthage: "Carriveau must be executed."

He then resumed his seat, looking ferocious and satisfied.

The president of the tribunal paused to take some mineral water before nodding to Olivier's defense advocate.

Lieutenant Plamondan got to his feet slowly. He held a single piece of paper in his single remaining hand. Though not yet thirty, owing to his wounds, he moved like a man of advanced age. Where Marcou had spoken harshly and bluntly, stressing uncontested facts and absolute law, Plamondan's voice was softer and his argument, though logical, implied an appeal to feeling.

"Private Carriveau single-handedly eliminated an enemy position and saved the lives of twenty-two of our soldiers. Had he not left the fort at Souville, those men would most likely not be alive today. Should we judge him by the momentary impulse that impelled him to leave that fort—which, I will remind the court, was not under attack—or by a deliberate act of courage that preserved so many lives at the risk of his own. Private Carriveau is charged with desertion and flight in the face of the enemy. But the court must ask itself why, if he was so anxious to flee the enemy, he would engage half a dozen of them unaided. Concern has been expressed here about the message that would be sent by sparing Private Carriveau. It has been asserted that such a verdict would undermine morale and even endanger the Republic. Consider, though, the blow to morale of shooting to death a man who is a hero to the rank and file, and justly so. I submit that such a verdict would be a kind of idol-worship, a human sacrifice to an excessively narrow notion of the law and its purpose. To condemn Carriveau by considering the so-called principle of one act while ignoring the far greater benefits of another is as unreasonable as it is cruel. With respect, I propose that the court martial follow the spirit of the law that gives life, not the letter that kills. I suggest you apply the principle of seeking the most desirable consequences, not blindly scrutinizing supposed motives which may be no more than passing whims or momentary lapses. I submit that the court pursue what our ally's philosophers call the principle of utility."

Here the lieutenant read from the paper trembling in his hand.

"'By the principle of utility is meant that principle which approves or disapproves of every action whatsoever, according to the tendency which it appears to have to augment or diminish the happiness of the party whose interest is in question. . .' Though that sentence was written by an Englishman, I find the reasoning both lucid and pertinent. Who are the parties whose interests are in question today. I submit there are many interests beyond those of Private Olivier Carriveau, though I would certainly not minimize his. There is also the interest of his parents who would like their son to remain alive; there is that of the Army, which has more uses for a gifted sharpshooter and popular hero who is breathing than for one who is not; there are also the interests of the troops rescued by Carriveau. Their happiness will certainly not be enhanced by executing the man who kept them from being killed, nor the happiness of their families who are grateful to Carriveau for saving their sons and husbands. Do you truly imagine that the morale of the men in the trenches would be improved by standing the man who saved so many like them before a firing squad. Sirs, with respect, let me state what is obvious not only to every enlisted man but to every front-line combatant: Olivier Carriveau deserves a medal, not a bullet."

The latest effort to push the Germans back was having some success. The enemy was giving ground. After reading the afternoon's dispatches, General de Tourdonnet's mood was almost buoyant. Then his adjutant handed him the report of the court martial. The tribunal could not concur; in fact, they could not have been further from agreeing. The presiding officer was strongly in favor of Carriveau's prompt execution. A second member insisted with equal vehemence that the man be spared and his conspicuous valor properly recognized. The third member of the court apologized to the General, saying he was simply unable to decide between execution and reprieve. In good conscience, he therefore could not cast a vote, let alone a deciding one.

The general swore under his breath and endured a difficult night.

Five platoons of Carriveau's regiment, the 412th, were lined up in front of headquarters on the dirt parade ground that three years before had been the green lawn of the château. They stood at attention, presenting arms, as Olivier, escorted by two corporals, was marched on to the field from the basement brig. He stood with his back to the troops, facing a major, a colonel, and the general himself. The major read out the citation and General de Tourdonnet stepped forward, pinned the Croix de Guerre to Olivier's chest, kissed him on both cheeks, stepped back, and saluted smartly.

Confused, Olivier returned the salute then also stepped backward. He would have liked to continue stepping backward until he vanished into the ranks and became again just an undistinguished poilu. He would have done just that too, if the two corporals had not prevented him from moving.

Everything went still for a minute and then the colonel ordered Lieutenant Boivin and his "special squad" to detach themselves. Five soldiers marched together with the lieutenant to the edge of the field, where there was a stone retaining wall. The colonel then read out a brief statement saying that Olivier had been found guilty of desertion from the fort at Souville. As General de Tourdonnet watched grimly, the colonel nodded to the corporals who grasped Olivier's arms, turned him around, and half-dragged him across the lawn to the wall where, with shocking rapidity, Lieutenant Boivin affixed the blindfold, stepped aside, and called out the orders to aim and shoot.

In his memoirs, General de Tourdonnet rehearses the details of the Carriveau case, calls it the worst dilemma of his career, and recalls the bad night it had given him. With the sophistication of the student of philosophy he had once been, the General considers again the demands of military justice and the objectivity gained by ruling out of consideration feelings, personalities, and consequences. He weighs these against the claims to consideration of all three in this case, especially given Carriveau's bravery after his desertion. What the private had done on that ridge, the General concedes, was more likely to have been undertaken deliberately than the desertion. There were hundreds of instances of men, undone by months in the trenches fighting the war's longest battle, slipping away or simply cowering in the mud, unable to move when ordered to do so. The General's uncertainty is revealed when, instead of defending his decision, he poses a chain of unanswered questions. "Should we judge a man's actions by his intentions when intentions are so hard to discern, or by their outcomes which he himself could hardly foresee. Are the law and the facts all that is required to ensure impartial justice or is such rigidity too inhumane and too blind to be called justice at all. Yet, if we depart so much as a centimeter from the law and the facts, do we risk partiality and unequal justice. If the purpose of military law—or any law—is not merely retribution but to convey a firm message, did the execution of Carriveau do anything to discourage desertion. Can we say that pardoning him would have encouraged it. Did awarding Carriveau the Croix de Guerre inspire the same valor in others or did executing him embitter desperate and shell-shocked soldiers who saw it as one more sadistic joke on the part of the general staff?"

In the end, General de Tourdonnet, evidently not comforted even by the cheerful blaze in the fireplace of his post-war study, throws himself on the mercy of his readers: "If heroism was to be rewarded then surely desertion had to be punished. What alternative did I have?"

HSI-WEI IN HUAIYANG

Luli's family lived in Heshun, one of the villages ringing Huaiyang. For the Spring Festival, she went to stay with her grandfather who lived in a three-room apartment in town. When Luli woke on the morning of the New Year, her grandfather presented her with a puppy. Luli embraced the dog ecstatically and the dog licked Luli's face with equal gusto.

"What's her name, Grandfather?"

"The one you'll give her, little flower."

Girl and puppy snuggled and played together all day. Her grandfather showed Luli what to feed the dog and how she was to be trained. At sundown, he tucked the two into bed together, but Luli couldn't sleep because naming the puppy was the biggest thing she had ever had to do.

In the morning, her grandfather asked if she had chosen a name.

"Xingfu," Luli declared resolutely. "She'll be Xingfu."

The old man grinned, delighted with the success of his gift. "Happiness," he said. "What a fine name!"

After the holiday, Luli's parents came to take her and the puppy home. They fussed over the little dog too. Xingfu made everyone happy.

Shortly before the Moon Festival, while Luli was helping her mother cut vegetables for dinner, Xingfu, who was lying in the doorway, spotted a squirrel. She took off after it, vanishing into the trees. When Luli couldn't find her dog, she began to wail. She and her brother and her parents looked everywhere, calling the dog's name, but they couldn't find Xingfu.

Luli was inconsolable, even when her father offered to find her another puppy.

"No!" she said weeping and petulant, "I only want Xingfu."

The next week, in the nearby village of Duoyishu, a boy of about Luli's age, Xiaodan, found the puppy looking damp and hungry. He gave the dog food and water and begged his parents to let him keep her. He named the dog Kuai because he thought her clever to have found him.

Three months later, Luli went with her aunt to visit her grandfather. Then they went to the marketplace to buy some meat and a new pillow. A stranger had stationed himself by the well beside a wooden sign with a picture of straw sandals on it. Luli's feet had grown, and her aunt decided to order her a new pair. Just then, Luli caught sight of a boy and a man buying dumplings. The boy had a dog on a leash. It looked just like Xingfu, only bigger. While her aunt was still talking with the sandal-maker, Luli dashed across the square. Before the child could lean down to embrace her, the dog leapt up and began to whimper and lick Luli's face.

"Hey!" said Xiaodan, pulling hard on the leash. "That's *my* dog."

"No!" cried Luli. "She's my lost dog and stop pulling her like that. You'll hurt her."

"She's *my* dog. Who takes care of her? Me, that's who."

The boy's father told Xiaodan to calm down.

By now the aunt had come over. As Luli entreated her help, Xiaodan appealed for his father's. The adults looked at one another indecisively; the children glared.

"Mine. Auntie, tell them."

"No, *mine*."

The sandal-maker, who had trailed the aunt across the square, heard the argument, noted the perplexity of the grown-ups, the distress and clenched fists of the children. After hesitating, he intervened.

He introduced himself, apologized for inserting himself into the dispute, then asked Xiaodan's father when his son had acquired the dog and Luli's aunt how long it had been since her niece had lost her pet. They both replied, "Three months."

The sandal-maker nodded then asked if he might make a humble suggestion.

The children looked at the dusty stranger uncertainly, the adults dubiously; but no one objected.

The sandal-maker knelt down to talk to the children. He turned first to the boy.

"Don't tell me what it is, but did you give the dog a name?"

"Yes. Of course I named my dog. What do you think?"

Hsi-wei turned to the girl, who was pouting and furious. "Please don't tell me what it is either, but did you also give your dog a name?"

"Yes, I did."

The sandal-maker stood. "I suggest we let the dog decide."

"The dog?" scoffed Luli's aunt.

"How's that?" said the boy's astonished father. "What do you mean?"

The sandal-maker asked if he might borrow the dog.

"What? *You* want to steal my dog too?" Luli protested

loudly.

"She's my dog," insisted Xiaodan, pulling even more tightly on the leash.

"Only for a minute," said the sandal-maker and turned to Luli and her aunt. "Would you please go and stand by that vegetable seller over there?" Then, turning to Xiaodan and his father, he said, "And would you please stay here by the dumpling stall?"

The children looked beseechingly at the grownups who nodded at the sandal-maker.

"Then, if you'll permit me, I'll take the dog over by the well. May I?"

Xiaodan's father told his son to hand the leash to the sandal-maker.

"Thank you. Now, children, when I release her leash, I want you both to call her name. Then we'll see which of you she chooses."

Neither child was pleased with this idea.

"But it's been such a long time since I've seen her. It's not fair," Luli complained.

"No, not fair. She's only been mine for three months," said Xiaodan.

But the girl's aunt said it was fair enough and the boy's father that he couldn't think of a better solution.

So, it was agreed to let the dog decide to whom she belonged.

In his travels through Yuzhou, Hsi-wei stopped for a few days in the town of Huaiyang. First, he found a rundown tavern and rented a place to sleep. It was only a storeroom with a pallet that smelled of vinegar and mold, but it was cheap.

Next, he strolled through the town which appeared

prosperous. The people were well dressed and there was plenty of food for sale. Gentry as well as peasants from the countryside crowded the streets. With summer just beginning, Hsi-wei could expect many customers for his sandals.

He made his way to the town's marketplace where it seemed anything could be had. There were stalls selling everything from whole pigs to bolts of silk, jade carvings to porcelain teapots, bedding to pipas and liuqins. Hsi-wei found an open spot beside the well, lay down his bag, and set up his sign.

He took several orders, bought a bundle of straw from a peasant who was unloading produce from a cart, and returned to the tavern. The place had a small stable and behind it was a clearing with a warped wooden table. It would do as a workshop.

It was the following day that he interceded in the dispute over the dog.

"Huai! Huai, come here, girl!" cried Xiaodan as Luli yelled "Xingfu! Xingfu!"

The dog didn't hesitate. She tore across the square and jumped into Lilu's arms.

After begging Xiaodan's father's permission, Hsi-wei bought the boy two red bean buns to soften his disappointment and sweeten his mood.

The story of the children, the dog, and the sandal-maker provided an entertaining tidbit of gossip for Huaiyang. It soon spread from the marketplace. Chao-Jing-hua, the wife of the new magistrate, heard the tale from her cook and told it to her husband over dinner.

Chao was amused. "This sandal-maker might make a decent magistrate. But I've got a more difficult case to settle, two claims to the same land."

"I wonder. . ." Jing-hua began to muse.

"What?"

"You remember my friend Daiyu?"

"Vaguely."

"Well, she was a lover of poetry. She told me about a young peasant who had become a poet and travels around selling straw sandals. She read me two of his poems. They were good. In fact, as a parting gift, she had a copy made for me of one of them. It's about Lake Weishan. The poet's name is Chen. Do you think this sandal-maker might be that Chen? If so, perhaps we could invite him to dine with us."

Chao, who liked to indulge his wife, said he would have inquiries made. While he had met some peasants who could read, he had never heard of one who wrote poetry. He was curious to see one, as he might be to see a horse that could dance.

The magistrate's men quickly tracked Hsi-wei down at the tavern. The asked him sneeringly if he made verses as well as sandals and, when he confessed he did, conveyed the invitation to dinner at the magistrate's villa, though they made it sound like a summons.

Hsi-wei cleaned himself up as best he could and arrived at the imposing villa at the time he was told to. Jing-hua herself greeted him warmly at the door. She was a woman of about thirty with the sort of round face that seems made to frame smiles. Hsi-wei liked her at once. She conducted him into the reception room and introduced him to her waiting husband. Chao Guo-zhi also made a good impression. He was tall and dignified without being remote. He surprised Hsi-wei by responding to his low bow with a small one of his own, an unusual gesture for a high official meeting a peasant.

The dinner was a success. The fare was sumptuous: spicy Manchow soup followed by mushroom fried rice with water chestnuts, bok choy and carrots in a honey black bean glaze, and braised pork belly. Hsi-wei ate as much as he could while answering questions, starting with one from the magistrate about how he had secured an education. Hsi-wei gave an abbreviated account of his service carrying a secret message to General Fu in the south, then declining the customary rewards in favor of an education under the stern Master Shen Kuo. Jing-hua wanted to know more about his time in Daxing, how he had become a poet, and his most memorable adventures on the road. She called her servant who brought her copy of "Yellow Moon at Lake Weishan". The scroll astonished Hsi-wei, who had not yet encountered many people who knew his poems. It made him blush. The magistrate said he had read the poem and was impressed. Jing-hua asked if Hsi-wei would sign the scroll which, after the maid returned with brush and ink, he did, apologizing for his deplorable calligraphy.

"Master Kuo compared my writing to the marks left by a lame crow that had stumbled through a puddle of ink." He didn't mention the beatings his calligraphy had earned him.

Magistrate Chao called for a jug of yellow wine and, after the first cup, his wife said it had gone to her head and demurely retired, thanking Hsi-wei for coming and accepting his gratitude. And so began the second half of the evening.

The magistrate had taken to the young sandal-maker, judging him articulate, intelligent, and modest, hardly at all like a dancing horse. He said he had heard of how Hsi-wei managed the affair of the lost dog and praised his solution.

"There's a similar case, though a much more complex one, that's been troubling me. It would be a relief to speak of it," he said. "It might help me clarify my thinking."

Hsi-wei asked if it was perhaps a dispute over the owner-ship of land.

Chao raised his eyebrows. "How did you know?"

"Emperor Wen's land reforms are good, but the Kaihuang Code has given rise to disputes. I've heard of many in my travels."

"You're familiar with the Code?"

Hsi-wei said that he had read it. "It felt like a duty for a peasant lucky enough to become literate."

"Extraordinary," murmured Chao, thinking again of the dancing horse. "Well, perhaps this case of mine isn't excep-tional, but it's still a quandary. Both sides have good claims and sound arguments."

"So did the children in the marketplace."

Chao chuckled. "Yes, but this case is more serious. I've just begun my three-year term here and a bad decision could upset people. In fact, even a good verdict is bound to leave some disappointed and angry."

"That's true. But a just decision will upset few people in the short-run and win you the respect of many later."

Chao was surprised that he could feel comforted by a young peasant. He refilled the wine cups.

"An encouraging bit of wisdom," he said. "Of course, I want to arrive at a sound verdict. The problem is knowing what it is."

"I understand, Your Honor, and I would be pleased to listen to the facts of the case."

"Very well. You know the new Code, but are you also familiar with *Huomai*?"

"A conditional sale? As I understand it, the *Huomai* principle is, wherever possible, to keep land in the hands of one family. It makes for stability."

"Just so. A conditional sale means that a family compelled to sell its land has the legal right to buy it back at the original price and without interest."

"Yes. That's also how I understand the law."

"Good. Here are the facts of the case. For generations, the land in question belonged to the Wu family. The grandfather of my petitioners fell into debt and sold the land to a man named Li. The petitioners claim the sale was conditional, the other side contends it was made permanent by agreement of the parties. However, the matter is moot as there is no surviving bill-of-sale, no evidence either way. Is that clear so far?"

"Yes."

"Well, when the purchaser, Li, died the land passed to his son. The son had only one child, a daughter. She married a man named Shen and so, when his father-in-law died, the land passed into the possession of the Shen family."

"I see."

"The petitioners are two Wu brothers, Bo-quin and Chong-lin. Twins. For years they hired themselves out as tile-layers and field workers, saving all they could to buy back the family land."

"So, I take it the Wu brothers are not well off. Are the Shens?"

The magistrate frowned. "That is legally irrelevant."

"Yes, but do you know?"

"Of course, a magistrate is obliged to know the tax records. Shen inherited land from his own ancestors, quite a lot, almost a thousand *mu*. He also owns a timber business that is doing well."

"Thank you."

Magistrate Chao took a long drink of wine. "Now," he said raising a finger in the manner of a learned judge, "the Wu brothers contend that, according to *Huomai*, they should be able to purchase the land at the original price, which could be determined by searching the records of sale from the time of Li's purchase. Shen argues that the land would have doubled in value by now and such a price would be unjust; however, his chief point is that the land belongs to him and, through his wife, has been in the same family for three generations."

"And the *Huomai* principle isn't clear about how many generations ensure ownership?"

"Precisely."

"It's certainly a conundrum."

"And there's no dog to decide," joked Chao.

The case interested Hsi-wei. He had a notion that there was a flaw somewhere in the arguments but needed to think it through.

It had grown late, and he saw his host stifling a yawn. Hsi-wei stood up.

"Thank you for your splendid hospitality, Magistrate Chao. And please thank your wife for receiving me so graciously and for her interest in my poor verses. One thing more. May I ask a favor?"

"What can I do for you? It's gone quite late. We could put you up for the night."

"That's very kind, sir. But no. I have accommodations and a good deal of straw to turn into sandals. The favor is your permission to visit you tomorrow. It's about your case."

Chao looked puzzled but said that he would be at the magistracy all day and Hsi-wei would be welcome to visit him there. He then escorted Hsi-wei to the door where they wished each other a good night.

Hsi-wei set to work on his sandals early in the morning. Sandal-making is hand work, intricate but almost second nature to him, leaving his mind free. Many of Hsi-wei's poems were composed while weaving straw.

The inchoate idea of the night before became clearer to him. He knew there was something the matter, a legal point; but in the morning his thinking became firm enough to present to the magistrate. He knew the official might justifiably dismiss what he had to say and resent Hsi-wei's presumption. Nevertheless, just after noon he went to the marketplace and asked the way to the magistracy.

The guard at the gate looked Hsi-wei up and down.

"Oh, so you want to see the magistrate. Why is that? Have you been summoned? If so, you need to present yourself to one of the deputies."

"Magistrate Chao asked me to see him today."

The guard laughed. "Ha! And when did His Honor do that?"

"Last night at dinner."

This reply made the guard laugh even louder.

Hsi-wei drew himself up. "Please let Magistrate Chao know the sandal-maker is here to keep his appointment. If you send me away, he won't be pleased."

The guard hesitated. "Very well," he said doubtfully. "You stay right here."

Magistrate Chao's office was spacious and well-appointed. Scrolls were neatly stacked on a wall of shelves. There were both chairs and cushions and a handsome teak desk at which the magistrate sat before an open scroll. He stood and greeted Hsi-wei.

"I've been reading more of your poems," he said unexpectedly. "It seems they are circulating. My men found three of them, including the one people call your 'famous letter,' the one addressed to the emperor when he was still regent of Northern Zhou, the one about the bandit Yuchi Jiang. It's very powerful and, according to what I'm told, it had an effect."

"I didn't know that poem had found its way into the world, let alone to Huaiyang."

"It seems the people like your poems and those who can't read them like hearing them. You may become famous for more than your sandals, Master Chen."

Hsi-wei blushed. "Master? That is pleasant to hear, Your Honor. Thank you. But I've come about something else. It's about the case you described last night."

"So you said. What is it you want to tell me?"

"I was trained in the classics, not the law. But, as you know, I've read the Emperor's Code. I would like most humbly to offer a suggestion about the dispute between the Wu brothers and Mr. Shen; that is, about how it might be decided."

The magistrate's smile was indulgent but also a little chilly. "Take a seat. If you have an opinion about the verdict, tell me what it is and how it can be supported."

Hsi-wei chose a cushion, sat, and did as he was asked.

"According to the Kaihuang Code and *Huomai*, where possible land is to stay with the family who traditionally held it. If it is sold, then the family can regain it by paying the new owner the original price."

"Yes. We agree on that. But Shen claims his family has owned the land for three generations. Even though the Wu family held it longer, that claim has real force."

"But it isn't quite true that the Shen family has owned

the land for three generations—or the Li family either. As I understand things, the land was sold to Li and eventually came into possession of his granddaughter, the wife of Mr. Shen."

"Yes, on her marriage, the property naturally became the possession of her husband. But Mrs. Shen is still a member of the Li family."

"That's so. But I believe there is a technical problem with Mr. Shen's claim, Your Honor."

"Oh? And what's that, Master Chen?" said the magistrate with some severity.

"Under the Kaihuang Code, it is not legal for a woman to own land directly. I personally don't agree with that rule, but that is the language of the law, *no woman can own land directly*. Land is to pass down by male primogeniture. Therefore, the wife of Mr. Shen did not legally own the property when it passed to her. And, that being the case, it was not owned by the Li family when she married, so Shen's three-generation claim is not valid. On the other hand, the claim of the Wu brothers is clearly in accord with both the Code and the spirit of *Huomai*. The land, you said, had belonged to the Wu family for many generations."

Magistrate Chao looked hard at Hsi-wei and rubbed his chin. "This is the outcome you wanted, isn't it? It's because Shen is rich and the Wu brothers are not."

This was perceptive. Hsi-wei did want the hard-working brothers Wu to best the rich timber merchant Shen, but he knew better than to admit it. He lowered his head.

"As you said last night, Magistrate, the wealth or poverty of the parties is legally irrelevant."

Chao spoke with some asperity. "It's bold to quote me back to myself. Some might even call it insolent."

"Nothing could be further from my intention, Your Honor."

The magistrate paused. He still looked displeased but not so angry. "Well, I'll admit you've given me something to think over. For that, I thank you, but I will have to review the Code for myself." Chao rose from his desk. "I will say nothing of the quality of your legal reasoning, but if your sandals are as good as your verses, at least you won't starve. Will you be leaving us soon?"

"Very soon. Tomorrow. Thank you for receiving me today, for last night, and please give my regards to your kind and generous wife."

"Of course. Then farewell, sandal-maker."

Hsi-wei bowed deeply and departed.

He never learned how Magistrate Chao decided the property dispute but that night he wrote the following poem, a copy of which he left with Chao's wife before continuing on his travels through Yuzhou. As usual, Hsi-wei did not give the poem a title but people have given it two. Some call it "In Huaiyang" and others "To Have and to Be".

Out of those woods, warns the sage, springs danger.
Yet who is like the Buddha? Some may fell a tree
but how few clear the brush and raze the forest of desire?

The child hugs her pet, the farmer fences in his plot,
his wife cherishes her favorite wok, and the Son of
Heaven himself jealously safeguards his mandate.

What is it to own? Only selfishness and ruinous
attachment? All should aspire to be like the Buddha
yet isn't it as human to want to have as to want to be?

The law is often harsh, but gentler far than lawlessness.
As virtue sometimes means committing the lesser offense
so justice may lie in choosing the slighter injustice.

In Huaiyang I twice intervened in disputes that weren't mine.
Have I done as the Buddha prescribes and, like a bee, taken
the nectar and fled without harming the scent of flowers?

THE RIO ROSA CRISIS

In those days the Alarcon palace was still in family hands. Don Feliz had graciously offered it for the emergency conference. We had to stand about in its well-lit reception hall. The space was elegant and formal, with high bookshelves, seats and couches covered in maroon leather, several small French tables, and a heavy sideboard on which coffee and maté tea had been laid along with salvers heaped with pastries. As I recall, the pastries were good, but the coffee and tea were not.

The two delegations took up opposite sides of the hall to match their opposed attitudes. My deputy, Romero, did a splendid job of affecting nonchalance, lounging against a bookshelf with his arms crossed as he chatted to me about football. This was gotten up to discompose our opposite numbers. Guillermo Calderon, whom I had known since the Cretaceous period, stood stiffly. With his thick eyebrows beetling fiercely he offered me just a single formal nod. His second, a protégée of the president who later rose to be vice president herself, looked like Garbo in the first reel of *Ninotchka*. If there really were to be a war, I remember thinking, I hoped not to encounter her. This was Señora Isabel Furtado, of course; however, among ourselves we called her Isabel Fuegado because, icy as she was, she looked as if she was about to spit fire. The seldom seen Señor Furtado was a figure of some curiosity and not a little pity. Our respective entourages, like good infantry, marched to the measure set by their officers. While my lot ate pastries like mad and talked of the World Cup,

Calderon's looked as if they were auditioning for the wax museum under the label, "a herd of officially outraged functionaries." None of this posturing mattered in the least.

We all were aware that on the other side of the double doors the die was being cast. The two presidents, dismissing all reasonable objections, insisted on meeting alone. Nothing could have made us more anxious. That buttoned up Calderon looked as if he might fly off in all directions at any moment. Incidentally, Calderon liked to let it be said he was descended from the great playwright, but of course it was nonsense. He was vain but he was no fool. He did not trust the caprice of his country's first popularly elected female president, not even the formidable Marta Mayol. As for me, I felt the same uneasiness but for different reasons. Aldon Gomez Ruano—and God help you if you left out either the Ruano or the Gomez—was inexperienced, impulsive, and, worst of all, an orator. As you may recall, he initiated the crisis during his inaugural address when, à la Mirabeau, he was apparently carried away by his own eloquence and claimed every hectare of the Rio Rosa delta, a border region that had been left happily in dispute for well over a century. People had made their accommodations and its unregulated, lightly taxed people prospered. Both nations shared in the profits. The crisis was maddeningly unnecessary. It hardly helped that Mayol should respond by instantly sending in a battalion of crack troops without even filing a demarche. Calderon must have been terribly put out to have been ignored. But there was something in it for him, an opportunity to show what a foreign minister of intelligence and firmness could accomplish. I confess I felt the same way.

So, picture the awkward scene. Were we enemies or not. Would we and our compatriots be trying to kill each other in a few hours. The pastries were soon gone. It gave my people satisfaction to have gobbled them all up, as if they had been the hectares of the Rio Rosa delta.

We cooled our heels like that for *two* hours. I can tell you we were like rubber bands stretched a little tauter during each of those one hundred and twenty minutes. We were all dying to listen at the doors but, in such a mob, who could dare?

· · ·

That, gentle reader, was intended to tickle your interest. I am a scholar who does not aspire to write for the popular taste. However, I do know that to engage an audience it is advisable to begin, like Homer, *in medias res.*

I say "gentle reader" though I am by no means certain that you exist, let alone that you are gentle. I have had decades in which to write up the notes of my interview with the late statesman, Don Alvaro Barrios, whose reconstructed words I have just set down. I had two reasons for not doing so. The first was a concern for my career. The *primum mobile* of all young academics, and most old ones for that matter, is the fear of appearing a fool, a purely negative motive that may preserve one from imbecile excesses, but which also narrows one's horizons. The result is that in our country respectable historiography conforms to established prejudices, such as that the past must be regarded as a serious matter, its major actors always dignified, and the causes of events largely rational. Violators of these strictures, the debunkers and farceurs, may be widely read and even believed in private; however, they seldom win promotion and never an endowed chair. Your academic historians are no mere chroniclers; their job is to make sense of events, or to make events sound sensible, and the more profound the sense appears the better. My second reason for silence was an apprehension that the wily old diplomat Barrios was amusing himself by pulling the leg of an over-earnest tyro. Will I try to put this piece before the public. Would anyone consent to publish it. My gardener replies to all but the most practical questions by saying *Quién sabe*. That all-purpose phrase sums up the wisdom of our skeptical people, who never expect an answer or credit the ones they receive.

Why return at this late date to my yellowed notes? For one thing, I no longer fear being called gullible. I have become a professor emeritus; that is to say, *magister superfluus*. My reputation is a settled matter or, should it be shattered, I no longer care. I imagine Don Alvaro might have felt the same way when he allowed me to interview him; and, if that is so, why shouldn't he speak the truth. At the end of a life of prevarication, intrigue, and careerism, frankness might feel like just the thing to him. It does to me.

But the immediate occasion of this little essay is the new book by my former colleague, and would-be successor, Bastiano Rivera. At 642 pages, *The Crisis of Rio Rosa* purports to be a comprehensive account of the episode, absolutely the last word. A better illustration of pompous conformity to the rules of academic historiography is hard to imagine. In one sense, what I am writing is a bad review of Rivera; in another, it is an alternative to his exhaustive but false account of the Rio Rosa Crisis. I am wielding Occam's razor to slice through his dense pages, the sword of Alexander to cut his knotty speculations. Rivera will be offended to have his painstaking work called speculation. Well, any historian would be. And yet, if one is not beguiled by his multitudinous footnotes, speculating is plainly what Rivera is up to. His book is laden with phrases that give the game away, viz.: *it seems plausible that* (12); *one may reasonably conclude* (14); *almost certainly* (135); *the most convincing* [alternatively, most persuasive, most appealing, most sensible] *explanation is* (259); *the evidence overwhelmingly suggests* (410)—what does it mean to "overwhelmingly suggest". Rivera is likewise fond of *without a doubt* (19 et passim) which invariably means there *is* doubt. Above all, he sprinkles his text with the modifiers *probable* and *probably* with the abandon of a farmer casting seed (144 times when I lost count). Rivera sets great store by probability, like a quantum physicist trying to pin down an electron. His book is really a wonder of weightless construction, piling supposition on presumption until the edifice looks persuasively ponderous, made of brick rather than air. The tome certainly accords with the axioms of seriousness, dignity, and reason; that is, it reads like a job application, which is what it is; for Rivera covets my old chair. No doubt it was reading his book, less convincing with every page, that induced me to reconsider the plausibility of my old interview with Alvaro Barrios.

I have one further consideration to mention. Don Alvaro is dead; all the principals are. No one can be harmed by this story, excepting a few undistinguished descendants whose pride may be bruised but who are too obscure to make any trouble.

. . .

Don Alvaro Barrios, quondam Minister of Foreign Affairs, consented to see me in his home, in his study. After rising to welcome me courteously, he seated himself behind the rampart of a massive mahogany desk. Señor Barrios still looked like an ambassador, courtly and sleek, with a sharp eye and thin but well-groomed gray hair. I was impressed that he wore a tie and a vest. Since retiring, he had put on a little weight, which at the time I thought added to his gravitas. He had also grown a short beard.

This neatly trimmed van dyke took my fancy, as if it marked both a strengthening of independence and a relaxation of official restraint. Perhaps because the beard was still new, he touched it often, sometimes rubbing his cheek, at others stroking his chin. The study itself was something of a surprise. On the walls hung a few landscapes, views of the campo, the sierra, the beach at Miraflores. There was only one low bookcase and a two-drawer oak filing cabinet. I had expected a sort of museum, a study crowded with souvenirs of his long service, its walls covered with signed photographs—that sort of thing. I wondered if the space had been stripped for action or stripped of it.

Don Alvaro's politeness flattered me. When I expressed my thanks for his agreeing to give me his time, he quoted a seemingly self-deprecating line of the sort favored by the securely famous. "It is better to treat the young with respect than the old. You never know what the former may become while with the latter it's only too obvious." Don Alvaro made me believe he liked me, that I was capable of sympathizing with his feelings even if I could have no notion of the tightropes he had traversed. I was young back then and basked in his confidence. Now I believe that it was just the tactic of a good diplomatist, getting others on your side by flattering their vanity.

We spoke of the nation. Don Alvaro had little love for his countrymen—love of the unconditional kind. What he loved were our empty spaces, unpopulated ones, like the landscapes on his wall. While he extolled the progress our nation had achieved, he added mordantly that ours was a history of two steps forward and one back. "Our intelligent progressives leave footprints on the shore, then the tide of idiocy and corruption rises once again and erases most of them." Patriotism being much in fashion at the time, I asked him about it. Don Alvaro observed that in his experience patriotism was a licentious noun, promiscuous as the women of the Barandango district. He said he approved of what an unhappy German wrote to Albert Camus, that he loved his country too much to be a nationalist. With a pedantic smile he observed that everybody attributes that bon mot to Camus whereas he only quoted it.

I do not believe Don Alvaro had become cynical in his retirement. Cynics are, for the most part, disappointed idealists, people who swing from expecting too much of the world to expecting too little. He was a practical man, the sort who begins with facts rather than dreams. That is why he was found indispensable and placed in important positions by so many administrations. Don Alvaro had no ideology and so no regard for purity. He desired for his country what most of his fellow citizens did, at least when they were not deluded by grandiose harangues or passing enthusiasms. prosperity, the rule of law, a flourishing culture, good relations with neighbors, and social stability. The socialist regime made him their ambassador to the Soviet Union; the Conservatives sent him to the United States. It was the moderates who twice made him foreign minister. I could well believe that the old man's life of subtlety and secrecy might have left him with a yearning to engage in a little blunt truth-telling in his retirement, especially with a young man like me.

It was evident that Don Alvaro was relishing our interview. He stretched his arms, was animated, and smiled on me, offering liberally from his trove of wisdom—and gossip. He related a few anecdotes which I expect had become polished by being repeated at many dinner parties. I laughed in the right places and took careful notes. The old man was keenly conscious of my pencil flying across the legal pad; he watched it as he spoke. Perhaps a few years out of the public eye had made him eager for attention. We were flattering each other.

The sunny tone of the interview darkened when I asked about the Rio Rosa crisis. There was, of course, an official story. In fact, it is likely that Don Alvaro had himself invented it. He regarded me more appraisingly than he had before, the way a rancher might size up a bull calf to decide whether it should be castrated. He stroked his little beard and then something peculiar happened. Don Alvaro winked at me.

This wink was disturbing and ambiguous. It has tormented me for years and does so now. What did it signify. That I was to take what he was about to tell me as a wild *jeu d'esprit*? That he had decided to give me a privileged peek behind the discreetly closed doors of history. Was the wink a sign of confidence and favor, as if to say, "Here, boy, I'll give you a story that will make your career," or, as seems more likely, a way of conveying that we both knew no one would believe such a story.

• • •

The origin of the Rio Rosa crisis did not lie in colonial maps, he said, not even in Gomez Ruano's notorious peroration or Mayol's belligerent response, though at the time that's what people believed. Of course, as always, some claimed to see in the crisis the work of our large friend to the north, a conspiracy to weaken one regime, or both, to sell arms, to make of one country or the other what is politely called a client state, to foment a little war for its own big ends. Others thought it was a tangled plot of the oil and fruit interests. Well, and so forth and so on. I always wonder at these people who find diabolical conspiracies behind everything. During those years when I had a seat near those in power what I found wasn't careful planning but desperate improvisation. "If these gringos are as smart as you say," I used to taunt my colleagues, "why don't you join them?" I'm sure there were plenty of memoranda proclaiming the existence of these wheels within wheels. These are the stories dug up by people like Rivera who documents everything but believes only himself. Well, as it happens, there really was a conspiracy, though not one with its source in some plot hatched in Washington.

The true origin of the Rio Rosa crisis lay twenty years earlier when two of those young people we are always sending up north to procure doctorates met in Boston, two talented and homesick graduate students, one male, one female. They found each other at a public lecture on something or other—Magic Realism or Palma's *Tradiciones Peruanas* or the peccadilloes of the CIA. So, they met, liked what they saw, went out for drinks, and probably argued with one another, relishing the Spanish in which they did it. Afterwards, they went to bed. So far, it was a commonplace little romance. Up there, you see, they were virtually compatriots, not citizens of two neighboring countries but what the Americans indiscriminately call "Hispanics". The young people became quite attached; however, there were obstacles. The girl was already married and the boy engaged. The spouse of the one and the intended of the other were both waiting back home in respectable celibacy. The young man was Aldon Gomez Ruano and the young woman was Marta Mayol.

No one knew about this attachment formed in Boston, let alone that the two future presidents had gone on meeting secretly at intervals for years in obscure resorts, second-class hotels, on Italian beaches and Swiss glaciers, egging each other on in their ambitions, loving, pining, and lusting after one another.

$\bullet \quad \bullet \quad \bullet$

Don Alaro said that when those double doors in the Alarcon Palace finally opened, he chanced to be standing just beside them. "I caught no more than a glimpse, you understand, a tiny gesture, a furtive look, the end of a whisper, a hand misplaced, something that astounded me and led me to question what had been going on in those inner chambers for two hours. Did it matter that the idea was absurd. Not in the least. As soon as such a notion grips the mind its absurdity diminishes. It turns from a whimsy into an explanation and, at last, a hypothesis."

He said that he drew his trusty deputy Romero aside and, without explaining why, instructed him to slip inside the room where the presidents had resolved the crisis and make a careful examination, particularly of the adjoining bedroom. He instructed Romero to make his report to no one but himself. "I had his findings within the hour, during the celebration that followed the issuing of the joint communiqué."

· · ·

-So, the Rio Rosa crisis was just an excuse for a tryst?

-A tryst. Well, yes. I suppose that's the right word.

-Did you ever confront Ruano?

-About a week later, yes. After the official story of the negotiations was well established. His Excellency denied it at first. I told him what Romero had found. He gave up then; all his dignity dissolved. He appealed to me as a man, babbling like a teenager about this grand passion, the difficulty of seeing one another before the election and the impossibility afterwards, and so forth and so on.

-And you?

-Oh, I. Naturally, I pretended to be horrified but was naturally amused.

-He wasn't concerned you'd tell?

-Actually, he said something rather piquant on that score, something I think will interest you.

-Me?

-He said, 'Don Alvaro, five hundred years ago such a story would not only be believed but treasured. It would be turned into a great poem or at least a popular ballad. Nowadays, we are beyond such childishness; nowadays, we know better. We know that history is propelled in accord with profound substructures, by world-historical forces, by political calculation and, above all, economic necessities. It is therefore entirely credible,' he said, 'that Marta and I tussled over the delta's oil, its fish and its port, but not that we tussled in bed.'

-I see.

-Yes, I can see you see. So, there was no war because there was never going to be one. However, the good feelings that issued from the happy solution to the crisis—all the details of which were also worked out in advance by those two excellent adulterers—brought our countries closer. As you know, trade picked up and military budgets were cut, and so forth and so on. Incidentally, if you should care to check, you'll find that the number of state visits, for consultations and the signing of agreements, also increased.

Don Alvaro made a wry face at me. He raised an eyebrow meaningly, but there was no second wink. If there had been I should have been certain that he was teasing me. Instead, he knitted his long fingers over his chest, leaned back in his big rolling chair and added nothing further. There was no need to state the obvious, *And if you every tell this story, my boy, do you suppose anybody would believe you?*

HSI-WEI IN THE GARDENS OF SHUN

It was early spring when, making his way through Jingzhou, the vagabond peasant/poet Chen Hsi-wei stopped at an inn called The Fallen Apple. As usual, he asked for the cheapest accommodation—a corner of the kitchen would do, he told the innkeeper, even the stable.

It happened that a deputy minister from Shun, going to visit his family in Yechan for the Spring Festival, was also stopping at The Fallen Apple. He sat with great dignity in the middle of the tavern drinking with his two guards. The local men watched him apprehensively. When Hsi-wei came into the room to ask if perhaps anyone required a new pair of straw sandals, the minister looked him up and down.

"What's your name?" he demanded.

Hsi-wei gave his name and the slightest of bows.

The minister's eyebrows rose. "Chen Hsi-wei. And may I ask, Master Chen Hsi-wei, if you make poems as well as sandals?"

"The sandals are better," remarked Hsi-wei.

The minister chuckled at this, and everyone else laughed—the very idea that such a man was able to read, let alone write verses, was ridiculous.

The minister commanded his escorts to leave and the innkeeper to bring a cup and another jug of rice wine. He motioned Hsi-wei over. "Come and sit and drink with me a little."

Hsi-wei sat.

"Coincidences come in pairs," observed the minister as though sharing a unique insight. "Only last week I had to listen to my colleague Rong Hongxu go on about the poems of some Chen Hsi-wei. He said the fellow was an educated peasant who drifted about the country leaving poems and straw sandals in his wake."

"Coincidences do generally come in pairs," said Hsi-wei dryly. "Is your colleague by any chance the same Rong Hongxu who compiled *The Midnight Verses of the North and South*?"

The minister looked startled. "You know his book?"

"I once had the good fortune to see it, yes. Unfortunately, I do not possess a copy."

"Rong is very proud of his little collection. All the poems were written in the decades before our Emperor Wen reunited the empire."

"Certainly not a great period for poetry but interesting all the same. I thought the poems well-chosen and Rong's commentaries, even when severe, both perceptive and considered."

"It's true. Rong can be harsh. He likes *your* verses, though, most of the ones he's seen anyway—but by no means all of them. 'This Chen must be the only peasant in China who writes poems, and he's not without talent.' That's what Rong said about you—and if it *is* you, I'm sure he'd welcome a visit. The man works too hard, and he could use the distraction."

"I would be honored to profit from the criticism of Rong Hongxu," said Hsi-wei.

"Well then, unless you've some other destination in mind, why don't you go back the way I've come. Go to Shun, I mean. You'll find Rong where he always is, slaving away in the Cavalry and Provisions Ministry. The place would fall apart without him."

Hsi-wei enjoyed a pleasant journey to Shun. He stopped three times to put up his sign and look for customers. The weather was fine and business was brisk. He was able to afford a proper room. In springtime, peasants know they'll be needing new sandals, and it was a spring to gladden a peasant's heart. When the sun wasn't out, light rain fell on pale green fields.

The capital of Shun was festive. Magnolias were in bud and geraniums everywhere, white, red, and pink. The people were well dressed, and even the beggars appeared to be in high spirits.

Hsi-wei had little difficulty finding his way to Rong's ministry, the one in charge of the duke's cavalry and military provisions. The first person he asked, a jolly porter with a head as big as a melon, showed him the way.

Hsi-wei had heard that before making a fortune in the timber trade Wu Shiyue, the Duke of Shun, had done military experience. For special services and his business acumen, the Emperor awarded him the governorship of Shun and revived the old title too. The duke was known to take as much pride in his palace gardens as in his cavalrymen and their horses. Whether he was a good ruler or not, Hsi-wei didn't know.

The offices of Rong's Ministry were housed in a rambling two-story building with gray roof tiles. It stood next to the duke's extensive stables and a broad field for exercises. Statues of two mounted warriors guarded the gate. Hsi-wei had no difficulty entering the building but had to persuade two lower officials to lead him to the office of Second

Minister Rong. The first, a young fellow with a rather foolish face, looked the dusty peasant over disdainfully.

"Minister Rong cannot be disturbed. What's your business?"

"Poetry," said Hsi-wei. He could hardly say straw sandals.

"What's that?"

"I was told that Minister Rong would welcome me."

"Who told you that?"

Hsi-wei gave the name of the deputy minister he had met at The Fallen Apple. This impressed the man sufficiently for him to conduct Hsi-wei to the office of a higher lower official.

This man, older and more intelligent looking, was also reluctant to show Hsi-wei to his superior and likewise demanded to know what business he had with the Second Minister.

"I have certain matters to discuss with the compiler of *Midnight Verses of the North and South*. I fear Minister Rong will be displeased if you prevent us from meeting."

The man scoffed. "You know the minister's book. A peasant?"

Hsi-wei stood up straighter. "I would be obliged if you would ask Second Minister Rong whether he would be so gracious as to grant the humble Chen Hsi-wei the honor of an audience."

"I doubt he'll do any such thing," the official said sharply. "Minister Rong hasn't time to waste on peasants."

"As you wish, Sir. I've warned you," said Hsi-wei, and turned to go.

Made uncertain by the implied threat, the official grumbled, "Very well. I'll ask. Wait right here and don't get your hopes up."

As the man made for the corridor, Hsi-wei shouted him. "Be sure to tell Minister Rong the name of the unworthy sandal-maker is Chen Hsi-wei."

Left alone, Hsi-wei thought about how hard Rong must work. He would oversee everything from horseshoes and radishes to invoices for iron, helmets, and hay, not to mention recruitment, promotions, weapons, and discipline. Even in this office, there were dozens of scrolls spilling from the shelves on to the floor.

The high low official returned in a state of bewilderment, rubbing his chin.

"The Minister says he'll see you at once. Follow me."

Rong Hongxu's office was on the second floor, with a good view of the stables and exercise field. He was seated on a padded bench before a desk piled with scrolls. When the higher lower official announced Hsi-wei, Rong looked up and, laying down his brush, got to his feet. He was a tall man, thin as a ferryman's bamboo pole. Hsi-wei estimated his age at between forty-five and fifty-five. He had a tired face, one that suggested a capacity for shrewdness and concentration, with disconcertingly sharp eyes, and a straight nose under a high brow. His green silk robe was tied at the waist with a narrow white sash.

Hsi-wei bowed low.

"I'm pleased to meet you, Master Chen. It was good of my colleague to send you my way."

Hsi-wei was surprised by this greeting. "Master?"

"Mastery is where you find it," said Rong sternly, as if in reproach. "Where are you staying?"

"Nowhere as yet." Hsi-wei pointed at his bag, which he had set on the floor. "I came straight here."

"Then you'll stay at my villa." The invitation was delivered as a command.

"You are too generous," said Hsi-wei. "I'm sure I can find a lodging somewhere in the city."

Rong regarded him reproachfully. "I'm starved for the sort of conversation I expect from you. You'll be staying with me."

"As you wish, Second Minister."

"Good. That's settled. Now look, I've still got a lot of work to finish. Why don't you look over the city and come back in an hour—or, better yet, two. The Duke has built a new menagerie, open to the public. It's worth a visit. You'll find it by the river. Ask anyone."

Hsi-wei found the menagerie. He spent two hours looking at the monkeys and watching the people watching them. When he returned to the ministry, he found that Rong left, leaving an order that the peasant Chen was to be escorted to his villa.

Rong Hongxu's villa was neither large nor ostentatiously furnished but it was elegant. The minister had two women living with him. Hsi-wei at first took them for servants, elderly females devoted to their master. It turned out that one was his mother and the other his aunt. There was no one else. Both women greeted Hsi-wei at the door and took him to see Rong in his study. He made the introductions; Hsi-wei bowed to the ladies, and they smiled at him.

Rong sat in a chair. He motioned Hsi-wei toward a small, cushioned divan.

As if getting a trivial matter out of the way, Rong said, "My wife died young. I felt no need for another."

Hsi-wei appreciated Rong's understatement. This diligent man must have loved his wife dearly, he thought.

Hsi-wei had noticed that the Second Minister was

no longer wearing the white mourning sash. Discretion prevented him from mentioning it when they first met; but now that they were alone, he asked about the sash.

"You noticed it. Hm. Perhaps I'll explain later," said his host.

The women had prepared a fine meal of silver carp with bok choy, spring onions, and rice in a delicate oyster sauce. They washed it all down with yellow wine. To finish, the aunt smilingly brought in a plate of sesame cakes. Either she's proud of her recipe, thought Hsi-wei, or they're her nephew's favorites—perhaps one because of the other.

Over the meal, the men spoke of poetry, first of the Shijing Masters whom both revered. Rong happily discoursed on the work of the three Caos then, as Hsi-wei asked his opinion, he enumerated and commented on each of the formal innovations of the Jian'an. Hsi-wei did his best to attend to his host's learned discourse, reflecting on how often a lecture is best enjoyed by the one delivering it. At length, he shifted the topic. He complimented Rong for laying out so well weighing the respective merits and demerits of the poetry of North and South in his fine collection, then asked if he preferred the new court style that aimed to be a sort of amalgam of both.

"Well, that's the Emperor Wendi's idea, of course, a new merged poetry for the reunited Empire. It's an improvement, yes, but not a wholly satisfying one. In most of the recent poems I've seen coming from Daxing, you can pick out the Northern harshness from the southern smoothness, like cakes with clumps of flour that hasn't been well mixed. *Your* poems, I've noticed, are nothing like the new court style—or the old one either."

"Ah, my poor verses. I'm deeply flattered that you've troubled to take any notice of them."

"Mind you, I don't like them all. You're at your best when you stick to your own subjects and style—for instance in "Yellow Moon at Lake Weishan" or "The Broken Fence". Both are good. And I appreciated your handling of the classic theme of the exiled poet." Rong paused then recited, *An exile is a man broken in half, living in two provinces at once.*"

Hsi-wei couldn't conceal his pleasure that Rong had memorized a line he had written. He blushed.

"But, despite its fame, I really can't approve of your 'Letter to Yang Jian." It's too brutal."

Hsi-wei lowered his head. "You're right—I mean about it being outside my sphere. My excuse is that I wrote it quickly and in a spasm of indignation. Those verses were a means to an end, an attempt to spur action, to put a stop to the atrocities of a ruthless bandit."

"A good policy, but a poor reason to write," said Rong censoriously, reminding Hsi-wei of his old teacher, the impossible-to-please Shen Kuo. Rong, he thought, is the sort of man whose good opinion is the more valuable for being hard to win. The Empire had a thousand poets to every critic.

Rong fell silent and looked suddenly cast down. Hsi-wei recalled the white sash.

Feeling he might be overstepping some boundary, Hsi-wei nevertheless asked, "Are you in mourning?"

Rong looked at Hsi-wei almost with suspicion. "You saw that sash. Why ask?"

"I'm sorry for asking. I didn't mean to upset you."

"My mourning is private."

Hsi-wei said nothing. He waited for his host to do what he supposed he wanted to do.

"I'm mourning the late Lord Lyu Xinghui. He was my chief. I've never known a better man."

"I'm sorry for your loss."

Rong looked away. "He was executed. Beheaded. The injustice eats at me, Master Chen. There's no one here with whom I can share it. Not safely."

"Indignation is hard to suppress. To cry out sometimes relieves pain."

Rong smiled ruefully.

"You're a stranger and you'll soon be on your way."

"That's true. I expect to leave tomorrow."

"You'll stay until the day after."

Hsi-wei nodded. "As you wish."

"Very well. I'll tell you what happened. It won't be a consolation, but perhaps, as you say, a relief."

"If it will do you even a little good, I'll gladly listen."

Rong cleared his throat then drank some wine. He took a deep breath and dove in.

"Before becoming First Minister, Lord Lyu commanded the duke's cavalry. He was an experienced captain, trustworthy and honest and as a squared-off beam, and an incomparable horseman. As you'll know, four years ago the Turks made deep incursions in the west. After slaughtering the border guards, they quickly overcame the local army. When the bad news reached our duke, he offered the emperor the services of his cavalry. The offer was accepted, and Lord Lyu was put at the head of all the imperial forces in the west. He led his horsemen across the country, joined with two detachments of infantry, engaged the Turks, beat them soundly, and returned with many spoils. Among these was an exceptionally beautiful princess. Her name was

Burcu. On his return, the duke made him First Minister of Cavalry and Provisions. The post had fallen open while he was gone. His predecessor had fallen off a horse and broken his neck."

"Were you at all disappointed the post didn't go to you?"

"Disappointed. Not in the least. I was relieved. I had feared the duke might appoint me and I have no wish for higher rank. As the saying goes, the wind bowls over the pines while the shrubs are undisturbed. Lord Lyu made Burcu his second wife. The couple were happy and became ornaments of the Court, our duke's favorites. But Lord Lyu's good fortune and proven merits made a dangerous man jealous. This is the Lord Han Yun-peng, First Minister of Rivers and Roads, who is also a cousin of the duke. The exotic beauty of Burcu had much the same effect on Han's wife, Cuifen. Together, the two devised a wicked plan to eliminate the couple. I learned of it only after the catastrophe. It's likely that others know as well, but it would be lethal to say so—or to engage in public mourning."

Here Rong paused to ask his aunt for more wine. He waited for her to leave before resuming his story.

"Lady Cuifen launched a rumor, claiming she had it from one who would know. She whispered it to the Lady Dangmei, who would be certain to run to her friends with the story, the Ladies Lanten and Huiqing. They were both as jealous of Burcu as Cuifen and passed the rumor on. In this way, the false story was spread among the court ladies, and they passed it on to their husbands. No one bothered to trace the rumor back to its source."

"What was the rumor?"

"A horrible lie. That Lord Lyu and Burcu were plotting to murder the duke and take his place, one out of unbridled ambition, the other to revenge her people's defeat.

The devilish plot succeeded. The couple were arrested, and a secret trial held that very night. How could the upright Lord Lyu defend himself. What could he do but deny the charge. He and Burcu were beheaded the next morning."

"A terrible story!" said Hsi-wei.

"I could do nothing," sighed Rong. "I didn't even know until it was all over. And I was never questioned."

They were quiet for a minute or two, finishing the wine in their cups.

"So, you have a new chief. Is he a good one?"

Rong scoffed. "A nephew of Lady Cuifen. First Minister Guo is a diffident and incompetent man with no military or administrative experience and no ambition. He's indifferent to our work; his chief interest is his jade collection. The man's actually afraid of horses. He has two wives and two concubines, and no one would call any of them an exotic beauty. First Minister Guo is nobody's rival."

"So then, all the responsibility for the Ministry has fallen on you?"

Rong didn't reply.

Hsi-wei spent the night at Rong's villa, where he was made more than comfortable. The following morning, his host took an hour from his to show Hsi-wei him the palace's celebrated gardens.

And this is how Hsi-wei came to write this poem which has become known as "In the Gardens of Shun":

> *I passed through Shun last year in the*
> *month of blossoms when new leaves made*
> *the katsura branches look like mist.*
> *The Duke's Second Minister entertained me.*
> *We talked through the night and the next day*

he showed me the palace's renowned gardens.
The learned Minister, my host, spoke of
the Orchid Pavilion Gathering and asked if
I had ever seen the calligraphy of Wang Xizhi.

Behind the peonies stood a small pagoda,
an elegant thing, rose-colored an. feminine.
There the noblewomen of Shun stood together
swaying silkenly, like willows, shy as foals.
I found it hard not to look at them.
With a bitter smile, the Minister remarked
that, as Shun's ladies spoke only in demure
whispers, one would have to draw quite
near to hear their slanderous gossip.

EGON GLEICHER

PROFESSOR KREMPE. I intend to make my position clear from the start. It is my opinion that the case of Egon Gleicher is indeed a case, one more suited to psychiatry than music criticism. As to the two symphonies, the string quartet, and the so-called *Eberlin Variations*, I believe them to be vastly, not to say perversely, overrated. They are at once deranged and derivative and I personally cannot listen to them without profound discomfort; they make me squirm with pity and distaste. That Gleicher had no real talent is obvious to all from his pre-War compositions. What he wrote after the unfortunate event of 14 March, 1945 is indeed wholly different from what came before; it is also pathological and a species of pretending. To say that genius is akin to madness, ladies and gentlemen, is an excusable romantic cliché. It is quite a different matter to claim that madness is genius.

FRAULEIN WALDMAN. I wish I could be as forthright as Professor Krempe has been. However, in my opinion, the case of Gleicher is complicated, though Professor Krempe may say the case is simple and it is I who am muddled. Well, I grant that Egon Gleicher's mind was disturbed by the trauma of 14 March, 1945—indeed, by far more than that shock. I grant that the state into which he fell was delusional but not that it was simple. For one thing, his condition was intermittent and, I would argue, never more than partial. Furthermore, there is evidence that Gleicher was himself *aware* of this delusion, in which case we may require another word for it. As to the astounding musical compositions he produced between 1945 and his death in 1950, I am hardly alone in regarding them as master-pieces of the first order. Professor Krempe dismisses them as *derivative*. I agree they are derivative and that, normally, this would be against them. But in this case *derivative* is precisely what they were intended to be, and in the most profound sense. Gleicher made this explicit when, shortly before his death, he wrote that they are the work of Beethoven who had lived hidden and ashamed through the dozen years of the Thousand-Year Reich.

KREMPE. The work of Beethoven. Not of *a* Beethoven. Not of an imaginary Beethoven. Not music that appro-priates Beethoven's more obvious devices, but actually *by* Beethoven, Ludwig van. Is *that* what Gleicher meant to say, Fraulein. What you mean as well?

WALDMAN. Yes, Professor. That is precisely what I mean to say.

•   •   •

The recent debate between Professor Gustav Krempe and Fraulein Julie Waldman was the brainchild of the new Chancellor of the Herrenstadt Conservatory. Shortly after taking up his post, he received a proposal from certain members of his faculty that a bust, or at the least a brass plaque, be installed to honor Egon Gleicher, who had taught at the school for fifteen years. The Chancellor personally admired Gleicher's final works, though the composer's controversial reputation gave him pause. He considered the matter and decided to make use of the proposal to earn the Conservatory, whose fame was not it had once been, some publicity. He was certain the proposal to memorialize Gleicher would draw a protest from Adelbert Krempe who had famously ridiculed the adulation of Gleicher and with whom many agreed. So, the Chancellor seized the opportunity to make an event out of it. He invited Krempe to debate the status of Gleicher's late works and, to make the offer more attractive, promised that his opponent would be a woman of no reputation, an adjunct instructor on his own staff who studied Gleicher. "To debate such an individual might not burnish your fame, Professor," he wrote suavely, "but it would furnish you with an excellent chance to present your views." As for Julie Waldman, she was a musicologist who had yet to complete her doctoral thesis and was in no position to refuse the Chancellor's invitation which was, in effect, an order. To soften the blow he ventured a ponderous joke: "Gleicher was trying to complete his book on Beethoven, so wouldn't you agree that it is altogether fitting that you, Fraulein Waldman, who are trying to finish your book about Gleicher, should defend him?"

• • •

KREMPE. Gleicher presents the most extreme imaginable instance of a scholar merging with his subject. This identification was most likely an unhealthy one from the start; it certainly turned into an *idée fixe*, into madness. The dissociation of personality suffered by Egon Gleicher should move us to pity, not admiration. The compositions my young colleague wishes to commend are, in fact, a form of playacting. Gleicher, a mediocre musician, as everyone agrees, *pretended* to be a great talent. Owing no doubt to the shock he suffered in March 1945, this pretense was persisted in far beyond the frontier of sanity. And so, what can one say. You all know the story of Beethoven's indignant letter to his patron Prince Lichnowsky, who had offended him. No? It's quite brief. "Prince, what you are, you are by accident of birth; what I am, I am by myself.

There are and will be a thousand princes; there is only one Beethoven." There are a thousand Gleichers, but there is only one Beethoven.

WALDMAN. Neither Egon Gleicher nor I would dispute Beethoven's uniqueness, Professor. Had he believed otherwise, had he only sought to write *in the manner of* Beethoven, had he merely wished to, as you say, *pretend*— or, as they say these days, *to channel* Beethoven—the case would be utterly different. In Gleicher's mind, when he wrote those last works, he *was* Beethoven. Thus, he actually became deaf while he wrote. His normally calm person- ality turned prickly. Even his appearance changed. With respect to Gleicher's so-called pretending, I should also like to quote Beethoven. "Anyone who tells a lie has not a pure heart, and cannot make a good soup." Gleicher made good soup, good music. His heart was pure; he was not telling a lie.

KREMPE. Certainly not, Fraulein. A lie requires sanity, as soup does water.

• • •

March 14, 1945 was a chilly, overcast day; the talons of that ferocious last winter of the war had yet to loosen their grip on the Swabian Jura. Egon Gleicher was in the Eberlin Lecture Hall speaking in a politically reckless manner of Beethoven's late quartets and piano sonatas. The class was small; a third were young women, the rest men of military age (by then, what wasn't?) who had lost limbs, suffered from fits, or had been declared unfit for service. All were pale and undernourished. The vise was closing on a ruined Germany. Herrenstadt, however, isolated and of no military significance, had been spared. The mountains rose above the valley as if protecting the town and its conservatory. Gleicher's horror at what had become of his country and, still more, its culture, had driven him inward. The only form of social intercourse he could tolerate was with his students. Years before, he had given up composing. Dissatisfied with his indifferent efforts and persuaded by the bad reviews, he took up teaching composition and scholarship. For years he had worked away at his big book on Beethoven. It had seen him through the war.

"Though Beethoven said all his music was for the future this is particularly true of these late works, written when he was more isolated than ever and not only by his deafness. Ordinarily, his reference to music of the future is taken to refer to Romanticism, which can indeed be understood as a century-long effort to digest the work of the colossus. However, my dears, I think otherwise. How can we not think of Beethoven and his dashed hopes for humanity— the lost love, the feckless nephew, the liberator with clay feet, the brotherhood of the millions destroyed by war— when we look around us. How can we not be in sympathy with the prophet who spoke from his heart when he said, 'I despise a world which does not feel that music is a higher revelation than all wisdom and philosophy'. Yes, music is far higher than politics and science, I would like to agree. Can any of us listen to the *Adagio expressivo* of Opus 131 or the prodigious *Fuga* that concludes Opus 110 and not feel they are meant for us. This is music for our own time, though not of it. Beethoven teaches us struggle and lament, shows us how to battle through the tensions of the world and in our souls. My dears, we must cleave to the best of our nation as the worst of it is purged. . . ."

During a daylight raid on a diesel engine factory in Munich, a B-17 of the 8th Air Force lost power in two engines, fell out of formation. In an effort to stay aloft, the pilot ordered the bombardier to jettison the plane's

6000-pound payload. Most of the bombs fell in the mountains; a few struck outside the town killing three cows and demolishing a tool shed. One fell on the Conservatory. All but three of the human beings inside the Eberlin Lecture Hall were blown to bits or crushed to death by falling timbers and masonry.

. . .

WALDMAN. I am saying that Gleicher was Beethoven and also that he wasn't; that is, he both knew and didn't know about his condition.

KREMPE. Both dead and alive, sane and mad. Like Schrodinger's cat?

WALDMAN. After the war, instead of completing his book, Gleicher became Beethoven. Yes, in a sense, that's what he did. This new identity imposed on him what he felt to be a solemn responsibility, a nearly crushing obligation. What would Beethoven have written after the debacle and in response to what brought it about. Gleicher replied to that question in the only possible way. What is remarkable, and the reason why we are here, is that he not only did so, but did it so. . . majestically.

KREMPE. *Majestically.* Now, now, Fraulein, I fear you have been carried away by a romantic notion. Either you are, as I've said, mistaking madness for genius or, if you really take these second-rate works to be masterpieces, you are defying good taste in order to excuse the madness. But please tell me, honestly, when you listen to the *Eberlin Variations* do you really hear the Beethoven of the *Diabelli.* Can you really say in good conscience that it is *Beethoven's* music to which you are listening?

WALDMAN. I understand why you wish to make me look foolish, Professor. But I am not alone. I would remind you of what the respected musicologist Adelbert Steiner said of the *Eberlin Variations*. He wrote that "they are worthy of Beethoven." Isn't it obvious that something extraordinary happened to Gleicher. I agree that his earlier work is mediocre; I willingly grant his lack of talent. It is that lack which makes his post-war accomplishments so astonishing. Is it too much to say that this man became what he imagined himself to be, that simile transgressed into metaphor. That is, I suppose, my point. How, except by virtue of what you call his *idée fixe*, could the talentless Egon Gleicher have written such stupendous music?

KREMPE. I do not agree with Doctor Steiner and would like to point out that he made that unfortunate remark prior to learning that the composer was in an asylum when he wrote the *Variations*. In fact, *The Eberlin Variations* is at best an impersonation of Beethoven, second-hand, with some superficial modernisms tossed in—that is to say, wrong notes.

WALDMAN. Few lunatics who believe they are Napoleon can win at Austerlitz.

KREMPE. On the contrary, Fraulein. In their poor, disturbed minds, every last one of them is a conqueror.

• • •

Notes of Dr. Wilhelm Schottinger, Staff Psychiatrist, Institüt Wenzel Hartmann

6 January, 1948

Patient 772, Gleicher, Egon

Today, patient was clean and shaved, altogether proper, dignified, and self-controlled. He was not "deaf". Patient described himself as "well" then asked two things. for more music paper and whether I am able to play the piano. I told him I would see to the paper and admitted I am an amateur. "Oh, that is good," he said with enthusiasm, treating me to his first smile.

Patient became expansive, and I permitted him to lead the conversation. Of course, it was about music. The more the patient spoke, the more at ease he appeared. His initial stiffness gave way to fluid motions, lively hand gestures, a free movement of limbs. During our conversation one moment was of particular significance. Patient quoted Beethoven *as* Beethoven and on a revealing subject. "Rossini would have been a great composer if his teacher had spanked his backside more." I believe there is a double significance here. First, the act of quotation demonstrates that Gleicher is able to dissociate himself from his delusion—a phenomenon with which I am unfamiliar— and also that he connects artistic achievement to punishment. The guilt of being Egon Gleicher the survivor, the guilt of watching his young students die before his eyes, the guilt of being—by his lights—a German, cries out for expiation. To the patient, without punishment there can be no release. There is nothing but guilty mediocrity.

So far as I have been able to determine, patient's childhood was pleasant or at least unremarkable. In response to my question, patient said with a smile that his mother may have favored his younger brother. His father was an insurance attorney. They got on well and often went fishing together. Beethoven's relation to his own father, of course, was quite different, as patient is certainly aware. Johann Beethoven was a second-rate musician but a first-rate alcoholic. After his mother's death, while still in his teens,

Ludwig petitioned the prince to award him custody of his two siblings and secured half his father's salary for their support. Johann Beethoven was a disgrace; he was publicly ridiculed. Notably, this deplorable father was Ludwig's first teacher and, according to the source I consulted, turned violent when his son's playing failed to please him.

At the close of the interview, alluding again to the Rossini story, patient's manner altered again. He became morose and said that perhaps after all it was a good thing that his father had beaten him so.

Notes of Dr. Wilhelm Schottinger, Staff Psychiatrist, Institüt Wenzel Hartmann

13 January, 1948
Patient 772, Gleicher, Egon

In contrast to last Tuesday, patient's appearance today was slovenly, hair uncombed and unclean, shirt not tucked in. He also seemed to be suffering from a head cold. On the other hand, he held himself unusually erect with head so high that his double chin almost vanished. Patient's eyes were sparkling and clear. He arrived squeezing papers in his fist and held on to them throughout the interview. Patient appeared frustrated and angry, at times furious. When I spoke to him, he furrowed his brow and looked hard at my mouth then shook his head. "Deaf" once more. Patient found it impossible to sit still. He rose three times during our brief session and paced the office. Someone seeing him for the first time might well be anxious about his committing a violent act.

Before leaving, patient handed me the roll of paper. It is music for the piano, far from neat, full of blots. It is far too difficult for me to play.

· · ·

KREMPE. The *Second Symphony* is simply an imposture. With that four-note motif in the allegro and the seven— or is it nine?—false endings, it reminds me of a slapdash fake of an old master, one made to look as if he had lived last week, so crude that even a rich American would not be taken in. There is no mystery about such work, at best only mystification. Gleicher underwent an episode of dissociation and this is unfortunate. But he persisted in it perversely, like one who leaves his costume on long after the masked ball has ended.

WALDMAN. Professor, your rhetoric is dazzling. I admire it. I fear, though, that we can never agree because you stubbornly refuse to open your ears to Gleicher's work; in fact, you condemn it *a priori*. Little wonder you can't hear it without squirming. For those of us without prejudice, however, like Adelbert Steiner, the *Second Symphony* is a whole world compacted of the best and worst of the last century. The finale takes chromaticism over the limit until tonality itself crumbles. It is as if Gleicher means to lead us to the edge of the stratosphere and show us where the true blackness begins, the emptiness all around us. In one respect at least, Gleicher is no different from Beethoven, from other great artists. That is, his anguish was mastered as he expressed it, *by* expressing it. Only in music of this order of seriousness could he find release, relief, or redemption. To me, the *Second Symphony* is a grand smashed cathedral, a great war monument free of both chauvinism and sentimentality.

· · ·

Notes of Dr. Wilhelm Schottinger, Staff Psychiatrist, Institüt Wenzel Hartmann

21 June, 1948
Patient 772, Gleicher, Egon

Patient is to be released this afternoon. He came to bid me farewell, though he is aware the decision was made over my strenuous objections. I informed him of that myself.

Clothing clean, demeanor calm, but hair rather wild and grayer than when he arrived half a year ago.

"Where will you go?" I asked.

"Herrenstadt, of course."

"Do you believe that wise?"

Patient shrugged.

To say something, I remarked, "It's the first day of summer."

Patient nodded, shook my hand and said, "I hope you can make a good soup, Doctor."

• • •

KREMPE. An old rabbi observed that the one thing that cannot be imitated is the truth because the instant it is imitated, it ceases to be the truth. The same may be said of genius. Gleicher's case is an oddity, a melancholy medical footnote. The Conservatory may choose to put up a plaque, even a bust in the Roman style, but by doing so it will gain no honor. I am thinking now of Beethoven's last words, "Friends, applaud. The comedy is over."

WALDMAN. Identity is a construct. We believe we are always the same—*ourselves*, we say by way of convenience. But can adults recall themselves as they were as children, as adolescents, and honestly assert that they are the same today. Egon Gleicher's story is indeed an oddity—for all I know, unique—but I insist that there really is truth in those late works of his. Why else would they be performed all over the world and counted by some among the glories of German music. They mark the beginning of a recovery, a foundation for the reconstruction of the ruined and polluted temple of our culture.

A plaque. A bust. Absolutely. But with or without them, Herrenstadt will forever be known as the home of Egon Gleicher.

I see the Chancellor is anxious that we have gone on too long. I will conclude then with the epigraph Gleicher intended to place at the head of his unfinished book.

"Music is the one incorporeal entrance into the higher world of knowledge which comprehends mankind, but which mankind cannot comprehend."

HSI-WEI IN WUYAN

The Sui Dynasty sandal-maker and poet Chen Hsi-wei lived his last years in a tiny cottage outside the city of Chiangling. The modest property was granted him by the governor of the city who declared it was a reward for his poems. Hsi-wei was overwhelmed by this gift and also surprised. Governor Bao Rui-hang, a former timber baron, had never been known to take the least interest in literature.

Once the vagabond Chen Hsi-wei had a fixed residence, people were able to pay visits. One of these was the widow of Governor Bao, who had been struck down by a stroke. She came one week after the end of the period of official mourning.

Lady Bao was a tall woman with a narrow face and lively, intelligent eyes. Her natural expression was severe, her customary tone one of command. She arrived at Hsi-wei's cottage late one morning in a carriage pulled by two chestnut horses accompanied by two stout men. One drove the carriage; the other was armed and rode his own mount. The governor's widow was dressed in a gown of plain white linen. Her hair was arranged in three elaborate braids held in place by silver combs. It was a style Hsi-wei had seen decades earlier when he was in the far south of Yangzhou. He had heard that Lady Bao was a daughter of one of the leading families of that region, her marriage a political alliance. He wondered if those exotic braids were a way of declaring the independence that came with her new status.

She was no longer obliged to conform to the fashions of the capital, just as she was free to leave the city on her own to visit retired a peasant-poet.

The armed escort dismounted and held out his arm to help Lady Bao from the carriage.

Hsi-wei greeted her with a low bow. His visitor glanced around disapprovingly. He had no idea who she was, but her first words made her identity clear.

"My husband was a mean man, but I didn't suspect it extended to this. Master Chen, I should be bowing to you. You've given me much pleasure with your verses and now I see that this is all I've given to you." She ran her gaze again over the unpainted boards, the sagging roof, the tiny unpaved patio with its puddles, Hsi-wei's exiguous woodpile.

"My Lady, I am unworthy of your attention but moved by your visit, especially at this difficult time. I didn't know I had you to thank for my home, with which I am more than content."

"Well, why shouldn't you know that I was the one who nagged my husband until he agreed to give you a place to live. He swore to me it was a proper villa, with five rooms, a kitchen, and a garden. I should have known better than to trust him. I ought to have made sure of it."

"My Lady, you have my humble gratitude for my first and last home. It suits me very well. I've no need of three more rooms or a garden. Please accept my belated thanks for your generosity and my condolences for the loss of your husband."

Lady Bao scoffed. "How were you to know I had anything to do with it. If I'd had *more* to do with it, you'd have those five rooms, a proper roof, and a decent garden. Now, Master Chen, I propose we dispense with any further empty courtesies. Since my husband died, I've been enjoying doing without such things. Now, I've brought food and yellow wine, which I'm told you like. I'm not here for your sympathy or gratitude. I want to talk about your poems."

She turned to her servants.

"Lixin, bring the hamper. Rui, fetch the bronze casket."

Lixin set a willow hamper down on the low wall of the patio. "Open it," ordered his mistress. It was crammed with good things—fish, beef and pork dishes with four sauces, spring onions, pickled radishes, cabbage, and two boxes of rice along with a fine porcelain wine carafe.

Hsi-wei's patio had two low chairs and a small, weathered table. Rui stood by with the casket until Lady Bao indicated he should lay it on the table.

"I suppose you at least have a hearth and a wok inside, Master Hsi-wei?"

Hsi-wei nodded and she told Rui to carry the food inside, Lixin to take in wood for the hearth, and both to get busy preparing lunch.

The day being fine, Lady Bao proposed they stay outside. Hsi-wei was inclined to like this extraordinary woman. She was not only his benefactress but intelligent, aristocratic without being condescending, and candid almost to the point of bluntness. After sending off the servants, she opened the bronze casket and took out a small scroll set atop dozens of others. She handed it to Hsi-wei. It was a list of some of his poems with annotations.

"It's a list of those verses of which I can't entirely approve. Look it over."

Her notes referred to passages and what she found objectionable about them. But the list was short and Hsi-wei quickly finished reading it. When he returned the scroll, Lady Bao said she was glad to get that out of the way. Then she spoke about of Hsi-wei's poems she particularly liked, even reciting some favorite lines.

"I would like to know how you came to write your poems, beginning with the one known as 'My Skull.'".

Hsi-wei willingly obliged. He told her how he had been plucked from dozens of young peasant boys to have a secret message inscribed on his head. He enjoyed reliving the perils of his journey to find General Feng in the south. Lady Bao's comments also gave him pleasure. She recognized when he used a southern idiom. While her catalogue of criticisms had hurt, Hsi-wei felt that they were all justified—in fact, more than numerous compliments. Here was a sympathetic reader and a learned one. She recognized the classics which he had emulated; she picked out his allusions too. "You use old forms but also make new ones. That's rare," she said appreciatively then went on to explain why she rated Hsi-wei's most popular poem, "Yellow Moon at Lake Weishan," as inferior to "The Sadness of the Emperor".

"I even prefer 'In Praise of Magistrate Jun Ti-an,' though that might just be because I liked the story of how those monks chastised the insolent schoolboys of Chiangling. I've had to deal with a few of that sort myself," she said in a tone that made Hsi-wei glad not to have been one of those boys.

"Now, Master Hsi-wei," she went on, "my collection of your work is incomplete. It's a deficiency I wish you to remedy. I'm sure there are very many poems I have never seen and I'm curious about them. I can tell from the poems I have read that you are fond of children. I wonder if you ever wrote anything for them, a fairy tale in verse for instance, or perhaps a fable."

As he grew older, Hsi-wei often forgot his poems, but this was not a bad thing. In fact, he liked a poem best when he had forgotten it and could read it as if it had been composed by somebody else. Then he would try to recollect when, where and why he had written the piece and, if he succeeded, that too gave him pleasure.

Lady Bao's question brought back a memory.

"Yes, long ago I did write a fable, though it wasn't for children, and I didn't write it for the usual reason—I mean not as a thing on its own."

"You mean the fable was a means to an end. It seems to me that quite a lot of your poems are exactly that—like your famous but excessively brutal 'Letter to Yang Jian'."

"But that was a public plea, a protest, a call for action against a ruthless, murderous bandit. I had only the faintest hope that it would reach its august addressee. Yet what you say is true. I did often make a poem with the aim of accomplishing something in the world. But the fable you've just made me remember was different. It was written just for one occasion. The others, even the ones meant to do something, even my letter to the emperor, were also intended to stand on their own even if they failed to change anything."

"Which means you wanted them to stand outside the world?"

Hsi-wei sighed. "In my opinion, My Lady, the world of poetry exists in its own empire and inside its own time."

"I think you're right, though I'd never thought of it quite that way. . . . But, it's getting late and I want to be home before dark. First business, then your fable." Lady Bao opened the bronze casket and took out a sheet of yellow paper which she handed to Hsi-wei. "This is a list of all the poems in this casket. When I come back in a week you will lend me all the ones I don't have. I'll see the scrolls are returned to you once I've had copies made. Now, pour us another cup of wine and tell me how Master Chen Hsi-wei came to write his one and only fable."

The poet obeyed, remembering what he could and reconstructing the rest.

After spending the last week of winter with a friend in Yuzhou, I decided to make my way to a mountainous area in the westernmost part of Liangzhou. I had heard the region praised for its good air, the beauty of its mountains and old forests. I thought it would make a good destination for a trek in springtime. The district was said to be a prosperous one with vast estates. The local landlords possessed almost as much land as the dukes did in the days of weak emperors.

The journey took me nearly two months and, by the time I arrived, spring had turned to early summer. I spent one night at an inn at the crest of a mountain road. As the place was nearly empty, I was able to negotiate a low price for a small room. At this inn, I met a young man named Chan Zihan, a boy really, still in his teens. Zihan had hair as thick as my own, keen eyes, and a temperament that was both fiery and sentimental. He invited me to share a jug with him. It was obvious the boy was troubled, lonely, and needed to talk.

"Are you on your way to Wuyan?" he asked.

I said I didn't know, that I was just following the road, and asked if he were from Wuyan.

"From it. Very much so. I'm in exile from Wuyan"

"Exile?"

"My father sent me away. I'm going to ask Ho Chang-li for refuge. His land is on the other side of these mountains. I'll do any work he sets me to. When I was little, Mr. Ho twice came to visit my father on business. He and I got on well. I'll miss Wuyan, though. I have many friends there among the peasants. And there's my mother."

"I don't wish to intrude on family matters, and I hope the question doesn't offend you, but why did your father send you away?"

Zihan was quiet for a moment then the words poured out of him.

"Father owns of the whole district to the west of here. What he owns includes four villages. As a young man, he did good service in fighting off an incursion from the western barbarians. The land was his reward. He was given a lot of land, but in those days it wasn't prosperous. Too rocky and hilly for farming. He chose to build our—his villa in Wuyan. It's the largest of the villages and, in recent years, it's become rich. That's because of the pigs. This sudden wealth changed my father and led him to do things I didn't like and then to sending me away. Have you ever tasted Wuyan pork?"

I admitted I hadn't heard of Wuyan pork, let alone eaten any.

The young man's tongue was loosened by the wine or perhaps just the relief of talking. He stretched out his legs and told the recent history of Wuyan as he understood it.

"About six years ago, Li Xiang, an honest man as well as a clever one, had the idea of feeding his eight pigs acorns instead of slops. The forests here are thick with oaks, both sawtooth and Daimyo, so there's no shortage of acorns. Xiang's pigs thrived and their meat was to ordinary pork as Mount Wutai is to an anthill. The peasants increased their herds, built large pens next to the forest, and began breeding pigs and feeding them all on acorns. It was also Xiang who thought of providing pork to all the local inns so travelers would learn of it. Before long, buyers from all over the province were showing up in Wuyan. They bid up prices. The peasants grew rich, and they all paid their rents right on time. That might have been enough for my father."

"But something went wrong?"

Zihan struck the table with his fist, overturning our wine cups.

"What went wrong was my father's greed and his pride. He couldn't bear seeing the peasants becoming wealthy—'*my* peasants,' as he always calls them. He complained that they had too much and he had too little. So, he doubled their rents. There was grumbling and a few of the peasants came humbly to object. My father's response was to hire five tough veterans."

"There was violence?"

"The threat was sufficient. Everybody paid up and the grumbling quieted down. But even that wasn't enough for Father. Now that he had more money, he bought himself a second wife. Liling grew up in Qingyuan, the daughter of a scholar—a scholar with debts which my father paid off. She's accomplished. She can write, sing, play the liuqin, and recite poems. She's likes city things, expensive ones. My father's infatuation and the need to satisfy her desires made him still greedier. A few weeks ago, he decreed that he was ending rents and that instead every pig and piglet on his land would now be his personal property. The peasants could keep their homes and cultivate their own plots on the condition that they continue raising and selling pigs—that is, working for him. Last week, Xiang Li led a small group of men to our house to put his objections. My father refused to reconsider his decision or even discuss it. *Your arrogance is inexcusable. I can throw you oafs off my land and replace every one of you in two weeks.* That's what he said to the good Xiang Li. That night, the poor man was dragged from his cottage and beaten so severely in front of his family. He died the next day. Xiang left a wife, Chu Hua, a little boy and a little girl, Wei and Ai. I had it out with my father. And now you know why I've been banished."

"If what you say is so, even leaving aside the beating of Xiang, what your father's done isn't only unjust but, under Emperor Wen's land reform, illegal. Has an appeal been made to the magistrate?"

Zihan scoffed. "As the saying goes, Heaven is high and the emperor is far away. Here, it's the landlords who are in charge. The magistrates serve their three-year terms and never interfere."

Shortly after that, we said good night and went to our beds.

I passed through the gate of Wuyan early the following afternoon. Because the pens were at the foot of the mountains, on the edge of the forest, the village was free of the stink of pigs. Wuyan looked more like a prosperous town than a village. Every building was freshly painted, and the central street was paved. But when I reached the marketplace, I felt the tension. Children were chasing each other around while their elders engaged in arguments. Tempers and voices were high. Over and over, I heard the name of Chan Yuxian, Zihan's father, invoked with bitterness. His second wife also came in for some harsh talk. "Things weren't so bad until that city girl showed up," I heard one woman say. Instead of setting up my sign and soliciting orders for straw sandals, I approached her group and asked the way to the villa of Landlord Chan.

A wiry man with a scraggly beard replied. "Why would you go there, stranger. They'll only yell and drive you off— or worse."

"Is that so. Well, nevertheless I'll go," I said. "Please show me the way."

The fellow shrugged and rolled his eyes. "Suit yourself," he said and pointed the way.

Two big men in leather tunics stood on either side of the bright red door of Chan's villa. They leaned on long *qiangs* and the short swords called *jians* hung from their belts.

"Go away," shouted one, looking at me with contempt.

"If that's the wish of your employer, of course," I said. "But I think he might not be pleased if he finds you've sent me away." "Oh, and why's that?"

"Because his friend and neighbor, Landlord Ho, sent me to see him but especially his new wife."

The two looked at one another. "Stay put," one ordered. gruffly then went inside. He returned with a slim, overly dressed young woman. She wore long golden earrings shaped like little bells. Liling.

I bowed to the new wife.

Her voice was high and thin but confident, like that of a spoiled child. "What brings you here and who sent you?"

"Your neighbor, the landlord Ho Chang-li, suggested I visit. If you are the Lady Liling, then, according to Mr. Ho, you're fond of poems and poets."

The young woman took in my dusty clothing, the worn leather bag over my shoulder.

"And you are a scholar?" she asked suspiciously. "A poet?"

"I have studied and yes, I have written some poor verses."

She examined me doubtfully. "What's your name?"

"Chen Hsi-wei."

"No. You are the author of 'Yellow Moon at Lake Weishan'?"

I nodded. "I'm flattered you know it."

"But it's one of my favorite poems!. She paused, looked up at the sky, and prettily recited, *Weishan lies cool and still as a forgotten bowl of tea*. I'd heard the poem was written by a peasant who travels all over making straw sandals, but I didn't believe it."

I opened my bag, took out my sample sandals and a small scroll with my most recent poem on it, some comical verses about a mother-in-law outsmarted by her son's new wife. Liling took the scroll, read it, and smiled.

As I'd hoped, I was invited to dinner. I spent the rest of the afternoon in the marketplace learning more about Wuyan and its landlord. The peasants were not only angry about the death of Xiang and the expropriation of their pigs but also the sending away of young Zihan, of whom they were fond and regarded as one of their own.

I did my best to clean myself up for dinner at the landlord's villa. Liling greeted me at the door and introduced me to her husband as the peasant she had told him about, the one who had become a poet, the author of her favorite poem.

Chan Yuxian was polite but clearly unimpressed. Dinner was served at once and he presided at the table.

The landlord was a barrel-chested man whose sour expression sweetened whenever he looked at his young wife, which he did from minute to minute. The first wife, Lan, a heavyset woman of about forty, sat like a statue of the Buddha, if not as serenely then as quietly, a model of self-restraint who ignored me and gave no sign of resenting either the presence of Liling or the absence of her son Zihan.

The table talk was almost entirely a dialogue between me and an excited Liling. The young woman recalled how one of my poems had been read to her when she was little.

"It was the one people call 'Mai-ling's Good Idea'. Could you recite some of it for me?"

I said I couldn't recall it well but she rattled off a dozen lines.

Her husband beamed as if she'd just levitated or served him a perfectly cooked duck.

After her recitation, Liling said, "I was fond of poems and stories from the first."

I asked if she had also been read any of those fables written for the instruction of children and, if so, whether she liked them.

She shook her head. "Oh, I was read many of those things. But I didn't care for most of them because of their respectable morals. *Always respect your elders. Don't give up what you've got for something you don't. Fire makes a good slave but a terrible master.* Ugh. I did like the ones that were clever and didn't try to teach me anything, like the one about the tiger and the fox."

Chan Yuxian, looking at her fondly, said he didn't know that story. I pretended never to have heard it either so that Liling could have the pleasure of telling it.

"A ferocious tiger corners a vixen and is about to eat her up. Thinking fast, the fox warns the tiger not to try anything because she's the most feared animal in the whole forest and can prove it, too. The tiger laughs. 'Oh, and how can you do that?' 'You just follow me,' says the vixen and prances off into the woods with the tiger right behind. As she approaches, all the mice and squirrels, all the rabbits and monkeys, even the wild dogs and boars run away in terror."

Liling laughed and turned to her husband. "It's because they saw the tiger behind her, of course."

For a moment, I wondered if this rather silly young woman—to whom every peasant in Wuyan must bow—ever thought she was the vixen and her overbearing husband the tiger. Chan certainly looked as if he would like to gobble her up. I don't believe it would have occurred to her, though. Liling was one of those people for whom poems and stories are doorways leading away from of reality, not windows drawing us towards it. . . . But excuse me. I've gone on far too long. You have to leave soon and you wanted to know about my fable. I'll come to it now.

Liling asked if I knew a fable that was also a poem.

I said I knew an ancient one that's attributed to a nobleman of the Zhou Dynasty, and that there was a story attached to it. The noble was Jie Zhitiai a good man who met a tragic end for offending his lord. The Daoists later made him a saint. I explained that Jie lived during the period of the Five Hegemons, those powerful dukes who reigned over their domains with absolute power, like so many emperors. The Duke of Mu was especially despotic. After brutally putting down a peasant uprising, he imposed a new penal code with all sorts of grisly punishments. It required dismemberment for all political crimes, which included not only any criticism of himself but of even his lowest-ranking official. Worse yet, the children of those found guilty were also to be executed—those under the age of five by strangulation, all others by decapitation. On the day that twelve children were to be executed, the court and hundreds of peasants gathered in the palace courtyard to bear witness to the event. Just before the sentence was carried out, the duke's eldest son who was seated beside his father leapt to his feet and loudly protested. The duke wanted to execute his son, but the boy's mother begged him on her knees to commute the sentence to exile. The exiled boy was taken in by the Duke of Qin. Only days after these events, the Duke of Mu held a banquet. The poet-courtier Jie was requested to entertain the guests with his latest poem. Jie was known for elegant but conventional verses, poems about gardens, landscapes, and the seasons. But that evening he rose and recited a fable.

"Can you recite it?" asked Liling, intrigued by the story.

This I could easily do as I had made up Jie's fable that very afternoon.

Deep in the Forest of Yu,
in the trunk of an old beech,
bees built their village.
They worked hard making
lots of fragrant honey.
Wandering through the woods,
Daxiong, his two wives, one
son and three daughters,
came upon the bees' hive.
They all made for the honey.
The sweet combs so intoxicated
Daxiong that he lost his head.
Growling and baring his claws,
he swiped at his two wives
and threatened his three children.
Angry bees swarmed all over him
wielding stingers like little swords,
but Daxiong's fur was thick.
Only his son dared stand up to him
accusing him of selfishness and greed.
Infuriated, Daxiong reared and roared.
His family ran off and he ate up all the honey.
Now Daxiong lurches through the forest alone,
an old bear with just four rotten teeth.

I went on. "A year later, the banished son of the Duke returned from Qin with a small force that, after being joined by thousands of peasants, overthrew his father."

"And did your fable have any effect?" asked Lady Bao.

"Oh, an immediate one. Lan, the first wife, applauded, Liling, the second one, looked perplexed, and Chan himself summoned two of his men to toss me out. I left Wuyan that night."

Lady Bao gave a little sigh. "Do you know what happened to the landlord's son, that Zihan. Did he too try to overthrow his father with the help of the swineherds of Wuyan?"

Hsi-wei smiled. "As it happens, I learned later from a traveler that Chan Yuxian had died unexpectedly of an apoplectic stroke. Liling was sent back to her father by Lan and Zihan returned to Wuyan. He rescinded his father's pig policy, restored the old rents, did all he could to promote the town's prosperity, and was beloved by the peasants. At least, that's what I was told."

"Perhaps," said Lady Bao, getting to her feet, "I'll buy some of this wonderful Wuyan pork. I'm assuming you didn't invent that as well, did you?"

"No, my Lady."

"Well then, if I can find some, we'll have it when I come back next week for those poems. Make sure you have them ready."

With a little bow, Hsi-wei assured her he would.

PHILHARMONIA

In the middle of rehearsing the *Symphonie Fantastique,* Augustin Bäcker, one of the second violins, suddenly leaned forward and whispered into the ear of Bernd Eichel, a first violin. Eichel spun around, upsetting his chair, and delivered a riposte so blistering that Bäcker's face turned red. Alois Labernz—who, years later, would have a *von* added to his name in recognition of his role as founder, director, and conductor of Marburg's highly regarded orchestra—was too far off to hear what either man said; but the enmity was unmistakable, and he could guess the cause. The uproar among the strings became general when Bäcker leapt to his feet, holding out his violin like a shield and wielding his bow like a sword, while Eichel grabbed his music stand and wheeled around with a curse. Labernz banged the podium with his baton. "Gentlemen!" he shouted. At the same time, his veteran Concertmaster, Matthias Urster, rose and turned. "*Basta!*" he cried, then, still louder, "*Herren, genug!*. He ordered the other violinists to separate the two before they could really lock horns. He then glowered in the direction of the woodwinds where Julie von Kibenau, who had just executed the oboe solo in Berlioz's Second Movement, regarded him with an equable smile, as if entirely unaware that she might in any way be implicated in the commotion.

With order restored, Labernz hastened through the rest of the symphony, keeping a sharp eye on the grumbling Eichel and scowling Bäcker, both of whom sawed away like lunatics in the Witches' Dance.

After the rehearsal was adjourned, Alois Labernz retreated to the office he kept up by the attics. It was a long room that might once have been used to store lumber. The conductor had furnished it with a dark Turkish rug, a hard wooden chair and small desk. On the long wall to the left was an old leather love seat and a spinet. To the right, behind the desk and on either side of a small fireplace, two walnut bookcases reached almost to the ceiling. There were a few books on the top shelves but mostly they were jam-packed with scores. Because of its shape, all the dark wood of the shelves, spinet, the brown leather of the couch, the faded maroon and blue of the carpet, the room, though hardly small, felt crowded and, with nothing to soften it, decidedly masculine. When the University, which for many years owned but neither used nor maintained Rheinach Hall, granted his orchestra a lease on good terms, Labernz had chosen this room as his lair. He particularly liked the high arched window at the end of the room. It looked out on the steep-roofed houses and market stalls of Rheinach Square.

In the eighteenth century, Marburg was governed by rulers of little account, a backwater with an underfunded university. It missed out on both baroque and neo-classical renovations, a medieval leftover irretrievably out of fashion. But cultural developments at the start of the new century gave the Gothic a cachet. A distinguished circle of writers and thinkers gathered in the town, including Friedrich Savigny, Achim and Bettina Arnim, Clemens Brentano, and the Brothers Grimm. For a time, Marburg could justly claim to be the epicenter of German Romanticism. Therefore, the cramped square on which the conductor could gaze from his window looked no different from the way it had when Jacob and Wilhelm Grimm escaped to the University or when Luther's *Ninety-Five Theses* were first being set in movable type.

After the rehearsal broke up, the exasperated concert-master pursued the conductor to his den and demanded a serious conversation, as Labernz feared he would. Urster, always stiffly correct, a great respecter of rank and deeply grateful to Labernz for his appointment, nevertheless found it impossible to hold his tongue. He was proud of the five years he had played with the orchestra in Mannheim, even if that ensemble had fallen a long way from the glories of a century before. Urster was among those who cuddle and pet their grievances like lapdogs. Sometimes he annoyed Labernz by exercising more authority than he was entitled to by his position. Now, leaning aggressively on the conduc-tor's desk, Urster presented his case to Labernz's back. The conductor, knowing what was coming, took refuge at the window where he watched three men, two women, four children, and a three-legged dog cross the square. This was far from the first time the concertmaster complained to him about the female oboist.

"That I was against her appointment and the way it came about you already know, Maestro, so I won't trudge back and forth over that road. I'll just remind you of my warning that hiring the girl was likely to have detrimental consequences. It's not just the little fracas we saw today with Bäcker and Eichel. That was merely one spark from a fire that's eating away the timbers. Last month, it was Rothbauer pining away and missing his entrances. And, just to remind you, we had to send Heiner Knochenmur away two months ago when he challenged poor Salzwedel to a duel. It was a real loss; he was hotheaded but talented boy. It's not just that she's twenty-one and pretty. The woman's a coquette as well—a coquette *at best*." Urster, having worked himself up, paused to catch his breath. "At Mannheim, we had no women. Nor are there any in Berlin or Leipzig or Vienna. There's a sound reason why women are not permitted on naval ships. It's no different with orchestras. The girl's become a threat to our work, Maestro, and just when your fame has begun to spread."

Urster, a widower, was conservative in his social views yet enthusiastic about the new music and personally fond of his conductor. The concertmaster was devoted to the orchestra and to Labernz who knew the fellow was sincerely distressed. Now Urster pushed his point as far as he could. "Mark my words, if you don't get rid of this girl, she'll end by destroying your life's work."

Labernz turned from the window with a smile. "My dear Matthias, you know how much I value your opinion and your work. I can't deny there may be something in what you say. I don't wish to appear pig-headed and I respect your advice, which I know is well meant."

"With respect, Maestro, why not take it?"

Why not. Perhaps it was because Labernz really was stubborn, because Fraulein von Kibenau was gifted, because he was proud of his innovation that had led to her appointment, and because he felt dismissing her would be unjust. Alois Labernz had been raised Catholic and learned from the priests about *occasiones peccati*, the occasions of sin. He understood them as traps that would rob men of their virtue, peace, liberty, if not their salvation. Even as his adherence to the Church faded, he had made a point of avoiding *occasiones*, particularly women. Yet he had come to understand that it isn't gold and good-looking girls that are at the root of evil but greed and lust. Alluring things are not to blame for our evil-doing but rather our excessive attachment to them.

Julie von Kibenau was young and pretty, just as Urster said. Apparently, she liked to enjoy herself. He had heard she relished good food, wine, and dancing with young men.

But did any of that mean she wasn't innocent. Was she really the coquette the prejudiced Urster accused her of being. Did she deliberately provoke his musicians to fall in love with her, one after another. Labernz, with his vestigial Jesuitical conscience, decided the fault lay with the men and not the Fraulein. After all, she had never flirted with him. And even if she had, wasn't he immune to her charms. His love was for his work, for music, and for his orchestra. Though he loved these things passionately, it never crossed his mind that any of them could be an occasion of sin.

At the start of the previous summer, the oboist Florian Zelleger had left Marburg to visit his nephew in Genoa. While he was in the port city, it suffered one of its occasional outbreaks of cholera. Zelleger caught the infection and died. In a letter addressed simply to *The Philharmonia, Marburg, Hesse*, the man's nephew explained that he himself had only been spared by the constant smoking of his pipe. He had urged this precaution on his uncle but was rebuked for it: "My late relative rejected my advice and chided me. He said that the smoking of tobacco was not only an expensive vice but certain to harm his breath-control."

So Labernz needed a good oboist and quickly. His autumn programs included the Mendelssohn *Third*, Mozart's *Jupiter*, and Beethoven's *Pastoral*, all of which featured oboe solos. Decent violinists were not rare and passable percussionists easy to find. If his orchestra had required one of these, Labernz might not have conceived the notion of holding an open audition. But the idea appealed to him. To advertise such an event might create a stir and bring the orchestra's name to the attention of a wider public. Then a second idea struck him, one inspired by his summer reading of his favorite Grimms' folk tales. He would make the audition a blind one. That is, the aspirants would be placed behind a curtain so that only the quality of their playing could be considered. It was not just an idea from a fairy tale, but a dramatic one, as drama is built on concealment followed by revelation. There would be suspense. Would the winner be an old hand, someone of reputation, or a talented newcomer.

Urster opposed the whole notion from the start and expressed his objection emphatically. "It's too democratic," he said. "Reputation matters, Maestro. As do connections and proper recommendations." But Labernz had fallen in love with his fairy tale and was not to be moved. He ordered advertisements to be placed in newspapers throughout Hesse and even beyond.

Meanwhile, in the nearby town of Siegen, Julie von Kibenau was longing to escape from her narrow-minded parents and rather stupid brothers. The von Kibenaus were a family of some consequence in Siegen, minor landowners, strict Pietists, and, in their daughter's estimation, every bit as stultifying as Siegen itself. Julie was a musical child. She took to the piano like a bird to the sky and loved to sing anything but hymns. When she was thirteen the family entertained a house guest from Bonn, a business associate of Julie's father. After dinner on the first night of his stay Julie was asked to sing for him. Accompanying herself on the piano, she performed Schubert's lullaby, *Schlafe, schlafe, holder süßer Knabe*. The guest, a cultured bachelor, was enthralled and remarked that her voice reminded him of an oboe. For the rest of his stay, he playfully addressed her as "my shepherdess" and, after his departure, Julie begged her father for an oboe. Herr von Kibenau gave in, but only on the condition that she would continue her lessons on the piano, promise to sit still in church, and stop gossiping with her friends on the Lord's Day. As she wanted that oboe, Julie acceded. She kept her word with respect to the piano, but not her other promises. She applied herself to the oboe and, even without instruction, improved from one day to the next.

In her eighteenth year, Julie began to receive offers of marriage from the scions of the local gentry. The best of these proposals was from the good-looking Ewald von Böhler, a blond boy who loved two things, shooting birds and the Prussian army. But Ewald unwisely gilded his offer of marriage by enumerating the joys Julie could expect as the mother of the six or even seven children he expected her to produce and the prospect of living with together under his parents' ample roof. Her own parents were eager for grandchildren and for Julie to be comfortably settled. They saw nothing objectionable in Ewald, his family, or their mansion—quite the contrary—and so they pressured Julie to accept the offer. Julie had no intention of doing so but was reluctant to say so. So, she stalled, hoping for some means of escape. Her heart leaped when she came across the announcement of the blind audition for the position of oboist in Marburg. It felt like divine intervention, and she resolved to run away and try her luck. Julie was a spirited young woman but also a prudent one. She had saved enough money for the adventure. Marburg might not be Paris or London, but it was a big step up from Siegen. The city was awash in university students and had plenty of establishments that catered to their love of dancing, good food, and strong beer. But, above all, Marburg possessed a good orchestra.

The auditions took place on a sultry day in August. The room Labernz chose, though large, was also stuffy. An old red velvet curtain had been retrieved from the attics and draped over a rope strung from one wall to the other. The panel of judges were to sit on one side; the applicants would enter by a door on the other. The room was provided with an oak chair with a cushion and a music stand that could be adjusted for height.

Labernz could hardly exclude his concertmaster from the panel but, to make a third, he appointed the fifty-year-old clarinetist Karsten Voss. Voss had emigrated from Leipzig to join the new orchestra a decade earlier. Labernz, also a Leipziger by birth, could count on Voss. Frau Voss, a round, cheerful woman, volunteered to organize the contestants in the adjoining room she was pleased to call *la salle d'attente*. She wrote down all their names, and admitted them one at a time, after cautioning them not to speak. The plan was simple. The contestants were to perform a piece of their own choosing. A second piece, not announced in advance, would test their sight-reading. After consulting with his colleagues, Labernz settled on the solo from Rossini's *La Scala di Seta*.

Julie arrived in Marburg the day before and found lodging in the respectable boarding house recommended by the retired professor of philology with whom she had shared the public coach from Siegen. Her landlady was welcoming but could not conceal her surprise at having an unaccompanied young woman inquiring about a room. Still, her attitude was courteous and, when she heard that Julie's surname had a *von* in it, deferential. Julie was ravenous. She asked the landlady to suggest a decent restaurant. "Go to the Atschel. It's right on the main square and serves good Hessian food, nothing to upset a young lady's stomach." The Atschel, an old timbered inn, was well lit, cordial and unpretentious. Julie ordered veal chops with breaded cauliflower and fried potatoes, all washed down with two glasses of Moselle. Thanks to the wine, she didn't wake until almost nine the following morning. She dressed quickly, swallowed the cup of tea offered by the landlady, took up her oboe case and asked the way to Rheinach Hall.

Frau Voss's *salle d'attente* quickly overheated and so she had everyone move outside under the shade of two linden trees. When Julie arrived, there were more than a dozen men lined up, all clutching oboe cases. As the contestants arrived, Frau Voss recorded their names and assigned them a number. When she saw Julie join the queue, the good woman asked if she had made a mistake. Was she perhaps looking for the baker's or the butcher's?

"No, Madam. I'm here to audition."

"What?"

The men who overheard this exchange scoffed. One tried to make a joke: "Just look," he said. "The dear creature's far too pretty to play the oboe well."

Julie rounded on the fellow and quoted Goethe's Gretchen. "Just look," she mocked. "*The new light blinds him so.*"

"Oh, ho," said the man with an amused smirk. "Mademoiselle, the audition may be blind, but the Maestro is not a fool."

"Then he has the advantage of you," Julie retorted.

"But," interrupted Frau Voss, genuinely puzzled, "you're a woman."

"Yes, Madam, like you. As I understand it, the audition is open. There were no conditions."

"Well, yes, but—"

"Then you may write down my name with the others." She moved closer, looked at the long list. "Julie von Kibenau."

"Oh, *von*," sneered her antagonist, winking at the others.

The day grew still muggier and the wait wasn't brief. The line disintegrated as men sat on the grass or leaned against the lindens, waiting to be summoned. Julie stood apart. The musicians who preceded her—as dressed in proper black with stocks around their necks—had come out dripping with sweat, but she remained as cool as a marble statue in her cotton frock. When, at last, Frau Voss called her number and ushered her into the audition room, Julie took her seat and three deep breaths.

She had chosen Bach movement from one of Bach's flute sonatas which she herself had transcribed and so knew by heart. When she finished, a deep voice came from the other side of the drapery. "That was good. Very good indeed. Now, if you please, open the folder on the music stand and play the piece inside."

La Scala di Seta. Julie knew the solo and, though unable to play it from memory, didn't drop a single note.

There was no disagreement over who had been the best oboist. However, when Labernz summoned Frau Voss and gave her the number of the winner, the good woman put her hands together and turned anxiously toward her husband.

"What's the matter?" he asked.

"You'd best see for yourselves."

"Many thanks for all your help, Frau Voss," said Labernz. "You've made everything go smoothly. Now, if you would be so good, please fetch number twenty-eight."

The woman heaved a sigh, drew aside the drape, went out the door, and returned with a beaming young woman who began talking at once.

"Oh, thank you, gentlemen. I'm inexpressibly grateful. And, if you'll permit me, what a wonderful idea you had to make the audition not only open but blind—like Lady Justice herself." Having delivered this analogy, Julie curtsied and walked right up to each of the men and introduced herself.

"Very well done, Fraulein," said a stunned Labernz,

taking her hand. Voss offered a little bow, and Urster no response at all.

After Julie left, Voss said he would, of course, defer to the Maestro on the matter, but the concertmaster was adamantly opposed to the appointment. As for the conductor, though it was his inspiration to make the audition blind, he had never imagined it being won by a female. He was shaken yet his exacting sense of fairness prevailed. Should Fraulein Julie von Kibenau get the post. Yes, she should. She had earned it.

He tried to sooth Ursger. "It will be all right," he said. "Besides, she'll soon marry and leave us."

The concertmaster was not mollified. He predicted that the young woman would wreak havoc on their orchestra.

"Calm yourself, Matthias. Think of Vivaldi and his Ospedale. He managed a whole orchestra of young women. It'll be fine."

Urster grumbled. "I feel like Cassandra."

"*Another* woman," Voss cracked. Neither of his colleagues smiled.

For Matthias Urster, the Philharmonia was at first only a refuge from his troubles in Mannheim. an unsatisfying marriage, an abrasive relationship with the music director, carping in-laws, too many debts. The winter his wife died, he learned of the new project in Marburg and applied to join the orchestra. Labernz saw in Urster what he needed in a concertmaster: a dependable violinist, a veteran who was no musical reactionary, someone with the authority, confidence, and experience to discipline young players. And all this proved true. Urster quickly showed his worth and devoted himself to the orchestra almost as completely as Labernz. The concertmaster was like a doting uncle, the conductor an adoring father.

Alois Labernz could fix precisely the moment that determined the course of his life. As a boy in Leipzig, he was taken to the Gewandhaus to hear Felix Mendelssohn conduct. It seemed to him that all his senses were shaken into life that evening. The glittering chandeliers, the immaculately groomed men, the coiffed and perfumed women, even their coughs and sneezes—everything all excited him. And then there was the unforgettable entrance of the Maestro—so slim and modest yet commanding. Alois was impressed that Mendelssohn's mere stepping to the podium set off loud and prolonged applause. The slight inclination of his curly head with which Mendelssohn acknowledged the adulation took Alois' breath away.

The concert began with Beethoven's *Consecration of the House*. Alois felt the five great opening chords in his chest. He had heard good music before; there was plenty of it at his mother's soirées—recitals by pianists, fiddlers, singers, even an amateur string quartet—but this was his first experience of a symphony orchestra. After those attention-grabbing chords came the first theme, a dignified melody stated with unexpected tenderness by an oboe behind which the propulsive power of the orchestra seemed to wait in high tension. The overture was an ocean and Alois was a cork, tiny but buoyed up and unsinkable. Beethoven's brilliant variations delighted him. They came like waves, the same but different, full of vitality and making him feel powerful too. He felt the music was rushing him toward a shore where all the instruments' strength would be released in a majestic detonation. The false endings teased, augmenting rather than dissipating the music's power, delaying and delaying its final release. Alois was in love. And up there, commanding it all, stood the hero Mendelssohn on whom the audience and the musicians fixed their gaze, the pin in the magnificent pinwheel—the great Felix Mendelssohn-

Bartholdy, who, though his name meant happy, would die tragically at thirty-eight.

It was for the sake of the city's Romantic connections that Alois decided to matriculate at the University of Marburg. His father preferred him to attend his own alma mater, Heidelberg. He was even willing to accept Wittenberg or Tübingen. Alois only got his way by promising to study law rather than music. Nevertheless, from the moment he heard those five chords, his heart belonged to music and his fixed ambition was to conduct. He was already an accomplished pianist but at Marburg he took up woodwinds, brass, strings, and pored over scores of scores. In his second year, he organized a chamber music society; in his third, he expanded it to a chamber orchestra to perform his own arrangements of Mozart and Haydn symphonies. Marburg was without an orchestra, and the public began to attend his performances at the University. Alois gained a local reputation and was taken up by the local nobility, made much of by the culturally ambitious wives of Marburg academics and burghers. After completing his law degree, Labernz stayed on, though the town was still without either important industries or political significance. That changed after 1866, when the Hessian prince backed the losing side in the war between Prussia and Austria. This miscalculation proved beneficial for Marburg, however. It became part of Prussia. Despite the annexation, Marburg remained effectively independent even after Bismarck chose to make it the region's new administrative center. But long before this, at the urging of his wife, the Hessian prince conferred on Alois the right to add *von* to his name. This distinction reconciled Alois' father to his son's refusal either to practice law or return to Leipzig. In only two years, Labernz elevated his amateur chamber orchestra into the professional Marburg Philharmonia. Subscriptions sold well enabling him to hire talented young players, to negotiate an open-ended lease on Rheinach Hall and carry out the essential renovations. The inaugural concert of the Philharmonia began fittingly with Beethoven's *Consecration of the House* and concluded with Mendelssohn's final symphony, the *Reformation*.

Alois lived simply, in two rented rooms, which he used only to sleep. Unless he had to attend a dinner party, he took his meals at a workmen's restaurant and was at Rheinach Hall the rest of the time. He was proof against every effort of the local ladies to arrange a marriage for him. At last, they threw up their hands, accepting that all the young conductor's affection was bestowed on music and his orchestra.

"The man's an ascetic, a musical monk," they said with disappointment, but renewed their subscriptions.

Julie von Kibenau's family knew where she had gone because on the morning of her escape she left a letter on her bed informing her parents of her intentions. Immediately after the successful audition, she wrote them reporting that she had been asked to join its celebrated orchestra and would therefore be staying in Marburg. She said that she was in good health, had found respectable lodging, was pleased with her new surroundings, delighted with her position, and had no intention of returning to Siegen, let alone marrying one of its inhabitants. "I am," she wrote forthrightly, "of age, free, independent, and employed." She concluded with a plea not to think her "ungrateful or unnatural," certain that this was precisely what her Pietist family would think.

Julie attracted a great deal of attention in Marburg and not only from the orchestra's young musicians. Docents and doctoral candidates were also drawn to her, registrars, councilors, visiting virtuosi too. It could not be fairly said that she flirted with all these men, but neither did she discourage any but the most boorish or unprepossessing. Julie simply did not regard her relations with them as a serious matter, not compared to music, to her work with the orchestra. This ambiguous attitude frustrated some admirers but inflamed others, especially the musicians who saw her regularly and imagined they were competing with one another rather than with something else, something they too loved.

"It's a scandal," the local ladies declared, and their husbands would have to pretend to agree, though for most of them observing Julie von Kibenau was the chief benefit of escorting their spouses to the concerts.

One Tuesday in January, following a rehearsal, Julie came up to Labernz at his podium and asked permission speak to him.

"Of course, Fraulein von Kibenau," he said. Alois had seen his oboist almost every day for months, but never from so short a distance. He noticed that she appeared distressed and found this upset him, as if whatever was troubling her were contagious.

She glanced around and in a low voice asked, "Might we speak privately?"

This request did not please Alois who liked to preserve a certain distance from his player. Nevertheless, he agreed. "Certainly, Fraulein. We can speak in my office."

Julie had never before been up to the Maestro's sanctum sanctorum. Under different circumstances, the room's dull colors and masculine clutter would have amused her. She might even have been drawn to the tall arched window, if she were not preoccupied.

"Please sit down," said Alois, indicating the love seat. Julie did so while he stood beside his desk. "Now, what's the matter?"

"It's my family, Maestro. Or, at least, my brothers."

"Yes?"

"Yesterday, I received an urgent message from a friend in Siegen. That's where I'm from."

"Siegen. Yes, I know."

"You do?" Julie looked at him quizzically then went on. "Well, my friend happened to learn that my brothers will be coming here to Marburg. They mean to persuade me to return with them, but if they fail—as they will—then, according to my friend, they're determined to abduct me."

"*Abduct* you. But why?"

Julie looked at Alois saw that he really did need the matter explained to him. She began slowly. "My family is very religious and terribly respectable. The church is the center of their existence and so they live in the eyes of others; that is, the eyes of the people of Siegen. When I came here and was so fortunate as to win a place in the orchestra, I expected they would be content to disown me and never to mention my name again. And perhaps they would have done so, if only others had also forgotten me. But it seems my brothers have been teased about me once too often—chided, mocked, ridiculed."

"I'm not sure I understand. Why would people tease your brothers?"

Julie blushed for herself but also for the conductor who was astoundingly naïve. Haltingly. she spelled things out. "My being here, here on my own and unmarried—don't you see?—it's led to talk in Siegen."

"Your home."

"No. In Siegen. My home is *here*. If my brothers come, they'll have to take me away against my will, by force."

For a moment Alois thought how pleased Urster would be were this pretty creature really to be whisked away, restoring harmony to the Philharmonia. But then Alois' conscience rebelled against the thought and he said, "We can't have that."

Julie beamed at him as she had on the sultry August day of her audition. "Oh, I'm so relieved to hear you say that, Maestro. I'm very happy here."

"Much happier than in Siegen. Yes, I can see that."

She nodded.

"But," he began with no clear idea of where he was heading, "but, um, no doubt you'll recall the trouble with Heiner Knochenmur, not to mention Bäcker and Eichel?"

"Yes?"

"What I mean is that your, er, your *situation*, that it's a problem here too, Fraulein, here in Marburg I mean, and with our orchestra. You must know there's been talk."

Julie raised her hands like a supplicant. "My *situation*. Am I to blame for people's gossip, for their childishness or jealousy. Is my *situation* an unforgivable fault?"

"No, of course not; but there have been complaints. Herr Urster in particular is most upset. The men. . . they do argue over you. The concertmaster says—"

Julie stuck out her chin. "Are you saying you would prefer a different oboist?"

"No, no. Your playing is more than satisfactory. In fact, it's excellent."

"Then I am—what?—inconvenient?"

Now it was Alois who blushed. He turned toward the

arched window, addressing himself to it rather than Julie.

"Let me think things over and decide what's best to do."

"You know that my brothers may show up at any time?"

"Yes, I understand."

There was nothing more Julie could say. She had made an appeal for protection but could not count on it. She rose to her feet, took a step toward Alois, and said, "Thank you, Maestro, for listening to my worries." She held out her hand. Alois hesitated, then took it awkwardly in both of his.

Then, with a quick curtsey, Julie was out the door.

Alois spent the rest of the afternoon in his office leaving only briefly for a light supper after which he returned. He couldn't face spending the cold night in his chilly rooms thinking through this new problem. Urster always made sure there was wood in the office's fireplace. Alois lit a fire, sat before it, paced from one end of the room to the other, and looked out the long window onto the empty Rheinach Square.

He certainly did not wish to lose his fine oboist; moreover, he flattered himself that taking on Fraulein von Kibenau aligned him with society's progressive elements. Yet he knew that he was claiming credit for a course he hadn't actually chosen. Hiring the fraulein had not been an act of political daring or moral courage. She had simply won a blind competition. Perhaps Urster was right to have advised against such a thing. Nevertheless, Alois believed in the young woman's right to choose the life she wanted, and the idea of her being removed by force from both Marburg and his orchestra disgusted him. On the other hand, he had to admit that Urster hadn't been wrong about the effect on the young men of placing an attractive unmarried female among them. Then there was the gossip in the town which could possibly do harm to the orchestra. And now he'd learned that her family suffered from the same kind of talk. At least her brothers did. Alois felt some sympathy for them, albeit not very much. It was a long night.

At nine the following morning, Concertmaster Urster climbed the stairs of Rheinach Hall. There was a tricky passage in Schumann's *Fourth Symphony* he wished to go over with the Maestro. When he knocked, the door was flung open and Alois stood before him red-eyed, unshaven, and disheveled.

"I've reached a decision, Matthias," he burst out before Urster could say a word.

"Yes?"

"Don't ask me. I can't tell you about it. No. I'm sorry. At least not yet. No, not yet."

Urster gaped at Alois. "Are you unwell, Maestro?"

"I don't know. Perhaps a little feverish. I haven't slept. Look, when Fraulein von Kibenau arrives, please send her to see me. To see me here. I'll be waiting."

Urster rejoiced. So, he had carried his point at last. The final straw had fallen and the disruptive weed was at last to be extirpated from the garden of the Philharmonia.

"I'll be sure to do so," he said with an almost jaunty bow.

Within the hour, Julie knocked at the open door and saw that the conductor was in a state. There had been no abduction during the night. She wore a yellow pinafore and looked fresh as a daffodil.

"Will you please sit down, Fraulein."

She did so. Alois paced back and forth.

"As I promised," he began, "I've given thorough consideration to your situation, also the orchestra's and—and your family's. Your brothers object to your presence here and, as you know, so does our Concertmaster." He paused. "I myself do not," he said with particular emphasis. "Nevertheless, I can see that the status-quo is untenable, that it has created a strain on you, your people, and also on us, on the orchestra. After careful thought, I believe I've found the only and also—at least from my point of view—the best solution."

Julie looked up at him with bright eyes.

Alois Labernz appeared to collapse at her feet, but his voice was firm.

"Fraulein von Kibenau," he said, "will you do me the honor of becoming my wife?"

HSI-WEI AND THE GARDEN OF YANGDI

"It was a dangerous poem, Master Hsi-wei. Yangdi was a parricide, a murderer of the people, the worst of all the emperors."

"But, to give him his due, a competent poet."

"Granted, but a vain and jealous one with a penchant for disposing of rivals. You must know about Wang Zhou and Xue Daheng."

"It goes to prove the saying that saplings survive gales that topple great oaks. I suppose you're right, My Lord. Had I been a court poet like Wang and Xue—or a better one—I'd have been lucky only to be exiled."

Two years after the assassination of Yang Guan, the last Sui emperor, Fang Xuan-ling, a second minister of the new dynasty, stole two weeks from his duties to pay a visit to Chen Hsi-wei. Fang learned that the vagabond poet, peasant, and sandal-maker had retired to a two-room cottage, a mean and grudging gift from the governor of Chiangling. When informed that a second minister of the new regime would be visiting his city, the Governor Bao was quick to offer him an entire wing of his official villa.

Fang had long admired Hsi-wei's work and was curious about the origins of his unconventional verses. Each morning during his stay, he had his attendants load the carriage with food he ordered from the governor's kitchen before making the five-li trip from to Hsi-wei's damp lodging outside the city. As they sat in the small, cobbled area Hsi-wei called his courtyard, Fang made notes of their conversations and carefully transcribed them into his journal each night.

Toward the end of the second week of his visit, after a hearty lunch of cabbage dumplings and baked carp, Fang asked Hsi-wei about the poem people called "Tall Trees in Xiyuan". Xiyuan was the name of the garden Yangdi had built when he moved the imperial capital from Daxing to Luoyang. Like everything the ruthless and profligate Yangdi did, this garden was on a gigantic scale and extravagantly costly.

"You never actually saw the garden, did you, Master?"

Hsi-wei smiled. "You know how the poem begins, My Lord. People like you were invited in to admire it; people like me weren't permitted near the place."

"No. But, since you never saw it, what I'd like to know is what prompted you to write about Xiyuan. Of course, I understand your verses aren't chiefly about the garden but still it *is* about the garden."

"The poem is about Emperor Yang," said Hsi-wei almost with distaste. "But, as I'm always flattered by your interest, I'll gladly tell you how I came to write it."

Fang ordered one of his attendants to prepare a pot of the rare Yunnan tea he'd brought along, took out his paper, ink, and brush, then settled back to listen.

That year, I was making my way to Huangshan, Hsi-wei began. I had a wish to see the famous mountains there. Along the way, I came on an astonishing sight, a convoy of enormous carts made of thick oak planks reinforced with iron bands and with the enormous wheels—eight of them on each cart, each higher than a tall man with his son on his shoulders. The carts were wider than the road and each was pulled by a dozen oxen. On all sides, peasants yanked at the animals' halters and shoveled away the mud that clutched at the wheels. They sweated, levered, shouted curses at the poor beasts and each other. The peasants were overseen by cavalrymen with short swords at their sides and long whips in their hands. Each cart bore a massive pine with fantastically contorted branches and trunks it would take three men to circle with their arms. The roots had been wrapped in burlap made tight with hemp ropes. Two men on each cart doused the roots with water drawn from tuns hanging from the sides.

I got well out of the way of this hellish procession. I judged it prudent not to ask any questions. I found out what it was all about later that day when I arrived in Xidi, a village at the foot of the mountains.

The houses in Xidi are small wooden structures of a square design I'd seen in old paintings. The villagers keep a few pigs and chickens, and each home has a small vegetable garden; but the land is too steep and rocky for proper farming. The villagers make their living from the forest. The peasants in that region have beliefs as old-fashioned as their houses. To them, the forest is sacred. From what I could make out, they believe every tree contains a spirit. Some hold the souls of ancestors, others of animals, and still others are homes to spirits that can be either friendly or hostile, little gods to be feared and placated. Mrs. Hong, the woman who let me stay the night in her shed, explained all this to me. She said that whenever a big tree was cut down, there was a ceremony. She described it as part funeral and part prayer for forgiveness.

I asked Mrs. Hong if people believed that cutting down a tree destroyed or freed the spirit inside it.

Mrs. Hong surprised me by shrugging and saying, "Well, some people like Donghai Li believe the one and others like Mrs. Shin the other. But nobody really knows. Either way, since the emperor's men came last week, everybody's upset and frightened. They destroyed scores of trees and dragged off our biggest and oldest. They also took twenty boys and men with them, promising we'd get them back within the month. They said that, if the boys worked hard, the emperor would let us off from half a year's taxes. We're in mourning for the damage to our forest and scared for the boys. Nobody can say what will become of the poor spirits in the pines or what's in store for us without them."

A few weeks later I met a retired clerk in Lingwu. He had worked in the capital and helped me piece the story together. It seems that when the landscape architect Li Yungang proudly showed Yangdi his new garden, the emperor was not well pleased. Extensive and beautiful though it was, a vast elaboration that outshone his father's imperial park in Daxing, with lovely small gardens inside larger gorgeous ones, something was lacking, something Yangdi insisted he must have. He wanted more trees and not just any trees but the tallest in the Empire. He ordered brigades of cavalry into the provinces to conscript peasants, seek out and dig up the trees, and haul them back alive to Luoyang. The task was all but impossible, mad. New carts had to be devised, roads cut through forests and countless trees cleared to make way for the excavation and transport of the giants. Nobody knows how many peasants were brained by falling branches, crushed beneath overturned carts, squashed by rolling trunks, or drowned when barges capsized. Also uncounted were the victims of fever, hunger, exhaustion, and beatings.

I can't say if the people of Xidi had to pay only half their taxes that year, said Hsi-wei bitterly. I suppose it's possible.

Minister Fang put down his brush and sighed.

"Everybody knows about the millions Yangdi sent to die at the Canal or the Wall. Most know about the armies annihilated in Goguryeo and the battalions that perished in Champa's jungles. But I didn't know about the trees. Are you sure of this story. I visited Luoyang last year and didn't see anything like what you've described."

Hsi-wei poured out two cups of tea.

"My Lord, I was told that when the news of Yangdi's death in Danyang reached his capital, the people looted his palace and despoiled Xiyuan. They cut down all the tall trees, hacked at them with axes, sawed them up to use for lumber and firewood."

"It was, I suppose, a kind of revenge."

"As I said, My Lord, the poem is about Yangdi. When I heard what happened to the garden, I thought some of those wielding the axes must have felt as if each tree held the spirit of the hated emperor, and directed every blow at him."

The sun was almost down. "Well," said Fang with a sigh, "I should be leaving now. You must be tired, Master Hsi-wei." As he put away his ink, brush, and paper, Fang added, "It really is lucky that nobody showed your poem about the trees to Yangdi."

Hsi-wei smiled. "Like most peasants, I prefer an absentee landlord."

"Ha!" Fang exclaimed and got to his feet.

"Now, with your permission, Master, I'll be back tomorrow."

Hsi-wei stood, bowed deeply, and, as he did every day, thanking the Minister for his condescension and for the fine meal.

Fang Xuan-li summoned his attendant and handed him the rosewood box in which he kept his writing materials. Glancing up at the darkening sky he raised a finger. "I think tomorrow I'll have the governor's cook prepare bird's nest soup and, hmm, yes, duck with plum sauce. What do you say?"

Hsi-wei bowed once more.

TALL TREES IN XIYUAN

The sumptuous garden is not for the likes of me,
yet if I shut my eyes I can travel all the way to Luoyang.
I imagine fragrance of osmanthus and aroma of peonies
hovering above Xiyuan's six ponds like morning mist.
Across lawns smooth as a magistrate's new
baize-covered desk, cunningly disposed shrubs
explode weekly like strings of timed fireworks.
Decorated and delicate as court ladies, eight
Pretty painted pavilions stand about with beckoning doors.
Beside magnolias and wisteria, water diverted from
the Luo burbles through rocks clad in emerald moss.
And over all tower twisting Huangshan pines, gigantic
fan-like ginkos, lofty cypresses, all torn from their homes
like conscripts at the Great Wall and Grand Canal.
The great trees that grew up elsewhere stand to attention
like the emperor's bodyguards, indifferent observers
of the pleasures below.
I've heard Xiyuan is made of
gardens inside gardens, outstripping in complexity
even the legendary park of Han Wudi.
Xiyuan gives no hint of the crushed oaks and firs,
the hacked arborvitae, felled birches, and dead

maples rotting away in provincial mud.
These monumental copses stretch from dirt to sky.
In the Emperor's garden everything is
clipped and cared-for, clean and serene.
There's not a single corpse to be seen.

THREE NOONS

I.

He was tired of the sight of bare lath and low beams and in no hurry to open his eyes. He rubbed his stubble then felt gingerly down below to see if the bandage were wet, sniffed at his fingers. He remembered the field hospitals. That was where he had first heard the word *sepsis*. He still shied away from hand saws.

In the next room, assuming he made it through the night, Folsom would be lying just like him. He'd plugged Folsom in the shoulder of his shooting arm and Folsom had hit him in the thigh. It all happened in an instant, coming on each other like that in the alley, guns drawn, surprise and fear in their eyes, both Colts going off simultaneously, not aimed, just desperately pointed, not meant to kill so much as keep from being killed. The proof, he reflected, was that neither of them had ventured a second shot, though it would have been easy. It wasn't because they were deafened by the reverberation or stunned by their pain, or even that they were both on the ground in horse shit. Folsom's pistol lay in easy reach and both had been conscious. Funny thing. His gun was still in his hand and he could have blown a hole in Folsom's head if he'd chosen and Folsom still had the use of his left hand. Instead they waited a few yards away from one another, breathing hard against the hurt, looking at each other, anger and fear drained as by anticlimax. Then Folsom began to hum. He recollected how in the war gut-shot men would do that until they went into shock. And then, after about a century or two, somebody dared to peer around the corner; he wasn't sure who. The word went out—"both down!"—as if they'd been a pair of pugilists. No doubt there'd been odds given and bets laid. It was that sort of town. Who would expect otherwise. Very well, it was a draw, then. But no, not a draw, not if Folsom were in custody or had bled to death.

The town, reduced to filthy boots, argued over what to do. "Well, damn it. Can't just leave 'em here," said Hank. "Shite, man. Go and fetch the doc," said Hanrahan. Who else would say "fetch" with that Hibernian lilt, let alone "shite". So, they were picked up, one man per limb. Folsom screamed when they took up his right arm. After that he fell quiet though, unconscious probably. He'd nearly passed out himself when they took his leg.

They were laid out side by side in the saloon. Damp sawdust. The doctor arrived and began to swear in German, women rubbernecking over his shoulder and all of them stinking of whiskey. Back in Bremen, Otto Furst had trained as an eye doctor but he did what he could and people trusted him because there wasn't any point in not doing so. He poured whiskey liberally on the wounds, wrapped bandages that were most likely ripped from whores' sheets. Then more whiskey, bottle against his lips. "Trink, trink," Furst ordered. After that they were lugged upstairs, and there was a brief argument over the assignment of rooms in which he was in no condition to participate.

Folsom paid the first visit. His door was open and Folsom looked in sheepishly, unsure what to say.

"Well, Folsom, so you're alive," he said. "But why ain't you locked up?"

Folsom squeezed through the narrow doorway and with a grimace shrugged his one good shoulder. "You okay?"

"Guess so. Doc says."

They were like toothless old men; neither considered the other a threat.

Folsom asked permission to come and sit on the foot of the bed. "Hurts more when I stand," he explained. He was being absurdly polite.

"Suit yourself, I don't mind."

Folsom put his rear end on the bed delicately, so as not to disturb the sheriff. He was quiet for a full minute, maybe two.

"I did hit that Johnson fellow."

"I know you did. There were only about a dozen witnesses."

"Well, we'd been drinking, of course. You know how it is. We got to re-fighting Gettysburg because we was both of us there and he said some things I just couldn't abide. About General Longstreet first. Well, I took that. But then he began on Robert E. Lee. So I hit him—just with a bottle and not even that hard."

"You damned near killed the man, if he isn't dead yet."

Folsom lowered his head. "An accident."

"You picked up the bottle, didn't you. You hit him over the head with it?"

"I didn't mean it was an accident that Johnson got his head split. I meant it was an accident I split it. Any man who'd served under Longstreet would've done the same— would have if he heard what Johnson said—but I was patient with him. Nah, it was General Lee that did it." After this speech Folsom paused, breathing hard. "Tell me something. If I heard right, you were at Gettysburg too. Didn't hear what corps. Not one of Pickett's poor Virginia boys, were you?"

The sheriff frowned.

"So," said Folsom very carefully, "the way I see it, it could've been you hit Johnson. No offense."

He looked Folsom, a man who had nearly killed him and whom he'd nearly killed. "None taken, Folsom. But it's of no account."

"No accident that you come after me, though."

"It's the job."

"Exactly," drawled Folsom and nodded two times. "That's the truth of it and no mistake. And yet some might consider even that an accident. I mean that they hired you to be the Law hereabouts and not somebody else."

"What. You, for instance?"

"Well, why not. We're the sort they hire, ain't we?"

"They?"

"Barbed wire people, dry goods and opera house people, church and schoolhouse people."

The sheriff laughed but not because Folsom was wrong. He'd got his job because after three men had been killed one Saturday the town was desperate and he'd just happened to knock down two drunken cowboys and take their guns away. He wasn't any better than Folsom and saw no point in pretending to be.

"Where's my damned deputy. He ought to be keeping a watch on you."

"Deputy. Went to buy himself a beefsteak, I think. Nice enough fellow, but kind of stringy. Looked to me like he could do with a *couple* of beefsteaks."

The sheriff smiled. "I call him Rail."

"Rail?"

"He looks something like a fence rail."

"So, was Rail coming after me, too. Down that alley?"

The Sheriff laughed at this. "What. Rail?"

Folsom laughed too. "No, I allow as he probably weren't."

The whores took care of them for two weeks, though they badly wanted the rooms. The sheriff paid for his own food and Folsom paid for his. Rail visited after supper bearing news which seldom amounted to much. The sheriff and Folsom played some cards and talked. Mostly Folsom talked. He seemed to need to talk about the war and the sheriff let him.

As soon as he was able to hobble about .he ordered up a bottle from the bar and took it into Folsom's room and they got drunk and had some laughs.

Rail reported that Johnson was considerably better, though he still had headaches and didn't always see straight. When the sheriff told him that, Folsom said he was sorry and wondered what the charge would be, assuming Johnson kept on getting better.

"Battery, I suppose."

"Battery?"

"That's legal for beating."

Folsom considered this. "Battery," he said, no doubt remembering the artillery. "Oh."

By the third week both men were so recovered that Furst told them they could go about their business if only they did it slowly and the rooms could go back to their original purpose which would be a general relief. Folsom didn't have the four dollars the doctor insisted on, only two, so the sheriff made up the difference.

"Thank you," said Folsom. "I owe you."

"You can pay me back some time."

"Why, sure, sure. Word and bond."

The two looked at each other and felt suddenly abashed.

"What do we do now?" asked Folsom.

The sheriff shrugged and took a quick look over his shoulder though nobody was around. Then he brushed at the star on his vest, turned his back on Folsom, and limped down the stairway.

II.

The fifth of June, another hot, dry day. He leaned against the lintel and looked apathetically at the empty street, the three bleached cottonwoods, the absence of clouds.

He had done his utmost to get help, humbled himself, offered to deputize almost all the men—Hank, Hanrahan, and the rest. Charlie Ransome sitting on his accustomed bench had grabbed at his arm as he passed and, for a moment, he had been tempted to accept the old man's offer. "*I'll* stand with you," Charlie had wheezed and tried unsuccessfully to stand up there and then.

It was disappointing to see how they hid from him or, if they weren't quick enough, turned away. The most humiliated tried to pick a fight. As for the women, they began to glance at him furtively, as though he were already a corpse, as if he were Death and wanted to steal their men away. Ever since the Johnson boy came into town it had been like that.

The boy had been out fixing a fence when Folsom's man rode up, handed him the note and a fifty-cent piece to deliver it.

You kilt my brother. Now me and my boys are going to
even things. Be seeing you on the sixth inst.
Very truly yours,
J. Folsom

Very truly yours. Now where had a mean character like Folsom picked up that lawyerly phrase. Mean Folsom famously was; he was said to have shot a man in a bunkhouse for snoring too loud and another in an Abilene saloon just because his mustache reminded him of his father's. Folsom's letter was roughly written in pencil on the back of an old wanted poster. The news went through town like spoiled meat through a Philadelphian.

You kilt my brother. All he'd done was track Henry Folsom down and arrest him, which was what he was supposed to do, what the town expected of him, what even Folsom ought to have understood it was his job to do. There had been a proper trial as the circuit judge came through that same week. Henry Folsom had been judged and the law had executed him fair and square. He'd shot down an unarmed sodbuster named Jenkins and then raped the man's wife. Mrs. Jenkins couldn't speak for shame, but she bravely pointed her finger at him in court. So it was all square. But that didn't count with Folsom, who had a code of his own and had to take somebody's life for Henry's, which was his idea of how to *even things.* You didn't smack your lips over legal niceties with the likes of Folsom.

He put his feet up on the desk and thought through his position one last time. Nobody in his line of work could help but feel let down. Still, he couldn't help the resentment boiling away in his gut. He also hated that he was scared. If he just lit out, Folsom might shoot up the town but then maybe the town deserved being shot up. On the other hand, Folsom might ride out to track him down the same way he'd done with Henry. Folsom might even find that fitting, evening things out. Any way he turned it over, sticking around was not just risky but downright foolish.

He unpinned the badge from his vest and laid it down on

the desk, bright side up. It made him feel lighter but also more exposed. He pulled his canteen from under the cot and took down the Winchester, which he examined carefully, since he hadn't used it for a while. From the ammunition drawer he pocketed two handfuls of rifle rounds, not even bothering to count, then filled his cartridge belt and picked up his pistol. Sitting on the cot he cleaned and oiled the Colt, waiting for sundown. He could buy food from the Olsons, whose place was two miles outside of town, and then light out. Maybe go up to Wyoming or west all the way to California. There was plenty of space. Anyway, he would run.

After Appomattox he had imagined a limitless refuge between the whited sepulchers of the East and the honest debauchery of San Francisco. Because he could write a fair hand, he'd found work as a clerk in St. Joe but soon tired of registering the departures of others. So, he bought himself a used outfit and a decent horse and for a year was a cowpuncher, which he thought a good life once he'd callused up and accustomed himself to the long days, the shit, and the Indians. By the campfires he dreamed of women; every cowboy did. He almost pities the whores who were the only females he saw in those days; but they were so hard, sentiment of any variety seemed misplaced. "Well, tonight I guess it's poker and poke her," Purdy, the squinty trail boss had joked bitterly the night before they finished the drive at Abilene. The old coot said it as if what he meant weren't crude pleasures but a kind of sentence, as if the unruly cow town were a canker on the clean plains, a sewer into which all the foulness of men ran. Come to that, what did he really think of the civilization he had been protecting since he put on the star almost two years ago. Had he come to agree with Purdy. Well, what did it matter what he thought. That's the way the tide was running and had been ever since Lewis and Clark first settled their rear-ends into a canoe, ever since Henry Hudson blundered on his river, ever since deluded Columbus sloshed onto that unfortunate island. Maybe there would come a time when men hung up their guns. But that time sure wasn't yet.

After dark, he slipped into the livery stable, saddled his horse, and, keeping clear of the lit-up saloon, headed out of town. If anybody caught sight of him, they were no keener on a discussion of the merits of discretion than he was. No matter. His absence would be noted soon enough and eagerly reported to Folsom when he got into town. He could picture his fellow citizens, the ingratiating smiles, the anxious pointing.

Around nine o'clock he rousted Olson and bought beans and salted meat off him. Olson threw in some tobacco too, but they hardly said a word to one another. Neither Folsom nor the absence of his badge came in for a mention. He had done Olson a few good turns and both men under-stood that was what the tobacco and the silence were for.

Shortly after dawn he caught sight of a couple turkey buzzards spreading their wings on the early updrafts. Mockingbirds and meadowlarks sang among the high tufts of prairie grass. For a minute the boulders turned violet then pink and there was velvety warmth to the air as the sun commenced its rise. This wasn't the first dawn he reckoned might be his last, yet it was the first since the war that found him on the run. Perhaps there comes a time in a man's life, he reflected, when cowardice turns into prudence. He wondered what would be said of him by the town that day; for the town he now pictured as a single person, a timorous but disapproving farmer maybe or a gangly teenager ashamed of his pa. Since he'd taken the sheriff's job there had been some good days when he felt the town was his, under his protection, and he'd sauntered through it like a sole proprietor. Now that vanity was borne in on him. Belonging had been an illusion—that the town and he had belonged to each other—the worst of it being that he'd permitted himself to believe what he supposed the town thought of him. Up against the starkness of a killer like Folsom, his self-confidence was shown to be a mirage like the false ponds that would presently spread on the flatlands. All that had gone when he took off the five-pointed piece of tin.

From time to time he'd dismount to rest or water his horse. He'd drag some sage over his tracks. It wasn't a serious effort, just one he felt obliged to make since he was now to live by prudence. He changed his direction three times, too.

It ought to have been a shock to see the dust rising behind him on the second day; and yet, he wasn't at all surprised. He realized he'd never believed he could evade Folsom, not from the moment the Johnson boy had handed him that wanted poster. The surprise was that he'd lied to himself about that as well.

He headed for the high ground to his left, trying not to raise dust of his own. He was in unfamiliar territory, but the big boulders promised some small chance of safety. He rose on his stirrups and swiveled his body to look back. They were closing on him. He counted four riders, like the ones in the Bible, riding so hard they must not have cared about wearing out their mounts.

He picked his way among the outcrops, the horse stepping delicately along the edges of scree. There was no hope that Folsom had missed him; he had seen them turn in his direction. Should he look for some high defile and set up an ambush or make a run for it. During the retreat in the final weeks of the war, they had done both and neither mattered in the end. He had yet to decide the matter when he ran up against a wall of limestone. There was no way out; he had blundered into a box canyon. "Figures," he said to himself as he dismounted and pulled out the Winchester. As he scanned the rocks for good cover, he wondered if Folsom, that free-ranging renegade, had known where he was headed all along and was laughing at him.

He climbed, pulling the horse after him, then wedged the reins between two rocks well behind the spot he had chosen to make his stand. By now, the sun was directly overhead. He held the rifle close, unwilling to give himself away by a glint from the barrel just to get off one or two long shots. He peered over the edge and saw them just below. They had their pistols drawn and were looking up. Suddenly the one with the black beard shouted and made a sweeping motion with his arm. All four hastened to dismount with pistols in their hands. Sudden shots reverberated all through the canyon. Two bullets struck close to him and then he felt like someone had struck a poker across his flank. He looked around wildly and saw an Indian moving rapidly across the ridge above him. Then there were more shots from across the canyon.

Folsom and his men never got off a single round. He saw their bodies jump as they were hit, saw them fall, still jumping. The noise in the canyon was awful. He slipped part way into a crevice, pressing his hand against his bleeding side. For a full minute everything went silent then he heard a movement above him, the soft sound of moccasins. A war party looking for horses—maybe Sioux, maybe Comanches. He was never any good at naming all the tribes. There were Indians who didn't kill you and Indians who did. He waited for them to come looking for him and prayed his horse would know enough to keep quiet.

The Indians must have been in a hurry. Or maybe they forgot about him or counted wrong or were satisfied with the horses of Folsom and his gang. It was hard to figure. They never came for him and, after a good long while squeezed in that crevice, he decided to risk a peek.

He crawled over the rock. Four corpses lay spread out below, blood all over their chests and legs. It looked like only one had been scalped, so the Sioux or Commanches must have been in a rush. Maybe they were on the run like him and really needed those ponies. The week before Hanrahan had mentioned seeing some cavalry on patrol.

His side hardly hurt at all, unless he took a deep breath. So, inhaling as shallowly, he retrieved his horse and led him down to the dead bodies. The terrified mare shied and he stroked her nose. The corpse with the long black beard, shot neatly in the forehead, had "Folsom" scratched on his belt.

Two days later, late in the afternoon, he rode into town. It had taken a long time to get back. With the extra weight of body behind the saddle he had to go easy on his horse. Folsom kept falling off.

He led the horse up the street. People gaped, said things, a couple called out his name, but, noting the set of his face, no one ventured to approach him.

He halted outside the saloon and, grabbing a leg, yanked the body off the horse and left it lying in the street. Then he took the horse to the livery, ordered water, oats, and a good rubdown. Then he walked back to his office.

The badge was where he'd left it. He picked it up, pinned it to his vest, then lay down on the cot.

Hanrahan and Rail turned up a few minutes later, followed by pretty nearly the whole town. The Irishman spoke first. Perhaps that's why it was his version of events that became history, displacing all suspicion, embarrassment, and guilt.

"Well, Sheriff, you're a clever one all right. Jesus, Mary, and Joseph, but we were sure you'd run off. Soon as the Folsom bunch showed up, they took off after you. Lord knows what they'd have done if they'd found you here." Hanrahan looked at him a moment, considering what he was about to say, and then he turned to the crowd and said what he must have felt he ought to. "Why, he saved the town, he did!. Then he turned back to the sheriff. "Handsomely done, boyo. What say I stand the first drink. Sure, if there be any justice in the round world, you'll never pay for one again."

III.

The moment he laid eyes on Eurydice Folsom, even before he caught her scent or touched her hand, his knees buckled. That's how it was.

He knew who this woman was, at least who her husband was. Every lawman in the territory knew about Jacob Folsom who had gone completely to the bad after blowing one of his hired hands nearly in half with a shotgun. He had been a successful rancher; now, turned outlaw, he seemed determined to make an equally good job of that. He gathered a gang of toughs and made a specialty of robbing banks, though there was also the occasional train or dry goods store. The banks and the railroad had put a rather flattering price on his head.

Folsom's spread was twenty miles away and in the neighboring jurisdiction. It was the ranch about which Eurydice had come to see him. The first bank her husband robbed held their mortgage and was now trying to foreclose notwithstanding that she'd done well running the place on her own and hadn't missed a payment. But the local sheriff was the banker's brother-in-law and declined to get involved. She'd consulted the town's only lawyer, but he was on the bank's board and would do nothing for her. In fact, he was working to get the foreclosure finalized.

"I didn't know where else to turn," she said in a voice that sounded to him like an April afternoon in Charleston. "You've a good reputation," she added, lowering her eyes. "My husband's a monster. A *monster*. I hope he's brought to justice for what he's done but it's not right for them to take my land." She paused and looked at him in a way that made her look serene rather than distraught. "Is it, Sheriff?"

He promised to do what he could. He would take the matter up with the county attorney, he said, and the U.S. Marshall's office. He admitted that he didn't know anything about property law.

"I'm hardly an expert either, but I believe the law's on my side in this. May I sit down?" Apologizing, he rushed to put a chair behind her. Taking her time, carefully smoothing her skirt, she placed herself in the chair and looked up at him. "Tell me, Sheriff, are you a married man yourself?" This made him blush and that made her smile.

He brought in two dinners from the saloon and Eurydice Folsom stayed with him that night. Since then, he had ridden twenty miles to her place every Thursday and twenty miles back the next day. It wasn't much of a secret, but he didn't care. If men like Rail shook their heads and frowned or those like Hanrahan grinned and winked, what was that to him?

She liked to talk about her husband, even in bed, though he never encouraged her. According to his wife, Folsom drank to excess, regularly molested squaws, beat up piano players, cheated at cards, lied out of habit, was an ungenerous lover, and had, in his early years, jumped claims and rustled cattle. Marrying him was a ghastly mistake, she said, a young girl's foolishness. Folsom had deceived not just her but also her parents, both now deceased. He had been all put-on manners and meretricious charm. The man had shamelessly claimed to have been a colonel under Lee which was as big a lie as everything else he said of himself. It was her bride money that went for the down payment on the ranch and her business head that made it prosper. To her he behaved like a brute. And *jealous*—that was what led to his murdering that Johnson. He accused the poor hand of looking at her in the wrong way. Folsom often struck her, she confided tearfully. Her tears were hard for him to bear. He held her close and stroked her shoulder blades.

He believed everything she said because he couldn't face what it would mean not to have believed her. That's how it was with him.

Meanwhile, he prevailed on the county attorney, who owed him three favors, to intervene in the foreclosure case to delay a final court order. An official letter was sent to the bank president with copies to Eurydice and him. The matter required study, wrote the county attorney, and he might become further involved. He needed to examine the bank's records, the mortgage agreement, and the deed. In the meantime, no action should be taken. Eurydice's gratitude was boundless. When he next rode out, she met him at the door, half undressed, threw her arms around his neck and her legs around his waist, and kissed him until he was breathless. She had made him a cherry pie and a roast of beef and kept him in bed from after dinner Thursday till late Friday morning.

Several days later Rail brought the post to the office, a sorrowful look on his long face. "Personal letter for you." He spoke ruefully, knowing already who had written it and what it signified.

Folsom was calling him out. The language was flowery, the handwriting almost feminine.

> *Sir,*
>
> *I regret to hear that you have been fornicating with my wife. I don't know what the bitch told you; however, you will appreciate that scarcely matters, as, whatever else she is, she remains my wife and not yours, for which, in my opinion you ought to be grateful. I intend to be up your way next week when you can*
> *try to kill me, but don't*
> *think of making an arrest. This is between us and, like all affairs of honor, a fatal if stupid necessity of manhood.*

J. Folsom

Was he in the wrong or the right in this business. Folsom was an outlaw, a killer, and yet he had wronged him. Eurydice was Folsom's wife yet Folsom betrayed and beat her, besides which she loved him and not Jake Folsom. That he could be in some measure both wrong and right was perplexing; he was a man who insisted on clarity, though he admitted to himself the straight and simple course of his life was finished the moment he saw Eurydice. Was it conceivable that Folsom had been right about Johnson. Had whatever happened gone beyond looking. He tried to dismiss such doubts and blamed himself for them. Folsom was a liar. However, the last sentence of the letter affected him. He read it over and over, thinking how the man had linked honor with stupidity. It was a curious thing to write, the declaration of an interesting man.

Eurydice came in the morning to warn him. Folsom had sent a man to tell her what he intended to do to her lover and precisely when. She had ridden through the night to alert him. "Why, he might be here already," she said fearfully, "lurking in some alleyway with his men to help him, which would be exactly like him. Get a posse together," she ordered, "shoot him on sight."

He did what he could to calm her down.

As it happened, Folsom rode into town an hour later, openly and alone. He dismounted outside the sheriff's office and called. The street emptied at once. Eurydice began to shake. "Don't let him see me!" she cried.

He put on his gun belt, considered taking off his badge, then decided not to. Folsom called again, called him out by name. Rail stuck his head in at the back window and started to say something, then thought better of it and went away.

A fatal if stupid necessity of manhood. The clock ticked and he glanced at it. Noon.

Folsom was leaning against the hitching post, arms folded, not exactly expectant or nonchalant but a little of each. He was a tall man, no longer young but not old either. He was covered with dust from his ride. He was lean, but not in a healthy way; in fact, he looked as if he'd shed a good deal of weight owing to an irregular life. His sunburned face displayed authority and refinement. It wasn't difficult to believe he really had been one of Lee's officers.

Folsom tossed his head toward the office, an impatient and dismissive gesture. "I suppose she's in there."

He nodded, unable to say it was none of the man's business.

"Well then, sir," drawled Folsom, "we'd best get on with

it." There was fellow feeling as well as weariness in his words and no hatred whatever, as if he took it for granted that they both agreed what had to be done was indeed necessary but nonetheless stupid.

Of course, it was impossible, but he would have liked to talk with Folsom, even knowing they'd still have to go ahead and shoot at each other afterwards. Instead, he stepped off the duckboards into the street. They were suicidally close to each other.

For about five seconds they faced off. Then, by tacit agreement, both took three steps back and drew. They fired almost simultaneously. He felt Folsom's bullet shatter his right arm and dropped his gun. Evidently untouched, Folsom pointed his pistol him, deciding where to place the bullet that would finish him off.

The next shot was a surprise. It came from behind, like a resounding, stunning slap from some giant congratulating him. The blow whirled him around so that, as he fell, he saw Eurydice throw down his Winchester and heard her shout "Jake!" With his cheek pressed against the ground he watched her little lace-up boots scurry by his face. Then there was no more breath and, though it was only minutes past noon, everything went black.

HSI-WEI AND THE THREE PROVERBS

The Tang minister Fang Xuan-ling devotes a lengthy section of his memoirs to the visit he paid the peasant/poet Chen Hsi-wei. This was near the end of Hsi-wei's life, after the poet had given up his itinerant existence and settled in the tiny cottage granted him by the Governor of Chiangling. The place was in the middle of farmland three *li* outside the city, two rooms with a modest patio and a small vegetable garden.

Each day, Minister Fang would arrive from the city in the late morning and stay until sunset. He brought food, tea, and wine, along with a scroll, an ink stone, and two brushes.

One afternoon, as they sat in the little patio taking tea, he asked about the poem Hsi-wei had titled "The Three Proverbs".

"Pardon my ignorance, Master, but the title is obscure to me. There are no proverbs in the poem. Perhaps you are aware that people have given it a different title. They call it 'Three Little Tales'."

Hsi-wei grinned. "Titles aren't important to me. I was always pleased when people came up with their own names for my poor verses. I prefer them which is why I didn't give titles to most of my poems. All the same, when I did decide to name a poem, I took the matter seriously. Sometimes the title was where the poem began; at others, it was a summary I only thought of after I'd finished. Mostly, I thought of a title as a promise."

"A promise?"

"One that the poem tries to fulfill. In a few cases, I thought of a title as be a key that would unlock hidden meaning. The poem you've asked about is one of those."

"The poem is in code?"

"No, it's not a secret message. Only a silly puzzle."

"How so?"

"My Lord, an archer doesn't set up his target in order to miss his aim; but I fear that's what happened with 'The Three Proverbs,' and you've confirmed it. The game was really for me more than the reader, which is where I went wrong. I was indulging myself. No doubt, people sensed this and so their title, 'Three Little Tales,' is better than mine. 'Three Pointless Tales' would have been better still."

Fang leaned forward. "I'm not sure I understand. When you say you were indulging yourself and that poem is a puzzle what do you mean?"

Hsi-wei refilled their teacups before replying.

"That unworthy little poem was an exercise I set myself. Two of the proverbs I heard as a child in my village; the third I picked up while traveling along the Grand Canal, which is where I wrote the poem."

"Ah," the attentive Fang said with satisfaction. "Then each of the stories illustrates a proverb but the proverbs aren't in the poem."

"Yes, that was the puzzle for the reader, to figure out the proverbs. Unfortunately, the poem turned out to be like one of those complicated jokes nobody gets. Or a lock without a key."

"But the *title* was the key."

"That was my idea. But, as I said, it turned out to be a useless one. Actually, there's a bit more to the matter. Behind each of the little made-up stories is a true one."

"So then, there are *six* stories and *three* proverbs?"

"Exactly. But now you've gotten me thinking about the difference between poems and proverbs. My relation to proverbs is that of a peasant while my relation to poems is the consequence of the education Master Shen gave me in Daxing. So, this poem reflects my own ambiguous situation, too low-born ever to belong to the gentry, too educated to be entirely at home with the peasantry."

"Another and maybe better way of looking at the matter would be to say your poems appeal to both the high and the low. That is unusual, Master."

"It's generous of you to say that. If you're right, then perhaps that too is the consequence of my belonging to neither group."

Here Minister Fang drew out his scroll and prepared the ink. Hsi-wei waited while he wrote down notes on what they'd been saying.

Fang looked up when he'd finished. "Please go on, Master. I would like to hear more of your views on poems and proverbs."

Hsi-wei was pleased to oblige.

"A poem is made by one person. It may be bad or good. If bad, it will be forgotten at once, even by the one who made it. But if it is good, a poem may be remembered for a long time. It may be memorized and recited at parties to divert or impress the guests. This is what passes for immortality among poets, who can be childishly vain. But a proverb comes from the people, even those sayings ascribed to

Confucius or Lao-tse, because, by repeated application to their own lives, the people appropriate a saying and make it their own. Because a good proverb belongs to everyone, it's owned by no one."

Fang made a few notes then returned to the poem about which he was now even more curious.

"What are the stories behind the stories in your poem?"

Hsi-wei waved a hand. "Oh, it's been so long. Wendi was still Emperor when I made up that little puzzle."

Fang readied his brush and begged Hsi-wei to try to remember.

"Very well, I'll do my best. As you'll remember, this was during my journey along the Grand Canal which has improved a great deal in the empire but which cost more lives than all the Sui wars put together. Somewhere between Suzhou and Wuxi I came to a town, set my sign up in the square as usual, and took orders for straw sandals. The town was busy; it had a depot and many barges stopped there. A bargeman with a red face and a body like a crate ordered a pair of sandals from me. He growled that he would buy them on condition that I had them ready by the following morning when he would be moving on. He was curt and seemed inexplicably angry." Hsi-wei paused. "Have you observed, my Lord, that people find it harder to conceal their anger than their sorrow?"

"Yes. That's quite true."

"In that respect, being angry is like knowing a humorous story. It wants to be told. Anyway, the bargeman said, 'I'd buy another pair for my wretched assistant but the dog's-head can go barefoot. Let him get splinters!'

"I asked what the wretched assistant had done to merit the splinters.

"'The fool neglected the sweep and drove us square into the dock. I have to pay for the damage. He's barricaded himself in the cabin, the coward, or I'd have given him a beating he'd never forget!'

"'With respect, sir,' I said, 'how old is he, this assistant?'

"'Fourteen. Big for his age, though.'

"'And has he done anything of the kind before?'

"'Yes. Last week he nearly made us collide with one of the heavy timber barges. We'd have been sunk for sure.'

"'And what did you do then?' I asked sympathetically.

"'What did I do. Gave him two hidings, didn't I, one with my tongue and one with the bamboo. Both good ones, I thought, though it looks like I was too lenient.'

"It was obvious why the boy was hiding. The bargeman could not control his temper. I ventured to ask him if he would listen to some advice.

"The astonished fellow looked me up and down. 'From a sandal-maker?'

"I stood up straighter. 'Yes,' I replied, 'from this worthless sandal-maker.'

The bargeman scoffed but said, 'Well, out with it.'

"At a stall close by, a woman was selling sweets.

"'First,' I said, 'calm yourself. Walk around the square. Take twenty deep breaths. Then go to that woman over there and buy a paper of her sweets. When you get back to your barge, use them to coax the boy out of the cabin. Speak softly and promise him a really good meal—a banquet with both pork and fish—if you make it to Jianxing without any more mishaps.'

"'What. Sweets. Pork?'

"'Yes, and fish, too,' I said."

Hsi-wei folded his hands and fell silent.

"What. That's all?" asked Fang lifting his brush.

"Yes. It was seeing how incensed that bargeman was and picturing the terrified boy that made me think of the old proverb I heard as a child."

"What proverb?"

Hsi-wei smiled slyly. "Just now my memory seems to be working rather well, so I'll relate the second story which also concerns a bargeman. I heard it from the drinkers in a tavern where I spent a sleepless summer night. It was a rambling, ramshackle place on the docks with gray boards above and green slime. It was terribly hot inside because of the low ceiling and crush of canal men.

"The story was about a certain bargeman whose name I can't recall but let's say it was Chin. Well, this Chin was ambitious. He used the family savings to buy a barge and was doing well, but to be merely comfortable didn't satisfy him. He wanted a four-pillared villa. He wanted to be bowed to on the streets. He wanted other men working for him. So, he took the easy path, said the men at the tavern. I had the impression that they all knew this path rather well.

"Chin made contacts among the disreputable dealers and struck deals with them. He began transporting untaxed cargo to the capital where the profits were greatest. His crooked colleagues assured him the local magistrate would make no difficulties.

"Before long, Chin bought a second barge, then a third. He picked out a piece of high ground and ordered plans made for a four-pillared villa.

"But then a new magistrate was appointed in Jining. He was from Qingzhou and incorruptible. After he was approached with the offer of the same bribe accepted by his predecessor, the new magistrate arrested the man making the offer and proclaimed that a substantial reward would be paid for information about anyone transporting untaxed goods.

"Within the week, Chin was arrested and a day later was kneeling before the magistrate's bench. There were two informants. One was the man he hired to take charge of his third barge; the other was his own younger brother. The first he had paid too little; the second was envious and also vengeful. Chin had not only bullied and tyrannized over his brother all his life he had also appropriated his share of the family savings.

"Chin was lashed fifty times, had to pay a heavy fine, and his three barges were confiscated."

"A familiar story," said Fang. "It shows the wisdom of the three-year term for magistrates and forbidding them to serve in their native province. But, Master, what's the proverb?"

Hsi-wei smiled. "Please be patient, My Lord. There's still one more story to tell. It isn't either pleasant or short. This one has nothing to do with the Canal or with bargemen, but it does have another honest magistrate. His name was Guo Hui-liang, and I came to know him a little when I was in the capital studying with Master Shen Kuo. Guo Hui-liang impressed me. He had just passed his examination with top scores. He was learned and humane, a good Confucian intrigued by Buddhist teachings. Though he was from a well-off family, he showed sincere concern for the poor. Perhaps that is why he wished to meet me, the peasant who turned down a fortune for an education. As you know, I was then a curiosity, something like a trained dog. Guo and I met twice, and I enjoyed our conversations. A more upright and thoughtful young man I never came across in Daxing. That I turned up at the post to which he was assigned was a sheer accident.

"Magistrate Guo had only been in Yangchuan for two months when I arrived. This was at the time when Emperor Wen's land reform was being carried out, the Equal Field system. By the way, I'm pleased that Emperor Gaozu has decided to retain the system, a good and wise decision."

Fang nodded his agreement.

"Well, as you know, My Lord, Wendi's law made the government sole owner of all the land in the Empire so it could be allocated it to individuals regardless of class. Instead, land was distributed based on each household's ability to supply labor. The new law transformed the situation of the poor, thought it was not entirely fair or without problems. For example, the lands of high officials were exempted from taxes and inherited by their families on their deaths. As taxes for all other households were the same, the burden fell heavily on the poor and not at all on the rich. Normally, when the householder died, the land reverted to the state. This was to keep the local gentry from accumulating land and the power that went with it. But there was a tear in the law's fabric. Land could be passed down within the family so long as it required long-term development.

"Guo's predecessor in the district had done nothing to implement the reforms. The wealthy of Yangchuan still controlled all the good land and the lot of the peasants was to be their sharecroppers, serfs, and servants.

"Guo arrived in Yangchuan with four constables and escorted by six cavalrymen. With such a small force, and the landowners so entrenched, no one expected him to change things. But they were wrong. The day after his arrival, he ordered notices posted and sent his constables out to summon the population to a public meeting. Three days later, Guo stood on a platform set up in the square. He was dressed in his formal robes and wearing his winged hat. He explained to the crowd that the new system meant all land in the district would now be reallocated by him as soon as a census was taken of men, women, and livestock. Each household, he promised, would be counted and issued its land according to the new law. I was told that the peasants set up a loud cheer after he finished speaking and that the well-off were silent.

"The rich did all they could to thwart Guo. They tried to bribe the census-takers, to intimidate the constables, and warned their sharecroppers and serfs not to cooperate with the new magistrate. The most cunning of the landlords tried to use the law to defeat the law."

Minister Fang, who had ceased taking notes and seemed to be losing interest, perked up at that last phrase and asked, "How did he do that?"

"You remember the exception for long-term development?"

"I believe that provision has also been retained. It's sensible to let one family hold on to their land if they are carrying out useful projects like swamp-clearing, the cultivation of orchards, and digging irrigation canals. Those can take years."

"Exactly. This rascally landowner instructed his friends to import eight mulberry trees each and to plant two in each corner of their land. They all filed petitions claiming they were establishing a local silk industry."

"I see. How did the magistrate react?"

"He found out which of the census-takers had taken bribes and had his honest constables deliver their punishment publicly. He reassured the frightened peasants that he would protect them. As for the mulberry plantings, he dismissed all the petitions, pointing out that they had planted red mulberries while silkworms would only eat the fruit of white mulberries. For good measure, he added that neither silkworms nor mulberry saplings would be likely to survive the severe winter of Yangchuan."

"Good for him. Imagine knowing about the red mulberries."

"I told you he was remarkable. Well, the nobles didn't give up. Instead, they slandered Guo, spreading the rumor that he was guilty of three outrages. First, that he had seduced the third wife of a rich landowner. Second, that he had misappropriated government funds. Third, that he had sent his constables to burn down one of their villas. Through their connections in the capital, these landowners managed to get these false charges into the hands of the First Minister."

"Had they any proof?"

"The third wife was bullied by her husband into signing a false affidavit. A villa really did burn down, but because of a careless cook. As for the misappropriated funds, they claimed that Guo had bought himself a dozen silk robes and a pair of prime horses. As evidence, they submitted forged receipts."

"What happened?"

"I arrived in time to witness the outcome. I heard the whole story from Guo himself when I happened to arrive the day before the provincial prefect was to conduct a hearing on the three charges. I attended it, of course. One landowner after another repeated their lies. The disgraced third wife was cross-examined but said almost nothing before breaking down in sobs."

"Was Guo able to defend himself?"

Hsi-wei shrugged. "He did what he could."

"Didn't anyone speak up for him?"

"Only one person."

"Not his constables?"

"No. One was beaten half to death and the others were offered the choice of the same treatment or a bribe."

"None of the peasants spoke for him?"

"None said a word. Some were obviously frightened; others may have believed the rumors, and many seemed pleased to see a magistrate in the dock, even a good one. The hearing ended with the prefect ordering Guo taken to the capital under guard. As the crowd was drifting away, I overheard one peasant say to another, 'It's just as well. It's dangerous to have a magistrate who can't be bribed.'"

"You said one person who spoke up for Guo. Who was it?"

Hsi-wei looked glumly down at his lap.

"Only this worthless maker of straw-sandals and useless poems. Guo was dismissed from his position and sent to join the army stationed in the west."

After that, the two men sat quietly for a while watching the sun set. Fang had been shocked by what that peasant had said about upright officials. Then he again spread out his scroll and took up his brush.

"So, Master Hsi-wei, I understand these are the stories behind the three in your poem. But what are the proverbs?"

Hsi-wei counted them out on his fingers.

"Strike with a meat bun. Water floats a boat but also sinks it. Virtue is more persecuted by the wicked than loved by the good."

THE THREE PROVERBS

Fu discovered Dao chewing a pair of his breeches.
He bawled at the dog and beat him with a stick.
Dao hid himself behind the pig shed all afternoon.
Just before supper, Dao dragged off a sandal.
Fu swore at the dog and threw an iron ladle at him.
Fu's old mother watched from the hearth.
She held a meat bun out toward the cowering Dao
then called him close and quietly stroked his head.

Dreaming of fat fish, rich trade, warm starry nights
on the canal, Dingxiao and his son decided to build
a sampan, one with comfortable quarters for two.
They laid the first plank flat, affixed two for the sides,
smoothed and sealed it all with tar. Two weeks hard work.
"Let's launch!" begged the son. Dingxiao tied the prow to a willow.
The hull floated. Proud and weary, they slept through that night's
cloudburst. Come morning, only the rope was above water.

Bingwen was diligent, the smartest, best behaved.
Master Shu praised him relentlessly. "Admire Bingwen's
calligraphy. See how neat he keeps his brushes!
Hear how perfectly he recites the Shijing Masters!"
Every day the other boys found new ways
to torment Bingwen. They tore off his cap,
pummeled his ribs, tripped him up, and the angriest
cursed his ancestors to the eighteenth generation.

Petite Suite Littéraire

1. Un Après-Midi à Paris - Trio Existentiel

One day in September, a week after the bourgeoisie returned from their August in the country, J.P. and Simone sat at their usual table outside the Café de Flore. He had ordered an anisette. "It makes a change," he remarked. Simone chose a pastis. "I am a congeries of habits," she explained. Between the two there was but one mood; that is, both were bored. To Simone, it was simply a case of seasonal ennui. If he had more energy, J.P. might have attributed his condition to being doomed to freedom, though in reality it was mostly a matter of a workaholic with too much time on his hands. His mind reverted to a slight he had received that morning from the editor of an excessively respected journal. He had already told the story to Simone, hoping for sympathy. "Bertrand must think I look too intelligent to keep my word." But Simone was uninterested in the matter of the editor; she was thinking of a certain purple dress she had seen in a window. "Shopping," she mused a little guiltily, "is reprehensible but still a profound pleasure." Of course, she didn't say this out loud. What she did say was, "Look. Isn't that Albert?"

It was indeed Albert, who was hurrying down the Boulevard Saint-Germaine looking like a man suffering from migraine. To one side of him was a man Simone felt certain must be a Pied-Noir; he was thin and sported a Franco-Hitlerian mustache—not Franco as in *French*, Franco as in *Francisco*. On the other side of Albert strode a young fellow J.P. recognized as an Algerian journalist, not the sort to pull his punches. More than a decade later, J.P. would invite the perceptive Arab to contribute to the pages of *Libération*.

The Pied Noir was yelling in Albert's right ear, the Algerian in the left one.

"Poor Albert. When he's at his best, he looks like Bogart, but today he resembles Superman in the issue where he's unable to turn off his super-hearing and the villains are bashing trashcans near his head." Simone knew about everything, not just American movies but even their comic books.

Catching sight of the bored couple, Albert managed to break away from his tormentors and drop into the spare chair at their little round table.

"Ouf!" he groaned.

"Egg?" asked Simone.

J.P. corrected her. "Not *oeuf*, ma chère. *Ouf.*"

The waiter, who was even more bored than J.P. and Simone, meandered over and stood by Albert as if, having committed some terrible faux pas in his adolescence, he was still being punished for it.

"Two aspirin and a Pernod."

The waiter yawned and withdrew.

Meanwhile, the mustachioed Pied Noir and the Algerian journalist came to blows. The fight was not edifying and did it last long enough to be entertaining. As the Pied Noir was the first to hit the sidewalk, Simone pronounced the Algerian the winner. The two combatants straightened their clothes. The Pied Noir also smoothed his hair, a gesture the curly-headed Algerian could omit. Dignity restored, they stalked off in opposite directions.

"That's what you get," said J.P. to Albert.

"For what?"

"For not choosing, for not properly committing. Without engagement, what can you expect but to be pulled this way and that. Oh, you shake things up; I'll give you that. But only those who aren't rowing have time to rock the boat."

Albert snorted and retorted, "What did you see in the monster Stalin?"

Simone answered for J.P. "Someone to admire at a safe distance."

J.P. answered for himself. "Stalin stood up for the people, the common people, for the collective interest."

"One leader, one people. What's that signify but one master and millions of slaves? The welfare of the people has always been the tyrant's alibi."

"Speaking of alibis," said Simone, "what's Freud's?"

"Freud. Freud showed the way," declared J.P.

"Unfortunately, it was the wrong way," said Simone. "What we need is a truly existential psychoanalysis and one developed by women."

"It would make a change," said Albert

Having turned the conversation in this satisfactory direction, Simone went on at length. "Freud had the prurient curiosity of an adolescent. He claimed to want to understand women but the best he could come up with was penis envy. He hasn't a clue what the erotic is for a female, has no idea that sexual pleasure in women is a magic spell, that it demands abandonment." She then called Freud a rude name.

Albert said that Freud reminded him of a certain painter. "I told him that it wasn't his paintings I admire but his painting."

The Pied Noir and the Algerian returned to resume their argument.

"You're a man of the Right," J.P. accused Albert.

"No, always of the Left, only not deluded by despots," Albert protested.

"Right."

"Left."

Overhearing this, the Pied Noir, a veteran, began instinctively to march in place.

"Phallocrat," said Simone to Albert.

"Democrat," he replied.

"Same thing," said J.P.

"That's true," said Simone. "The women of Athens weren't allowed to vote."

"No, not even Saint Lysistrata."

"Apropos," said Albert. "I've broken up with Catherine."

"Too bad, Albert," said J.P. indifferently.

"But entirely predictable," added Simone, who had always been vaguely impressed by the speed with which Albert changed partners. "So, you'll never see her again?"

Albert's reply was one that Simone could tell he had trotted out on many similar occasions. "Friendship," he declared sententiously, "sometimes turns to love, but love to friendship—never."

The Pied Noir and the Algerian, worn out with arguing, approached the table and appealed to Albert. He pretended they were not there at all. His headache had finally let up, and he didn't want it coming back.

And so, the discourse continued as dusk fell. The Eiffel Tower and the Arc de Triomphe, lit up and looked on impassively.

The waiter came over to say that he deeply regretted to inform them that unfortunately the café would be closing for two hours. The staff had to prepare for a special dinner.

"For the President of the Republic?"

"No, Monsieur. For Mademoiselle Chanel."

"What. That Fascist?"

The waiter gave a Gallic shrug.

The three rose to leave.

Albert and J.P. shook hands. "The compulsion to be right is the sign of a vulgar mind," the former whispered in the ear of the latter.

"We don't judge the people we love," the latter whispered into the ear of the former.

Holding one hand out to Albert and taking J.P.'s arm with the other, Simone smiled complacently.

Then they departed, Simone and J.P. turning to the left, Albert to the right.

Nobody left a tip.

2. Un Automne à Vienne et Lyme Regis - Ouverture et Duo Érotique

In 1803, Ludwig van Beethoven was erupting. He spewed out three symphonies, including the astonishing *Third*, completed before the summer was over. High into the cooling air of Vienna shot the *Waldstein*; from the open casements of Schwarzspanierstrasse 15 wafted the motifs that would congeal into Opus 47, the maestro's ninth and finest violin sonata. Yet this *annus mirabilis* had its disappointments. Twice the maestro was compelled by his conscience to alter his dedications. Everyone knows the first case. Bonaparte let the composer down, dashed his liberal hopes, by crowning himself emperor. The *Eroica* was furiously rededicated "to the memory of a great man." The second case is less well known.

Not yet deaf, not yet cut off from good fellowship, Beethoven good-naturedly accepted the impertinent yet sound suggestions of the virtuoso who was to premier his new sonata. His homely English name notwith-standing, George Bridgewater was an African-European born in Poland, a prodigy. The happy collaboration with Beethoven prompted a dedication that is at once mocking, affectionate, and racist. *Sonata per un mulattico lunatico.* How Bridgewater felt about this is unknown; however, we do know that the "*lunatico*" made an insulting remark about a certain lady within Beethoven's still functioning hearing, maybe even for the composer's amusement. Perhaps Bridgewater wasn't striking back at Beethoven for that dedication, and maybe he was unaware that the lady he traduced was one Beethoven knew and admired. Anyway, that was that. The *mulattico lunatico* was blotted out in favor of Rudolphe Kreutzer, a musical rather than imperial Frenchman. So far as anybody knows, Kreutzer never played the piece.

The *Kreutzer Sonata* is so amorous that, eighty-six years later, Tolstoy wrote a novella of the same name which pretty much blames the music's sexiness for adultery and murder. By then Tolstoy was well on his way to his final ascetic, music-mistrusting phase. What isn't so surprising is that those in authority entirely mistook the work's puritanism. The Russian government censored it, perhaps more for its narrator's critique of marriage (Tolstoy's wasn't exactly happy) than for the lurid *crime passionnel*. In another hemisphere, the United States Post Office, not noted for its literary insight, banned the book also. President Theodore Roosevelt, a prolific writer, did himself little honor in branding its author "a sexual and moral pervert".

Did Kreutzer make it a point not to play the sonata. Did he think it cursed, too difficult, or did he just not care for the piece—or for Beethoven. Ironic that its rededication to him should be the one thing for which he's remembered. But for Beethoven's crush and Bridgewater's impropriety, Kreutzer would today be as forgotten as his compositions. We can speculate that Beethoven fancied the lady who was so casually insulted by Bridgewater; we might even suppose that it is a longing for her that infuses Opus 47, and that Beethoven's wrath—a fearful thing to see, though glorious to hear—was more sexual than racist.

What else is there to say.

Will Eros always find a way?

Meanwhile, at the other end of Europe, a different eruption was preparing itself, one of enlightenment and release. Don't suppose it is just a vulgar tale about a hormone-crazed youth and a frustrated older woman. Think rather of a pair of billiard balls careering across a green table, solid, kinetic, hard. Imagine that they collide, rebound, then rush off in a new directions.

George is fifteen. Jane is twenty-eight. Both are virgins.

"I despise cricket even more than Latin, almost more than mathematics."

"Haven't you found that when people say they despise an activity it's generally because they aren't good at it?"

"Yes. I'm being unfair. Harrow isn't really so harrowing. You're right. The problem isn't with the school but with me. I'm paralyzed—I couldn't go back last month because of—"

"Yes?"

He shook his head, like a horse tossing its mane. "Oh, call it yearning."

"Yearning?" She was unable to conceal an amused smile. "I see. So, the way things are isn't the way you'd prefer them to be?"

"Are they ever. For *anyone*. They certainly aren't for my poor ruined and widowed mother. Are they for you?"

"Oh, me. Never mind *me*. But I think we owe much to the difference between is and ought."

"Dissatisfaction."

"Yes. But also, morality, religion, progress, invention, not to mention comedy and tragedy."

"In Denmark something's rotten. Am I just a boy to you. Are you making fun of me?"

Jane laughed. "Is there something else I ought to make of you?" She couldn't help but tease. It wasn't just because he was so young. To tease was her nature, her manner of dealing with a world she understood so much better than it understood itself.

But George bridled. After all, he was not the world. And he was proud. At school, he was prepared to fight at any hint of a slight—such as some all- too-justified crack about his father, the "Mad Jack" who got hold of his second wife's money as he did of her name, a name passed on to George along with certain traits, including pride. And yet, though he couldn't have said why, George found being teased by this woman more agreeable than being praised by his mother. He did resent a little the way Jane brought him down, yet he enjoyed it at the same time. It was perplexing. Anyway, talking with his mother was no help for what was ailing him. It was only during his strolls with this plain but witty woman that he was able to forget his charming Mary for a time. But even then, to his dismay, he could be afflicted by one of his stubborn erections. Evidently, a part of him had acquired a will of its own. He began to call it "Mad Jack," as if it were the spirit of his father. He couldn't decide if he resented Jack or approved of him, wanted to suppress or abet him. In short, George's feelings were a mélange of baffled, tangled potentiality.

Resignation to her unmarried state did not prevent Jane from being fascinated by everything that happens between men and women up until the wedding night. She thought about it, imagined it, wrote about it. As so often happens, her writing was the consequence of her reading, and the novels she read were about young people making their way to financial and marital security. So far, so good. But, for Jane, romance divorced from reality was simply ridiculous. In fact, she was ridiculing it right there in Lyme Regis, working away at her counter-novel. During the hours when she would write while her sister Cassie drew, Jane worked at sending up the Gothic fantasies over which the women she knew so immoderately enthused. To Cassandra, she had compared them to a gaggle of Quixotes, looking at the world through thick, wavy lenses, mistaking men for monsters, cellars for dungeons, and all to the end of puffing up factitious passions.

Satire was good literature's revenge on bad writing—at least, it would be hers. She doubted her anti-Gothic novel, or anything she wrote, would ever be published. She told herself it didn't matter as she already had her ideal reader in her sister, who, it seemed, would also never marry.

When the weather turned, poor Cassie caught a cold and was unable to join Jane for their daily walk along the promenade. Over her mother's objections, Jane went down to the sea wall by herself. It was on one of these jaunts that she met George, likewise a solitary walker and refugee from a vigilant mother. He was an unusually handsome boy, educated, and as eager to talk as Jane was to listen. He looked older than his age.

"I couldn't go back."

"Because of Miss Chaworth?"

"Mary's divine. But all this adoring from afar. . ." He threw up his hands, exasperated with his situation or, more likely, with himself.

"You know what you don't want. Do you know what you *do*?"

"Too much. I want everything. I'm all wanting."

"Ah, I see. And if you got everything, where would you keep it?"

He glanced at her with annoyance, then broke into a smile. "And what about you. What is it *you* want?"

"Oh, I. I suppose sometimes what I want is. . . to want."

"You're remarkable, you know, quite unlike anyone I've ever met."

Jane blushed. "You're too kind. And too young to think me unique. You can't have met so many people."

"That again?"

"It's true. The young are impatient."

"And so I am. Out of patience entirely. I want to grab hold."

"You have greedy hands?"

"You would say so I think, you who are without greed."

"Don't be so sure."

George halted and took her soft hand in his greedy one. She wasn't young and beautiful like Mary Chaworth, but she was there and, though she concealed it well, he sensed that she enjoyed his physical proximity. He certainly admired her and, besides, there was Mad Jack acting up again.

The one night they somehow arranged to spend together set George off on a life of motion, notoriety, acclaim, and scandal, a life famously crowded with affairs: Augusta, Elizabeth, Caroline, Claire, Isabella, Teresa, les Macris, Elena, Marianna, Margarita, and so on.

As for Jane, romance and reality would ever after have a complicated relationship for her. She imagined George over and over, aged him, filled him in, gave him some good lines, varied his location, income, hairline, title, and avocations; but she kept him as she'd have liked, witty, well-read, a little vain but sympathetic, ever desirable and always dependable.

Even before she left Dorset, the George she imagined he would soon become merged with Henry T., the level-headed hero of her satirical novel. Henry speaks for his creator when he says, "The person, be it gentleman or lady, who has not pleasure in a good novel, must be intolerably stupid." Jane was well enough pleased with her Henry; however, it was some years later that her successive portraits George attained perfection in the person of Fitzwilliam D. who, at the close of her sublime novel, is twenty-eight years old.

3. Un Voyage à Omsk – Quator Franco-Russe

Despair drove her from paralysis to frenzy. Her reputation, her position in society were lost, her child, money, both her lover and her husband. She scarcely knew what she had become; she could only recall—with a bitter chill that made her tremble all over—who she had been. Her life was already over in every sense but one. *Pourquoi pas cela aussi?*

Ivan was born in 1818. Fyodor and Gustave both entered the world three years later. Sunlight first struck Leo's face in 1828. That the four knew one another is not particularly surprising, but it was chiefly down to Ivan. He may have been practically an expatriate, very nearly a Frenchman; nevertheless, he felt himself to be *un vrai Russe*, and sometimes it was necessary to say so. Anyway, it was always about Russia he wrote.

Ivan and Gustave became fast friends from the moment they met. They were kindred spirits with sympathetic views. in religion agnostic, in politics liberal, in philosophy rational. They were aesthetic confrères, both pessimistic but slow to render judgments, meticulous formalists with an urge toward formal purity. Though he would have liked to, Ivan couldn't get on anywhere near so well with his countrymen, Fyodor and Leo. The former despised him for admiring the West and mocked him cruelly in a novel. As for the latter, after they spent some days together in Paris, Leo declared Ivan "a bore" and did not speak to him for seventeen years.

Gustave and Ivan were not without their differences, though. The former was a licentious, libidinous man. The latter was, mostly, not. Gustave couldn't count all the prostitutes—female and male—he'd paid, let alone how much. Ivan's life was more sedate. He never married, though, in his early years, he did interfere with the daughters of his family's serfs. The consequence of one of these dalliances was an illegitimate daughter. As a writer, he was more drawn to the nuances of romance than the brutalities of sex. But their few differences between Ivan and Gustave only added seasoning to their friendship.

Both loved to travel. In 1850, Gustave went to Egypt, a country that afforded plenty of scope for his Don Juanism.

Ivan did not accompany his friend to the Levant, but he too felt the itch to be away from France. When the first leaves began to fall in September, he was overwhelmed by nostalgia. He yearned to see peasants hunting for mushrooms underneath birch trees; he longed for the sight of troikas and the noise of sledges driven by bearded coachmen bundled up in bearskin robes; he missed men in fur hats and reeking of vodka. He wanted to see again Russia's endless forests and wide steppes, the braid on the uniforms of its cavalry officers, its timorous clerks hurrying from one government office to another, its shapeless babushkas who cross themselves twenty times a day and hoard half-rubles in old stockings.

He went first to St. Petersburg, the most European place in Russia. In a remarkable book that Ivan would admire almost as much he deplored, Fyodor would call the city "the most intentional in the world." Ivan found satisfaction in any truth succinctly expressed.

Soon after he settled into his hotel, Ivan thought of old friends on whom he should be paying calls. Among these was Vissarion Grigoryevich, the critic who had been so gracious when he was just starting out, praising him when praise meant the most and was least merited. He went to the critic's townhouse, knocked, then had a long wait. The door was eventually opened—partially—by an aged servant in a threadbare livery jacket and wide trousers. The man drew back in shock when Ivan asked to see his master.

"But it's two years since the master passed away," said the fellow quickly crossing himself once for each year.

For some reason, Ivan felt obliged to explain himself. "I didn't know. I've been abroad."

"It was the consumption," the servant reported. "And maybe it was just as well."

"Just as well?"

"If the master hadn't coughed out his life at just the right time, he'd have been arrested and sent off to Siberia to freeze."

Ivan was horrified and not for the first time felt fury at his country's backwardness, its insatiable taste for tyranny, its determination to snuff out any little spark of progress.

"I had no idea. And his wife. . . I mean, his widow?"

"The mistress is unwell. No visitors," declared the servant then rudely shut the door.

As he made his way back toward Nevsky Prospekt, Ivan recalled what the late Vissarion Grigoryevich had written about Fyodor, that he was Nikolai's true heir. It had required effort not to be jealous, which he found not only extravagant but puzzling. After all, wasn't it he, Ivan, who, like Nikolai, lived abroad but wrote about Russia. He had read the novel that so impressed Vissarion Grigoryevich and a few of Fyodor's short stories. He thought the novel mawkish and derivative, Russified Balzac, but admitted that Fyodor did indeed show promise. Fyodor, he supposed, must be, like him, a foe of Russian obscurantism. Ivan had not given Fyodor a thought in years. It was the servant's saying that his master had evaded arrest only by dying that reminded Ivan of Fyodor. Poor Fyodor really had been sent to Siberia.

Ivan had followed the Petrashevsky trial with dismay. He was indignant when he learned the story of the phony execution, the last-minute commutation to a decade in Siberia. Now the memory of these events and the feelings they had evoked returned.

Ivan made inquiries among his contacts and discovered that Fyodor was incarcerated in Omsk—Omsk, which is further from Petersburg than Petersburg is from Paris. But as Ivan had promised himself to see the interior of his native land, he resolved to make the trek to western Siberia and pay a visit of charity. Perhaps a visit from a colleague would give heart to the unfortunate Fyodor and help him to endure his suffering.

The journey was as arduous as Ivan anticipated. The inns were just as repellent as he remembered them—the same aromas of sweat, urine, onion, boiled cabbage, and cheap alcohol; the same thin, infested mattresses and low, smoke-darkened ceilings; the same toadying and over-charging; the same superstition masquerading as religion. The further you go into Russia, he reflected, the more nothing ever changes—to go east is to go backwards. Yet seeing the deep forests pleased Ivan. He recalled his childhood with the kind of sentiment customary on such occasions. He was twice hospitably received on estates owned by old Moscow friends who had given up the city to become country squires. The sister of one flirted with him. She was a widow and not bad looking.

When he at last reached Omsk, Ivan easily obtained permission to see Fyodor. The prison colony was horrible and bleak, but the officials were not punctilious. He didn't even have to pay a bribe.

Ivan had naively supposed that an educated political prisoner like Fyodor would be better treated than the common thieves and murderers, that he would be separately accommodated. Not so.

Fyodor looked thin and unhealthy; his beard was brittle, scraggly and full of gray hairs. He was excessively moved by Ivan's visit. He hugged him then kissed his cheeks over and over and wouldn't let go of his hands. "How wonderful of you to come!" he exclaimed. "Here, you know, one always thinks one is forgotten, like the dead."

Ivan spent two long afternoons with Fyodor in a little whitewashed room the officer in charge made available to them. There was even a rusty old samovar. Fyodor spoke like the deprived creature he was, one starved for an educated listener. He talked with an exalted feverishness for which Ivan did not really care and thought close to madness. He was even less pleased to learn that the Tsar's remedy was working, that Fyodor had become a counter-revolutionary, and even that was putting it mildly. He denigrated the West as godless, superficial, and un-Russian. Salvation, he said, lay with the Christ of the orthodox church and humility. One must, he said, rid oneself of the egoism that tainted everything that crept into Russia from Europe. Ivan attempted to discourage Fyodor's politico-religious harangues by simply not commenting on them and changing the subject. He asked Fyodor to tell him stories he had picked up from his fellow prisoners.

"You're looking for material, eh?"

"Yes, you could say that."

"Very well, then."

The tales were lurid, pathetic, vile, and violent. This one had stolen the life-savings of an old veteran who had lost both an arm and a leg fighting the Turks. Another had murdered a whole family—even an infant—in a drunken rage. An axe murderer, an embezzler, a confidence trickster, an abuser of children, pimps. One tale of child rape might have made even Gustave blanch.

The story that intrigued Ivan most was that of a certain well-to-do Muscovite, a court councilor, whose wife was seduced then abandoned by a Guards officer. The man took pains in plotting his revenge, even hiring two railway workers to help him. "They waited for the man outside an establishment called The Yar where he often spent a night of dissipation," said Fyodor. "As soon as it was safe, they threw a sack over his head and dragged him into an alley off Kuznetsky Most. They used iron bars. Apparently, even his mother wasn't able to recognize him."

"What of the wife?" Ivan asked.

"Oh, he'd never have harmed *her*," said Fyodor. "He loved her too dearly. He testified at his trial he confessed that it wasn't for seducing his wife that he beat the officer to death but because he abandoned her. You see, the woman killed herself. He swore to the court that if the Guards officer had run off with his wife, he could have born it because then he would have known she was safe."

"What a terrible story. How did the woman commit suicide?"

Fyodor shrugged. To him, the wife was a minor character, a prop; it was the fate of the court councilor that interested him. "The fellow died a year ago. Typhoid. I can't recall exactly how the woman did away with herself. Poison or hanging or a pistol or—who knows—perhaps she threw herself under a carriage. Every story here is one of ruin and despair. But there are many—even among the worst sinner—who become humble, remorseful, and redeem themselves. Yes, it's really so. It's beautiful when some lost soul, with the aid of the good Father Vassily and God's grace, at last repents and finds his way to Christ." Though he didn't say so, Fyodor clearly meant to include himself among the redeemed.

As he made his way back from Omsk, the landscape now seemed to Ivan endlessly flat and desolate, a pointless country of muddy roads, brown grass; the forests meant nothing but impenetrable timber. When he returned to Paris, Ivan felt like the diver in Schiller's poem who has extricated himself from a tangle of weeds and rises to breathe joyfully "up in the roseate light."

Gustave was back from Egypt and had left a message for him. The two friends enjoyed a reunion dinner La Petite Château. They also met again the following afternoon for a stroll through the Tuileries and the morning after that as well for coffee and brioche. They had much to say to one another. Save for the usual complaints about delays, disgusting food, wretched accommodations, bad roads, greedy innkeepers, corrupt officials, insatiable bedbugs, and stomach troubles, the chief topics were their adventures in Egypt and Russia. Gustave's stories were many, amusing, and mostly scandalous. Ivan could hardly match his friend but he did have his trip to Omsk. He told Gustave about going all that way to see the imprisoned Fyodor. In the course of his narrative, he told Gustave the anecdote of the court councilor, the Guards officer, and the formerly respectable adulteress who killed herself. He said that he found her of greater interest than either her husband or faithless lover. Gustave asked why. Ivan explained that the motives of the two men were obvious and their feelings almost clichés. Of course, some might say the same of the woman, and yet he thought she might have been something original.

Of all that Ivan reported about his journey, it was this story that Gustave couldn't get out of his mind.

Twenty years later, when Leo grudgingly agreed to receive him on his estate, Ivan asked if he were in communication with Fyodor.

Leo was curt. "No."

"I wonder," said Ivan thoughtfully, "if he really has convinced himself of God's existence. He seems to write about the question compulsively. Would he do that if the matter were settled?"

"I should say he has a good opinion of God and a poor one of you."

Ivan nodded modestly. "I know and I regret it. But what can I do. And it's all the more vexing because, when he was imprisoned in Siberia, I went all that way just to pay the fellow a friendly visit."

"You did?"

"Yes, to Omsk."

"Omsk," Leo repeated. "What did you talk about?"

Ivan spoke of Fyodor's conversion to Slavophilism, of his white, Siberian Christ. Apart from that, all he was able to recall was the story that had so interested his friend Gustave, the one about the adulteress who killed herself.

And so he told it to Leo as well.

HSI-WEI AND THE WOOD-BLOCK PRINTER

Note. In 593 C.E., Emperor Wen of Sui ordered the printing of Buddhist scriptures. His aim was to spread these beliefs across the Empire he had united after three centuries of division and civil war. His decree is the first mention of printing in Chinese history.

In the spring of the twelfth year of Wendi's reign, the peasant/poet Chen Hsi-wei made his way north to Yuzhou. For a few days, he stayed in the town of Huaiyang. As usual, the first thing he did was look for a cheap accommodation. He found one at the back of an inn called the Two Medlars, a storeroom he would share with two crates of dried fish, three sacks of rice, and a dozen jars of yellow wine. Once he struck his bargain with the innkeeper, Hsi-wei headed for the town square. With the weather warming, he expected plenty of orders for his straw sandals. The square bustled with vendors selling vegetables, fruit, pastries, and meat. Hsi-wei noticed a small opening between an old woman offering dumplings and a butcher standing behind a long table. Hsi-wei propped his sign against the wall, lay down his pack, and sat down beside it. From behind her brazier, the dumpling seller nodded welcomingly; however, though Hsi-wei was not a competitor, the butcher appeared annoyed. He grumbled, hefted his cleaver, and might have said something unpleasant if a customer had not approached and turned his sincere scowl into an insincere smile.

Hsi-wei watched the butcher cut a hunk of pork, put it on one scale then lay a lead weight in the other. "There," he said, "one *jin* exactly!. The butcher quickly wrapped the meat in a square of burlap. After the customer handed over her coins and departed, the butcher smiled slyly to himself. A second customer was greeted with a false smile and the procedure repeated, the cutting, weighing, and the sly look once the coins were pocketed. Hsi-wei was suspicious but was soon taking orders of his own.

About an hour later, a fat fellow in a leather jerkin came up to the butcher laughing. "Ho, Hulin. It's hot and you're in the sun. Let's go get a drink."

"A drink. Why not?"

The butcher Hulin turned to the dumpling-seller. "Keep an eye on my things, Granny."

The old woman nodded.

The butcher threw a burlap over his table and left with his friend.

Hsi-wei had come across butchers in many markets and knew their tricks. He got to his feet and told the old woman that he just wanted to look at something, not to take anything.

She nodded.

Hsi-wei drew back the burlap and picked up the butcher's scales. It was as he expected. A thin piece of lead had been fixed to the bottom of the scale that held the meat. Customers who paid for one *jin* would get only two-thirds. Hsi-wei replaced the burlap and resumed his place.

The butcher returned, his gait rolling. He belched, yanked the cloth off the table, and took up his position. Hsi-wei contemplated whether he ought to challenge the man or not. After all, the butcher was hostile, dishonest, tipsy, and armed with a cleaver.

Just then five boys—four full-sized ten-year-olds and one younger and smaller—ran exuberantly into the square, full of chilies and energy. They came to a stop not far from Hsi-wei, the dumpling-seller, and the butcher. His neighbors were busy with customers but Hsi-wei was free to watch the boys.

"I know. Let's play Toad in the Circle," cried the biggest of the boys.

"Yes. Let's!"

The smallest boy said he didn't know how the game was played.

"Oh, it's easy" said the big one. "One of us is blindfolded and everybody else makes a circle around him and he has to squat down and jump like a toad until he touches somebody else and then *that* one becomes the toad. I know. Since you're new to the game, we'll start with you and then you'll get the hang of it."

Hsi-wei noticed the other boys exchanging furtive smiles.

Eager to fit in, the little boy agreed, and a nasty-looking rag was produced and tied over his face.

"It's too tight," he complained.

"It has to be tight or you'll see," said the biggest boy.

The child squatted and began to bounce about with his arms extended, feeling for legs. But there were no legs because the others, suppressing giggles, had cleared out.

The little boy kept hopping, looking more ridiculous than pitiable. Then he lost his balance and careened into the butcher's trestle table, which collapsed, the heavy top just missing the boy's head.

Hulin had two customers and both walked away sharing a laugh. Enraged, the butcher grabbed the horrified boy's shoulder, swore at him, and made a fist.

Hsi-wei leapt to his feet and took hold of the man's arm.

"This boy has done you a real damage," he said calmly, and nodded in the direction of two men lounging by the well on the far side of the square. "I'll summon the magistrate's men."

The furious butcher said, "Go ahead. But first, I'm going to teach this boy a lesson and then have him arrested."

Hsi-wei leaned close to the butcher. "Arrested. Very well," he whispered. "But then I'll ask the officers to take a close look at your scales."

The surprised butcher swore at Hsi-wei and called him a damned vagrant; but he let go of the boy. Hsi-wei helped Hulin set up his table then packed up his things and took the shocked boy, who hadn't moved except to tear off his blindfold, by the hand.

"What's your name?"

"Guoliang," muttered the boy in a tiny voice.

"Where do you live?"

Guoliang conducted Hsi-wei to a neat but modest villa. Instead of the usual garden, it had a workshop in the back.

Hsi-wei knocked at the door. When Mrs. Teng opened it, the boy threw himself into his mother's arms and, without pausing to take a breath, blurted out the whole story of his mischance in the marketplace, the rules of Toad in the Circle, how the big boys tricked him and he knocked over a table and how the butcher was going to beat him when he was saved by the sandal-maker, who was so brave, a hero. Then he broke into tears and buried his face in his mother's stomach.

Mr. Teng, hearing his son crying, came running around the side of the villa and took in the scene. He looked first at Hsi-wei, then his wife. Mrs. Teng gave him an abbreviated version of what had happened, after which Teng bowed to Hsi-wei and thanked him.

"Please, Daddy," begged Guoliang, "please can he stay for dinner?"

"You must," said Mrs. Teng and her husband agreed. The boy stopped crying and turned his teary eyes worshipfully on Hsi-wei.

"Come inside," said Teng, and lay down that pack. Li-jing, how long before we eat?"

"An hour."

"Excellent!"

Teng asked Hsi-wei's name and, when he heard it, asked if he was really a sandal-maker as his son said. Hsi-wei said he was.

"And do you, by any chance, also make poems?"

Hsi-wei was surprised by the question and admitted that he did.

Teng, smiling broadly now, asked yet another question. "And might one of those poems be about Lake Weishan?"

Hsi-wei confessed that he had written some verses about Lake Weishan.

At that, Teng clapped his hands and called to his wife.

"Li-jing, we are having no ordinary guest to dinner. Here is the author of that poem Mingmei loves so much."

Teng explained. "Our daughter was recently married and lives in Liang now. She knows how to write," he said proudly. "She copied out your poem for my wife and me."

"I'm honored," said a surprised but gratified Hsi-wei.

"The honor is ours" said Mrs. Teng. "Imagine. What will Mingmei say?"

"I miss Mingmei," murmured the little boy then he spoke up more brightly. "Mommy, can I cut up the vegetables?"

"Only if you promise to be very very careful."

Teng took Hsi-wei by the arm. "Come with me while they get dinner together," he said. "I think you might be interested in my new work."

The two men went around back to the workshop, a shed with stacks of wood blocks, scrolls, inkpots, rollers, and a stout table with at least a dozen carving tools neatly laid out on it. A scroll had been nailed to the rough boards above Teng's workbench. The floor of the shed was thick with shavings.

"I've just secured a contract and there's a lot to do."

"A contract?"

And that was when Hsi-wei first learned of the emperor's decree and how a technique he thought good only for decorating textiles was to be used to carry it out.

Teng explained how the work was done, the painstaking carving of wood blocks, the spreading of the ink, and the pressing. He took a small scroll from a shelf. "It's the only project I've completed, just a small one. I wanted to test things out." He nodded to the scroll fixed to the wall. "As you can see, the next job is much bigger."

Hsi-wei examined the little scroll and recognized a passage from the *Tripitaka*: "Purity or impurity depends on oneself. No one can purify another."

"I can press out as many copies of that as I like," Teng said. "There are ten big scrolls, and the contract requires fifty copies of each. I've a lot to do, Master Chen. What do you think. As a poet, I mean."

Hsi-wei understood that he was looking at something important, something with far-reaching implications, something that would change the world.

"It's amazing," he said. "It can bring so much good."

Teng, catching something in the poet's tone, looked questioningly at Hsi-wei. "But?"

"Well, isn't it possible that there might be some bad as well?"

"Really. How?"

"What if a lie is printed a thousand times and spread across the Empire?"

Teng was almost offended. He shook his head. "A lie. But we only print Buddhist texts and charms, as the emperor commanded. No lies."

"No. Not yet. And, I hope, there never will be. But I have to say how much I admire your work. Your characters are so clear and regular. I think because of this innovation more people will learn to read, like your daughter."

"And that is good!"

"Yes, it is. *Very* good."

"And yet. You still want to say something against it?"

"No, not against it, not at all. But I worry."

"What about. Those lies?"

"Not only that. I don't want to suggest anything but good will come from your work. Still, I wonder. Will memories shrink. Will people record everything and remember nothing?"

Teng scoffed. "I see you like to worry, Master Chen. Perhaps you're right and someday we'll print more than Buddhist charms. But that too is good. Think of those future people who will be able to read the emperor's edicts for themselves—think of peasants reading verses from the Shijing Masters—and Chen Hsi-wei!"

The dinner was wholesome and tasty. The Tengs were full of questions for Hsi-wei. They wanted to know how he had come to be a poet, who taught him to make straw sandals, what he had seen in his travels. The little boy sat squirming beside Hsi-wei and, as soon as the meal was over, insisted on showing the poet his toys.

"Will you be here for some time?" asked Mr. Teng.

"I took many orders today. It will take me a whole week to fulfill them."

"Good. Will you do us the honor of coming back to see us before you leave?"

Hsi-wei promised that he would.

It was Hsi-wei's habit to leave a poem thanking those who showed him hospitality but, on this occasion, it was the other way around. When he stopped to see the Tengs before taking to the road, Hsi-wei gave Guoliang a pair of sandals and Mr. Teng presented him with a handsomely printed copy of "Yellow Moon at Lake Weishan".

Hsi-wei's visit did result in new verses. He composed them later, after reflecting further on the innovation of printed texts. As was his usual custom, he didn't give the poem a title, but people did.

Wood-Block Wisdom

The Emperor is wise. He knows that to
unify his lands words will be better than war.
What once was used to press peonies on
court ladies' gowns will now strew the *Vinaya*
and *Abhidharma* from Sanxi to Sichuan.
Innkeepers will hang the Four Noble Truths
in their vestibules. *What you are is what you*

have been, a girl will recite; her sister will
giggle and retort, *What you will be is*
what you do now. Then their mother will
raise a finger and admonish both:
*Wear your selves like loose-fitting garment*s.
Peasants who learn to read will buy scrolls as
readily as dumplings. There will be histories,
books of remedies, tales of ghosts,
stories of revenge and wonder with new
heroes and fresh villains. The sound precepts
of Kon Qiu, the subtle sayings of Lao-tse,
the eccentric advice of Zhuang Zhou
shall be in a million hands. If people care
to print them, poems will be cheap as straw.
Mothers will read to open-mouthed toddlers
and children to their blind grandparents.

But what of calligraphy. Will those
scratchings for which Master Shen Kuo beat
me be forgiven because they are obsolete?
Printed characters will stand at attention,
uniform as the pikemen of General Gao.
But will people no longer admire the
elegant brushstrokes of the great Wang Xizhi?
Will they record all but remember nothing?
What if falsehoods should be pressed a thousand
times and spread through Shun and Lignan.
Mightn't they be like a butcher's leaded scale,
deceitful mismeasures believed by all.
Might that far-off bad outstrip this nearby good?

I wonder if, when the Son of Heaven
proclaimed his decree, some counselor—

the oldest and most cautious—felt
some compunction and mumbled in
his beard, recollecting the old legend
that, in a playful hour, the Buddha
loosed a few words from his golden mouth
and that ever since Heaven and Earth
have been choked with entangling briars?

COUNT MACTENBURG

As usual with what is called high diplomacy, the idea was straightforward and the details frightfully complicated. The goal was to regulate the pillage, sparing the colonizers unnecessary conflict with one another, and to cast over the brutal business a kind of magician's veil of legality, even benevolence. Portugal had formally called the conference, but it was obvious who the real organizer and sponsor was, whose ambition and power had prompted all of Europe to dispatch half their foreign ministries to Berlin. They were even meeting in his personal villa.

During a break in the proceedings, two senior diplomats, men who had known one another professionally for decades, took a stroll around the grounds together. Both felt relieved to get away from the stale air and Biedermeier furniture, the damask draperies and pompous insincerities of the conference table. The afternoon was fine and the Chancellor's lawn was dotted with men in black frock coats. There was not a woman to be seen.

"Like bears in the zoological gardens," observed Hauff dyspeptically.

"That's not very kind," replied van Schlichtma. "There's going to be a scramble anyway. Surely, it's better this way."

"An *organized* scramble sounds like a contradiction. But yes, I understand what you mean. It will much better for the scramblers, to be sure. You didn't chance to notice any Africans at the table, did you?"

"We've agreed to outlaw the slave trade," the other offered thinly.

Hauff scoffed. "A fig leaf, and a transparent one at that. If you believe that—well. . ."

"To be candid, I don't." Van Schlichtma stroked his short beard and groaned. "The Belgians."

"Leopold, you mean."

Having reached this much of an accord, the two men walked quietly for a full minute before Schlichtma wondered out loud, "Do you think it's to the Americans' credit, I mean that they refused to participate?"

"Oh, the Yankees don't want a chunk of Africa. It's too far off and as good as bespoke anyway. They may posture as they wish—they're good at moral puffery—but just have a word or two with the Mexicans or the Sioux."

Schlichtma smiled.

Hauff halted and turned to him. "Do you know what our respected host said about the Americans. 'There's a providence that protects idiots, drunkards, children, and the United States of America.'"

"I hadn't heard that. So, the man's a wit as well."

"Oh, better than a wit—a philosopher with arguments furnished by Krupp."

The two diplomats shared the professional intimacy of men who followed the same exacting vocation, one that made them members of an international fraternity and set them apart from their countrymen. They had been encountering each other in one capital or another for almost thirty years, like sea captains running across one another in various ports. Hauff was the more cynical of the two and for a couple of reasons. First, he had begun with more illusions. Second, he had witnessed close up the bullying and the wars by which their host had unified Germany. *Realpolitik*; that is to say, Blood and Iron. "The real god of the nineteenth century is power," was one of Hauff's widely quoted apothegms. Though less cynical, van Schlichtma also had few illusions. In his view, the sanctification of power was no great discovery nor anything particularly modern; it was merely the natural order of things. He saw his task not to deplore power but to tame it, as the fellow in the circus does the lions. That way nobody gets killed and multitudes are entertained. These distinctions notwithstanding, the two men genuinely liked one another. Affinities like theirs often have overlooked physical origins. In the case of these two, it may have had something to do with their height. Though Hauff was broad in the chest and van Schlichtma lanky, both were uncommonly tall, over six feet high. Their strides accorded even more exactly than their views.

"You have to admit Bismarck is impressive or at least imposing. He thinks on a large-scale."

"That he does, but he thinks like a Prussian."

"I see. You mean like a militarist. Apropos, do you know where our titles originated, Hauff?"

"Our titles?"

Van Schlichtma raised a pedantic finger. "*Ambassador.* The word."

Hauff waved his hand. "French, I always supposed."

"In a way. It comes from the Celts' word for the close companions of their war chiefs. Our roots are in war."

Hauff cocked his head. "And the Romans took over the word, I suppose, the same as they did Gaul?"

"*Bien sûr.* It's an old story, *mon ami.*"

"You seem to think life is a perpetual war, albeit with an infinite number of truces, like the one between men and women. As for me, I've always regarded war as a failure—in particular, a failure on *our* part."

Schlichtma thought he would tease his friend and alluded to an epigram more famous than any of Hauff's. "War's *not* the continuation of politics by other means, then?"

"Ach, *another* Prussian, that Clausewitz. It's a seductive saying, of course, clever, certainly very much to our host's taste."

"Actually, I feel the same as you. For old hands like us war isn't *continuous* with politics; it's the collapse of politics."

"You know, you really ought to write that one down."

Schlichtma patted his companion's shoulder. "Before you steal it?"

"Precisely!. Hauff laughed, then turned another epigram. "We diplomats are the world's only practical cosmopolites."

"So, we're careerists rather than patriots. Is that what you mean?"

Hauff pretended to be affronted. "Certainly not. We're a loyal guild, with some notable exceptions, of course. I meant that we're capable of broader views than those of our superiors because we're more accustomed to appreciating the interests of others."

"And by others you mean rivals?"

"Yes, but more than rivals—even of all of humanity, if I might be forgiven a bit of sentimental hyperbole."

"Well, there's something in what you say," Schlichtma conceded. "Still, we're mostly like those boys who deliver the telegrams, aren't we. We don't get to write the messages."

"Once in a while we do."

"Yes, on rare occasions we are listened to."

"Especially when things get out of hand. But sometimes a diplomat offers more than advice."

"Oh?"

"It's uncommon, I agree, but sometimes we can act. I could tell you a story that some might call heroic."

"About yourself?"

Hauff clicked his heels and made an ironic half-bow. "Hardly. But thank you, Schlichtma. You do me honor."

"Well, you said we're a loyal guild. Once in a while, we're even loyal to each other."

"As regards loyalty, my story is the *non plus ultra*."

"You interest me." Van Schlichtma reached into his vest and consulted his watch. "We have another twenty minutes. Can you tell your story that quickly. Won't do to keep the Herr Chancellor waiting."

"Twenty minutes will suffice."

"Pre-Bismarck gossip, then?"

"From the days of Oldenburg and Hanover, Baden and Württemberg, Woldeck and Lippe-Detmold—when sovereignty was as common in Germany as pickled herring."

"In those good old days it was a seller's market in diplomatic talent, but so very confusing," joked Schlichtma.

"My story dates from the fifties."

"Ah, back when we were really alive."

"Speak for yourself, Schlichtma. Remember, I have a young wife, my second. I introduced you to her in Paris just last year."

"My apologies. That city is so crowded with beautiful things it's difficult to recall them all. Now, if you please— the story?"

"Since your memory's so poor, you probably won't recall the Nassau-Hessen crisis."

"No—but wait. Yes, I do remember something. Nearly came to blows, right?"

"On the cusp of war, yes. The Duke of Nassau, Adolf,

had reigned for fifteen years but was still an intemperate baby and, between us, not the most intelligent of dukes. He required managing."

"Backed a loser in 1866, didn't he?"

"In fairness, so did many others."

"As you say. So, what *bêtise* did Duke Adolf commit?"

"He composed a memorandum commanding his generals to prepare to occupy certain fertile borderlands he imagined belonged to him and not, as everybody else agreed, Hessen-Darmstadt. Worse, he ordered his secretary to draw up twenty copies of the thing, one for each general plus two for his uncle, the field-marshal."

"That was an imprudence."

"Yes. Within a week one of the copies found its way to Darmstadt and Hessen began to mobilize."

"Ah, it's coming back to me now. But it all fizzled out with no harm done, correct?"

"Thanks to Count Mactenburg, yes."

"Mactenburg. He was foreign minister?"

"Yes, and a true patriot. Yet I'd also count him in support of my claims that we diplomats can take a broad view of humanity's interests, that war ought always to be regarded as a failure—the policies of our triumphant host notwith-standing—and finally that our guild can do more than hand over telegrams."

"You knew Mactenburg?"

"I met him once towards the end of his life and only briefly."

"What sort of fellow was he?"

Hauff shrugged. "As honest as a diplomat can be without ceasing to be a diplomat. Physically, he was a good deal like you, actually. Bit of a beanpole, but very dignified, with an admirable chin every bit as strong as your own. When I met Mactenburg, he was in ill health and quite poor, reduced to living with his daughter and her husband in a wretched apartment in Koblenz."

"The man was a count. What about his lands?"

"Lost them all. Lost them on purpose."

"On purpose. You mean he forfeited them?"

"A little patience, Schlichtma. We have to go back to the feast in fifteen minutes."

"Very well. Tell on."

"Count Mactenburg went to his master as soon as he learned of his blunder. He had prepared to expostulate with the Duke but Adolf was already full of regret. In fact, he was frightened. He hadn't reckoned on war, you see, just a crafty *fait accompli* to be followed by quiet acquiescence from Hessen. Mactenburg easily persuaded the Duke that his claim to the marches was illegitimate and would certainly not be supported by any other state, neither duchy nor republic. *Fix it, Mactenburg*, said the duke if you please—just the sort of imperative with which we're both familiar. But in this instance, I imagine it sounded more like a desperate plea than a command."

"A tricky predicament," Schlichtma remarked. "And the contents of the memorandum had been become public?"

"Public enough."

"That would have added to the difficulty. So, Mactenburg had to find a way of forestalling war without the Duke losing face."

"*Exactement*. And he managed it too, and more. He detached the Duke from his folly. The young men of Nassau and Hessen weren't slaughtered, the fertile borderlands weren't raked by artillery shells or despoiled by foragers. In fact, everything quickly returned to the *status quo ante*, save for Mactenburg himself."

"Did he do some deal with Darmstadt?"

"No. He returned to the Duke and told him how he saw a way one way out of the crisis. 'But, my dear Mactenburg, how?' said the dull duke, tentatively overjoyed. And Count Mactenburg replied bravely, 'We blame *me*.'"

"Ah, I see."

"A heroic self-sacrifice, Schlichtma. We diplomats really ought to subscribe to erect a statue of Mactenburg on the frontier between Nassau and Hessen."

The diplomats of Europe were heading back toward the villa in pairs, as if summoned by Noah. Van Schlichtma hauled out his watch. "Time to go, Hauff. How exactly did Mactenburg manage it?"

"Just as I said; he took it all on himself. Said the Duke must inform Hessen that the memorandum was written by his foreign minister without authorization, that his personal signature was forged. Mactenburg told him to add that his foreign minister wanted to provoke a war because he personally planned to profit from it, forsooth. The Duke must also inform Darmstadt that he had naturally demanded Mactenburg's resignation and express profound regret that the Count's title, being hereditary, could not be revoked, but that his estates had been confiscated and the disgraced man permanently exiled."

"That is a terrible story indeed. Did anybody in Darmstadt believe it?"

Hauff coughed twice. "Come now, you know as well as I that doesn't matter in the least. Statesmen aren't historians; the only story that matters is the official one."

Van Schlichtma made a bitter face. "And the outcome of by this damnable conference will be officially presented as an act of benevolence. Spheres of influence established, Leopold given a free hand, all land-grabs sanctified."

Hauff shrugged. "More or less."

Together they made their way up the terrace to the French doors then paused, peering from the sunlit garden into the impenetrable darkness inside.

Van Schlichtma said, "It's ironic. A decade later Hessen and Nassau were merged, weren't they?"

"And promptly annexed by our gracious host."

"So, it was when you saw him in Koblenz that Mactenburg told you the tale?"

"Not exactly. The Count was not a man to divulge even dead state secrets, or secrets of dead states. No, I told *him*. You see, I'd pieced it together and he didn't deny it. He thanked me for visiting then spoke about Bismarck, whom he professed to admire—to a certain degree."

"Indeed?"

"As I was about to say farewell, he quoted the Chancellor at me. 'Anyone who has ever looked into the glazed eyes of a soldier dying on the battlefield will think hard before starting a war.' How's that for irony?"

"Sad, sad. And poor Count Mactenburg has been forgotten."

"How many of us are not forgotten?" As Hauff opened the door for his colleague, he added, "Gird up your loins, Schlichtma, and your conscience."

Hsi-wei and the Little Straw Sandals

The most durable achievements of the Sui Dynasty are the rebuilding of the Great Wall and the construction of the Grand Canal. But the brief reign of the Sui accomplished more. Emperor Wen's reinstatement of the examination system, his penal, land, and currency reforms along with his promotion of Buddhism can be said to have laid the foundation for the glories of the Tang Dynasty. To carry out the Sui construction projects and fight their wars, millions were conscripted, and countless lives sacrificed. The common people paid their taxes in labor or military service. It is not surprising that these losses figure in many of the poems of Chen Hsi-wei, who was, after all, a peasant himself. Hsi-wei lived to see the fall of the Sui Dynasty and the promising start of its successor. A minister of the new dynasty and an admirer of Hsi-wei's verses, Fang Xuan-ling paid an extended visit to the poet in his retirement and kept extensive notes of their conversations. His journal is the best source on the origins of Hsi-wei's poems.

• • •

As a special gift, Fang Xuan-ling brought along three cakes of green tea which, he said, was becoming popular at court. After Fang's attendant had brewed a pot, the two men settled down to talk in the tiny patio the poet called his courtyard.

Always courteous, Hsi-wei complimented the tea.

Fang took out his writing materials and asked if Hsi-wei recalled a poem popularly known as "The Little Straw Sandals".

The poet put down his cup. "I do remember it, My Lord. It's one where I tried to say something by not saying it."

"Saying by not saying. Is that something you picked up from the Chan Buddhists?" Laying his cup aside and taking up his brush, Fang prepared to make a note as he recited the well-known Chan principle, "Never tell to plainly."

Hsi-wei chuckled. "Oh, nothing so spiritually elevated as that, Lord Feng."

"Well then, I would like to know how you came to write that poem. Can you recall?"

"I can. In fact, I remember it very well and, if I tell you, I think you'll see what I wasn't saying."

Fang finished his tea. "That sounds like a challenge. Very well, please proceed, Master Hsi-wei."

"I wrote the poem one summer when I was making my way through Liangzhou. I came to a little village called Yanshi Kun. Like so many others I saw that year, the place was in a pitiable state. No dogs barked when I came down the dusty road. The peasants' huts were in various states of disrepair; the neglected fields were choked with weeds. A few under-nourished, half-dressed children ran around but most slumped under trees looking exhausted and despondent, like their elders."

"What was the matter?"

"Yanshi Kun was a village populated by those too old to do much work and those too young to do any at all. The whole district was poor, but Yanshi Kun was destitute."

"Ah, that explains the lack of dogs. They couldn't even afford to feed them.

"My Lord, I'm afraid it was rather the other way around. The dogs had fed them."

Fang, a city man from an old family that had always been well off, blushed. "Ah. I didn't think of that."

Hsi-wei, a little regretful to have embarrassed his guest, continued. "Though it wasn't likely I'd find customers there, I set up my sign by the village well. A few people gathered around, not to order straw sandals but to beg for news. Of course, I couldn't tell them what they really wanted to know—about those who'd gone away—but I shared what I could, things I'd heard along the way, though not everything. I didn't tell them about a recent tragedy at the Canal or the latest reverse in Goguryeo. Things for these people were bad enough as they were."

Fang tried to lighten the mood. "Did you sell any sandals at all?"

Hsi-wei grinned. "My Lord, you *know* I did. One pair."

"Then I suppose you had little to do in the village."

"On the contrary. I was very busy in Yanshi Kun. I made myself useful. I remember repairing a leaking roof and replacing some rotted boards on a shed. Though it was late in the season, I even planted some rice for an ancient farmer who couldn't bend over anymore. The old fellow kept nodding and smiling at me. I weeded an old woman's vegetable plot and I tried to entertain the children."

"Did you gather the children, or did they just come to you?"

"The youngest had never seen a man my age and others must have had happy memories of their fathers and uncles. Maybe that's why they flocked around me."

"And how did you entertain them?"

"I can't recall all I did, the games I devised. But I do

remember reciting a poem I thought they would like. It's about a smart little girl named Mai Ling. Is it possible you know that one?"

Fang made a serious face, concentrating. "I think I might. Do you have a copy?"

"As it happens, I do. I could get it for you. Would you like to read it?"

"I'd like it even better if you read it to me."

The poet went into his cottage and returned with a small, rather soiled scroll.

"I'll pretend I'm one of those children in Yanshi Kun."

"As you wish, My Lord," said Hsi-wei. He unfurled the scroll and read the poem that people titled "Mai Ling's Good Idea".

Long ago, there was war between Night and Day.
They taunted and insulted each other, all spite and spleen.
Like a woolen blanket, Night tried to blot out Day
while Day, like a bonfire, toiled to outshine the stars.
People and animals suffered from these mighty battles,
enjoying respites only at noontime and midnight.

With Winter and Summer, it was much the same.
They detested each other and all the more
for being so evenly matched. Midsummer and Midwinter
were calm, but, in between, the seasons' wrestled
raising tempests and earthquakes to afflict the world.

One day, as her grandparents were complaining of it all,
Mai Ling spoke up, a little girl of just eight years.
"Nobody can tell me what time is or how much there is of it.
So, why not just make more. Then Uncle Winter can have
his time and Auntie Summer hers; then Day can be day

all day and Night can be night the whole night through."

Mai Ling's grandfather laughed indulgently, as old men do.
But her granny reproached him. "Listen to the child.
New eyes see better than old ones." And so, the people
convened a parley with Day and Night; they invited
Winter and Summer too. When all were settled,
Day and Night and Winter and Summer glaring
at one another, Mai ling got up and explained her idea.

"Uncle Day, when you get sleepy you shouldn't struggle.
Auntie Night, when you're worn out, you ought to go to bed.
You shouldn't rub your eyes and spite each other.
Neighbors need boundaries, little walls, not too high.
We can make new time if only you'll agree.
We'll set fences between you: Dusk and Dawn.

"And as for you, Uncle Winter and Auntie Summer,
you should do the same and not crash into each other
ruining our rice with untimely heat and blasts of cold.
We'll set new seasons between you, just little ones, low walls.
As Winter tires, we'll have Spring, and as Summer fades, Fall.

That's my idea. In the night people and animals can go
to sleep and during the day we'll work and play.
In Spring we'll sow and in the Fall we'll reap.
Then you can stop this nasty wrangling and enjoy yourselves.
Then we shall all be grateful to you, blessing
each day and every night, each season and every year."

"I'd forgotten how charming it was," said Fang, picturing of happy young peasants hearing the poem. "The children must have been delighted."

Hsi-wei didn't reply at once and, when he did, it was in a

somber tone. "My Lord, the village was very poor, and the children were terribly hungry."

"I can imagine."

"With respect, I'm not sure you can. Those children didn't have enough strength to express delight. But they did sit quietly so I was at least able to give their grandparents a little time to themselves. And the people were generous with me, as the poor usually are. The less they have the more they share. The old couple whose thatch roof I repaired wanted to give me their bed, though it was only a burlap sack stuffed with rushes. 'We'll sleep on the floor beside the children. It will be a pleasure for us.' I declined, of course, and took myself to the shed I'd repaired. Except for the smell, the pigs were long gone.

"The next day I did some more work, mostly lifting things, as I recall. An old woman watched me, impossible to say whether with approval or suspicion. A tiny, barefoot toddler was clinging to her. He kept saying 'Zumu, Zumu,' and tugging at her skirt. It sounded like a whine, a plea. He was as thin as the others but his stomach was swollen."

"Ah, a big stomach. Then he was well fed?"

Hsi-wei shook his head, again embarrassed to have to explain. "No, My Lord. It's what happens to children who are starving."

Fang had nothing to say to that and Hsi-wei quickly resumed.

"In the afternoon, it grew hot. The old woman led the boy over to a dusty willow tree and sat him down with a group of children lolling in the shade."

"This was the old woman in the poem?"

"Yes. Mrs. Chu. Another old woman told me later that Mrs. Chu's son had been lost in Goguryeo and, to pay the tax, her daughter-in-law went to the Canal. That happened the year before, when the boy was barely two years old. No one expected his mother to come back except Mrs. Chu. I could see the boy was falling asleep, but I could hear him still murmuring 'Zumu,' not pleadingly now, but with resignation. That was when she approached me.

"'You make sandals?' she asked. I said I did.

"She nodded toward the willow. 'My grandson is walking now. His mother will be so surprised. I've been thinking. I want to buy him a pair of sandals. How much would that cost?'"

Hsi-wei stopped. "Another cup of tea?"

"Now I know what you were telling without telling," said Fang.

"Yes?"

"The poem tells about Mrs. Chu, the little boy, and the sandals. You also said interesting things about your feelings concerning your work. But the poem is really about what's missing, isn't it. About *who's* missing, I mean. The dogs, the pigs, and most of all the parents."

Hsi-wei smiled, got to his feet, collected their cups, and went to fetch more green tea.

• • •

THE LITTLE STRAW SANDALS

Mrs. Chu ordered sandals for her grandson
Wanglei. She beamed, proud that the boy could
already walk. "They'll be his first," she said.
She took something from the pocket of her skirt.
It was a little Wanglei-sole-sized cucumber.

"This is how small you're to make them."

Fashioning such tiny sandals isn't simple.
I used the finest straw, pulled the strand.
taut, made the knots tight, and carefully sliced
off the loose ends. I made them sturdy.
Wanglei was bound to be rough on them.
Straw sandals are humble, useful, honest,
like Mrs. Chu who wanted to pay me.

I've had more customers than readers.
I'm happy when people admire their new sandals,
hold them up and, turn them this way and that,
and say it must have been hard to make them.
But I'm even happier when they say that
making straw sandals must be easy for me.
To tell the truth, it's no different with my poems.

CITY OF CAESARS

Concerning Ciudad de los Césares, known variously as The Wandering City, Lin Lin, Trapananda, and Elelín

The Spanish imagination, inflamed by the immensity of the New World, the speed with which the conquistadors vanquished its inhabitants and appropriated their treasures, readily credited stories of cities of inexhaustible wealth and magical power, the Fountain of Youth, El Dorado. One might suppose these tales were mere fables of the genuine riches and fresh starts New Spain afforded the adventurous. Yet the Spanish really believed the wild tales of golden cities and searched relentlessly for them before, only with the greatest reluctance, giving up and dismissing the stories as legends. Yet, Troy, Machu Picchu, and Vilcabamba have all been discovered. Legendary cities are often real enough; only the tons of gold and rejuvenating fountains were mythical.

Among the so-called lost cities of the New World, the one to which the most peculiar beliefs were attached, and the most names, is Ciudad de los Césares. From the sixteenth century to the eighteenth, Spaniards searched for it in the mountains between Chile and Argentina, where it was said to nestle between two peaks, one of gold, one of diamonds. The city was said to have been founded by European survivors of a shipwreck in the Magellan Straits; other versions had it inhabited by Patagonian giants, the last of the Incas, or by ghosts. In the most popular versions, the city is enchanted, visible only intermittently, surrounded by a protective fog that will dissipate only when the world comes to an end.

These absurdities did not discourage greedy men from looking the place. On the contrary, between its first official mention in 1526 until well into the eighteenth century, numerous expeditions went in search of the city which withdrew further into the fog until, at last, its existence was dismissed by the Age of Reason with a knowing sneer.

Two Dominicans. One Famous, One Obscure

Bartolome de las Casas, born in 1484, one year after Martin Luther, was among the most decent men of his time. Shocked in his youth by witnessing the extermination of the Caribbean Indians, he took holy orders and became Spain's most persistent opponent of the exploitation of the peoples of the New World, of the slavery and genocide too often abetted by his Church. Las Casas is the author of *Account of the Destruction of the Indies* (1552), editor of Columbus's journal, and is revered as a far-seeing pioneer of human rights and international law. On the other hand, he also advocated the importation of African slaves to replace and spare the dwindling number of Indians. But, to his credit, he was honest enough, and lived long enough, to acknowledge his monstrous error.

Unknown to history is las Casas' young disciple, Bernardus Acacio Espinoza, likewise a Dominican, who was sent by las Casas to the southern reaches of the Empire to report on conditions there. Espinoza's report, apparently intended only for las Casas, was unknown until the recent repurposing of the medieval monastery of San Sebastian in Tudela as a deluxe parador. Archivists from Salamanca were given the entire library of the monastery and estimate it will take eight years just to catalogue it. By chance, however, a graduate assistant assigned to the work happened on the unbound Espinoza report and, as such people will, began to read it.

Espinoza's report concerning the lost city was written in 1547, a period when the tale of an Andean El Dorado, neglected for nearly a decade, was being recalled with new excitement. This was owing to the arrival in the capital of a handful of shipwrecked Spanish sailors who had survived for seven years outside civilization. It was their unexpected reappearance that reminded people of the story of a fabulous mountain city founded by just such shipwrecked Europeans. Now that its existence again seemed plausible, two fresh expeditions set off into the mountains. One returned empty-handed; the other did not return at all.

Espinoza, on the other hand, gives an account of his sojourn in the elusive city—or at least one he took for it. He also claims to be the person who bestowed on the place its most popular name, the one by which it is still chiefly known, Ciudad de los Césares.

BERNARDUS ACACIO ESPINOZA IN CHILOE

In 1546, Bernardus Espinoza traveled to the island of Chiloe, best known for contributing to humanity the world's most widely cultivated potato. The denizens of the island had only recently been converted, and, as has often happens, the theologically flexible missionaries found it expedient to integrate indigenous beliefs with those of the One True Church. The locals, Espinoza notes, were not being ill-treated and appeared to have had little difficulty in blending the new faith with the old. And, of course, everybody was pleased about the potatoes.

It was through his examination of the island's theological gallimaufry that Espinoza

heard of an oral tradition he connected to the lost city in the Andes about which he had heard so much talk before setting off from the River Plate. He remarks dryly that the beliefs of the Chiloeans exploded the notion that the city could be populated by shipwrecked Europeans. "I supposed," he wrote, "that the tradition, being heathenish, must also be ancient." His report on Chiloe includes this translation of what a local *cacique* told him:

There is in the high country across the water an enchanted city, not given to any traveler to discover. Only at the end of the world will the city of Lin Lin become visible to convince unbelievers of its existence.

With a mixture of amusement and admiration Espinoza recounts how the missionaries turned this fairy tale to account, using it to reinforce the doctrines of the Last Judgment and Kingdom Come, "when," he concludes piously, "unbelievers even in enchanted cities shall be overthrown, thrust down into the Pit and damned, when time shall come to an end and every mystery will be revealed."

A VALLEY IN THE ANDES

Espinoza's rendition of the vicissitudes of his return journey to the River Plate resembles an Anabasis boiled down to a series of disastrous vignettes. A raft is reduced to splinters in rapids, pack animals tumble from cliffs, soldiers fall out, illness and cold cause many to perish. There is a recurring motif of falling, of everything going down—except fevers. On these mischances Espinoza does not dwell; nevertheless, the sense is of a doomed odyssey. Ever mindful of his master and only reader, he has strong words for the Spanish soldiers' abuse of their Indian bearers and the animals. The weather was against them, as the group unwisely set off in the middle of June. The Indians, conscripted from among the lowlanders of the piedmont, could not bear the winds and snow squalls, and those who did not die ran off. The soldiers began to quarrel among themselves, then took to fighting; two were killed and three gravely wounded. After this catastrophe the remaining company separated into three bands. Two were willing to take the carping Dominican with them but the captain of the third, having often been upbraided by Espinoza, refused. Espinoza diligently records in his narra-tive— more, perhaps, out of humor than resentment—the man's long-winded denunciation of him as a "whining whey-faced Indian-loving eunuch bastard of a diseased Salamancan whore."

Disgusted with his countrymen, commending himself to the Virgin and his patron saint, whom, he notes, also endured alpine cold, Espinoza took what he was able to carry and bravely set off on his own, choosing a path the others rejected, one leading higher into the mountains where the peaks were wreathed in snow and mist.

After five days of exhausting trekking and privation, four nights when he all but froze to death, Espinoza emerged from the clouds to see a valley with many buildings— a walled city—nestled at the center of neatly terraced farmland. He mentions his amazement that some of the buildings had arches.

According to Espinoza, what he had stumbled on was the lost city, minus the mountain of gold and the one of diamonds.

Los Césares

Espinoza's account of what he found in the valley makes up the longest portion of his report, though one might wish it still longer, for it arouses a curiosity he is not always at pains to satisfy.

The narrative begins by describing how he was met on coming down from the mountain, half-frozen and starving. He was greeted humanely, with kindness, though he notes that the people, the men and the women both, were disappointingly laconic. They dealt with his immediate needs efficiently but did not show much surprise at seeing him. He quickly discovered that several spoke Spanish and, indeed, were either Spanish or mestizo. The greater number of the people had, he writes, "*el semblante inca*," the Incan countenance. The Indians could speak passable Castilian and the Spaniards were equally fluent in the native tongue with which he was unfamiliar.

As he staggered down the terraces toward the city, half a dozen men and three women came out through the gates and at once took him inside the walls. The men did not ask him anything but were gentle, treating him, Espinoza writes, "as if I were a deaf child." Once inside the walls, he was struck by the style of the buildings, some of the Incan lintel-and-post variety, others distinctly Spanish in character, with stuccoed walls, arched windows, and roof tiles of fired-clay. All the structures looked well-made and sturdy. The grandest building Espinoza describes as "a sort of mongrel cathedral, having pyramidal steps on four sides, a carved façade, and two towers, neither crowned by a cross."

He was conducted to the home of one of the Spaniards, a tall, bearded man of thirty or thirty-five, who introduced himself as Jeronimo Rugera. Espinoza confesses he must have looked as spent as he felt. Rugera showed himself so anxious for his guest that he declined to answer any questions until Espinoza had been given a warm bath. While he was bathing, Rugera laid out dry clothing, a pair of breeches cut from soft leather, a shirt of wool so fine it felt like silk, and a colorful poncho. Then he served Espinoza a large bowl of hot porridge.

In the course all this hospitality, people kept arriving at Don Jeronimo's door, curious to see the stranger though they appeared studiously nonchalant. By the time Espinoza emerged bathed, clothed, and fed a small crowd had gathered in the large room at the front of the house. His host asked, "Well, Señor, I'm glad to see you looking much improved. Now, who are you?" First offering thanks to the Virgin and his patron saint, then to his host, Espinoza gave his name and explained that he was a Dominican. Rugera frowned at this and said rather harshly that was of no significance to him. Another man who stood at the forefront of the visitors whispered the word "Inquisition" to the Indian woman at his side. She looked puzzled for a moment, as if trying to recall the meaning of the word, then she nodded, took a step forward to scrutinize Espinoza, shrugged, then left.

When Espinoza asked the name of the city in which he found himself, Rugera replied that it was called Elelín by the Spaniards and Trapananda by the Indians.

Espinoza writes that he was perplexed by the relationship between the Spaniards and the Indians. While it was apparent that some of the men were superior in rank to others, those granted deference were not always Spanish and those who showed it not invariably Indians.

Of the physical and economic disposition of the city he writes:

The settlement is well situated. Ingenious channels conduct the water that runs down from the irrigated terraces. The people keep livestock in pens and corrals outside the city walls. As it was winter, I could not judge the fruitfulness of the land, but the citizens I saw were all well-nourished and I was shown two well-stocked store-houses. The people were proud of these places and most pleased that I admired them.

Espinoza spent two days recovering his strength in Rugera's house. On the third day, his host conducted him to the largest of the private homes. Espinoza reports his host's words: "We are going to the *palacete*. The king would like to see you for himself."

They were met at the high doors by two unarmed attendants, one Spanish, one Indian, and led into a hall with three arches at the back opening on a garden with a fountain at its center. On a dais before these arches the king sat on an elaborately carved chair, his throne. Though he was short, fat, and dark, he looked impressive in a feathered headdress and a breastplate of beaten gold in the Andalusian style. Espinoza was astonished to see that he was an Indian. The attendants—the Spaniard as well as the Indian—knelt to him, as did Rugera, who prompted Espinoza to do likewise.

The king did not put any questions to the Dominican; in fact, he said nothing at all. He merely looked Espinoza—restored now to his brown robe—up and down, then motioned Rugera to approach and exchanged with him a few whispers, all the while looking suspiciously at Espinoza. Then, flicking his hand as if to scatter flies, he dismissed them.

Outside the palace, Rugera heaved a sigh and looked relieved. "At least for the time being," he said, "you will not be executed. I am very glad."

Espinoza was shocked. Though he does not record this conversation in detail, one can imagine him asking, "Executed. For the time being?"

"It will depend," Rugera might have replied.

"On what?"

"I have to talk with some people this afternoon. I will explain tonight."

Espinoza reports spending the remainder of the day with the women of Rugera's household. He gives his impressions of Rugera's wife and the others, extolling their good sense and friendly relations with one another.

Of his state of mind, he writes:

> I was in anxiety for my safety, and began to calculate the chances of a successful escape into the mountains. I was in no way reassured when I considered the way the king had regarded me. I began to conceive that he had examined my person not only with curiosity and suspicion only but also with apprehension, as if I was there to do harm him or his city.

At this point, Espinoza interpolates a paragraph describing his puzzlement over the relations of the people in the city. His devotion to the humane views of las Casas notwithstanding, he admits being astounded by the cordial dealings between Indians and Spaniards, so accustomed was he to assuming the superiority of his own kind. He observes that, while he was gratified to see the Indians treated with respect and had long been reconciled to the custom of Spaniards taking Indian wives, he was disturbed by the terms on which the Indians presumed to live in equality with Europeans and speculates on how, in its isolation, the city might have fallen into this indiscriminate mixing of races, cultures, and languages. Then, recalling his host's exchange of whispers with the king, he wonders if the Spaniards might not really be in charge, allowing the Indians a powerless king, a pretense maintained for the sake of peace. But then, reviewing what he had observed of the degrees of status among the city's inhabitants and noting that these did not appear to depend on race, he discards this hypothesis with an expression of puzzlement.

At this point there is a break in the manuscript. Evidently, several pages are missing. What remains is the conclusion of Espinoza's report which is an account of what Jeronimo Rugera confided to him that night, his last in the city:

> After we had taken food with the people of the household sitting all together, as was their custom, my host invited me into a small room at the rear of the house. Here weapons were stored. I saw some rusted armor and swords, three old-style casques, two pikes, and a crossbow. We sat across from one another at a rough table, so close that our beards nearly touched. Rugera began by telling me bluntly that he and the other Spaniards had forsworn the Church, having taken account of its many sins, that the Indians had likewise renounced their pagan priests and bloody rituals. When I asked about the church building, he replied somberly that it was not faith they had given up but those who abused the faith of others.
>
> I felt a powerful urge to castigate the man, to implore him to think of his soul's fate; however, being mindful of your book and all I had myself witnessed in the New World, I found myself too

ashamed to speak. Instead, I posed to him the question I had been pondering all that day; I asked how the city was governed. Rugera's answer, which was not brief, filled me with wonder, which delighted him, just as the people had smiled when I admired their storehouses.

According to Rugera, the Spaniards were indeed survivors of a shipwreck. They had made their way north through Patagonia and became lost in the mountains where they encountered a large band of Incas fleeing to the south. It was in this valley that they met. Both were prepared to fight but they talked instead. This was owing to an Indian sage. According to Rugera, the man was able to speak in our language. The talks continued for a period of two weeks, hc said, becoming ever deeper and more complex. Meanwhile, the two groups set up camp and mingled with one another in a precarious armistice. The Indians stated they were fleeing the Spanish but admitted that they did not like being ruled by the great Inca, a single man, even if he were also a god. The Spanish, for their part, agreed that a tyrant was not to their taste either, not even if God had placed the man's fundament on a throne of gold. Both parties also criticized their respective religions, finding them both sanguinary, making too much of death and too little of life. Yet neither knew any other method of government than kingship. And so when they decided to found a city together they also created a new constitution unlike anything ever known. The arrangements were arrived at together, with the Incan sage making the initial suggestion. His idea was to hedge in royal power.

How? *More kings*, he said. Thus, it was decided that every man in the city would be a king, though not of equal authority. The king I had met the day before was, Rugera said, the least powerful of all. When I expressed my astonishment and recalled to him the *palacete*, the kneeling, the throne, he explained that in this city the king who rules, the one who is treated royally, knelt to, and given the *palacete* in which to live, has the least authority. True, he makes all decisions—on legal and land disputes, construction, and family feuds—but his judgments have no effect until they are approved by all the other kings, who are applied to in a prescribed order based on wealth. Therefore, the last word on all matters, the power to accept or reject, but also to modify, belongs to the city's meanest citizen, who on this ground is held to be the most powerful king. To put it mathematically, in their city wealth is inversely proportional to power. Worldly goods are given respect but only that owing to an appearance. The system works, Rugera said proudly, because every man regards the city as his own and lives in the eyes of others.

Rugera explained, he had absented himself during the afternoon to make the rounds of the kings. The last approved the verdict that I could live but only if I would swear by the most sacred of oaths known to me never to divulge the location of the city. I told Rugera there was talk everywhere of his city, which was thought by some to be full of treasure and by others a mere legend. At this Rugera frowned and said he was not surprised, for others had preceded me and must have spoken of the place. Though so far it appeared all had kept their vow not to say where the city was located, doubtless some had been tempted to lie about the gold and diamonds. It was not forbidden to speak of the city, he said, only to reveal its where-abouts. Indeed, he added in words that touched me and would have moved you, they wanted their manner of life to become widely known, to prove that Spaniards and Indians could exist in dignity and mutual trust without murdering, pillaging, or enslaving one another— all under the eye of gods who had no priests. Here he seized my, cassock and gave it a good shake.

I would have to decide, he said. If I gave my solemn oath the next morning in the presence of all the kings of Elelín and Trapananda, I would be allotted provisions and sent on my way. Otherwise, he said with evident compunction, for I believe the man had conceived some fondness for me, I would be decapitated. "Will you swear by your Virgin?" he asked. "She is yours also," I replied sadly. Rugera was silent for a moment and then, smiling on me in a brotherly fashion, said there was a third alternative. I could renounce my holy vocation and increase the number of the city's kings by one.

As a faithful son of the Church, I informed him that of course this was impossible.

So ends Espinoza's account of the place he named Ciudad de los Césares.

HSI-WEI, SONG SIDAO AND SHI XING

The forgotten poet Song Sidao was the only son of a minor landlord in Yanzhou. As the boy showed early promise, his father engaged a tutor for him. When Emperor Wen came to power, Song's father conceived the ambition that Sidao would find a position in the new government. The rumor was that the new dynasty would favor merit over family. When the tutor admitted he had taught Sidao all he could, the boy's father scraped together the money to send him to Daxing. Song's father admonished him sternly: "You must enroll in one of the schools in the capital, distinguish yourself in every way, and pass the examination."

In Daxing, with the help of a distant cousin, the boy found a place in one of the new academies set up to train officials. He excelled in his studies, including military training. He was particularly good with the bow and arrow, seldom missing his mark. But Song's greatest delight was reading and reciting the Shijing and Chu Ci masters.

After successfully passing his examination, Song was appointed to a minor post in the Ministry of Revenue where he quickly became popular with his colleagues and superiors. "That Song is good company," they said. "He tells such amusing stories."

Song's first poems were on themes of nature. Later, he began to write satirically about court life, of which he was a sharp observer. His verses circulated widely and people in the capital knew who he was. Song also made up stories that amounted to thinly veiled gossip to entertain the guests at the dinners to which his colleagues invited him. Before long, his wit and eagerness to please gained him many invitations to banquets where he was begged to recite his verses and tell his stories. Song enjoyed mingling with his betters, and he liked the fine food. He became addicted to his social life and, while never neglecting his duties at the Ministry, used his spare time to prepare stories and poems for every dinner.

At a banquet hosted by a high official in the Ministry of Personnel, Song was encouraged to share his latest poem. He recited a conventional poem about a garden coming alive in early spring but was then begged for a story. "Something," his host stipulated, "more entertaining than peonies and irises." Without considering the consequences, Song obliged with a story he had thought up the day before.

"During the civil wars so gloriously ended by our Emperor, Lord Chang Shimin commanded the cavalry of the Duke of Shu. This Chang had a stable of fine horses, all of whom had proved themselves in battle, never shying even before a line of bristling pikes. One day, while reviewing the stock, Lord Chang caught sight of a snow-white colt. He inquired and was told it belonged to one of his captains. He decided he must possess the colt and train him up himself. He thought of how fine he would look leading his men on a white stallion. So, he took the colt; the captain could hardly refuse. But things turned out badly. The colt missed his dam and the apple orchard beside his old pasture. The older horses in Chang's stable resented the newcomer, their master's new favorite, and took every opportunity to kick and bite the colt. And so, no one was happy—not the harassed colt or his bereft dam, not the faithful warhorses who no longer rejoiced to see their master. So, not even Lord Chang was happy."

Everybody at the table knew that the Minister of Cavalry had recently taken a girl of fifteen as a concubine, the daughter of a man who had been badly wounded in a border skirmish with the Turks. The gossip was that the Minister's four wives were resentful and not slow to show it to either the Minister or the poor girl, who was said to be utterly miserable.

Song's story was far too direct. If he had been more circumspect, told some other story, or at least not made the greedy Chang a cavalry commander, then he might not have been summoned to his chief's office two days later, dismissed from his post, and exiled from the capital.

Song headed north. Sometimes he was able to find work along the way but often he was reduced to begging. He was now a long way from the warm offices, opulent pavilions, silk robes, and ten-course banquets of Daxing. Though his direction was toward home, he could not face his father. So, skirting his native district in Yanzhou, he continued going north without a destination. In the region locals called Tuoba Wei, he came on one of the Ch'an monasteries that had sprung up since the arrival from the West of bearded Bodhidharma a century before. Buddhism was flourishing under Emperor Wen who saw it as a unifying force for his Empire. He declared himself a Buddhist, praised its doctrines, subsidized its temples, and initiated the printing of Buddhist scriptures and their dissemination throughout the empire.

Song never took the slightest interest in Buddhism but now, in the north, famished, footsore, and humbled, he was glad to find refuge in a place that welcomed him as it would anyone else. He was intrigued by the monks who possessed nothing but appeared happy whereas he had nothing and was not happy at all. He conversed a little with the Master whose oblique way of speaking along with his mixture of dignity and modesty impressed him. Song worked alongside the young monks and entertained them with descriptions of court life. They made clear, however, their distaste for his satirical verses. Song found that he too no longer cared for them.

Song found he enjoyed asking the Master questions and how the Master answered them. From one week to the next, he put off his departure. In the end, he never left at all.

. . .

During his time studying with Master Shen Kuo in the capital, Hsi-wei came across several poems of Song Sidao; and, though he did not rate them very highly, regarding them as frivolous, he found them diverting. He asked Master Shen about the poet and learned that Song, like so many of his colleagues, had been exiled.

Years later, during his travels through the Empire, making verses and straw sandals, Hsi-wei learned that Song Sidao had gone to the far north and become a Buddhist monk. Hsi-wei was curious about such a transformation and, with nothing to prevent him, decided to go north and see the exile. His inquiries about Song along the way were fruitless until, in a tavern in Bohai, a jade merchant told him where Song might have wound up.

"There's a monastery at the foot of the hills outside Dingxiang. People call it the North Mountain Temple. I only know about it because I stayed there myself—it must be four years ago. The place was very quiet and spotless—but the food wasn't to my taste. No meat and no spices." The tipsy merchant giggled and held up his cup. "Worse yet, not a drop of yellow wine!"

Hsi-wei asked if perhaps the man remembered meeting a

certain Song Sidao, a former official in the capital.

"If I met the fellow, I certainly don't remember. They all look alike, don't they?"

. . .

Finding his way to Dingxiang was easy; there was only one road. Though it was June, the weather that far north was chilly, and the peasants were only just beginning their planting. Hsi-wei found lodging in sheds and stables, spoke with the local people, and sold some of them sandals. The district was hardly prosperous. The land was poor, but the peasants' cottages were clean and their mood cheerful as befits springtime. Many were devoted to the emperor, a northerner whom they saw as one of their own. One old woman proudly referred to Wen as "our boy from Wei". It was this woman who gave Hsi-wei directions to the monastery and warned him it would be a three-day walk. But Hsi-wei made haste and arrived around noon on the second day.

He was greeted courteously by the Master.

"Welcome, young man. Are you a pilgrim or a traveler?"

"Can't one be both?" Hsi-wei replied.

This evoked a laugh from Daizu Hongren.

"It's true. Some travelers only discover they are pilgrims after they arrive."

During his brief stay at the monastery Hsi-wei noted that the Master laughed easily and often, but that it was not always clear at what.

He was invited to share a meal with the monks—rice, vegetables, and water—no spices and no wine. But Hsi-wei ate with relish. The old proverb is true: the appetite makes the meal, and Hsi-wei was hungry.

It was the monks' custom to eat in silence but, after the meal, Hsi-wei asked Master Daizu if he might borrow a bit of his time.

"Only what can be returned can be borrowed," said the Master sententiously, then chuckled. "We like people to ask questions."

Hsi-wei explained that he had come looking for Song Sidao, who had been an official in the capital and a poet of some note.

"I've learned that he came north years ago, and people say he found a home in a monastery. Is he perhaps here?"

"Ah. I have to tell you that Song Sidao died twice. The first time was when he became a monk here and took the dharma name Shi Xing. He was one of the most enlightened. In fact, Shi Xing was my predecessor and my teacher. His second death, I regret to say, was two years ago. We keep his ashes in the temple in a place of honor."

Hsi-wei expressed his regret at the loss and asked to know more about the former Master.

"I could try to describe him, but I would fail. We prefer to preserve the memory of the enlightened in stories."

"Very well," said Hsi-wei. "I also like stories and so did Song Sidao. In fact, if what I've been told is true, it was a story that led him here."

"I know the story of that story," said Daizu and laughed again. "Look, the day has turned pleasantly warm. Our apple trees are just beginning to bloom. Let's go sit in the orchard. It was Master Shi's favorite place to meditate."

Under the apple trees, Daizu related story after story about his teacher. It gave him pleasure to speak of a man he obviously revered and loved.

On my first day as an apprentice monk—a *samanera*—I asked Shi Xing, "Master, how should I study?" I had only just arrived and was keen to learn. We were standing in front of the temple.

Shi pointed upward. "Pretend you are that roof. Each day one of your tiles falls off. At first, you will be only a bad roof but, eventually, you will be no roof at all."

One day Master Shi came across a group of us working in the vegetable patch. We were about to pull out some weeds. Seeing the Master, we paused.

"What are you doing?" Shi Xing demanded.

"Tearing up weeds, Master."

"I see," said Master Shi. "And what is a weed?"

Puzzled, we looked at one another, then Xuan replied. "A weed is a plant growing where you don't want it to."

"Exactly," said Master Shi. "A living thing which we think we can judge. Humble yourselves."

On his first day, a *samanera* asked, "Master. Please, can you tell me where I fit into the cycle of being?"

Shi Xing replied with a shrug, "Who said you do?"

A newly appointed magistrate stopped by the monastery. He was a haughty man who had come with an armed escort to inspect the district. Master Shi asked what his mission was. The magistrate said that revenues were lower than they should be, and he had come to extract their taxes from the cheating peasants.

"On what authority do you take from the peasants?" asked Shi Xing calmly.

The magistrate glared and drew himself up. "On what authority. The Emperor's, of course!"

Master Shi bowed to the magistrate. "The people may not always be in the right," he said, "but they will always be the people. The Son of Heaven may always be in the right, but he won't always be the emperor."

Master Shi Xing overheard us praising Shen Chou-lai, a monk from another monastery who had achieved fame by reciting the sutras with particular feeling. "I've heard Shen Chou-lai. It's true; he's a virtuoso who recites with love— but what is it he loves?"

We were sitting quietly after reciting prayers. A young monk to the Master's left broke the silence. "Master Shi Xing, we praise the compassionate Buddha. What is compassion?" At once, the Master seized his bamboo stick and struck the monk to his right a stinging blow. Then he turned back to the monk on his left. "There. Did you feel that?"

One day Master Shi Xing was walking in this orchard with a peasant who often came to pray with us and brought us gifts of vegetables. The good fellow asked the Master if it were his duty to obey all the emperor's commands. Master Shi pointed up at one of the highest branches. "That apple up there might not want to fall from the tree."

One fine spring day the Master was working beside us as we cultivated the field. A *samanera* paused and leaned on his hoe. "Master," he asked, pointing to the sky, "is the Buddha-nature as pure as that little white cloud up there?" Master Shi looked across the field to our shed where a dog was crouching. "You see that dog shitting over there. That is the Buddha-nature."

A well-to-do traveler from the capital stayed the night. Before leaving in the morning, he asked Master Shi, "Why do you monks support yourselves by begging. It robs you of dignity."

"Did you eat your dinner last night?" asked Shi.

"Yes. You know very well that I was served along with everyone else."

"That was nice, wasn't it?" said Shi Xing.

Daizu had many such stories.

• • •

Hsi-wei stayed with the monks for three nights and joined them each afternoon for an hour of sitting. Before taking his leave, he made the monks six pairs of straw sandals and this poem.

SONG SIDAO AND MASTER SHI XING

Song Sidao was vain in the way of poets.
In the way of courtiers, he was witty and acerbic.
By his wit he earned ten-course banquets and jade wine.
Telling a court poet to please is telling a fish to swim;
but to please some, Song would sting others.

Song went too far and was sent away to the north.
Unknowing, he found himself on Bodhidharma's track
starving and exhausted, chastened and humbled.
The North Mountain Temple took him in.
The noise of the banquet hall was drowned out by
quiet fasting, clever sallies by silent meditation.
As Song became less clever, he grew more wise.
When he renounced fame, he became famous.
As Song Sidao he wrote ephemeral verse but
as Shi Xing he became an abiding poem.

LUCIANA DI PARMA

1.

An April breeze ruffled the new leaves on the mulberry tree that stood in the center of the courtyard. The duke was proud of that mulberry; he examined it anxiously every day he was not away from the palace. The tree was visible through the broad triple-arched window of the library where Federico Polacchio, a Florentine scholar, sat across a heavy walnut table from his pupil, the duke's only daughter.

"You've read what I asked?" This was his standard opening, a meaningless formality because Lady Luciana always read what he asked.

"Signor Polacchio?"

"Yes?"

"Why did you want me to read the seventh part rather than to start from the beginning of Book Eight?"

"Because I knew you would read it all anyway."

She smiled. "But you wanted to draw my attention to Seven in particular. Is that it?"

Polaccchio shrugged.

Luciana was pretty and prettier still when she laughed, which she now did.

"My Lady, you occupy an exalted station, though Heaven knows you're far too naughty to deserve it. But it is because of this position that Part Seven is, for you, the most important not only of Book Eight but the whole of the *Ethics*."

"More important than even the Golden Mean?" she teased.

"See. Naughty."

"Ah, *too naughty*, you think. I, on the other hand, would argue that I am right on the golden mean between too much naughtiness and too little."

"Alarmingly ironic, frivolous, arrogant, proud—"

"Oh. And what else?"

"Intelligent and precocious, to a fault."

"A fault?"

"Yes."

"You would prefer a less apt pupil?"

"Plato might have thought so. In comparing Aristotle, who scarcely ever agreed with him, to a duller student who did, he observed, *One needs spurs, a bridle to the other*."

"So you would have me less. . . unbridled?"

"Certainly. I would rejoice in a pupil who isn't forever cross-grained and can't pronounce Latin better than I do, one who doesn't excel at algebra, who refrains from teasing her father and mocking her teacher."

"As I recall the story, Plato added, *What an ass I have to breastfeed, and against a horse*. At least you grant that I'm not an ass," said Luciana and broke into a laugh which make her look prettier still. "Well then, do let's be serious, Signor."

Polacchio grimaced and took up the book. "Part Seven, of unequal friendships."

"Such as ours. Is that why you asked me especially to read Part Seven?"

"I'd say we're more like wrestlers on market day, rivals rather than friends. No. I wasn't thinking of us but of you and your noble parents—and the unlucky man you'll marry one day."

Luciana blushed. The word *marriage* made her think of the well-made Guido d'Ostiglia with whom she believed herself in love and who professed to love her. According to Guido, he adored her just as Dante had Beatrice and Petrarca his Laura—girls of her own age.

The tutor brought his forefinger down on the table, a way he had of soundlessly raising his voice.

"When Aristotle speaks of unequal friends he means to include a variety of relations. father to daughter, elder to younger, ruler to subject, man to wife."

"That's four relationships. He insists they are all distinct and shouldn't be conflated, so does he do just that?"

"Because they are of a kind and what they all have in common is disproportion." Here Polacchio opened the book and read. "*Each party, then, neither gets the same from the other, nor ought to seek it. In all friendships implying inequality the love should also be proportional; that is to say, the better should be more loved than he loves.*"

Luciana sighed. "*He.* Always he."

"No, the elder too. And the ruler. Everything isn't about your fixed idea about the inferior position of women."

"A question for you, Signor. Should I love *you* more because you are older than I am, and a man—and from *Florence* to boot!—or should you love *me* more because of my superior social status, however undeserved?"

Polacchio threw up one hand and made an unpleasant noise.

"Come now," said Luciana sternly. "Do you really agree

with the Peripatetic that inequality can or even ought to dictate the measure of one's love. That sort of thinking is, if you'll pardon me, masculine, and I don't intend that as a compliment to either Aristotle or to *you*."

The tutor was accustomed to being challenged. He affected annoyance but actually delighted in it, as Luciana perfectly well knew. She would goad him and he would scrupulously avoided showing the pleasure he took in her provocations. It was their manner with one another; it suited them both.

Polacchio put on a somber face. "Your brothers are good boys. They know their place. They bow to their father and treat me like a dung beetle. Giovanni is dutifully courting the Farnese girl and, as for Filippo, didn't he wed Giulia Visconti girl without having laid eyes on her?"

"Where Giovanni is concerned, I believe it was the Maria Farnesi who did the really strenuous courting. As to my dear Filippo, what shall I say. He isn't the brightest candle in our Parmesan chandelier."

Polacchio pretended to be shocked. "They're your older brothers!"

"And so twice as worthy of love than I—once for sex and once for age. But look here, Signor, did you really think I wouldn't read on?"

"Pardon me?"

"I refer to Part Eight, of course, which, to a degree, *undoes* Part Seven."

Polacchio leaned back in his chair, feigning surprise. "To a degree. Do, please, explain."

"Very well then. Since you're so backward, I'll spell it out for you."

Luciana drew the heavy book to her, hefted it, and turned

a few vellum pages. "Like his teacher, Aristotle distinguishes loving from being loved. As you've insisted, he says the beloved is more elevated than the lover, yes. We know he loved to contradict his teacher."

"Like somebody else I could mention."

"Plato has Socrates say the very opposite, that *the lover is more exalted than the beloved.* To Plato the act of loving spiritualizes the lover while, for Aristotle, in Part Seven, it appears almost a degradation."

"Appears?"

"Oh yes. In Part Eight he considered the matter more deeply and ended up changing his mind. Listen." Luciana propped the book up and translated more quickly than her tutor would have been able to do. "*Since friendship depends more on loving*—he means, of course, more than being loved—*it is those who love their friends that are praised. Loving seems to be the characteristic virtue of friends, so that it is only those in whom this is found in due measure that are lasting friends, and only their friendship that endures. It is in this way that even unequals can be friends; they can be equalized.*"

She lay down the book, smiled at her tutor and began speaking before he could say anything.

"By '*due* measure' Aristotle obviously means *equal* measure. Now if, as *you* argue, I am to love young people, females, and my father's subjects less, my elders and rulers more, then there cannot be what Aristotle calls a lasting friendship between us—which I take to mean a genuine one. *Quod erat demonstrandum.* It is by their mutual love that unequals are equalized."

Polacchio looked at his pupil closely and said, "May I speak of something more serious than philosophy for a moment?"

"By all means.

"Everybody knows about you and young d'Ostiglia," he said almost with sadness. "He's a fine fellow this Guido. I acknowledge it."

Luciana counted Guido's merits on her fingers. "He sits a horse. He has a leg. He can even write passable sonnets."

"I agree he does more than fill out his velvet doublets and slashed sleeves. But your father, I think, is going to have other plans for his only daughter. And, of course, my Lady, you've only just turned fourteen."

"Ah, but Signor Polacchio, as you've often observed, my father has spoiled me by giving me whatever I want. As to being just fourteen, don't forget my insufferable precociousness."

2.

Despite Francesco Sforza's protestations of support for the Treaty of Lodi, the status-quo, and peace across Lombardy, the Duke of Parma did not trust him. Milan's history of aggression would not permit it. Moreover, his eldest son's marriage lost all its value after the Treaty replaced the Visconti with the Sforzas in Milan. He had done what he could to secure a defensive alliance with Mantua by arranging for his younger son to marry the third daughter of Duke Francis. Neither was ever likely to rule, but you could never be certain. Now he was nearly out of ammunition. He had only his daughter left to try to fortify an alliance with Modena. The trouble was that there was so much competition. The Duke of Modena had a son, but geography and the uncertain peace had had put a premium on the boy's head. On the other hand, the same misgivings that led him to want to ally Parma with Modena might sway Modena to desire an ally in Parma. An alliance with Naples, or even France, might be less desirable than one with nearby Parma.

Luciana's father selected his ambassador slyly. He did not choose one of his own nobles but rather the Florentine tutor. Polacchio had gained some renown as a scholar, which the culturally ambitious court of Modena would respect. He was also well-spoken, dressed presentably, and, like all Florentines, was crafty. The duke calculated that not being one of his subjects would count in the man's favor as well. It suggested neutrality and therefore honesty. Polacchio could be counted on to present his pupil's charms and accomplishments with both eloquence and sincerity.

Meanwhile, everyone in Parma, except her father, knew of the romance between Luciana and the dashing young courtier Guido d'Ostiglia. Guido was popular, of good family, fashionable, honorable, and spent freely. When news got out that her father was planning to marry Luciana to the heir of the Duke of Modena's, people began to speculate on whether the story was to be a fairy tale, a tragedy, or a farce. Odds were given and betting was lively. The possibilities offered were many. A) The girl would take the veil rather than marry a man she didn't love. B) She and d'Ostiglia would elope. This generated side bets: would they they'd take refuge in Naples, Sicily, France, or the Piedmont. C) The girl would impetuously do away with herself. D) She would poison her father. E) She would appear to accept the son of the Duke of Modena but then poison him. F) Guido d'Ostiglia would arrange his rival's assassination. G) The Duke's willful daughter would put up a holy fuss but finally give in.

At seventeen, Guido d'Ostiglia was a fully developed specimen of his type, all he would ever be. He had money, looks, physical strength, high connections, an expensive wardrobe, and a fair education. He liked horses, hunting, Toledo swords and weapons in general, gossip, also polyphonic music, Boccaccio's stories and Petrarch's sonnets. His feelings for Luciana di Parma were socially irregular but culturally impeccable. He sent her nosegays and poems, made secret assignations during which he sighed worshipfully, and listened attentively even to the most astonishing and irreverent things she said.

> *"I'm much like my brothers, save in one respect."*
> *"And that would be?"*
> *"I'm more masculine."*

> *"The current Pope spends more than he prays. In fact, I*
>   *calculate the ratio at something over 100:1."*

> *"Don't you agree that patriotism is among the highest of*
>   *virtues, My Lady?"*
> *"Certainly, one should always cherish the merits of*
>   *one's own land. Florence for brains, Rome for*
>   *extravagance, Venice for intrigue, Naples for*
>   *skullduggery, and Modena for vinegar."*
> *"And what of our Parma?"*
> *"Parma for cheese."*

Guido behaved toward Luciana with deference because of her position and with tenderness because of her youth. He was vain, but an adept courtier and not without perception. He soon developed a genuine, not merely formal, respect for Luciana. Most ladies, he thought, look best when they are still and silent, like statues. Luciana's beauty showed best when she was animated. He was fascinated by her face's movements and the original way she thought. Even her scorn, he admitted, was always well placed. He could see that she was her father's daughter and, though a female, better suited to command than either of her brothers. Guido also took after his father, an off-and-on *condottiero* during the wars, now commander of the Duke of Parma's forces.

One night when both were supposed to be asleep, they met at their usual tryst, a corner of the palace garden with an ancient Roman bust on a brandnew pedestal.

"This marriage to Modena, Luciana—it isn't just a rumor, is it?"

"No. My father has sent Polacchio off to strike a bargain, if he can."

Guido, fingering his linen sleeve, paused to control his voice. "You'll obey?"

Luciana also hesitated to reply, and for the same reason. "I don't know."

Guido thereupon put his hand over his heart and recited four lines of Petrarch, verses he had memorized long before, but in which he found a new, sorrowful meaning.

> *She ruled in beauty o'er this heart of mine,*
> *A noble lady in a humble home,*
> *And now her time for heavenly bliss has come,*
> *'Tis I am mortal proved, and she divine.*

3.

Luciana and her mother Matilda were never close, certainly not friends. Luciana had been an unexpected child, and her birth was both painful and perilous. The Duchess preferred her boys who were so much more pliable, sympathetic, and resembled her. "Well," she said complacently when her sister commented on her obvious partiality, "who doesn't prefer boys?" The Duchess was used to her sons doing what she and her husband told them to do. Not so Luciana. It would be saying too much to call their relations hostile; inimical is a better word. Matilda was alarmed by her daughter's independence, deplored her excessive love of reading, disapproved of her daring wit, deplored her cheeky jokes, especially when she told them in company. But she was tired of remonstrating with Luciana. That her husband indulged the girl in everything undermined all her efforts. The Duchess had therefore been relieved to turn Luciana over to Signor Polacchio. Matilda was aware of her daughter's attraction to d'Ostiglia and that it could only lead to trouble. At this perilous moment, the tutor was off in Modena and the Duke had gone to Rome. Matilda considered that it was her duty to do something to put an end to Luciana's unacceptable romance. However, as she wasn't eager to confront her daughter, she decided instead to have a word with the boy's father.

The old soldier listened calmly enough, though he added impertinently that the good Lady might do well to sing the same tune to her daughter. The Duchess pulled herself up and replied sharply, "It goes without saying that my daughter will do as she is told."

But would she. The Duchess was not in the least confident she would. Did she ever. It was inconsiderate of the Duke to have gone to Rome, ostensibly to pull the strings that would raise his sister's second nephew from monsignor to a bishop. *More likely he's with the Papal whores*, she thought, though without bitterness. It was decades since she had accepted her husband's dalliances. Indeed, like all the married women of her acquaintance, she considered them both natural and inconsequential.

The words of the *condottiero* stuck with her. He had been insolent, but he wasn't wrong. She valued peace, particularly in the family, and she was a little afraid of her daughter. For the sake of peace she refrained from being disagreeable with her husband and had ceased pitting her will against her daughter's. But now, for the sake of peace, she would have a go at the girl.

They sat on chairs in the parental bedchamber.

"Put an end to this flirtation. Your duty is to do as your father says, child."

"Did you?"

"What?"

"Did you do as *your* father ordered?"

"My marriage to your father—"

"Yes, I know. Back then it was Urbino and Parma; now it's Parma and Modena. Reasons of state. The incest of the ruling families. Yes, but wasn't Father meant to marry Aunt Giulietta?"

The Duchess felt her stomach seize up. She had been sure the children knew nothing of the story. "Who told you that?"

"I know the tale, Mother. It's a good one—splendid, really. A confusion of identities. What they call a comedy of errors, as in that old play by Plautus."

"Plautus. I don't know what you're talking about."

Luciana went on equably. "Father mistook you for Giulietta and you didn't correct him because you'd fallen in love with him at first sight. And he with you. You Montefeltros are a romantic lot, aren't you. You begged your father until he gave in—I'm told you actually *swooned*. So, he made a still better match for Aunt Giulietta. A Medici!"

The Duchess was more shocked than angry. The conversation had gone all wrong, and she wasn't sure what to say.

Luciana filled the void. "You married for love, Mother, though you would have me think otherwise. Not to worry. So far as I can see, it did you little good." Luciana sighed. "Either way, love left the table while duty stayed for the sweet. So, you see, I require no further lessons. Reasons of state or reasons of the heart—one's as dangerous as the other."

The Duchess dabbed her handkerchief to her eyes. "You—you are terrible!"

Luciana got to her feet and curtseyed prettily. "I'm merely trying to keep both my head and my heart, Mother. If that is possible."

The Duchess pointed a finger at her daughter. "Remember. When the time comes, you will do as your father tells you."

"And we end where we began. *Addio*, Mama." With that, Luciana gave a second, deeper curtsey, turned her back, and walked out of the room.

4.

Luciana and her tutor were back at the big table in the library. The afternoon was still and sultry. Outside, the mulberry leaves hung dejectedly in the heat.

Polacchio had returned without anything being settled. Modena was interested—more than interested—but not yet prepared to commit. Evidently, other negotiations were still in train.

"I met a brace of ambassadors from Siena who dressed like Frenchmen. And there was a most distinguished Pisan. Charming fellows all."

"Who was the distinguished gentleman from Pisa?"

"Giovanni Bragello. He wrote a rather good study of Roman villas and their gardens."

"Bragello. Isn't he the architect of the Villa Spirozzi in Lucca?"

"The same."

"Ah. Someone showed me an engraving. It's quite beautiful."

"And already being imitated."

Luciana put a finger thoughtfully to her lips. "Why is it, Signor, that when beauty and truth are imitated they cease to be themselves?"

Polacchio chuckled. He was happy to be reunited with his witty pupil, just as he had been happy in Modena where, it seemed to him, everybody knew his book and admired it. In addition, it appeared that ambassadors eat and sleep better than tutors. Both bed and board had been first-rate. There was the heavenly vinegar, of course, but also the divine *prosciutto crudo*.

"Anyway," said Luciana, "it's just as well the bargain wasn't struck. My father isn't back from Rome."

"I'm told he'll be here before the week's out. I have hopes of a definite answer from Modena by then."

Luciana looked into her lap. "I see."

They were quiet for a moment, tutor examining his student as she turned her gaze on her father's mulberry tree.

"Signor Polacchio, may we talk seriously?"

"It would make a change," he joked.

"You see, it's that I'm uncertain."

"Might some slight portion of this uncertainty have to do with Guido d'Ostiglia?"

She pouted just the way she had when she was little and she answered him like a child too. "A little. Not only."

"You haven't asked me about the Duke of Modena's son."

"No," she said, as if surprised herself. "All I know is that his name is Sandro."

"He's not like Guido."

"Oh?"

"He has, I think, other qualities."

"I notice you say *qualities*, not *virtues*."

"He is shorter than d'Ostiglia, less broad in the chest, and he is fair rather than dark. He dresses far more simply and is more studious. They say he's very good at mathematics and knows Greek. He has a slight stutter, but it's very slight. I found him to be polite, modest, and sympathetic."

"Does he want to be married?"

Polacchio offered one of his shrugs, as if to say, *as much as you*.

Luciana rose and began to pace.

"What do you think I ought to do?"

"Me?"

"Why not you?"

"My Lady, it's hardly my place."

"Oh, your *place*." Exasperated, she stamped her foot.

"Very well, then. Take what I have to say for the little it's worth. But know that my opinion's founded chiefly on my estimation of your character."

"Oh, do I have such a thing?"

"You said we were to be serious."

"I apologize. It's my. . . my character to tease, I suppose."

Polacchio made that familiar noise of his and waited for her to sit down. She didn't. She crossed her arms.

"Go on, man. Speak."

"Guido's a good lad. Healthy and passionate. He's infatuated with you. He's strong and a little conceited. He is much like his father—and also yours."

"I think I understand."

"Do you. Good. Well, I had the impression that Sandro is also a good boy, but far weaker. He's religious without being excessively pious, and he is accustomed to being ruled by his mother."

"Yes?"

Polacchio put his hands together. "Epicurus says it is better to be unfortunate through a reasonable action than to prosper in unreason, that it's better an action be well chosen and fail than that successful owing to chance. So, my Lady, let's consider things dispassionately. An elopement with d'Ostiglia would ruin your relations with your family. Moreover, being based on passion, which is fleeting, the union would be more precarious than one founded on duty, which is durable. I've no doubt Guido would swear to be faithful but, like his father and yours, he's more apt to follow passion than obligation."

"Duty. There speaks not the Epicurean but the Stoic."

"The Stoics had good marriages."

"Not your Epictetus. He was a bachelor. I haven't forgotten that delicious story you told me about how one day the old philosopher was haranguing his students about their duty to marry and reproduce themselves. What was the name of that clever wisecracker who piped up. Demonax, wasn't it. Yes, it was Demonax who asked, 'Tell me, Master, which of your daughters should I wed?'"

Polacchio raised his hands but not in surrender. "May I continue, please?"

"By all means, since you too are a bachelor."

"Should the marriage with Modena be arranged, I believe it will have more benefits than you suppose. It will please your father, of course. If properly managed, it will serve the interests of both Parma and Modena in deterring Milan."

"This I know already."

"Those are just the immediate benefits, true. But I am also thinking of the longer perspective—with respect, a difficult thing to do at your age. Consider: if I am right in my judgment of him then, to govern, Sandro will need to be governed, and he is already used to doing what a woman tells him."

"You're promising me power?"

"I promise nothing. However, I'm thinking less of the satisfactions of power than the frustrations of impotence. The wife of Guido d'Ostiglia will never be anything more than that. The Duchess of Modena, on the other hand, will have. . . let us say *scope* for her talents which, in your case, are very considerable."

Luciana looked at her tutor skeptically. "Flattery. From *you*, Signor?"

Polacchio raised his eyebrows, stroked his short beard, and grinned.

5.

The Duke and Duchess of Modena arrived with their son in a gilded coach that needed six horses to haul it. Their retinue was large enough to consume the equivalent of a couple fair-sized dowries. The betrothal was sealed with a formal celebration that called for everyone's utmost efforts, from scullions to ministers. The logistics were about as complicated as a small war's. There were banquets, masques, and a joust for the rich, pageants, public feasts, and horse races for everybody. Every musician in the area made money and all the guilds paraded.

The young couple were shifted about like furniture. Standing beside Sandro at the reception of the first evening, Luciana whispered to him, "Look, fellow pawn, there goes knight to queen's seven, and the bishop just put the king in mate."

Sandro stifled a chuckle, thereby passing at least one test.

The two spent ample time together, but none of it alone. In public, Sandro delivered what sounded like speeches memorized from Seneca, with a very slight stutter. As for Luciana, she was studiously and uncharacteristically demure. Before the arrival of their guests, her father, who had always encouraged her wit, took both her hands and said, "There'll be time for a thousand sallies later, my dear." Polacchio offered her much the same advice. "Diplomacy is a peculiar form of comedy, my Lady, one in which nobody's allowed to laugh."

Filippo was there with his useless Visconti wife, both of them looking sour. Giovanni and his Farnese bride stuck close by his mother and father. As he was the heir, protocol required it, though he'd have done it anyway.

During Mass, Luciana noted that the future Duke of Modena closed his eyes in devotion and that, when they were open, he looked first to his mother. However, when looked at Luciana it was always with a shy smile.

Sitting beside each other at dinner the second night, she ventured a comment. "My Lord, I understand you like mathematics and know Greek."

"A little Greek," he said, embarrassed. "Not much."

"Latin?"

"My tutor, Father Poggio, was very strict. So many declensions."

"*Hoc opus, hic labor est,*" she said.

"Cicero?"

"Virgil."

Polacchio hadn't lied. Physically, Sandro was nothing like Guido d'Ostiglia. He was slimmer than Guido; his neck was thinner, and he was obviously uncomfortable in his fashionable new clothes. He never made jokes.

Guido's father had tactfully arranged that his son should visit Florence for an indefinite period. Luciana received no less than fifteen sonnets from him on his departure. They weren't bad either, his best efforts by far.

On the third day, as they took the seats of honor for the guilds' parade, Luciana decided she might as well begin calling her future husband by his given name. "Sandro, may I ask you something?"

He nodded.

"Is your father faithful to your mother. Mine isn't."

The boy's mouth fell open in astonishment.

"Sorry. I didn't mean to pry. What I suppose I really want to know is how *you* feel about the vow of fidelity."

Sandro's eyebrows shot up in shock. "How do I feel about a vow made before *God*?"

"Exactly."

"Oh, I see. You're not serious."

That evening, following a masque on the theme of Apollo and Daphne, they had a few moments of rest on a banquette while the musicians left and the hall was cleared of scenery. Luciana pointed to one of the Sforzas.

"Do you believe the Milanese will try to take over Modena, Sandro. They've done it before."

The boy gave a prompt answer. "My father thinks it's possible. I believe that's why we're getting married."

"Do you know if he's in contact with the French. Your father, I mean."

"I don't think so. No, wait. He did mention something about the French but I can't remember what."

Luciana sighed. "But to bring the French over the mountains would be a capital error. Don't you agree?"

Sandro examined her more closely than he ever had before. "You know, Luciana, you're really very pretty, even on the rare occasions when you're being serious. Especially then."

Luciana smiled at this graceless but sincere compliment. "Thank you, Sandro. By the way, I meant to ask if you know the work of Luca Pacioli?"

"No."

"A gifted mathematician. Signor Polacchio received a manuscript from him last week. He has some original and useful ideas about how to keep accounts, though he steals shamelessly from Della Francesca. Would you like to see it?"

"Yes, I would like that very much. *Grazie mille*."

6.

Only after she accused him of abandoning her did Polacchio consent to spend a year in Modena watching over his newly wed former pupil while exploring the middling ducal library, enjoying his growing reputation as well as the heavenly vinegar, and the divine *prosciutto crudo*. His advice to Luciana was to be cautious not only with her in-laws but also with the courtiers. They were, he told her in confidence, not a first-rate collection. "The ones that are conscious of their limitations are even less trustworthy than the ones who aren't. Also, the mediocre are the most susceptible to envy."

Luciana replied with an allusion to Plato. "I've noticed that, too. The gossip here is even nastier than in Parma but somehow duller. Like Meletus they'd rather tearing others down than improve themselves."

Polacchio smiled with a teacher's satisfaction.

"I have to say you've done well."

"Have I?"

"You're loved by some, liked by many, respected by everybody. You've been generous with the poor and you know how to speak to the common people. And that's no small talent, seeing how peasants crave familiarity with their betters but like them to keep their distance."

"In Parma I had few opportunities to help the poor. Now I have many."

"Yes. Widows and orphans bless you twice a day. But winning over your mother-in-law, that must have been a Herculean labor, a true achievement."

Polacchio overestimated the difficulty of this task. The Duchess of Modena could never, like Matilda, be content under the thumb of a man. She valued the female mind, insisted on a measure of liberty for herself, even allowed herself a certain rebelliousness, albeit of the inconsequential, point-scoring variety. Taken as a group, the Duchess's lady-attendants were superior to her husband's ministers in both morality and intelligence; and her young daughter-in-law seemed to fit right into the circle, making it more charming. In fact, it was Luciana's reputation for learning and wit, confirmed by her tutor, that had made the Duchess her backer in the marriage sweepstakes. As for Luciana, she found with her mother-in-law the friendship she had missed with Matilda. The Duchess, who had always wanted a daughter, was pleased by how well Luciana got on with Sandro, how she brought him out of himself and made him happy. It also helped that they both adored Dante and couldn't stand the cardinal.

Sandro was only twenty years old when his father died, Luciana seventeen. The Duke's death came after a brief respiratory illness his doctors were powerless to arrest. To the surprise of those who mistook her independent manner for indifference, the Duchess was inconsolable. Luciana was only able to talk her out of taking the veil by pointing out that such a step would place her under the authority of men like the Bishop of Modena—"or, worse yet, the Pope!"

The same week her father-in-law died Luciana sent an urgent letter to Polacchio, who was then in Venice, summoning him to Modena and asking him to bring along a competent engineer. "I am told that Signor Cramonti is in Venice at present. He would do. If things proceed as I intend, there will be work and good pay for you both."

Luciana knew from her father and other sources that there were powerful men in Milan who were never reconciled to what had been done at Lodi and were plotting to take back both Modena and Parma. In her view, the death of the Duke made the whole region vulnerable. Her inexperienced and indecisive husband lacked a martial reputation. Her father was far better prepared but, on its own, Parma could not fend off a serious attack by the Sforzas. She worked on an idea of how the two cities could be defended. After all, why else was she in Modena if not to defend both it and Parma?

In the second year of her marriage, shortly after the departure of Polacchio, Luciana had explored Modena's two rivers, the Secchia and the Panaro. It was while floating down the latter that a notion had come to her through an association of ideas. Before he left, she and Polacchio had been reading the Roman historians. In an effort to bring the old chronicles to life, the tutor had asked her to compare Livy's and Polybius' accounts of a battle fought hardly more than two day's distance from where they sat. This was Hannibal's victory over of the Romans at the River Trebia. The story was still in her mind during her voyage down the Panaro, when the kernel of a scheme of defense came to her like a daydream.

Within days of the Duke's interment, Luciana worked her idea out in detail and disclosed it to her husband. She also dispatched a trusted messenger, one of the women she had brought with her from Parma, to deliver a confidential report to her father and the old *condottiero*.

The dam was constructed roughly and rapidly and situated at the head of the narrow valley to the west of Modena. The Panaro flows robustly through this ravine before meandering more sedately over the plain. Polacchio and Cramonti disguised the dam to look like nothing more than a somewhat large mill, with wheel and weir.

When news came that a Milanese army was marching toward Parma and Modena, Luciana's plan, much improved by d'Ostiglia, was put into motion. Parma's forces left the city heading west. After engaging in a few skirmishes to give the Milanese a good look at them, they retreated eastward, drawing the enemy away from Parma and toward Modena. Meanwhile, Modena's troops, reinforced by peasant volunteers, concealed themselves on the heights to either side of the Panaro valley. The old *condottiero* led his troops on an orderly retreat straight up the valley but instructed the hindmost to hang back then give the appearance of fleeing in panic. Seeing this, the Milanese impetuously rushed into the valley. As soon as the last of Parma's men began to scale the slope at the end of the valley, a signal was given and the dam was pulled down. The pent-up Panaro, suddenly freed, gushed into the valley. It was hardly a biblical flood, but the torrent was sufficient to knock the Milanese vanguard flat and get all the troops mired in mud. At that moment, Modenese archers on the heights rose up and showered the enemy with arrows while the infantry rolled rocks and tree trunks down on them. The Milanese were compelled to withdraw in disorder.

The Sforzas denied responsibility for the attack, blaming the old party of the Visconti for acting independently, which may even have been true. Francesco Sforza tossed a couple dozen men into his dungeons, formally apologized to the Dukes of Modena and Parma, and once again confirmed, with the most solemn oaths, his commitment to the Peace of Lodi.

7.

The name attached to the library of Modena is Sandro's but the credit for its outstanding collection of incunabula belongs properly to Luciana. A good deal is owed also to Polacchio, who sent many books to her, first from Venice, then Florence, Basel, Wittenberg, and finally Amsterdam. "My teacher's star," Luciana liked to joke, "drifts ever northwards." His own *Morum Lata, De Pantheiusmus Occidentalis et Orientalis* had been condemned as heretical by several powerful churchmen which did not deter Luciana from including three copies of each in the ducal library. Most of the other volumes she had from Polacchio were even more offensive to the Church.

When the old duke died, the Archbishop of Modena moved his residence to Rome, while holding on to the emoluments of his office. When he at last won the red hat, he returned from Rome specifically to confront the new duke about his library. Sandro simply referred him to his wife. In consideration of her youth, position, and popularity, prudence suggested to the Cardinal that it would be best to do so with discretion. To this purpose he invited Luciana to his palace on the pretext of presenting her with three new books he had brought for her from Rome, all freshly printed and unobjectionable.

"Knowing your cherished aim of building up the ducal library, I am delighted to make you a gift of these good books, my Lady."

"Many thanks, Your Eminence. I assure you they shall be cared for as they deserve."

"You are most welcome. But, while we're on the subject of the library, I must point out that it contains many books that have been condemned, particularly those printed in the North. Our Mother Church has made it clear that such works are to be burned, not collected, and certainly not read."

Luciana's reply was typical of her. "Your Eminence, how can people know what books to reject if they can't read them. Surely, you can't believe that the lucubrations of some dyspeptic German or Hollander could turn the heads of true children of our mother the Church, especially as you have yourself instructed them in right thinking since they were baptized?"

Even the local clergy were relieved when the Cardinal returned to Rome.

Luciana gave birth to a son. The boy was christened Francesco—not, as some supposed, to propitiate the Duke of Milan—but after the laureate Petrarca.

The Peace of Lodi having been re-established, Luciana and Sandro devoted themselves to their son, the happiness of the duchy, and the patronage of the arts. Many famous men spent time in Modena. Not only paintings and statues accumulated but also smaller *objets d'art*, exotic curiosities, well-wrought salvers and saltcellars of silver and gold. Just as Polacchio had predicted, Sandro needed to be governed and, with help from her mother-in-law, Luciana managed this not only without undermining her husband's dignity but in a way that increased his self-confidence. He was devoted to his wife, she to him, and both doted on little Francesco. They enjoyed a few good years.

From the third month, Luciana's second pregnancy did not proceed smoothly. By the seventh she could not leave her bed. The five doctors summoned by the terrified Duke—two local men plus one each from Florence, Pisa, and Venice—frowned and whispered, whispered and frowned. Luciana's mother-in-law would not leave her bedside until implored to do so by Luciana herself. Despite his age, when told that his daughter's life was in danger, her father would not wait for his coach but galloped all the way from Parma.

The baby, a girl, though delivered prematurely and terribly small lived; however, after ten days, her mother died. Luciana was twenty-six years of age. The girl was christened Agnella Lucia. All Modena went into mourning for a month, as did Parma. Sandro commissioned Baraschetti to design the charming Church of Saint Margaret of Antioch in his wife's memory.

A year and a half later, Charles VIII entered Italy. The

peace ended, and the wars resumed. Sandro, who had never recovered from the loss of his wife, was overthrown and took refuge with his children in Parma, now under the rule of Luciana's elder brother, whose hospitality was meager and grudging.

Guido d'Ostiglia, after distinguishing himself in the wars, became in Siena what his father had been in Parma. He married twice and people say his mistresses were beyond counting.

HSI-WEI AND THE GREAT WALL

Note. In the year that Yang Jian declared himself Emperor Wen of Sui, the Turks and Tuyuhan breached the Empire's northern border and overran the local garrison. Once the invaders were driven out, the new emperor ordered the neglected fortifications to be repaired and extended. Over the next six years, thousands of laborers were conscripted to complete the massive project. Wendi's aim was to defend the Empire. Two decades later, the profligate and unscrupulous Yang Guan, Wendi's second son, successor, and probable assassin, ordered further expansions of the Wall merely to flaunt his power. He raised taxes to unbearable levels and sacrificed countless peasants to his own glory. The human losses at the Wall, along with the thousands of lives lost digging the Grand Canal, the costs of Yangdi's personal extravagance, and finally the military disasters in Goguryeo, led to the uprising that provoked the Emperor's ministers to assassinate him and bring the Sui Dynasty to an end.

What follows is based on the journal of Fang Xuan-ling, a minister of the new Tang dynasty and an admirer of Hsi-wei's work. When Fang learned that the poet was living in retirement near Chiangling, he visited Hsi-wei for two weeks. Each day, he inquired about the origins of certain of the peasant/poet's verses and recorded Hsi-wei's replies.

• • •

As usual, Fang Xuan-ling and his one attendant arrived on horseback from Chiangling late in the morning. The weather was fair. April sun glinted off the puddles in the nearby field. Fang had his attendant take the basket he had brought into the cottage then he and the poet settled down in the tiny cobbled patio with its weathered table and two chairs. Fang was staying in the villa of the Governor and always brought a good things from his host's kitchen. That day, there were just two courses. a cold cucumber soup with mushrooms and spring onions plus stewed beef with cabbage and rice.

As soon as they finished the meal, Fang took out his brush, inkstone, scroll and began the day's interview.

"Master, I'm curious about the poem people call 'Walls Have Two Sides'. You remember it?"

Hsi-wei gave a little groan. "It's an old poem but yes, I remember it—well *some* of it."

Fang tilted his head to the side quizzically. "And with some compunction?"

"It's true. I wasn't happy with that poem; or rather, I was of two minds about it."

"So a poem about the wall's two sides," said Fang, "is *also* two-sided?"

Hsi-wei nodded to acknowledge the witticism. "I think the poet must be even more two-sided than his verses, My Lord."

"Yes, Master. I noticed the ambivalence in the poem and that's why I wanted to ask about it. You appear to object to the Wall but also to acknowledge its necessity."

"Many bad things appear necessary. The reverse is no less true, but some things really are both."

"Can you recall what prompted you to write it the way you did?"

"When I visited the Wall back then I felt how much I was like the peasants carrying out the heavy work. My heart was entirely with them. All the same, my Daxing-educated mind appreciated why Wendi pushed them so hard to complete the project."

Fang nodded. "In the poem you say little about anything that happened during your journey. It's all empty villages and fallow fields, desolation and depopulation."

"That was for effect, I'm afraid. It wasn't all like that; every village wasn't abandoned. I did meet people. I remember finding many customers for my sandals in Hengshan and in the little hamlets along the way. I slept outside but when the weather was bad, I bedded down in stables and barns. I also did something of which I'm both proud and ashamed."

Fang was intrigued. "More ambivalence. Please tell me the story."

Hsi-wei hesitated then said he would on condition that Fang made no notes. The Minister agreed and laid his brush aside. We have the story because that night Fang wrote it down from memory.

"West of Hengshan, not far from where the work was going on, I happened on three frightened peasants, all about my own age. They were wretched, dressed in rags, and begged me for food. I carried little but I gave them all I had in my bag. I usually carried a couple of rice balls, fruit, perhaps a cucumber or pickled radish. They might have attacked me, even in their weakened state. That they didn't deepened my sympathy and I laid before them whatever I had. It cost them something not to snatch at the food and cram it into their mouths, but they divided everything up before wolfing it down. I understood their predicament.

"'You're on the run, aren't you?' I said. 'From the work.'"

"They exchanged terrified glances, then attempted to look menacing. But I could see they weren't really a danger to me. I'd just given them all my food which they could have taken by force. How could they threaten me?

"I asked if they were being pursued.

"One nodded. Another asked if I'd seen any soldiers. The third, the youngest, began to cry.

"'They took the lot of us—all the men in Wuzhen. We're the only ones still alive. If they catch us we'll be tortured. They do it as a lesson to others.'

"I wanted to help these miserable men. I began to think of a plan, one as desperate as they were. I asked if their pursuers would recognize them. One said he didn't know, but another said he didn't think so.

"'We're all the same to them. Like so many oxen.'

"I said I hoped that was the case.

"I always kept two small scrolls in my pack to write down my verses. I laid one out on the ground and used my knife to cut four equal squares from it then took out my brush and inkstone. The peasants' mouths fell open. I made four copies of a document declaring that the bearer was on official business and not to be detained. I made use not only of the official calligraphy Master Shen tried to teach me but also his name. I signed each paper *Shen Kuo, Magistrate of Meishan* and affixed my own chop at the bottom, being careful to smudge the ink so that it might be mistaken for an official stamp."

"Why did you choose Meishan?"

"I asked the men the name of the city nearest their village."

"Why four copies instead of three."

"Out of prudence, my Lord. One was for me."

"Ah, I see. And what happened?"

"I told the peasants that they should continue on with me and not to worry about the soldiers. They were shocked.

"'Are you mad?' they said. 'Don't you know they'll take you too?'

"I explained my plan and why I thought it might work. I cautioned them that it was essential not to appear afraid of the soldiers when—or if—they caught up with us."

"And did they catch up. The soldiers?"

Hsi-wei nodded. "Only an hour or so later. Three mounted men with lances and a captain with a sword."

Fang felt like a child listening to a fairy story. "And what happened then?"

"The peasants tried to behave just as I'd told them to. Nevertheless, the captain ordered his men to put ropes around our necks. I did the talking. 'Your Honor,' I said, 'you've clearly mistaken us for somebody else. We've been summoned by the Magistrate of Meishan on urgent business.'

"'The Magistrate of Meishan. Some story,' growled the captain. I was relieved that he didn't recognize the men.

"I took my copy of the false document from my bag. The others took theirs from their shirts. 'Here,' I said with all the confidence I could muster, 'examine our passes for yourself.'

"We held out our squares. The captain took mine and examined it suspiciously. My legs were trembling, but I smiled confidently. If he could read, he might be deceived. If he couldn't read and we all kept our nerve, he might be unwilling to take the risk of ignoring an official order.

"As he stared at the paper I observed that his eyes didn't move which meant he couldn't read it. He handed it back to me.

"'Well, there are four of you,' he said sternly. 'We're looking for three men, deserters from the work on the Wall. Have you seen them?'

"One of the peasants surprised me by speaking up and cunningly, too. 'I believe we did, Your Honor. About two hours ago. They were heading south.'

"The captain frowned. He didn't look entirely convinced, but motioned to his men to follow, remounted his horse, and set off to the south at a gallop.

"So," said Fang assuming the harsh tone of a displeased Minister, "you deceived an officer of the Emperor."

Hsi-wei bowed his head.

Fang laughed. "That was risky indeed. I wonder that the officer, illiterate or not, fell for what sounds like a crude forgery."

"With respect, it's not difficult to explain, My Lord."

"No?"

"It never occurred to him that a peasant could read and write, especially when he couldn't do either himself."

Fang laughed. "Well, as this was decades ago and the Sui Dynasty is no more, I suppose I can pardon you."

"Thank you, My Lord. Though I'm glad of what I did and proud that it succeeded, I do still feel some remorse."

"Yet more ambivalence!" said Fang and got to his feet. "It's grown late, more than time for me to return to Chiangling. But, with your permission, Master, I'll be back again tomorrow."

Hsi-wei rose and bowed deeply. "It will give me pleasure," he said.

"I hope so," said Fang. "Tomorrow, I'll think I'll bring both pork and fish."

• • •

Here are the verses about which Minister Fang was curious. As with most of his poems, the title of this one was not chosen by Hsi-wei but by the people.

Walls Have Two Sides

Last summer I walked the length of the Wall
from the Huang Ho west beyond Hengshan.
The Wall looked like an uninteresting city, cut up
then sewn into a narrow never-ending scroll
unfurled over the whole length of the north.
a moral in stone dividing good from bad.
On one side, thickness and height frustrate
hard horsemen keen to pillage; on the other,
rising high as the taxes and lethal as the toil.
The Wall oppresses those who build it but
is meant to protect their children's children.
I understand why the Emperor is devoted to
the Wall; nevertheless, I wonder if it has
cost more lives than it will save. Who can say?

There's a story that, in his later years, the
Duke of Xu fell in love with the peerless
beauty Ehuang and made her his third wife.
When told that a young man had
managed to send a secret message to Ehuang,
the jealous Duke built a little palace for her,
with high palings all around it and set guards.
No matter how often the Duke reminded
Ehuang what he was keeping out, she cried
that she was being kept in. In the end, the
poor girl grew depressed, sickened, and died.

In his grief, the Duke buried her where she perished,
Made of her palace a tomb, the tomb a temple.

My journey was not agreeable, all heat and dust,
dead stone always to my right. I trekked through
many deserted villages, beside abandoned fields.
By the time I reached Jingian, I'd seen enough.

IRRETITO ANIMAE

On a rainy Tuesday in September, 1751, Roland Busette, Bishop of Nantes, ordered his carriage to take him to the town of Cholet where Jules La Detterie lay on his deathbed. Cholet sits on the northern approach to the hills of Vendée so the bishop had an uphill journey from the Loire, one made more arduous by the ceaseless rain. Still, he was determined to speak with the philosopher, who had twice been expelled from France and had only recently returned from Prussia. In his robe the Bishop placed a small blue velvet pouch and a copy of La Detterie's latest tract, already included on the Index and under review by the state as well. In it, the freethinker reiterated his arguments against the existence of God, confirmed his materialism, detailed the Church's baleful influence on human affairs, and laid out a two-stage hedonism in which the only value that trumped private pleasure was that of the public. As always, the bishop found La Detterie's style captivating, even seductive. calm, level-headed, logical, untainted by rancor, sentiment, defiance, or compunction.

La Detterie's ideas had never troubled the bishop as much they did his colleagues. He had met the man on half a dozen occasions and even disputed with him at one memorable soirée. La Detterie was a reprobate and yet he spoke simply, with complete candor. He never sought simply to shock; in fact, there was something appealingly forthright, even childish about him. As for his ideas—the exclusive reliance on reason, the belief in nothing beyond bodies, space. and motion, this whole new paganism of the intellect—such notions were human creations and Busette knew men were infinitely weaker than God. Jules La Detterie was, to be sure, an enemy but by no means an unworthy adversary. The bishop could not help esteeming and even liking the fellow. Otherwise, he would have avoided a difficult carriage ride in the autumn rain.

The inn was what one would expect in a place like Cholet: not clean, not comfortable, not painted. It crouched close to the highway like a beggar. Behind its two crooked chimneys the hills rose to the south. In the best of weather these hills were hardly impressive; owing to the rain they were almost invisible. Where the inn's courtyard was not inches deep in water the stones were slippery with muck. Manure, sweat, spilled wine, urine and bean cassoulet furnished the chief aromas of the place whose proprietor, in a state of unctuous exhilaration, rushed out to meet his dying guest's latest distinguished visitor. He had never seen such a parade of luminaries: scholars, academics, aristocratic women, and now His Grace the Bishop of Nantes. Who would have suspected that a consumptive scribbler in a patched German frockcoat would be such an attraction?

The host bowed low. "Your Grace, welcome. I'll have your horses seen to at once. I would apologize for these puddles but the rain too is sent by God. I say *too* because, beyond doubt, He has sent you to my unfortunate guest for the easing of his poor soul. Please, please come in."

"The man is still alive, then?" asked Busette curtly.

This question slowed the loquacious innkeeper only momentarily. "Alive. Oh, yes. Barely, barely, but yes, most definitely alive. In fact, he has been entertaining two ladies for the last half an hour."

"Two women. Tell me, what does the doctor say?"

A doctor, thought the innkeeper. Cholet had only Molinier

the barber and his verdict was a shake of the head. The innkeeper too shook his head and tried to do so more sadly than Molinier.

"You would like to see him now?"

"Yes."

"But the women—"

"Never mind the women."

The innkeeper nodded. "As you wish, Your Grace," he said and directed the bishop through a low doorway to the stairway.

Two well-dressed females were just departing. The bishop met them on the landing. He recognized the elder, who had been crying. It was the once-notorious and still-handsome Comtesse de Royen. She bowed coldly to him and introduced her daughter, Hélène. The girl turned to the bishop with big, surprised eyes and, making a slight curtsey, stared at his ring as if uncertain if she was obliged to kiss it.

"You won't find him in a repentant mood, Father," said the Comtesse.

"Repentance, my Lady, is not a mood. It is a turning of the soul. Pardon me, but I'm surprised to see you here with your daughter."

The Comtesse did not blush. "Hélène was always a great favorite with Jules, and he with her."

The girl shuffled her feet. The bishop wondered if she might not be a bit backward.

"Yes," said the bishop. He understood the Comtesse perfectly and rather admired her aristocratic self-possession, even if it was owing to the cardinal sin of pride. After all, pride is not invariably a sin, nor, Heaven knows, are cardinals immune to it. He bowed to the women then swept straight into La Detterie's room unannounced, brushing his cassock against the narrow doorway.

The bed was hardly a foot or two above the bare floor-boards. There was an old armoire, a small table, a basin, pitcher, and chamber pot. Everything looked gray, as though fashioned from ashes.

Jules La Detterie lay on his back, looking equally gray, face pinched, cheeks hollow, eyes glazed. But his wit had not deserted him.

"Illness is a potent magnet," he groaned. "First it draws the physicians, then the women, and finally the priests. Seneca had the right idea—may the lightning get me before the doctors."

"*Fulgur coram medicis.* I believe that *bon mot* was a prayer," said the Bishop.

"Not quite, Your Grace. Seneca was a Stoic. Stoics accept all that happens; consequently, for them prayer was superfluous. Why pray that nature will take her course?"

"Prayer is not always aimed at miracles."

"Not for the saints, perhaps," La Detterie gasped, but for your flock praying's a plea against nature, isn't it?"

The bishop looked sorrowful. "I'm truly sorry to see you so low, Monsieur La Detterie—*Jules*, if I may—but I'm pleased to find your mind so sharp. You know, I admire that mind of yours very much, more than you suspect."

The sick man's voice was bitter but without force. "Your admiration is a surprise, and, for you, risky. The Church damns my work and the State spits me out—and all for talking sense."

The bishop smiled. "When *wasn't* it risky to talk sense?"

"That's so."

"I came as soon as I heard you'd fallen ill and were here."

"A visit as generous as it is futile, presuming you've come

all this way to save my soul." The sick man coughed. "Pity about the weather."

"Yes. The road was terrible."

La Detterie pushed himself up a little on his elbows and gave out a rueful chuckle. "Our circumstances remind me of a story I picked up in Prussia."

"What is it?"

"A Swabian convict was to be hanged. The day appointed for the execution was as miserable as this. For his comfort and salvation, he was escorted by a Franciscan. All the way to the gallows the condemned man complained about having to be hanged in such dreary weather. The Franciscan stopped mumbling his prayers and indignantly told the man he had no right to whine. '*You* only have to walk to the gallows, while *I* have to walk all the way back again.'"

The bishop could see that it gave the sick man pleasure to tell this story and laughed to the degree expected. "Amusing and, yes, apt. . . may I?" He gestured toward the bed.

La Detterie managed a nod and the Bishop of Nantes seated himself at the foot of the bed, taking care to avoid the sick man's feet.

"Have you any better comfort for me than that Franciscan?" asked La Detterie with pathetic irony.

"On the contrary, Jules. I've come to tell you I've read your latest tract and that you've won."

"Pardon me?"

"You've convinced me. I've decided to leave the Church."

"What?"

"Your arguments have overwhelmed me. Today will be my last as a bishop. How could I spend it better than by saying farewell to my instructor, my Socrates, my Galileo?"

"You've lost your faith?"

"Lost. I'm surprised by your choice of words, Jules. I hardly need to tell you that illusions are not lost like keys or watches. One's eyes are simply opened, and you've opened mine."

La Detterie was too weak to raise his head further. Still, he looked suspiciously at the bishop who said, "Your reaction disappoints me, Jules. I thought you'd be pleased."

"Naturally."

"Nature, as you so eloquently write, is the only subject worthy of a philosopher's attention. There is nothing higher, nothing beyond her. . . physical operations."

"Of which death is one," whispered La Detterie.

"Yes indeed, merely another process, like the one that I presume produced that charming Hélène sixteen or so years ago."

"So then, you're *sure*?" asked the dying man.

"Utterly convinced," retorted the Bishop cheerfully. "And by *you*, Jules."

La Detterie spoke hesitantly, his voice faltering. "But—I'm a—skeptic myself."

"How well I know it!"

"I mean that, unlike you, I'm *not* sure."

"I beg your pardon?"

The sick man's wasted body trembled as he coughed. He shut his eyes in pain and shook his head slowly back and forth. "You're evidently a man who demands certainty—first of faith and now of faithlessness."

"Of course. A man wants to know precisely how things stand. You don't agree?"

"We're not alike. You answer questions; I question answers."

"Oh, you're far too modest, Jules. You do more than question worn-out answers. You absolutely annihilate them. Besides, it's not true that you give no answers. You offer entirely convincing ones, as I said."

Here the Bishop carefully took from his robe La Detterie's tract and read a marked passage. "*Is there a God. Though countless generations have wished it so, their numbers constitute no valid argument. Is there an after-life. No doctrine makes it more obvious that religion exploits our terrors and hopes. Is death a transition or is it final. Alas, it is final. Death is no mystery. It is the same as being unborn, neither better nor worse. The dead are beyond justice because they are outside of being. Those bodies that are buried decay and those that are burnt liberate phlogiston.* I particularly appreciate that scientific touch about phlogiston, Jules."

"I am a man of science," La Detterie declared firmly but in a weak voice.

"Indeed, and, as I keep assuring you, you've converted me to this new faith, which is not a faith at all but something higher and better," said the bishop with enthusiasm.

La Detterie began to twist on his bed as if he were being racked by an inquisitor. "No, no," he wheezed. "You miss the point. Science isn't founded on certainty but doubt."

"What's that. I don't believe I heard clearly."

"Doubt. Descartes. Hypothesis. Proof." Each word required one breath, none of them substantial.

The bishop looked scandalized. He held up the pamphlet. "Then you aren't *sure* of what you wrote here?"

"Provisional. Subject to revision."

"But. . . if that's so, then you don't know whether there's a Judge or not?"

"Knowledge is of several degrees. *Techne* is not *Episteme*." Le Detterie groaned pedantically.

"What are you saying. That there may really be an after-life?"

La Detterie's mind may have been wandering but his tone was still sarcastic. "Apostolic succession. Authority founded on a pun."

"*On this rock*, yes. St. Peter. Yes, I know. But you're evading the issue, Jules. Look, my eternal life's at stake here. What is it you really mean to say. This is all-important to me."

La Detterie's eyelids fluttered and his chest seemed to collapse. He was near the end of being able to speak. "This place. Awful. Frightened," he rasped, looking not at the bishop but the ceiling beams.

"Ah, I see," crooned the bishop, as if he had suddenly become deeply thoughtful. "I suppose that too is nature speaking. . . . Look here, Jules. I haven't resigned yet. I'm still the Bishop of Nantes, even if you have shattered my faith. What can it matter if one unbeliever goes through an empty ritual with another?"

"Uhh?"

The bishop extracted from his pocket the little blue velvet pouch. "Non-existence is so close," he whispered softly, inveiglingly. "Just like before you were born, Jules. Nature alone endures. We must fill this little time somehow. I won't leave you alone, like the Comtesse." He leaned over the dying man. "You just tell me anything you want to get off your chest, I put an insignificant smudge of oil on your forehead and mumble some meaningless Latin—what can it matter. And besides, as you say, your brilliant tract is provisional. There could be a revision quite soon."

Ten minutes later the Bishop of Nantes, that cunning hunter of souls, strolled out of the room of the defunct freethinker with a smile on his lips. The tract he left on the bed.

Hsi-wei and the Worn-Out Brush

By the time Chen Hsi-wei retired from his life of wandering through the Empire, the Sui Dynasty had come to an end. To the relief of everyone, Emperor Yangdi had been assassinated and a promising new dynasty had just begun, its glories still in the future.

Sending and receiving letters had been haphazard while Hsi-wei was on the road; but now that he had a fixed abode, he was able to carry on a proper correspondence with old friends. He dispatched one of his first letters to the landscape painter Ko Qing-zhao, a friend from their student days under the stern Master Shen Kuo. Years earlier, Ko, an accomplished painter who held a government post in Hsuan, hosted Hsi-wei for a lengthy visit. That was in the days when Ko was still mastering the art of Shan Shui. Ko's reply to Hsi-wei brought the news that Ko had been promoted to first deputy magistrate and had gotten married. "Yes, I've given up my bachelor's room and my studio in the old shed and moved with my wife into a proper villa. The room I don't regret but I do miss my shed; however, it collapsed long ago. There's more money now but also much more work and hardly any time for making pictures. Apart from that sadness, I can report that I am a contented man. Mai-ling is gentle, capable, and wise. I love her even more now than I did on our wedding day. It seems a paradoxical request, but now that you've finally settled down, would you consider paying us a visit? I would come to Chiangling, but I cannot get leave from my work at the magistracy. No need to tell you what a joy it would be to see you, old friend, how welcome we would make you. Mai-ling has heard a lot about you, and it counts in her favor that she loves your poems."

Hsi-wei replied that he would be pleased to visit though the journey to Hsuan would be long. Now that he was a proper peasant with crops to tend, he would need to see to planting his garden but, once the vegetables were established and the weeds torn up, he would undertake the trip. So, if it was acceptable to Ko and Mai-ling, he would try to come in early summer.

After more than a year away from the road, Hsi-wei found the journey physically taxing at first but emotionally a pleasure. He took his old sign and his tools with him and, as he had done for so long, took orders for straw sandals along the way. He stayed in taverns and stables, barns and on riverbanks, taking note of the crops along the way and meeting all kinds of people. In the larger towns, his name was sometimes recognized and he received offers to stay in the villas of merchants or officials. Twice he was asked to dine by rich widows who claimed admiration for his poems but may only have wanted to show off a celebrity to their friends. The weather was fine that summer; even the rain was gentle. In the towns the granaries were full. In the countryside he saw prosperity, not famine; peace, not war. The poet was pleased that the Mandate of Heaven was sitting so well on Emperor Gaozu.

Hsi-wei arrived in Hsuan in the middle of the afternoon and stopped by the public well for a drink of water and to ask the way to his friend's home. Women selling vegetables and fruit, men selling fish and meat were spread around the square. He went up to a dumpling-seller, ordered two, and asked if she knew the way to the villa of Deputy Magistrate Ko.

She smiled. "He is a good man, that Ko. He married Mai-ling," she said, and told him the way. Hsi-wei pondered her peculiar remark about the marriage. He considered whether to go first to the magistracy then thought he might find his friend at home.

Ko's villa was modest in size but trim and very well kept. There was a small portico with red-painted pillars and flowering plants in front as well as two young plum trees.

Hsi-wei knocked. The woman who appeared was too well dressed to be a servant. She must be Ko's wife. Mai-ling was younger than Hsi-wei expected, perhaps thirty, one of those women whose beauty fades slowly because it comes from the inside. She struck Hsi-wei as humble and modest but also contented; yet her face expressed kindness rather than complacency. She looked at the dusty traveler with an uncertain smile.

Hsi-wei bowed. "Mrs. Ko?" he said.

"Yes?"

The poet bowed. "Chen Hsi-wei."

The woman clapped her hands and gave a little cry. "Oh, you've come! We weren't sure you would. My husband is going to be so happy."

"I'm glad to be here, Mrs. Ko."

"You must call me, Mai-ling, Master Chen."

"And you must call me Hsi-wei."

Mai-ling beamed. "Ah, I'm forgetting myself!" She pulled the door open wide. "Please, please come in. Set down your bag. Would you like some tea, something to eat?"

Hsi-wei stepped into a small vestibule beyond which was a broad parlor with corridors off it to the right and left. Everything was clean, tidy. Through a wide window at the back Hsi-wei saw a lovely garden with peonies, geraniums, and irises, a magnolia tree and, on one side, a substantial vegetable plot. He knew this was Mai-ling's work. While Ko loved painting landscapes, he didn't care for putting his hands in the dirt.

Mai-ling fussed over him. "Would you like to wash, to change clothes while I make tea?" she asked. "I can give you one of Ko's spare robes."

"Thank you. If it's convenient, it would be good to get the dust off me, and the sweat."

"We have our own well. I'll fill a bucket for you."

"Let me do that."

"No, no. I'll see to it."

She looked at Hsi-wei and smiled.

"I suppose you're wondering if Qing-zhao has left me without any help, aren't you. Not so. I do have a helper, but her mother fell ill last week, and I sent Mei home to care for her."

Hsi-wei noted with approval that Mai-ling said *helper* rather than *servant*.

She pointed to the corridor on the left. "Your room has been waiting for you as eagerly as we have. It's just down there. Would you like to see it while I fetch the water?"

The room was cozy, immaculate, and decorated with three of Ko's drawings, studies, Hsi-wei guessed, for his landscapes. There was a fine brush drawing of a waterfall crashing down on huge boulders, another of a stand of bamboo trees, each leaf painted lovingly, the third showed a wide view of a river winding through a forest. There were a pair of small boats on the river heading in a opposite directions. Hsi-wei smiled. So typical of Ko, to conceal a subtle bit of political commentary in one of his landscapes.

Mai-ling returned.

"The bucket is ready. I'll warm the water first then you can wash in the garden. I've laid a robe out for you on the bench. Just leave your things by the bucket and I'll launder them for you." She gave a slight bow, said she was going to start preparing for the evening meal, and discreetly withdrew.

Hsi-wei washed in the garden. The warm water felt wonderful. When he was clean, he poured the water out where he thought it would do the most good.

He was still in the garden when Ko arrived. He heard Mai-ling. "He's here!. It could as well have been meant for him as her husband.

Ko rushed into the garden, threw his arms around Hsi-wei, and began chattering.

"Wonderful. Retirement obviously agrees with you. You look almost alarmingly healthy. Please forgive me for not being here when you arrived. Are you all worn out. Was the trip all right. Are you famished. Oh, it's so good to see you. Really, you haven't changed a bit."

Hsi-wei smiled at his friend's exuberance and his final fib, quite aware that he had changed considerably. So had Ko. He had put on weight and lost a lot his hair. In his formal robe, he looked like a proper deputy magistrate and not at all like a painter. But he was still the same Ko, a spewing volcano of questions.

"How long did the journey take?"

Hsi-wei told him.

"Did you have any adventures on the way?"

"Nothing worth mentioning. My thoughts were on my destination."

"Ah. And how do you like being a man of property, all settled down? Have you given up making straw sandals?"

"I made many on the way here. At home, I sometimes make presents of them to my neighbors, especially the children."

"Well, I hope you're still making poems, too."

Hsi-wei fingered the folds in his robe. "I hope you don't mind that Mai-ling loaned me this robe. I noticed there are no paint spots on it. Are you still making paintings?"

Ko made a sour face. "You know how to strike the sore spot."

"Pardon me. I know your duties have increased but hoped that you still had time for work."

"Work? I have plenty of work, far more work than I'd like. Painting is play and for play there's been no time. But never mind that. Tell me what you think of Mai-ling. Did she receive you properly?"

"Properly. She took my shirt to wash; she gave me your robe. She made tea for me. She prepared a comfortable room, too. No dirty, sweaty stranger who shows up unannounced ever received a more gracious reception. She's a gem, Ko. You chose well."

Ko raised an eyebrow. "But?"

"But?"

"I saw something in your look. Is it a reservation?"

"Not about Mai-ling. It's just that I was surprised to

learn that you'd married. I'd thought you were as unlikely to do that as myself."

"Well, it surprised me, too. There's a story in it. I'll tell you later."

Mai-ling joined them in the garden.

"The meal's nearly ready. What do you think. Shall I put out a jug of wine?"

"Two!" cried Ko and gave her a hug. "It's a grand occasion. We're entertaining your favorite poet, the author of 'Yellow Moon at Lake Weishan' and 'My Skull'. This is the man with whom we outwitted two wicked landlords who forged wills. You've heard the story."

Mai-ling touched Ko's elbow and smiled at him as if to say, "I've heard it dozens of times!"

Dinner was simple, abundant, and delicious. Mai-ling had made pork pancakes and chicken with snap beans in sauce. She sat with them but said little while they ate and drank cups of wine. When Ko and Hsi-wei started to reminisce about their days in Daxing, she fetched the second jug of yellow wine and excused herself.

After she left, Hsi-wei congratulated Ko on his wife and asked to hear the story of how he came to marry.

Ko put his finger to his lips, got up, disappeared for a few seconds, then returned.

"I wanted to make sure she'd closed the door and couldn't hear us. Now tell me honestly, am I too old for her?"

"Not if you married for love."

"And if it were for something else?"

Hsi-wei looked at his friend quizzically.

"I didn't say it was," Ko muttered. "If I remember rightly, you don't approve of old men marrying young women, though it's common enough."

"No, I don't care for the custom," said Hsi-wei slowly. "As you say, the marrying off of young girls to old men as second or third wives isn't uncommon. In my opinion, it isn't uncommon enough. But I suspect that's not the case of you and Mai-ling."

Ko pretended to be offended. "Then you *do* think I'm too old to have married her?"

"Not at all! Anyway, you're not too old and she's not too young. What's the age difference, ten years? Twelve at most?"

Ko persisted with the argument, though he was only teasing Hsi-wei, igniting his friend's peasant resentment. "There are many more poor girls than rich old men. For a girl to become a wife means to have a home, a family, some security for the future. People say it's a sensible arrangement."

Hsi-wei replied tartly. "There should be even fewer rich men and more well-off young ones."

Ko patted the table and laughed. "Always for the under-dogs, aren't you? Well, in this case I agree with you; and, speaking as a deputy magistrate, more equality would mean more justice. But then poets are dreamers."

"Perhaps so. But sometimes I think every reality was once a poet's dream."

"Or a painter's. Only the dreams get distorted, don't they?"

"Nightmares are also dreams," said Hsi-wei bitterly. Then, in a brighter tone, he reassured Ko. "In any case, you certainly aren't too old for Mai-ling. She's your only wife, not a second or third. Besides, you didn't buy her, did you?"

"No, I don't believe I did."

"You aren't sure?"

Ko sighed. "It's time to tell you the story I promised, a tale of solitude turning to loneliness and pity to love."

"It has a happy ending, I think," said Hsi-wei with a grin.

"For me, very happy," said Ko grinning. "Here's what happened. Three years ago, the magistrate and I were investigating the murder of a lumber-merchant. The unfortunate man had been attacked on the road, his money taken and a wagonload of rosewood planks. Two years before that, this merchant had taken a second wife."

"How old was the murdered man?"

"About sixty. The girl not yet twenty. She was the youngest child of a peasant, a widower who owed money to the merchant. You understand?"

"Clearly."

"Well, it was the usual thing. The first wife was furious over the marriage and jealous of the girl. She lorded it over her, treated her harshly and complained to her husband. The merchant neglected to change his will when he married for the second time; and, as he was childless and had no living relatives, all he had went to the first wife who didn't even wait for the funeral before throwing the girl out. People weren't pleased, but, when she was criticized, the woman justified herself on the ground that the second wife hadn't borne a son."

"I see."

"The girl was now a widow, destitute and with nowhere to turn."

"What about her father?"

"Another too-familiar story, I'm afraid. The summer before we had two floods. The first was bad, the second worse. Her father's land was near the river and, when his crops and pigs were drowned, the poor man hanged himself."

"So far this is a terrible story."

"Yes, but wait. As it happened, I knew a local landlord, a good man with a kind wife, both up in years. The couple had just sent away their servant for stealing from them. They thought that punishment enough and declined to file a charge. I persuaded this couple to take on the young widow to do their cooking and cleaning. I visited from time to time just to see how the arrangement was working out. I noticed how humble the young woman was, how modest and grateful, how well she served the old couple. They quickly grew fond of her. Their villa had a large garden that had been badly neglected. On her own initiative, the girl made beautifying it her special project. During my visits, I'd sit on a bench while she worked there. I found myself looking out for plants to offer her— ferns, rose bushes, myrtle. I visited more and more, even after my promotion. She was always glad to see me, and so grateful it made me blush. . . . I don't know. Hsi-wei. Do you think seeing her took the place of all the painting I wasn't doing. Does that seem possible to you?"

Hsi-wei smiled. "Well, hardly *im*possible. One kind of love can be replaced by another."

Ko grunted and poured out more wine. "Maybe that was it, then. A new love."

"And the young widow—the humble servant, the grateful gardener—of course that was Mai-ling."

"So, you really don't think it's just another case of an old man with a little money offering refuge to an attractive young woman with none?"

Hsi-wei shook his head. "I've seen how you are with her and, still more to the point, how she is with you. Mai-ling was no longer a child and she wasn't desperate. She had a choice."

"That's true. She was happy with the old couple and might have refused me. But, as you say, she's not a child. She's suffered much. That's the only reason I wonder."

The following morning, Ko left for the Magistracy and Hsi-wei for the marketplace to find customers. Mai-ling gave him the name of a peasant from he could get fresh straw and said she was going to make bing cakes to take along with a basket of fresh vegetables for Mei and her mother.

Ko and Hsi-wei walked toward the center of Hsuan. "It's a good woman who helps the help," the poet said to the painter as they went their separate ways.

In the marketplace, Hsi-wei took several orders then found his way to the peasant with straw to sell. Hsi-wei also bought four of his wife's dumplings and got a cup of tea for free.

Hours later, he returned to the villa and found Mai-ling in the garden pulling weeds. Hsi-wei watched her for a while, thinking of Ko visiting her in another garden and falling in love. He thought about whether life really had replaced art for his friend and if his own case had been the opposite. As he so often had before, Hsi-wei recalled how giving up the young widow Tian Miao in Daxing all decades ago had sent him on his wandering life and made of the composing of verses a consolation.

Mai-ling looked up and saw Hsi-wei standing holding a bundle of straw.

"Welcome back! I see you've had some orders. Good. I

hope there are hundreds!"

Hsi-wei laughed. "Hundreds?"

"You'll have to stay until you've fulfilled them."

Hsi-wei laughed. "It's more likely you'll beg me to go. You know the proverb about fish and houseguests. But I'm in no hurry to leave, Mai-ling. The food's delicious, the bed's soft, and the company's excellent. And it's a long way back to Chiangling."

Mai-ling sat down on the bench and motioned for Hsi-wei to sit beside her."

"How are Mei and her mother?"

"Mei's worried and so am I. Her mother is very ill. Fever."

"I'm sorry to hear it."

They sat silently for a moment.

"Your poems," Mai-ling began hesitantly.

"Yes?"

She faltered then said, "It's an honor to meet you."

Hsi-wei inclined his head. "Do my poems measure up to your husband's paintings?"

Mai-ling looked shocked but then put her hand to her mouth and laughed.

"You're teasing me. Well, I love those paintings as much as I do the painter—*almost* as much. Tell me, is it really true, that story of how the two of you outsmarted the greedy landlords with their forged wills?"

"Every word. Your husband is no liar."

"And the greedy landlords had to pay big fines?"

"They did."

"And you persuaded the court to turn the land over to the peasants and the villa to the old servant and his family?"

"Yes, it's all true. We had a fine time doing it, too."

"And you did all this by impersonating a high official?"

"Not a *very* high one."

Mai-ling beamed. "I was never sure how much of that story to believe."

"All of it. I sometimes wondered if Qing-zhao thinks of it now that he is a high official."

"Not a *very* high one."

Ko returned home early and looking glum. He hugged his wife, and greeted his friend.

"You look as wrung out as my shirt did yesterday," said Hsi-wei.

"Was it so bad a day?" asked Mai-ling.

Ko sighed. "On Tuesday, Mrs. Shin came to the office with her husband to file an accusation against a young man—a boy, really, the Chows' youngest son Gulan. Mrs. Shin accused him of assaulting her. The magistrate ordered him brought in. Gulan denied everything but the magistrate put him in the cell for the night. This morning his feet were beaten with the bamboo until he confessed. The Shins were there, of course. So was the boy's mother."

"It's a bad practice," said Hsi-wei.

"Mrs. Chow was made to watch?" asked Mai-ling, distressed.

Ko frowned. "Coerced confessions. Emperor Wen's Kaihuang Code was a vast improvement, but it didn't go far enough."

"The Kaihuang Code?" asked Mai-ling.

"The penal code," said Ko. "The law for dealing with crimes."

Hsi-wei explained. "Wendi was revolted by the harsh punishments he saw growing up in Zhou. Beheading, tearing limbs apart with chariots, even the execution of the children of criminals."

"But that's barbaric!" cried Mai-ling.

"It was," said Hsi-wei. Wendi did away those excesses, but he kept the death penalty and also permitted beating," said Hsi-wei. "And both have been abused."

Ko felt he had to defend the law, even if he didn't agree with it. "What we did today was only what was required," he said gravely. "The minimum."

Hsi-wei was silent.

Ko gave a deep sigh. "Unofficially, I agree with you. What does beating to obtain confessions do but show the brutality of some magistrates and the laziness of others? What's worse, the confessions are unreliable. If Shin weren't so rich. . ."

Ko had grown heated but stopped himself and, without a pause, said, "Excuse me, please. I need to bathe and lie down before dinner."

After the troubled and exhausted Ko retreated to the bedroom, Hsi-wei went out to the bench in the garden to work on his sandals. Mai-ling looked after the baked carp, brought in wood for the hearth, chopped scallions and bok choy, mixed up a sesame sauce, measured out rice and set the water to boil. She put their next-to-last jug of yellow wine on the table.

Ko woke from his nap at sunset with improved spirits and a keen appetite. "Everything smells wonderful," he yawned.

The carp turned out perfectly, crisp and flaky. As they

ate, the mood grew convivial. Mai-ling, relieved by her husband's improved mood, surprised both men by saying that she might take just a taste of the wine and got up to get a cup. Ko whispered merrily to Hsi-wei, "This is an event. She never drinks." So, perhaps the turn in the conversation was because the wine went to Mai-ling's head.

"Hsi-wei, if you've written any love poems, I haven't seen them," she said in a challenging tone.

"That's true!" seconded Ko and turned to his friend. "Why is that, Hsi-wei? Are you shy or prudish or do you keep such things to yourself?"

Hsi-wei said nothing, but this discouraged neither man nor wife.

"Women, especially young ones, are often attracted to poets," mused Mai-ling.

"And not painters?" teased Ko.

Mai-ling giggled. "Of course, painters. Landscape painters in particular. But poets too. Hsi-wei, surely you've had some experiences of that sort, especially once your name became well known. A famous poet who isn't bald or fat. A celebrated, not bad-looking poet!"

Hsi-wei corrected her. "A vagabond peasant who sells straw sandals."

"Yes, but also the author of 'Yellow Moon at Lake Weishan' and 'We Love the Good' and the famous "Letter to Yang Jian". Unmarried and solitary, too? I don't believe you never had a young woman pursuing you."

Ko was amused by his wife's unwonted forwardness and his friend's embarrassment. He chuckled and refilled Mai-ling's cup. "Out with it," he said to Hsi-wei. "There must be a story."

Hsi-wei shook his head, but when Ko said, "A poet has to sing for his baked carp," Hsi-wei gave in.

"Very well. Some years ago I was invited to stay at the home of the magistrate in Dongdu, Rong Guangli. Rong, an excellent scholar, had three daughters. Two were married but the youngest, Lihua, was still at home. She was perhaps seventeen at the time, maybe eighteen. I was twice her age. Lihua was excited by my arrival and bubbled over with questions about my poems, which her father collected and she read. At dinner, she threw me glances that made me uncomfortable, and the next day took every opportunity to be alone with me. She had more questions but now they concerned me rather than my verses. Lihua was emotional, effusive, and I suppose she felt some of what you described, Mai-ling. The magistrate's youngest daughter was very direct in her indirection."

"Direct in her indirection? You'll have to explain that," said Ko.

"Like you, Mai-ling, Lihua offered to wash the dirt of the road off my shirt. Her father offered me an old shirt of his to wear during the following day. When I went to my room just before dinner on the second night, I found my old shirt cleaned, pressed, and neatly folded on my bed. When I picked it up, a small piece of paper fluttered to the floor. There were four verses on it written in delicate calligraphy.

> *When the hills are all flat,*
> *When the rivers are all dry,*
> *When it thunders in winter*
> *When it snows in summer. . ."*

"Were they yours?" asked Mai-ling?

Hsi-wei smiled. "No. The lines are from one of the Yuefu folk poems. They're very old, from the Han Dynasty. Lihua assumed I'd recognize them and that I'd know the first line."

"What was the first line?" asked Ko.

Hsi-wei blushed. "*I want to be your love for ever and ever.*"

"Ahh," said Mai-ling.

"So, Hsi-wei. The girl Lihua was infatuated. What did you do about it. Were you tempted?" asked Ko.

Hsi-wei didn't reply at once. He took a sip of wine, as if turning the question over.

"Lihua was lovely, well-read, and passionate. But I was twice her age and a guest in her father's house. Good manners, self-knowledge, and age were all against it. I left early the next morning."

Mai-ling seemed shocked. "And you never said anything to her?"

"I left her a pair of sandals with bronze fittings—small ones—and also a poem."

Mai-ling made an impatient noise. "What did the poem say?"

"It was years ago."

"Oh, try to remember."

"I might have a copy rolled up with the others in my bag."

"Please go look!" Mai-ling begged.

Hsi-wei came back after a few minutes with a small scroll which, with a courtly bow, he handed to Mai-ling who read it to herself then passed it to her husband. The next morning, Mai-ling asked to borrow the scroll. She made three copies and gave two to her friends. That is how the poem came to be circulated.

Hsi-wei gave it no title but people called it "The Worn-Out Brush".

The dirt on the floor laughs at a ten-year-old broom.
A young stallion is of more use than a knackered gelding.
A cracked wedding wok may be cherished but
it's no longer good for making pork with spring onions.
The young should revere more than love the old,
and the old should beware temptations to forget their age.

Cao Cao wrote Walking from Xiamen *with his favorite brush,*
but for The Tortoise Lives Long *he had to buy a new one.*
Before long, the brush I'm holding now will also be discarded.
The closer to the drain the faster the water spins.

THE DREAMS OF COUNT WENZEL VON GEIZ AND THE JEW EISIK

From his childhood Eisik had been called a dreamer. His parents, aunts, uncles, neighbors, and then his wife Brina all said it and smiled as they did so, yet it was no compliment. The smiles were rueful, as if being a dreamer were to be the most useless thing in the world. It was true that Eisik did dream often and vividly. In his youth he had felt compelled to tell everybody about these dreams. Over the years he had learned discretion.

Eisik could dream anywhere. For example, only a day after the catastrophe fell on the village he had been out working in a buckwheat field, the one that belonged to Dov Hayyim. The summer sun was strong. Eisik put down his hoe to take a drink from the jug Brina had given him when he left in the morning. He thought it best to find some shade while he drank and so he went to the little copse at the end of the field. The water was warm but felt good all the same. Then, what with his worries and the heat he began to feel listless. He lay back and looked up through the birch branches at the small white clouds gliding across the sky. In minutes he was asleep.

In his dream Eisik wasn't lying in a copse but on a high and fragrant haystack. About twenty feet over his head a little angel was perched on a cloud looking down at him. This angel appeared to Eisik altogether too smug. "So, you're an angel," he'd said in the dream, "big deal. Look, that's nothing to boast of. Life is easy for you angels. You don't have to eat or drink. You don't have children to clothe. In short, you don't have to earn money which, no matter how hard you work for it or how cleverly you hide it, the Count's men will find. And then they'll take it all away and laugh at you while they're doing it. You just come down here and then we'll see if you go on being so pleased with things. If you can manage things down here, then, so far as Eisik's concerned, you can look as smug as you like." But the angel had merely gone on smiling at Eisik, as complacent as ever.

He woke up with a start. "So that's how it is," he said to himself sheepishly. "I whine even in my sleep—and to angels yet!" Then he rubbed his eyes and reproached himself, "Everybody complains, but I even whine about my whining."

It was true that Eisik was not alone in complaining or worrying about money. Two years before came the bad news of Napoleon's defeat, then there was the story of Prince Metternich's big conference in Vienna where the high-and-mighty arranged the world to suit themselves; and then, two months earlier, the old Count died in his sleep. Count Reinhardt von Geiz was a stern man and hardly a friend, but still one who was fair according to his own lights and whose extravagances were kept within limits by his decent wife. As the Rabbi said, "It's a fine thing the Count loves his beef and Hungarian wine. If he ate only bread, he'd think we Jews could survive on grass." But now the old Count's nephew Wenzel von Geiz had taken over. This nobleman was a spoiled child of thirty-two years, self-indulgent as a sultan and cruel as a caesar.

It was open house at the castle. The old major domo

was shuffled into retirement and Grete, who had been the von Geiz housekeeper from the time of the Flood, was pensioned off, replaced with a Silesian slattern thirty years her junior who brought with her a gaggle of maids with flaxen hair and turned-up noses. An Alsatian chef de cuisine was taken on and, like crows at harvest time, von Geiz's drinking companions descended by the dozens to do what they did best. The new count ordered up all kinds of entertainments. There were masques and fireworks; he brought in traveling actors and even a hypnotist who claimed to have studied with Mesmer. The forest's game was slaughtered wholesale and the old Count's pious and horrified widow was quietly restored to her people in Württemberg. The contents of the castle coffers evaporated like a shallow pond in a dry July.

Instead of taking their leave when the pickings grew slim, von Geiz's parasitic sycophants jokingly declared themselves his "vassals" and thought of how to keep things going. It was one of this band who suggested that, as the Wenzel found himself short of cash, he take what was required from the local good-for-nothing Jews. The new count liked the idea.

"But they've already been taxed," his estate manager had the temerity to say when ordered to make the expropriation look legal. "Besides, you see how they live. They have hardly anything to take."

"Nonsense," the count retorted. "Everybody knows the Jews conceal money everywhere, even up their arses."

"So, the new liegemen were given leave to descend on the Jews like magpies, calling downright robbery just taxation and beating anybody who objected or got in their way. They took not only money, but anything made of silver, copper, or brass, not excepting the holy salvers and menorahs from the synagogue and Brina's Pesach pot. The village was picked clean as a dead corporal at Austerlitz. This was the disaster that had occurred just the day before Eisik had the dream in which he upbraided the little angel.

Everybody was miserable and frightened. "How are we supposed to survive?" "What's to become of us?" Mothers ran about, some tearing their hair; fathers yelled at their hungry children or simply sat down and wept. Moshe the tailor did not need his clarinet to wail pathetically. Only the rabbi remained calm, telling the people stories which all had the same moral: that one should submit to the will of God and accept that they must suffer for their sins.

The story the rabbi told at the Friday night service exasperated people. Herschel Wolfsheim stood up and objected. "But the sinner's the new count, Rabbi, not us."

"Very well then," said the rabbi contentedly, "then we'll suffer for Wenzel von Geiz's sins."

One evening, Eisik recited the prayer over the meager meal, a couple of duck's eggs he'd found and a stale heel of black bread. Then he tucked his two little children into bed and told them a story about how the beggar Shmuel, who had never harmed a soul and who froze to death in a snowdrift, was greeted in Heaven by all the angels, big ones and little ones, who served him a royal banquet. His wife Brina listened at the door. To her dismay, Eisik concocted a fabulous bill-of-fare for the late Shmuel including beef soup with barley and a whole roasted chicken to borsht with cream, candied potatoes, a great golden challah, all finished off with jellied plums.

"It's foolish," Brina chided him, "and it's cruel to tell them what they can't have and will never have."

Eisik, who considered himself an expert on dreams, defended himself. "They're going to dream of food anyway, so why not give them a few specifics?"

That night Eisik himself had a particularly vivid dream. He dreamt he was digging in the Christian cemetery, just behind the grave in which the old Count was buried beside his ancestors. The ground had been newly turned, barely covered with a few pine branches which Eisik threw aside. The digging was easy. Soon his spade struck metal. He dug hurriedly and unearthed a huge strongbox. An iron bar appeared in his hand and with it Eisik broke open the lock. Inside he found all the good things that had been taken from the Jews—the money, the menorahs, even his Brina's Pesach pot that had been a wedding gift from her Uncle Chaim.

That same night, up at the castle, Wenzel von Geiz also had a dream. He saw his new servants stealing caskets full of gold coins from his treasury, taking plates and the family silverware. Some of his so-called vassals were pocketing money hand over fist as well. He awoke perplexed, indignant yet uncertain whether to take the dream seriously. Just to be safe, he resolved to bury his treasure were no one would think of looking for it.

All day Eisik tried to forget about his dream about the buried strongbox, and he didn't tell anybody about it. He could guess what they would say if he did. "Ah, you're a fool Eisik, always dreaming. Isn't it obvious? The Count's men take our things so you dream of getting them back again. It's childish. Better you should cultivate Dov Hayyim's buckwheat. Better you should scare up another pair of duck eggs."

Eisik saw nothing all that day but anxious faces, hungry children, vacant eyes. Everything reminded him of his dream which, after all, had been unusually specific. Eisik had long ago accepted that he was indeed "a dreamer," that it was his nature. How could he help believing in his dreams; that is to say, that they signified something, even if he couldn't always say what it was. Did these dreams come from inside him or outside. He didn't know that either but, in his opinion, either way his dreams were important because they came only to him and felt like whispers and suggestions—intimations, in short.

Early in the morning, while his so-called vassals still snored and the servant-girls who were not still in bed with them yawned and gossiped, Wenzel von Geiz heaved a strongbox onto a cart to which he had himself hitched a pony. It was heavy work and he sweated. On the other hand, the ride to the cemetery, to the von Geiz ancestral tomb, was extremely pleasant. It had been years since he had been up with the birds, and he was amazed how overnight the dew seemed to have washed everything clean. Though it was menial work and hard, he felt rather happy as he dug the hole behind his late uncle's grave, unloaded the strongbox, slid it in, and covered it with dirt and a few pine branches, which left his fingers sticky but smelling pleasantly of resin.

Around midnight, Eisik slipped out of bed, careful not to wake Brina, even though she could sleep through five thunderstorms. In accord with an irresistible urge, which he prayed was not from the Evil One, he took up his spade, Wolfsheim's wheelbarrow, and an iron bar he found in Brodsky's yard. He pushed the barrow all the way to the Gentile cemetery where he quickly found the old count's grave. As he considered its tall, finely carved stone, he recollected something he had once heard at a funeral, a saying of Rabbi Gamaliel, if he recalled correctly. "No tombstones should be erected on the graves of the righteous; it is their words that are their monuments."

Everything was just as in his dream. There were the pine branches and, under them, freshly turned earth. It was easy to move and soon his spade struck metal. Reciting a short prayer, Eisik used the iron bar to break open the lock, and there it all was, all the Jews' things and more. It took every bit of his strength to wrangle the box into the barrow but he managed it. "Only what is imagined is really true," reflected Eisik. This was to comfort himself, because now he was afraid. Still, it was the biggest thought he had ever had. With great difficulty he wheeled the strongbox to the copse at the edge of Dov Hayyim's buckwheat field, where he placed it under three good-sized logs and some brush. Looking up at the stars, he said, "You see, little angel, what it means to be human?"

The servant brought two letters along with the count's breakfast. A nasty butcher and an insolent tailor were threatening legal action, to send in bailiffs. He would have to give them some money and promptly if he were to save his credit. In the afternoon, giving the excuse that he would be paying his respects at his deceased uncle's tomb, he told his friends, quite superfluously, to amuse themselves while he was gone. "A visit to your sainted uncle's grave?" laughed one of his drinking companions from their university days. "A nice euphemism for an afternoon of cocksmanship!. Wenzel was content to let himself be teased; it suited both his vanity and his purpose. Anything to get away for an hour.

The consternation the Count Wenzel had experienced in his dream was nothing compared to what he felt on discovering that his strongbox was gone. Could he accuse his friends? The servants? Surely someone must have watched him bury the box that morning, but who. It was too monstrous. His mind began to race. He imagined a terrible scene, one in which he would have to make accusations.

He foresaw indignant denials, curses; there might even be points of honor to settle and, in the end, he would be left alone—alone and insolvent. Well, he thought, damn them all anyway. Maybe they were all in on it, the whole lot, eating him out of house and home, the freeloaders and the sluts. And as for skinning the Jews, hadn't that been their suggestion. If he did accuse his friends they'd only blame the Jews, even though no Jew would dare such an act. But what if he anticipated them and blamed the Jews himself. That way he could inform the household he knew of the theft without accusing them. Then there would be no need to tell them about his dream or how he had suspected them and hid the money. He could send the men back to that wretched Jewish village where they would, of course, find nothing. Who knows. Maybe then shame and guilt would lead to the return of his strongbox. And, if not, as seemed more likely, he could—sadly, of course, with infinite regret at the unfortunate necessity—propose that the castle be searched from top to bottom.

Eisik too found himself in considerable perplexity. Now that he had it, what should he do with the treasure. Was he, in fact, a thief. Had he succumbed to the Evil One who had sent the dream to destroy him. He hardly minded that there was no food that morning as he had no appetite. All day he fretted and finally resolved that he would have to lay the matter, in confidence, before the rabbi who if not himself a wise man was always quoting the sages.

He was fortunate to find the rabbi alone, reading from one of his big, black-bound books.

"Rabbi," he said, turning his cap in his hands, "I need to speak with you."

"Yes, Eisik. Take a seat. What is it?"

Eisik told the Rabbi all that had happened, from the

night of his dream, the borrowing of the wheelbarrow and the iron rod, the midnight trek to the Gentile cemetery, digging up the strongbox, bringing it back, the three logs in the copse. He left nothing out, not even Brina's copper Pesach pot.

To all this the rabbi listened without interrupting. When Eisik had finished he said, "As it happens, I've just been reading about your case."

Eisik was astonished. "You have?"

"Yes. It's a story called 'The Second Thief.' Here, I'll read it to you." The rabbi opened the book, licked his finger, turned some pages, and began to read.

"A man whose most prized possession is a watch given him by his father is traveling to Lublin. On the way, he stops in the town of Kalisz to take some refreshment. Knowing nothing of the place, he goes into a low tavern favored by the local riff-raff. While he is eating a pickpocket steals his watch and slips out into the lane behind the tavern. The thief is very pleased because the watch is made of gold. Putting it into his pocket, the thief peers in the window and sees that the traveler he has robbed has gone. So, he goes boldly back into the tavern and orders a glass of schnapps. While he is drinking the schnapps a second pickpocket, who has observed everything, rubs against the thief and pinches the watch from him. No sooner has this second thief slipped the gold watch into his pocket than the traveler bursts through the door accompanied by two policemen. Everyone is searched and the second pickpocket is discovered to have the watch, which the traveler readily identifies. So, the watch is returned to its owner and the second pickpocket is arrested, protesting loudly that he never took the watch from the stranger. Yet it is the second thief who is sent to jail while the first thief goes free."

"That seems unjust," said Eisik, "or at least not quite just."

"And yet," said the Rabbi, raising one finger in a characteristic gesture, "the story is about justice."

"Look, Rabbi, I'm confused. You said this story fits my case—the strongbox, the Count."

"So I did because it seems to me the question you have to answer is which of the three men in the story is you. Are you the traveler, the first thief, or the second one. Go and think it over, Eisik. When you decide then you'll know what to do."

Eisik did think it over. In fact, thinking was almost all he did that day, even when the ruffians from the castle came with their curses, their horses and whips, and tore the village apart. Through all this disruption he sat on his porch, chin in his hand, pondering the rabbi's story. So lost was he in thought that he didn't notice when the men from the castle demanded to know where the Count's strongbox had been hidden, a question they put to everyone. "Come on," said one, "the wretch must be simple or deaf." Was he, Eisik wondered, one of the thieves or was he the traveler. Was he the robbed or a robber. Should he keep the treasure for himself and his family or return it to the Count, take whatever punishment was given to him, so that he and his men would leave the other Jews alone. Eisik thought how much simpler it was to be an angel on a cloud than Eisik on a porch.

By dusk, which happened to be the beginning of the Sabbath, the Count's men had gone and Eisik had reached the end of his thinking. Just as the rabbi said, he now knew what he had to do. After lighting the stump of candle with his family and saying the prayers, he went to Wolfsheim to ask for the loan of his wheelbarrow. "Take it. What's left to put in it but misery?" Eisik did take it and set off for the copse. In better times, the whole village would be eating the Sabbath meal before going to the synagogue, but that night the Jews had no dinner, for in their frustration, the lords had taken away every scrap of food they could find.

Up at the castle, after receiving the report that nothing of value had been found among the Jews, Count Wenzel reluctantly made his suspicions known and it fell out just as he had feared. His friends all left in high dudgeon and the pretty maids went with them. Only the housekeeper remained to help him with his futile search.

That night every house in the village received a visit from the dreamer Eisik who made the rounds with Wolfshein's wheelbarrow. All took what was theirs. Eisik got back his pittance and Brina was reunited with her Pesach pot. The rabbi too had his money returned to him, but he said nothing to Eisik. As for the strongbox, the dreamer prudently threw it into the deepest part of the river.

POSTSCRIPT

That was not the end of Eisik's dreaming, nor of his entanglement with buried treasure. Ten years later, after he and his family moved to Cracow where they fared no better than in the village on von Geiz's land, he had another dream that has since become famous; for he is that same Eisik about whom the renowned Rabbi Bunam told in his celebrated "Story of the Treasure" which Martin Buber preserved in the first volume of his *Tales of the Hasidim*. Here is the story, which, curiously, also concerns a double dream.

Eisik, son of Yekel, lived in Cracow. After years of great poverty which had never shaken his faith in God, he dreamed someone bade him look for a treasure in Prague, under the bridge which leads to the king's palace. When the dream recurred a third time, Eisik prepared for a journey and set out for Prague. He found the bridge but it was guarded day and night and he did not dare to start digging. Nevertheless, every morning he went to the bridge and kept walking around it until evening.

Finally the captain of the guards, who had been watching him, asked in a kindly way whether he was looking for something or waiting for somebody. Impetuously, Eisik told him of the dream which had brought him from a faraway country. The captain laughed: "And so to please the dream, you, poor fellow, wore out your shoes to come here. As for having faith in dreams, if I had had it, I should have had to get going when a dream once told me to go to Cracow and dig for treasure under the stove in the room of a Jew—Eisik, son of Yekel, that was his name. Eisik, son of Yekel. I can just imagine what it would be like, how I should have to try every house over there, where one half of the Jews are named Eisik, and the other half Yekel!. And he laughed again. Eisik bowed deeply to the captain, returned home, dug up the treasure from under the stove, and built the House of Prayer which is still called "Reb Eisik's Shul."

HSI-WEI AND THE FALL OF THE SUI

The two weeks the Tang minister Fang Xuan-ling stole from his work in the capital to visit the poet/peasant Chen Hsi-wei in Chiangling were up. Late in the afternoon of the final day, Fang asked the retired poet and sandal-maker about the end of the dynasty in which he'd live almost his entire life.

"You must have been deeply affected. After all, you helped to start it," said Fang.

"You mean that message I delivered as a boy?"

"Yes, the secret message to General Fu, the one inscribed on your scalp."

Hsi-wei made a gesture as if brushing away a fly. "Who can say if it really made any difference? Five armies were sent from Northern Zhou into Southern Chen. General Fu's was only one. Besides, the message might have been out-of-date by the time I delivered it."

Fang smiled at the impregnability of Hsi-wei's modesty.

"Would the First Minister have offered you rewards if the message had been of no use?"

"I don't know. Perhaps the rewards were only because I managed to survive. I've no idea how many peasant boys with quick-growing hair didn't."

Fang chuckled. "As you wish, Master Hsi-wei. But do tell me what you felt when you learned about the end of the Sui?"

"At the very moment I heard, you mean?"

"Yes, then. Everybody remembers when and where they first heard the news."

"And so do I. But the truth is that I was distracted by something else at the time. I took in the news but only reflected on it later. I suppose that like any other peasant I was relieved and hoped for something better."

"You respected Emperor Wen."

"Yes, although with some ambivalence. But yes, Wendi accomplished a great deal and I admired him."

"But not Emperor Yang."

"As you know very well, Yangdi was the worst of emperors and a monstrous man. He ended his father's dynasty with his grandiose projects, the catastrophic wars and unheard-of extravagances. The wonder is Heaven took fourteen years to lift its mandate."

"And you believe the story that he killed his father?"

"Certainly. It's exactly what he would do."

The two men and watched the sun go down over the fields and the low hills beyond. Fang was already thinking of all he'd have to do on his return to Chang'an. He had faith that the new dynasty would be a glorious one and long-lived and he was proud to serve it. Still, though work would have piled up, he didn't regret his two weeks with Hsi-wei and glad that he kept a record of their conversations. Listening to Hsi-wei's tales sometimes felt like looking back on the best of the worst. Much as he loved Hsi-wei's poems, his heart belonged to the future. As for Hsi-wei, he had enjoyed their conversations more than he expected. Explaining where his poems had come from was also reviewing his life which, like the minister's visit, was nearly at its end.

Fang was about to stand and begin the leave-taking when he recalled something Hsi-wei had just said.

"Master Hsi-wei, tell me more about when you learned about the death of Emperor Yang. You said your mind was on something else. I wonder, what could have been more absorbing than such news?"

Hsi-wei smiled indulgently. Not for the first time he felt he was an old man talking to a young one and not an educated peasant chatting with a high minister who happened to like his verses. Fang's curiosity was responsible. Like an inquisitive child, the minister had a bottomless bag of questions. As for this one, Hsi-wei remembered the day very well; it was hardly four years ago. Telling about it would make a fitting finale to Fang's visit. Doesn't everything end—visits, poems, lives, dynasties, even love?

"In those days, I still used to walk to Chiangling once a week. It's so quiet here. I suppose I missed my life on the road and also the noise and variety of a city. It's not unusual, is it—craving the peace of the country when in town and the liveliness of the city when in the country?"

Fang nodded. "People want excitement and, when they get it, long for tranquility."

"We're in-between creatures, higher than the worms, lower than the swallows, wanting one thing and then its opposite. Anyway, the day I heard the news I was in Chiangling. I liked spending time with the peddlers in the marketplace and some have become good friends. Nostalgia for my old life, you'll say, selling sandals everywhere, and that's true, too. At first, it felt strange to be in a market without my pack, my sign, not taking orders for straw sandals. Well, that day I fell into conversation with Mrs. Cheng, a widow who sells dumplings. She is fat in a jolly way and good-natured. We're of an age and like each other. I've presented her with more than one pair of straw sandals, and she's given me more than a few dumplings. Mrs. Cheng likes hearing about the places I've seen, and I like listening to her gossip. Somehow, she learned that I used to write poems, a fact she regards as simply hilarious."

"Hilarious?"

"Oh yes. Making sandals is respectable. You can use a pair of sandals. She teases me about it. Once she asked me what I write on. I told her I wrote about mountains and rivers but mostly about the doings of people I came across—peasants, soldiers, craftsmen, even ministers and their wives, the rich and poor.

"Then I noticed that she was laughing at my answer. She could barely contain herself. 'No, no,' she said bursting out. 'I asked what do you write *on*. Do you write your poems on wood or cloth. Paper is so awfully expensive."

"Amusing," said Fang, pretending to be amused.

"Well, o. that particular day, Mrs. Cheng was troubled and in no mood for teasing. I asked her what the matter was.

"'It's my friend Mrs. Liao—or, I suppose, her pretty daughter Li-hua. You see, the girl's got two suitors—well, dozens actually, but just the two serious ones. The old one is less good-looking than the young one and not nearly so well-off either. The young one's family—that's the Kangs—does a good business supplying tackle to the Emperor—pulleys and rope and what-not. They wear things like that out fast at the Canal and even faster at the Wall, those cursed projects that kill more people than all the Emperor's ruinous wars put together.'

"She was getting wound up and I reminded her of her friend. We'd discussed the Canal and the Great Wall before and I was more interested in the private drama than the public ones.

"'Oh yes,' she said. 'Well, that Li-hua was always as smart as she was pretty. She was a favorite of a neighbor of the Chengs, Mr. Gao, a retired magistrate's clerk. He's dead now. But when he was teaching his son to read, he taught her too. And that was very unlucky.'

I was surprised. "'How so?' I asked.

"'Just listen,' said Mrs. Cheng impatiently. 'The foolish girl has fallen in love with the wrong suitor, the old one without good looks or a tackle business. Mrs. Liao gave the girl sound arguments; she's told her off and threatened her and even made her brother Donghai come all the way from Shui Dong to give the girl a talking-to. But Li-hua prefers the old, poor, ugly man. And do you know why?'

"I said I didn't.

"'It's because of their gifts. Kang's given her a bracelet made of real silver and a jade statuette of Yang Asha, and a red silk robe. The other gives her nothing but poems. Can you believe it. No offense. You write poems too—good ones, or so I'm told. But even you'll admit that a rich young businessman will provide better for Li-hua and her children than a retired widower who writes poems hardly anybody around here can read—bad ones, for all I know—and whose good years are as far behind him as I hope the Turks are behind the Wall which has probably killed more people than the Turks would if there wasn't any.'"

Fang smiled at Hsi-wei's imitation of Mrs. Cheng's way of speaking, also the incongruity between some girl's choice of a suitor and the collapse of an imperial dynasty. And yet, he sensed that there was something serious for Hsi-wei in the matter of Li-hua. Then he realized that the story of the two suitors would have touched Hsi-wei because of how it resembled the poet's own case, the story of which Hsi-wei had been so reluctant to share, the story of what had happened all those years ago when Chang'an was still called Daxing. Hsi-wei had revealed it when he asked about the poem people call "The Cruelty of Springtime". Hsi-wei told him how he had given up the beautiful young widow Tien Miao so she would marry his wealthy rival, Hu Zhi-peng. Hsi-wei said this was this turning-point of his life, that it was what set him on the road. He confessed that all these decades later Tien Miao still appeared in his dreams.

"Mrs. Cheng was trying to remember the old suitor's name when we heard shouts coming from the direction of the Governor Bao's residence. It was like the waves from a rock tossed into a pond, the way the noise spread through Chiangling. The clamor of mobs always sounds unanimous, but its meaning isn't always clear. What we heard could have been grief as easily as joy, another rout in the East or lethal landslide at the Canal. I saw a man I knew hurrying by, Mr. Zhao, a candlemaker. He told us that the Governor had just read out a proclamation that Emperor Yang was dead."

The sun was halfway behind the hills and the field was already dark. The time had come to leave. Fang got to his feet and took Hsi-wei's hands. The poet bowed and thanked his guest for coming, also for his many gifts of which, he said, Fang's interest was the most precious. Neither pretended that they would ever see one another again.

Fang was curious to the end.

"One last thing, Master Hsi-wei. Do you know which suitor Li-hua married in the end?"

"The rich one, of course."

"Ah. Yes, of course. Tell me, did that disappoint you?"

"Disappoint me. Not at all, My Lord. I agreed with Mrs. Cheng and Mrs. Liao."

"Do you wonder what became of the other man, the old one who wrote verses for her, the one she rejected but loved?"

"Oh, I expect he wrote a lot of poems about it. By the way, I wrote a poem that night about the end of Emperor Yang. It's one of my last."

"I don't know it."

"That's not surprising. I've never showed to anyone."

"Would you show me now?"

Hsi-wei went into his cottage and came back with a scroll which he handed to his friend.

After reading it, Minister Fang asked if Hsi-wei would permit him to make a copy.

"I know many people in the capital who would like to see it."

"If it pleases you, My Lord."

Here is the poem. The title was chosen by Fang Xuan-ling.

The Death of Emperor Yang

The blighted plum tree can still bear fruit
though its sweetness will taste of poison.
I've read his verses. They aren't bad. I'd
rather they were or that someone else had
made them, some poet he'd sent to die in exile.

Waking, he'd think, today I'll write about gardens
and tonight sleep with whichever minister's wife admires

the poem most. We'll gorge on oysters and pomegranates.
Tomorrow, I'll order the next invasion of Goguryeo
and send ten thousand more to dig and die at the Canal.

He was brave and handsome once, the victor of Chen,
Cunning enough to brush aside his brother, the Crown Prince.
wicked enough to assassinate his too-indulgent father,
cruel enough to throw ten million lives at a wall, into a ditch,
stubborn enough to waste armies in southern swamps, eastern
    ravines.

Today I heard he had to flee to his palace in Jiangdu
where, they say, General Yuwei himself saw to the strangling.
But I had no thought for a dynasty turning into dust,
for vicious princes, fed-up generals, for the great world.
I was more captivated by the tale of a young girl's love.

ABOUT THE AUTHOR

Robert Wexelblatt is professor of humanities at Boston University's College of General Studies. He has published eight fiction collections, *Life in the Temperate Zone, The Decline of Our Neighborhood, The Artist Wears Rough Clothing, Heiberg's Twitch, Petites Suites, Intuition of the News, Hsi-wei Tales,* and *The Thirteenth Studebaker*; two books of essays, *Professors at Play* and *The Posthumous Papers of Sidney Fein*; two short novels, *Losses* and *The Derangement of Jules Torquemal*; three books of verse, *Fifty Poems, Girl Asleep,* and *To See What I Have Seen, See What I See*; essays, stories, and poems in a variety of scholarly and literary journals, and the novel *Zublinka Among Women,* awarded the Indie Book Awards first prize for fiction.

112 Harvard Ave #65
Claremont, CA 91711 USA

pelekinesis@gmail.com
www.pelekinesis.com

Pelekinesis titles are available through Small Press Distribution,
Ingram, Gardners, and directly from the publisher's website.